RIVER

THE KING'S
ORCHARD

O'HARA'S

THE KING'S
GARDEN

SEMPLE'S
TAVERN

RIVER

A View of
PITTSBURGH
1777

THE
King's Orchard

By
Agnes Sligh Turnbull

NOVELS

The Rolling Years
Remember the End
The Day Must Dawn
The Bishop's Mantle
The Gown of Glory
The Golden Journey
The Nightingale
The King's Orchard

NONFICTION

Out of My Heart
Dear Me: Leaves from a Diary

FOR CHILDREN

Jed, the Shepherd's Dog
Elijah the Fish-Bite

VOLUMES OF SHORT STORIES

Far Above Rubies
The Four Marys
This Spring of Love
Old Home Town

THE
King's Orchard

Agnes Sligh Turnbull

AMOR:PATRIÆ:VINCIT

HOUGHTON MIFFLIN COMPANY BOSTON

The Riverside Press Cambridge

1963

"And yet they, who are long gone, are in us,
as predisposition, as burden upon our destiny,
as blood that pulsates, and as gesture that
rises up out of the depths of time."

RAINER MARIA RILKE

ACKNOWLEDGMENTS

M Y FIRST and deepest thanks go to Agnes L. Starrett, Editor of the University of Pittsburgh Press, for suggesting to me that I use James O'Hara as the subject of a novel.

During the writing I have been encouraged by the steady interest of Mr. and Mrs. Harmar Denny and Mr. and Mrs. James O'Hara Denny of Pittsburgh who introduced me to family treasures relative to my work, the Dennys being direct descendants of James O'Hara.

I regret that it is impossible to give credit to all the many sources from which I have drawn material, but I wish to mention three with my especial gratitude: *Pittsburgh: The Story of a City* by Leland D. Baldwin; *General James O'Hara, Pittsburgh's First Captain of Industry,* a master's thesis by Eulalia Catherine Schramm; and *Background to Glory: The Life of George Rogers Clark* by John Bakeless.

A.S.T.

Maplewood, N.J.

THE

King's Orchard

CHAPTER ONE

THE FIRST THING he thought of as he set his feet upon American soil was the weather! After the scudding rains and mists of Ireland's County Mayo and the dank dawns and often darker noons of Liverpool, all topped by as stormy a crossing as the Atlantic could churn up, he stood upon the planks of the Philadelphia wharf and looked in astonishment at the sky. It was the color of the Virgin's own robe, with only a lacy white cloud here and there to break the richness of the blue; while over all was the golden effulgence of the sun.

"I can't believe it," he said under his breath, "I can't believe it, *in October!*"

But it was true. There was even a certain serene assurance about the brightness, as though it was an accustomed thing not easily disturbed or driven away. There was also a pervasive beatitude in the warmth itself which not only comforted the bones but lifted the spirits. James O'Hara smiled, lighting up his long, handsome face. He had suddenly remembered a line from the old pamphlet he had discovered in a secondhand book-store and had brought with him. It was the prospectus written by William Penn nearly a hundred years before about his "Holy Experiment, Philadelphia." *The place lies six hundred miles nearer the sun than England,* the Quaker had written ingratiatingly.

"So that's it!" young O'Hara thought with a chuckle. He had come across the seas with the pull of adventure in his heart, steeled to face the perils of a new world, but never expecting the welcome of this beautiful autumn midday. So, still smiling as though at a fair presage, he took a firmer grip upon his baggage which looked like — and was — that of a gentleman and began to move along the busy wharf.

He had made no friends of his own age on the crossing, partly because he was reserved by nature but largely because all the other young immigrants seemed to have come steerage while he had journeyed upper class. He had held a few conversations with older men whom he met daily but for the most part had read, walked the deck on the few hours when it was possible to keep his balance, and slept, as though storing up energy for what might lie ahead.

One of the men who had interested him was, he gathered, what in Great Britain would be called an iron master, Mark Bird by name. He was a man perhaps in his sixties, who apparently enjoyed the young Irishman's company and often sought him out for a chat. O'Hara was a keen, almost voracious listener as the talks went on. Bird was evidently a man of wealth, having not only *furnaces* but a pack of hounds as well.

"Have you ever hunted?" he asked the young man one day.

"A few times. Only on visits to my cousin who is keen on it."

"Uh hmm," Bird said, eyeing him with new respect. "May I ask where you intend to settle over here?"

"I don't know yet, sir. Not till I've looked around a bit."

"Does the frontier attract you?"

"It does, rather."

"Pretty rough going out there. And there's always the devil to pay with the Indians one way or another. As to that," he added slowly, "even if you decide to stay in the East, there may be trouble enough for everybody in a few years."

"What do you mean, sir?"

"You haven't heard about it?"

"Nothing that seemed serious."

The older man smiled grimly. "Well, you probably wouldn't, but over here there are a lot of people saying, 'To hell with the King,' and saying it pretty loud. That wouldn't be a popular cry in the old country."

"You mean there could really be a break with the Crown? On what grounds?"

"Well, it's hard to put it in a nutshell but you'll hear it little by little. Let me just say we've had our noses rubbed in the muck and we're tired of it. We're an upstanding lot in the Colonies and the air here smells free. After you've drawn it in for years — Well, I don't mean to scare you out." He laughed. "It's not too late to go back."

O'Hara did not return the laughter. "I never heard of an Irishman running away from a fight," he said soberly, "but that certainly wasn't what I came over for. There's one thing I'd like to ask, though I believe you've already made it clear. If it should ever come to *war*, you mean you'd stand against the King?"

"Well, let's just say I'm an American first and last no matter what comes. Of course the troubles may all smooth out. We've got some good men working on them. Ben Franklin and others. But," he added, lowering his tone, "in my furnaces right now we're making a few cannon balls, *just in case*."

The night before they landed Mr. Bird had spoken to him again.

"Do you know anyone in Philadelphia?"

"Not a soul. I've got a letter though from my employer in Liverpool to a Mr. William Carson, a Scotsman."

"Good," said the older man. "I know of him. I've been thinking, though, that if you give up the frontier idea and decide to stay in the East I'd be glad to have you come up and have a look at our furnaces. The Birdsboro Iron Works is the name, and the village is called Birdsboro. Anyone in Philadelphia can tell you how to get there. We're on Hay Creek that runs into the Schuylkill — just up the river. I could give you a job and maybe a day's hunting to boot."

"That's more than kind of you," O'Hara said. "I wouldn't be too good at the hunt but I'll surely remember about the job. I thank you, sir, for your interest in me." There had been a warm handshake between them as they said goodbye.

O'Hara now, with his letter of introduction in his safest pocket, still smiled as he stepped into the cobblestone street, for he faced a neat, new, clean little town. With the remembrance of worn old cities strong within him, especially the dark, decrepit buildings edging the Liverpool piers, he looked in amazement at the bright and tidy thoroughfare which here ran along the wharf. The houses were mostly brick, some, he could see, three stories high with iron grillwork decoration, but all pleasant, habitable, and fresh in the sunlight. There was still another contrast to the old world ports which he sensed at once. Here there was no salt in the air and no ocean breeze blowing. For there was only the broad, placid flow of the Delaware river to bear its shipping from the seven seas to Philadelphia's doorsteps.

As he stood looking at the buildings before him his eye

caught a swinging sign in bold coloring from which the words *The Crooked Billet* beckoned. He knew his first move was to get established in a tavern before presenting himself and his letter to Mr. Carson, but he hesitated a moment while he surveyed the street. It fairly bristled with other hostelry signs. From where he stood he could make out: *The Pewter Platter, The Star and Garter, King Henry on Horseback,* and *The Indian King.* But he had the strong Irish feeling for omen and coincidence. He decided to stick to the first sign he had seen and so went up the scrubbed stone steps and through the door into The Crooked Billet.

The bar room which he entered seemed dark at first after the brilliant sunlight without, but it was, withal, a cheerful place. There was much polished brass about the wide fireplace and a settle at the side, worn smooth with use. Tables and chairs stood waiting for the later influx of customers, a dartboard showed invitingly in one corner and a row of beer mugs hung from their hooks on a rafter above the bar. A man in a leather apron and full-sleeved shirt came through a door at the back and grinned at O'Hara.

"What'll you have, friend?" he asked.

"Could I get a room, please?"

"I'll have the master, Mr. Hastings, in to see you about that. I just pulls the beer! I'm Sam," he added still grinning and disappeared.

The master proved to be tall, thin and pock-marked, with cheerful eyes which now studied the young man.

"You wish lodging?" he said.

"I'm James O'Hara. I've just landed and don't know yet what I'll be finding to do. I would like a room until I learn my way round a little."

The older man sized up his clothes and his luggage.

"Irish, then?"

"I was born there."

"Green or orange?"

"Orange. My family's divided on that. I might say I'll gladly pay you a week in advance."

There was a sudden noise of loud voices just outside the tavern and then two men entered apparently on the verge of a fight. From the dark bearded one a torrent of French issued, accompanied by threatening gestures; his companion, slightly shorter and sandy, clutched a heavy load of pelts, cursing eloquently as he fended off the other's efforts to grab the furs.

O'Hara jumped up. "Arrêtez! Arrêtez!" he cried. The Frenchman, startled at hearing his own language, stepped back and directed his angry discourse to the young man who listened carefully, putting a question now and then.

"What's eating at him?" the other man said. "Why is he trying to steal my pelts?"

"He says these are his pelts. That you picked up the wrong bundle in the trading store. He says if you'll check them over you'll see they aren't yours. I think the man is honest."

"The devil he is! They're all slippery, these Frenchies. Well, I'll take a look to satisfy him."

He opened an end of the big bundle which was contained in a deerskin and then straightened in surprise.

"May I be a dead Injun if he ain't right! I hadn't any fox skins that color. We both set our packs down at the store about the same time but when I saw who was back of the counter today I grabbed mine — as I thought — and hustled down here until Clark himself is in. Tell this to Frenchy, young fellow. . . ."

"O'Hara, and just now landed, Mr. Elliott," Hastings introduced.

"Well, O'Hara, tell this man how it happened and that I apologize. And tell him not to make a trade until Clark is in the store. That other fellow there will cheat him as sure as there's an eye in a goat. I've got to get back now and see to my own pack. But give these two both a beer to wet their whistles while I'm gone, Hastings. And thank you, young man. I think you saved me a drubbing."

As O'Hara and the stranger sat at the bar the French flowed apace between them; when they had finished their beer, still conversing, they moved over to the corner where the bundle of furs lay. The Frenchman opened it up, displayed each skin, evidently explaining its value. O'Hara kept questioning him, until at last he put the pelts back into the deerskin, fastened it with leather thongs and then with a wave to Hastings and a hearty hand grip to his new friend, shouldered it up and departed.

Hastings came at once from behind the bar.

"Now, I'd like a few words with you. In English," he added, laughing. "I'll be glad to give you lodging but suppose you explain yourself a little. It's not every day that an Irish Orangeman turns up here, speaking French like a native."

O'Hara laughed too. "It's no mystery," he said. "I was born in County Mayo, Ireland, but my father's in the Irish Brigade in France so I went to school there. That's about the way of it. Except that for years I've had a wish to come to America, and here I am!"

"Good enough," Hastings said. "Come along upstairs then, and I'll show you the rooms. I've one at the front facing the river, and one at the back over the garden. You can look at them and take your pick."

"Sight unseen I'll choose the back one. I've been working in Liverpool the past two years and I've had my fill of ships. The garden will be a nice change."

"So be it, then," Hastings said.

He led the way into a passage and on up narrow stairs to a larger hall at the top with rooms the length of it. He opened the last door in the rear and O'Hara stepped inside with him. The young man looked at the stout bed, the high dresser and desk with satisfaction, but when the shade was raised revealing the garden below he could hardly restrain his delight. His mother, however, had grounded him well in the Bible and the words of the wise man ran at once through his mind:

It is nought, it is nought, saith the buyer, but when he goeth his way then he rejoiceth.

So now he said, merely, "This room will do very well, I think."

Hastings had evidently expected more praise for he went on to speak of the garden.

"It's Sam's work," he said, "and for its size I think it's a pretty nice one. Of course now the *best* of the flowers are gone but there's still a goodly showing for October. And the coloring of the trees! That must be new to you?"

"It is. It's astonishing."

"Sam's my cook, too, and a good one, I may say, if you're planning to have meals here. He was indentured to me for twenty years but after he nursed me through smallpox I made him a free man. So we keep bachelor's hall together. Well, I hope you'll be comfortable."

"I'll be that," O'Hara answered. "Would you be knowing a man named William Carson here in the city?"

"I do, indeed. He's one of our influential citizens and a rich one. Are you connected with him?"

"I have a letter of introduction, that's all. I thought I'd go to see him at once, toward the back end of the afternoon."

"Then you'll not be supping here, I doubt. Carson never lets anyone leave his house hungry. It was that way as long as his wife lived and it's still the same. You'll find he has a pretty little daughter," Hastings finished with a smile.

O'Hara passed this over as though it was without interest.

"This trading business," he said. "From what the Frenchman told me it must be a good one."

"One of the best if you like to get mixed up with the Indians. For my part I prefer to keep as far away from them as possible. And keep my *hair*," he added with a chuckle.

They settled the lodging terms and then O'Hara, left to himself, gloated upon his new surroundings. He liked the small room with its substantial furniture and his spirits soared as he looked again at the garden. It was bordered by gold and scarlet trees, the like of which he had not seen before, and as Hastings had pointed out there were still blooming flowers between the edgings of box. *And in October,* he thought again, in amazement.

It was his nature to do promptly what was to be done, so, after Sam had brought him a can of hot water, he washed carefully at the small stand, arranged his clothes in the drawers and the press, then put on a fresh shirt and stock and a plum-colored waistcoat, assured himself that he had the precious letter of introduction and at four o'clock, planning to avoid family teatime, he started out to wander a bit before going to the address on the envelope. Once out in the streets he marveled again at the little city in which he found himself. It all had a look of fresh neatness. None of the heavy grime of centuries rested upon it. Sensitive as he was to a prevailing atmosphere, he felt a young, brisk confidence in the air. The people he passed confirmed this. He thought he might be stretching a point, yet the feeling persisted that a certain cheerfulness of spirit went with the general youth of the town.

He paused occasionally; once before a sturdy red Georgian building with *1724* on the gable and *Carpenter's Hall* below the date; once with interest at a place called *Rickett's Circus* on Chestnut Street; and at greater length at the market in the street of that name. Here in the open air under a colonnade were displayed geese, pheasants, rabbits, hams and small pigs hanging from their hooks while below were receptacles of fresh fish and baskets of every kind containing all the kindly fruits of the earth! It was a place that suggested good and bountiful living, and O'Hara savored the scene with zest. Beyond, as he went along the street, was a large flat-board wagon with two oxen in the shafts. A man suddenly fell into step beside him, carrying a heavy basket of hams and flitches from the market.

"Just loadin' up," he remarked. "Be leavin' at daybreak."

"Where are you going?" O'Hara asked.

"West," the other said, as though surprised at the question.

"You mean the *frontier?*"

"That's right, if the wheels stay on. I've been aimin' to do it this good spell."

"Any special place?" O'Hara pursued.

"Fort Pitt if we can make it. That's about the jumpin'-off-spot in the West right now. I want to pick me up some spare land. Gettin' too crowded round here."

Impulsively O'Hara held out his hand.

"Good luck to you," he said. "I may head out that way my-self."

"Stranger here, ain't you?"

"Just landed from the old country."

"Want to join up with us? Two wagons of us are goin' an'
we got room for another able-bodied man. You look like you
could hold your own in a tough spot. That is, if you had them
fancy clothes off you."

O'Hara laughed and shook his head. "I thank you kindly
but I'll be staying round here a while till I feel my way. But
good luck to you again."

"We'll mebbe run into each other out there. My name's Silas
Porter."

"Mine's James O'Hara."

The other waved and passed him with his basket. After a
few steps he looked over his shoulder.

"Can you shoot straight?" he called.

"Pretty fair," the young man answered.

"You have to be better than that if you're goin' into the wilderness. Injuns an' rattlers don't give you a second chance."
And with another friendly salute he reached his wagon.

O'Hara continued his saunter thoughtfully until five fifteen,
then he addressed his steps toward the Carson home. When he
reached it he stopped, his heart beating faster. This was evidently an abode of wealth. The three-story building was brick,
painted yellow. The wide steps led to a pillared entrance and
the great brass knocker gleamed in the sun. He climbed to it
slowly and struck it with a hand that hesitated in spite of him.
He wondered about his welcome in a house like this.

A man servant opened the door. "Yes?" he queried over
a long nose.

"I've a letter to Mr. William Carson. Would he be at home?"

"I'll tell him. Will you come in and have a seat in the hall,
sir?"

It was a wide hall with an Oriental rug filling it. A gold-hinged Chinese chest stood along one wall with a heavy mirror above it. In its reflection O'Hara saw an oil painting of a beautiful woman and a child over his head. His eyes were still fixed on the portrait when the servant returned.

"He'll see you in the library, sir. Just come this way."

The man who rose to greet him had the big frame, rugged features and ruddy cheeks of a Scot. His eyes were keen but they had a fine twinkle.

"Come away in," he said heartily. "You wished to see me?"

"I'm James O'Hara, sir, just landed today from the other side. I have a letter to you from my employer in Liverpool — John McNeil."

"Ah, I'll give you a double welcome then. McNeil and I were boys together in Scotland and we've always kept track of each other. Sit you down while I see what he has to say."

He pointed to one of the fireside chairs and reached for the letter. When he had finished it he looked pleased.

"Well," he began, "in all the years I've known McNeil the greatest praise he's ever given anybody or anything was that it *was not too bad.* He's gone a little further with you so I know he must feel pretty strongly. He says your main interest is in some form of business."

"That's right, sir."

"I'm a business man myself, forty years a merchant, so I know the field a little. Suppose, though, before we talk about positions and such, you tell me about yourself. McNeil says nothing about you except your qualifications. The name O'Hara hardly sounds *Scotch.*"

They both laughed. "I'm as Irish as Paddy's pig, sir," O'Hara began, "as far as my blood goes. The family's lived in County Mayo for generations and I was born there, around

Tyrawley. But my grandfather Felix got sick of the Irish troubles and went into the French service. He was a major in Dillon's regiment of the Irish Brigade, and my own father John was born in France and went into the Brigade too, when he was old enough, so he's always had one foot there and the other in Ireland where he married my mother. It sounds a bit mixed up, I fear, sir."

"But very interesting. Go on."

"I lived in Ireland with my mother when she was there and with relatives when she was with my father, till I was twelve, then he wanted me to come to France to go to school so I went to the college of St. Sulpice till I was eighteen — and you know the rest."

"St. Sulpice, eh? You started out then for the priesthood?"

"Oh, not at all. The college is divided. It has a secular, classical course, too. Besides, I'm *North* Ireland."

"Theologically as well as geographically?"

"I guess you could put it that way."

"Good! Then for two years you've been in Liverpool in McNeil's ship broker's office and now you're going to have a try at America."

"I've had an urge to come this long while, and I like the feel of it even after a day."

"I was just twenty when I came over myself, and I've never regretted it. And as to Philadelphia, it's the finest place you could settle. That's your intention, I take it? I can help you here, you know."

O'Hara moved in his chair a shade uneasily.

"That's good of you, sir, but I'm not rightly decided. You see it hasn't been my idea just to exchange one city for another. I'd like to get into the *new* country, the wilderness, the frontier, whatever you'd be calling it. It sounds presumptuous but I'd like to help build a *new* city instead of settling down in one that's already built."

"In other words you want adventure."

"Well, I'm young, sir."

"True enough. And there's this, I must admit. If no young men were willing to head for the frontier the country would be at a pretty standstill. But yet . . ."

He was interrupted by a clear young voice.

"Fa — *ther!*"

"That'll be my daughter, Mary," he said. "She's only thirteen but she's had to be mistress of the house since her mother died. *In the library,*" he called back.

In a second a girl appeared in the doorway, and seeing the stranger hesitated there for a moment.

"Mary, this is young Mr. O'Hara, fresh over today from the old country."

She came nearer and made a graceful curtsy, as O'Hara rose and bowed.

"Your servant, ma'am," he said smiling, being pleased to use the words he would have employed toward an older woman.

When she looked up, smiling in her turn, O'Hara felt a rush of hot blood to his head. She could have been sixteen at least. The young breasts showed delicately full beneath the tight bodice. Her manner was poised and her face . . . O'Hara, growing up in France, was not without knowledge of women; however, it had all been to him purely physical and superficial. He had never before been emotionally moved in the way he was at this moment. For this girl — this child — had a beauty that arrested him. Her long lashes were dark over eyes blue as Irish flax; her features were as purely cut as a cameo; and the curls tied up on her head were auburn bright.

"Sit down, both of you," Mr. Carson was saying in a voice a shade less hearty than before. His eyes were fixed quizzically upon the young man but the kindness of his expression did not change.

"Mr. O'Hara, here," he said, addressing Mary, "has been working in Liverpool two years for my old friend, John McNeil, who sent a letter by him. Now he's going to be a business man when he decides where to settle, though already . . ."

"Oh, Mr. O'Hara," Mary exclaimed, her face lighting up, "you couldn't find a place in the country as delightful as Philadelphia! Isn't that so, Father? Have you told him how wonderful it is?"

"I believe he fancies the frontier."

Mary gave a little shudder. "Oh, surely not." Her eyes dwelt upon his elegant plum satin waistcoat. "I can't picture you fighting Indians. And besides, if it's business you're interested in, there's no place better than right here with Father to help you get started."

She paused a moment and then, "I do love my city," she added.

"That is plain to see," O'Hara answered, "and I have a strong feeling of admiration for it even in this one afternoon. Of course I'll make no decision to go west until I've learned all the possibilities here if your father . . ." he smiled and bowed to Mary . . . "and perhaps you, too, will teach me more about it."

"It's a bargain then," Mary cried. "Father can take you round to the merchant houses and I'll show you the gardens — too bad it's so late — and make you acquainted with society. For we have that too, haven't we, Father?"

Mr. Carson's face had a touch of pride. "We do, indeed. Many people fresh over are surprised to discover that our men know how to dine and our ladies to dance even in the Colonies.

And speaking of dining, you'll do us the honor to sup with us this evening?"

"The honor will be mine, sir, and thank you."

Mary rose quickly. "I'll run and tell Isaac to lay an extra place, while you go on, Father, telling him why he should stay here."

O'Hara's eyes watched her go, but as he turned he tried to keep his expression casual.

"Did I understand you rightly that your daughter is only *thirteen?*"

"That's true, though I know she seems older. Of course all our girls here grow up early, but Mary has matured incredibly since her mother's death. I need not add," he said, looking keenly at the young man before him, "that she is my chief treasure and I guard her accordingly."

O'Hara's face colored slightly. "She is worth guarding, sir," he replied simply.

"But now," Mr. Carson went on, "I'll try to put in a nut shell why our city at the present at least is the most important one in the Colonies. First, there's our port. You've seen that for yourself. Then we've got a sort of strategic inland position. We've got iron and anthracite coal all around us for manufacturing. And maybe as important a factor as anything else in our growth has been our *tolerance.*"

"I beg your pardon?" O'Hara questioned.

"That's right. I said tolerance. William Penn started it and the plain fact is, to put it on the lowest level, it's been *profitable.* The Quakers have a mystic streak in them but they're damned good business men and when other towns in other colonies ran them out, they came here and a lot more so-called Hereticks besides. And they all brought their skills with them. It's been good for the city. Well, as I can, I'll show you round."

The supper which followed soon was dazzling to O'Hara. The dining-room furniture was more elegant than any he had ever seen even in the home of his elderly cousin, Lady O'Hara, in Tyrawley; the crystal chandelier with its dozens of lighted candles threw wine-colored pools on the dark mahogany table; the silver gleamed. At the end of the table opposite her father, sat the girl Mary, now in rose brocade.

"Mr. O'Hara was educated in Paris," Mr. Carson said as Isaac passed the platter of fried chicken.

Mary gave a cry of delight. *"Paris!"* she echoed. "Oh, I want to go there even more than to London. Please tell me what it's like. Were you fond of it?"

"Yes, quite. I lived there for six years. But to describe it — that's a bit hard. You will have heard or read anything I could tell you, I'm sure."

At her look of disappointment he was apologetic.

"I was in school, you see, and pretty young. I don't believe I was very conscious of what you might call the historic beauty of the city. We had to work hard and when we had holidays we usually . . ."

"Yes?" Mary prompted.

"Well, we usually made for the *Bois,* you know, that's the great park, to get out of the city. It's a pleasant spot." He suddenly laughed, showing a row of strong white teeth. "One thing we often did there when the weather was fine was to take a rowboat across the lake to a cheap little café on the other side. The tables were set close to the water and the ducks used to come right up to our feet to be fed. We had names for them and bets on which one would be the quickest and get the most food. . . ."

He stopped embarrassed. "You ask me to describe *Paris* and I tell you about feeding ducks! I am sorry."

"But I liked that," Mary said.

"More real, I should say, than if you had described Notre Dame's 'storied windows richly dight,' " Mr. Carson added.

"That's Milton," Mary put in. "Father's always quoting him."

"Well," Mr. Carson defended himself, "I'm a business man but I do a bit of reading too, and I've always maintained that if a man knows Milton and Scott he can hold his own."

Before O'Hara could answer Mary broke in excitedly. "How stupid of me not to think of it before! You must speak French, then," she said to him.

"Well, naturally. I . . . I mean I had to."

"Why, Father, I must introduce him to Mary Vining and they can talk together! She speaks the most perfect French, everyone says, and she's so beautiful and witty. She lives in Delaware but she spends a great deal of time here. And she's coming up in two weeks for Anne Bingham's ball!"

The girl's eyes suddenly shone, as she gave an exclamation of delight. "Oh, here is the most wonderful idea! You see, Mr. O'Hara, I'm not really as old as I look." She paused innocently, as though to let the great confession sink in. "So while I've *known* all the older girls all my life, like Peggy Shippen and Peggy Chew and Mary Vining and Anne Bingham, Father hasn't thought it seemly for me to go to the balls before. Until this one. My very first. And now, since I want you to see our society anyway, and since Father was going to take me and call for me himself, if . . . *if you could escort me* . . ."

She blushed a rosy red as she looked pleadingly from one to

the other. O'Hara's reply was immediate. "I would be greatly honored, ma'am!"

Mr. Carson's face was sober as he watched the young people for a moment.

"With your permission, sir, of course," O'Hara added quickly.

"I think we will accept your offer, Mr. O'Hara," he said, "though I must remind my daughter that it is the gentleman who asks the privilege of escorting a lady."

Mary laughed as though she knew her father's reproof was not too sharp-edged. "He thinks I'm bold," she said. "But I'm not really. I'll call upon Anne Bingham tomorrow and see about an extra invitation. She'll be very surprised that I'm going to have a real escort. And pleased for me, too. Oh, Mr. O'Hara, I think you must have come straight from heaven!"

"Perhaps I have just arrived there," he said gallantly. And then, carefully avoiding even a glance again at Mary, he gave most respectful attention to Mr. Carson's conversation until dinner was ended.

As soon as he felt it was proper O'Hara made his adieux. It was settled that he would meet Mr. Carson at the latter's office the next afternoon and be shown something of the business life of the city.

"By the way, where are you stopping?" Carson asked.

"At The Crooked Billet."

"Good house. You'll be well looked after. As a matter of fact Ben Franklin stayed there once himself."

When O'Hara said goodbye to Mary, he made his best bow and kissed her hand. All at once the poised young lady vanished and the little girl appeared as she giggled delightedly.

"Oh, I like *that*. Did you see, Father? No one ever kissed my hand before!"

They parted at the library door but as old Isaac was showing him out O'Hara heard laughter and running footsteps behind him.

"Mr. O'Hara!" Mary was calling, "it's so funny for me not to think of it before, but *can you dance?*"

He laughed back at her. "All French schoolboys have to learn that," he said. "Your steps here may be a bit different but I'll be doing my best."

Back in his room, he prepared for bed quickly, standing for a moment naked, flexing his muscles. As a boxer would have said, he "stripped well." The full strength of the limbs did not hint beneath his clothes. There was a clean vigor about his body with its white Irish skin which would have struck any athlete. In college he had managed exercise with some sparring bouts, and even during his time at the ship broker's he had walked miles every day, after office hours. He came of a hardy breed and his bare frame showed it.

He put on his bedgown and with a sigh of comfortable young weariness settled himself to review his evening with satisfaction. He had expected help from Mr. Carson because of his letter of introduction, but he had received more than the promise of this; there had been added a warmth of friendship as well. As to the girl . . . He recalled now his first feeling at sight of her with a kind of sane superiority. Odd, that sudden rush of hot blood he had felt. It was her unusual beauty that had impressed him of course and he could continue to enjoy that even if she was only a child. Yes, a pretty, charming child who would be an entertaining companion and be also of the greatest use in acquainting him with the social side of the city. At twenty his pulse quickened at thought of a ball. While deep within him he knew he still craved the adventures of the wilderness it was only common sense to study all the possibilities of Philadelphia first. But before dropping off he suddenly thought of the man with the wagon. Fort Pitt, he had said, was the jumping-off-place in the West. *Ah, I might be having a look at that one day myself,* he thought. Then he fell asleep to dream that a laughing voice behind him kept calling, "Can you dance?"

The next afternoon in Mr. Carson's office the latter outlined his plans. It was to take his young protégé to meet some of the most successful business men of the city so that he could feel for himself the strong commercial pulse of Philadelphia.

"And we'll start, I think, with Robert Morris, one of our most ambitious young men. Only now in his late thirties. He was born in Liverpool but came over here when he was in his teens."

He stopped and eyed O'Hara keenly.

"Funny thing. The two of you don't look unlike when I come to think of it. Also Morris made his connection with the Willing counting-house when *he* was just twenty. You'll see he's done pretty well."

They went out through the warehouses which interested O'Hara more than the well furnished office. But Mr. Carson did not stop to comment upon the great boxes and bales piled up on every side.

"I'll save my own business for the last," he said as he noted O'Hara's interested glances. "I'm starting you at the top as it were. This young Morris is amazing. When he was only twenty-one he helped found our stock exchange and he's been in the thick of money affairs ever since. You might fancy banking," he added.

"It's possible, that," O'Hara returned seriously.

"About tomorrow," Mr. Carson went on. "I have a busy day.

Can you amuse yourself? I'll be able to take you around any time following that. And you must come in soon and have a dish of tea with us."

"I'll be fine," O'Hara said, "and thank you. You mustn't be making a burden of me and besides I'm wanting to have a good look about the town. As to tea, I'll be very pleased to come when it's convenient."

They entered the big counting-house and passed between rows of clerks standing behind their tall desks until they reached Morris's office. Here the young men smiled at each other at once, for there *was* a certain resemblance between them. They had the same wide-set eyes, the same lengthy nose, the same generous mouth all in a long face. They got on well from the start, beginning with Liverpool and progressing to finance. Mr. Carson left them together and they talked for an hour.

"If you're really interested," Morris said at last, "I think I can offer you a job. It would be at the bottom, but the rising is good here for the worthy ones. You'll let me know?"

"I'll do that, and my deep thanks to you. It's been a pleasure to meet you."

"I have a feeling we'll hear of each other again, whether you take to counting or not," Morris said.

"The same thing occurred to me. Would you be knowing a trading store with a man named Clark at the head of it?"

Morris looked at him quizzically. "So?" he said. "A little interest in *Indian trading?*"

O'Hara colored. "A bit, maybe."

"It leads you nowhere, you know."

"Wouldn't that depend on where you're heading for?"

Morris laughed. "You're a deep one," he said, "and I'd like

to know you better. I can direct you to Clark's and keep me posted, will you, on what you decide?"

The big trading store was like nothing O'Hara could have imagined: a barnlike building with a rough plank floor and rows of heavy wooden tables ranging along two sides and part of the front upon which lay the bundles of furs. Across the back of the room was another long, wide counter, one end evidently reserved for accounting and the rest given over to a display of clothing, trinkets and gewgaws. The smell of freshly dried skins lay heavy on the air mixed with a reek of tobacco and sweaty unwashed bodies. Several traders stood about waiting their turn to have their pelts weighed while two others were poring over the table of knickknacks. O'Hara watched it all avidly. He listened as the skins were checked and appraised by the man at the front, Clark apparently. There was somehow in the atmosphere the breath of the untamed forest; there was an emanation of struggle and danger and conquest. He turned suddenly and went out into the street.

For two hours he walked and thought, unmindful of the passing scene. He was about to make a decision that would mold the rest of his life. The logical one of course would be to stay in Philadelphia. His whole bent was toward business in some form, and here he would have Mr. Carson's mature guidance. Here (he felt it!) he, too, might become successful even as Robert Morris already was. Moreover, a job had even now been offered him. Above and beyond all this there was a certain small new cry within his heart. If he stayed here he would be near the young Mary whose beauty had so strangely disarmed him. As time passed and she grew older . . .

But there still moved upon him another compulsion, that irresistible impulse which had begun back in the old country as he had heard of the new world's slow progress westward through the wilderness. It was this, he now knew clearly, which had made him cross the sea. It was this urging, unformed then, almost unrecognized, which had brought him hither. Was he now to disregard it? Could it be, perhaps, his *destiny?* And if so would a strong man turn his back upon it?

At long last he raised his head which had been bent forward in deep concentration, squared his shoulders and headed back toward The Crooked Billet. While with wisdom he realized that such contacts as the one today with Robert Morris and with the other business men Mr. Carson was planning for him to meet could be valuable to him later in one way or another, he must not go on under false pretenses.

At supper that night with Hastings and Sam in the back room of The Crooked Billet he confided to them his decision.

"Well, trading's the big business out at Fort Pitt, I hear. At least that's what Elliott tells me. He's in it up to his ears and making some money too."

"I'd like to meet him again," O'Hara said.

"Oh, he'll be around. Usually drops in of an evening for a pint. He can tell you what you want to know. Of course I think you'd be smarter to stay right here in Philadelphia."

"How's your shootin'?" Sam asked abruptly as he got up to bring in the pudding.

"Pretty good at mark. My father's a soldier and he saw to that, but at moving objects I'm not so sure."

"We'll have to practice you up," Sam said. "There's lots of movin' critters in the wilderness, I've heard tell. You can try your luck out in the garden. I'll throw some *objects* up in the air for you an' you can aim at 'em. Eh, Mr. Hastings?"

"Good idea. Have you a rifle?"

"No, but I'll get one."

"Well, Sam will put you through your paces. He shoots as well as he does most things. And talk to Elliott. He thinks Fort Pitt out there has a chance to grow. Not much to it now, of course. I gather that's where you're really heading for?"

"That's right. I hardly know why, myself, but it is."

That evening O'Hara sat in the taproom, listening and observing. There was plenty of rough men's talk, but there was also serious discussion of the state of the Colonies with reference to the Crown. Something like a deep growl of dissatisfaction could be heard beneath the words. Dark words, some of them.

It minds me of Mr. Bird on shipboard, O'Hara thought. *I must be writing him, for I doubt I'll not be going to see him now.*

It was nearly ten when Elliott came in. Upon seeing O'Hara he came across to him at once.

"Well, well! My rescuer! Glad to see you again. How's the maggot bitin' you anyway?"

They talked till midnight. Elliott was delighted to pour out his information.

"A good town this, but after I've been here a week or so, I get to feelin' cramped. Now Fort Pitt. Not much of a place yet and it's had plenty troubles, God knows, but it's on the edge of things. Room to grow and grow she will if I'm any judge. There's a point of land runs right down to where these two big rivers meet — the Allegheny and the Monongahela. That's where the fort is, sittin' right there like a tomcat eyein' two tabbies, kind of sure of itself in spite of everything. Pretty little grove of apple trees along one side called *The King's Orchard.* Anyway right now Indian tradin's the big business there and I'm glad you've decided to get into it. And if you'd like to join up with me on my next trip I'll be pleased to have you."

Before he left they had discussed practical details: clothes, horses, ammunition, the trade supplies. Elliott had also inquired about his marksmanship and approved Sam's plan.

"I'll give you a look-in while you're at it," he said. "Mebbe give you some hints. When a cat's ready to jump from a tree at you, you have to be damned quick on the trigger."

"*Cats?*" O'Hara echoed in surprise.

"Painters. Fancy name is panther but we say painters over here. Bad customers no matter what you call 'em. We don't run into too many, though," he added encouragingly. "Of course," and his tone was serious, "this whole trading business ain't child's play. Mebbe you ought to think it over twice."

"I'm prepared," O'Hara answered simply.

The next morning before O'Hara had left his room, Sam, grinning widely, delivered a note.

"Ole Isaac from Mr. Carson's brought it an' is waitin' outside for an answer. Smells good," he added.

O'Hara opened the small missive with a slightly quickened pulse. The writing was delicate as was the scent of lavender.

DEAR MR. O'HARA:

If the weather holds and the day be fine will you drive with me on the morrow afternoon at two to Bartram's Garden of Delight and return here for a dish of tea after. Father says he can continue escorting you around on the day following. Kindly send reply by Isaac.

Respectfully,
MARY CARSON

This timing could not have suited him better, considering his recent decision. He could now impart it to Mr. Carson over the tea table. As to the drive? He went to the tall desk at once where he had put paper and a quill when he came. Honored

Madam (he wrote, a small smile quirking his lips at the phrasing) I shall be most happy to present myself at your home tomorrow at two and thank you for your gracious invitation. (Signed) Your humble servant, James O'Hara.

The weather held. The next afternoon was pure gold, and warm. When he reached the Carson house he saw a low barouche drawn up before the door with a driver in the front seat; a few minutes later he himself was handing Mary into the back seat and settling himself beside her. If possible, he thought, she was prettier in the full sunlight than she had been at the candle-lit table. She was dressed in a full-skirted pink dress with velvet laced bodice, a bewitching poke bonnet of the same color, with a small dun-colored cape thrown over her shoulders. Her eyes were bright and merry.

"The Garden of Delight is so beautiful!" she said. "Mr. Bartram started planting it long ago and now it's known even in Europe. When you've seen it, and attended the ball, you'll surely admire Philadelphia."

O'Hara said nothing, content to watch the changing light on her face and listen as she chatted on.

"It's four miles out along the Schuylkill and a pretty drive. Oh, I went to Anne Bingham's yesterday and she is pleased indeed that you will escort me to the ball. It's to be in their town house. And such a mansion! Just wait till you see it. Mr. Bingham's the big West Indian merchant and he married Anne when she was only sixteen."

"Would you fancy the thought of marrying young?" O'Hara found himself asking.

"I don't know," she said. "In two and a half years *I'll* be sixteen. But I'd have to love any man very much to leave my father."

Mary turned again to the subject of the Garden.

"Mr. Bartram has such a knack with all growing things. One curiosity you'll see is a big cypress tree that grew out of a riding whip!"

"Oh, come, come!" O'Hara laughed. "You needn't tell me stories like that!"

"But it's *true*," Mary said earnestly. "Mr. Bartram brought the whip home once years ago from Delaware and for an experiment he planted it. You'll see the tree."

When they reached the Bartram place Mary led the way at once around the stone house to the Garden. O'Hara had come with small interest in what he might see of plant life; his main desire had been to be with Mary again. Now, however, he drew in his breath with astonishment and even rapture. For here, edging winding walks and behind box borders, seemed to his untrained eye what must be every variety of tree and shrub in the world. Before Mary could begin her descriptions an elderly man in wide trousers and a leather apron came up the walk that led from the river.

"Oh, here is Mr. Bartram himself," she said.

He smiled at her. "Well, Mary, thee can't keep away from the Garden. And who is thy friend?"

O'Hara took to the old man at once after the introductions, and the feeling seemed to be mutual for Bartram insisted upon leaving his work at cider making to become their guide. He took them first to his cider mill by the river which he had hewed out of stone himself. There they tasted the freshly made juice, O'Hara for the first time. Then he showed them slowly through the Garden, speaking of the unusual summer flower varieties now dormant for the winter, then of the more famous trees: the riding whip cypress, the Christ's Thorn sent him from the Holy Land, the Ginkgo, the Ohio buck-eyes, the Kentucky coffee trees, the great yellow-wood with its eight-foot stem, and the oak beside the house.

"Thee may have heard of André Michaux, the French botanist?"

"Just the name," O'Hara answered.

"We are in correspondence and he says this must be known as *Bartram's Oak* because I raised it myself from an acorn," the old Quaker said with pride.

As they bade goodbye at last, O'Hara tried to speak his thanks.

"I have never seen such beauty, Mr. Bartram. I shall treasure this hour in my mind. Your Garden of Delight."

"We'll come again," Mary called brightly as the barouche moved off.

"And you've seen the Garden at its poorest," she said eagerly as they drove on. "Imagine the beds filled with flowers in bloom! And some of the trees and shrubs too! That big yellow-wood is covered with hanging creamy clusters in May! What a sight! We'll come out then."

"Mistress Carson," O'Hara said, "there is something I must tell you. I have already settled upon the frontier."

The brightness left her face. "Oh no! You couldn't decide so soon! Before Father's shown you round as he plans. Surely you can't mean it!"

"I'm afraid I do. It's a strange thing working in me. Do you know the word *destiny?*"

"Of course," Mary said with spirit.

"It's like that. I felt it even before I came over. I wanted to get into the newest end of the country and grow up with it, sort of. Help to build it. I'd like to feel that some day . . ." he hesitated, but her eyes were so tender . . . "that some day my name might be remembered for that."

To his astonishment the eyes into which he was looking filled with tears.

"But I like you so," she said innocently. "Somehow I was sure you would stay. And it's dangerous out there. You may get killed by the Indians!"

"I'll try to see them first," he said gently. "You mustn't worry. And of course I will be back in Philadelphia from time to time. Only not to stay."

"You won't leave till *after the ball?*"

"No, I told this Mr. Elliott I'm going with, that I'd be waiting for that. I haven't all my preparations made yet anyway."

Mary drew a small breath of relief but was quiet the rest of the way back. She was still quiet as she poured the tea. Mr. Carson was genial, talkative and eager to hear the immediate news of the Garden trip. Then he brought the conversation around to the interview with Robert Morris.

"He was very kind. I liked him immensely and he offered me a job," O'Hara said in answer to the older man's question.

"Fine! I was going to introduce you to William Bingham next but if Morris will take you, then if I were you I would look no further! Just my own advice. Of course, you . . ."

O'Hara's firm voice broke in. "Mr. Carson, I can't thank you enough for your kindness, but I feel I must follow my first impulse, attractive as this city is. I've met a man, an Indian trader, William Elliott by name. He is willing to take me with him on his next trip clear out to Fort Pitt. I have decided, rather quickly at the last, to go with him."

Mr. Carson took a long sip of tea before he answered. "Well, well," he said at last, "I had a feeling this might be the way you would end but I was hoping to show you more of the advantages here before you made up your mind. Well, well, you're young and strong and eager to prove your mettle. I fear, though, I've been of no use to you."

"But you have," O'Hara said eagerly. "I came here a stranger in a strange land and you made me welcome and gave me friendship — you and Mistress Mary. I'll go my way with a stronger heart because of that!"

"I've heard of this Elliott. A pretty good man I gather with the Indians. That is, if anyone can be sure of dealings with them."

"Father!" Mary's cry was piteous. "*Don't* talk about Indians. I can't bear it. And Mr. O'Hara's not leaving till after the ball!"

"Oh, good! Then I'm still saved from a late night. You must drop in often between now and the time you set out. Can you stay to sup with us this evening?"

"I thank you but Mr. Hastings and Sam are expecting me, and I meet Elliott again tonight to go on with our planning."

He made his thanks and adieux and kissed Mary's hand.

"When I'm camping in the wilderness," he said to her, "I can be thinking of The Garden of Delight."

The next ten days were filled to the brim with activity. O'Hara rose early and put in an hour of marksmanship after breakfast with his new rifle. Another in the late afternoon was supervised by Elliott. It was hard work for both hand and eye but progress was steadily made. In the intervening hours the young man spent time in the Trading store, studying the furs and gradually making his own purchases. The Indians, he was told, were always eager for shirts, leggings, beads, powder, wampum and tobacco, along with any knickknacks that might

attract the eye. He spent much time picking out the latter articles: a little mirror, a doll, a ribbon, a bauble on a chain . . .
He slowly built up his own wardrobe, under direction, and
last of all bought a horse which he named *Pitt*, a fine beast with
a good pair of eyes and a strong if undistinguished pack horse.
He left his money reserves in the care of Robert Morris after
telling him his decision.

On his visits to the Carsons' there was a new tone of intimacy
due to his imminent leave-taking, just as at The Crooked Billet,
Hastings and Sam all but belabored him with kindness and
advice. By the time the night of the Bingham ball rolled
around the preparations were finished.

He dressed with the greatest care that night with Sam, grinning widely, assisting. After the wash, there was clean under-
clothing, then a rose satin waistcoat and black knee breeches
he had brought with him. The silver knee buckles had been
an ancestral gift from his cousin, Lady Mary O'Hara, on his
eighteenth birthday. He had bought in Philadelphia a new
and elegant lace stock and a dark woolen cape lined in white
satin, a pair of dancing pumps and a white wig with a queue.
Finally caparisoned, he knew even from the small mirror that
in looks at least he could hold his own with the other male
guests. Sam and Hastings, admiringly, let him out the house
entrance so he would not need to thread his way through the
taproom customers.

Mr. Carson had offered his carriage which was waiting. Old
Isaac, in a trembling pleasure, greeted O'Hara at the door and
ushered him into the hall where Mr. Carson waited too, holding a red cloak.

"Well, very handsome, Mr. O'Hara! Mary has the notion of
us being here when she comes down the stairway. Ah, here
she is!"

They both caught their breath a little for Mary came slowly, her head maturely poised, every movement assured, all in purest white from powdered hair to satin slippers. She looked like a vision — or a bride. Only her face was aflame with excitement and color. When she reached the hall she curtsied.

"How do I look, Father?"

"Very lovely, my dear," he said, forgetting his Scottish reserve of praise.

"And Mr. O'Hara?" She was smiling at him with eyes coquettish beyond her years.

O'Hara could not speak. So he bowed low, placed the cloak about her shoulders, and offered his arm.

"Well, have a fine time now," Mr. Carson said, as they moved toward the door. "Take good care of her, O'Hara, and come home in reasonable time. Don't stay till the end of the rout. It could go on till dawn, you know, and Mary's too young for that."

"I'll remember, sir. You need not worry."

In the carriage Mary was excitedly gay.

"It's wonderful past believing," she said, "that I'm going to a ball at last and with an escort. I hated the thought of being left there by Father and maybe not having a partner for the dances. The older girls are all kind to me but they'll be busy dancing themselves and could easily forget me."

"Even then," O'Hara said, "I think you would have had your share of attention." He could feel her soft body against his shoulder and the hot blood rose again in him.

"You think so? Then you do feel I look . . . nice?"

"That is too small a word," he said. "Before the evening is over, I'll tell you how you look!"

The Bingham town mansion stood in a garden of three

acres. As they turned in the drive the lights from the great house shone out over the wide portico and the tubs of orange trees and exotic plants which bordered it. Lackeys waited to help the guests alight and more footmen were in attendance at the front door, showing the ladies and gentlemen to their respective dressing room. When O'Hara and Mary met again, divested of their cloaks, they were both flushed with youthful excitement.

"I told you it was elegant!" Mary whispered as they started up the wide marble stairway.

"But I never dreamed of anything like this," he returned.

The great ballroom and the drawing rooms were on the second floor and already the music was rippling out like a banner. In the main drawing room where Mr. and Mrs. Bingham were receiving their guests, O'Hara was conscious of the carpet beneath his feet, its pile inches deep, and his quick eye recognized the French wall paper and the Italian frescoes! The luxury it all represented amazed him. This was not Paris nor an Irish lord's castle. This was *the Colonies!*

He bowed low over Mrs. Bingham's hand, noting her charm. He had seen her affectionate greeting to Mary and also the look of pride and devotion on her husband's face.

"He dotes upon her," Mary said as they passed on. "If I ever get married I want my husband to be just like that to me."

"That could easily happen, I should think," he answered.

The ballroom was a maze of handsomely dressed men and women. Mary looked about eagerly to recognize someone she knew.

"I didn't think there would be such a crowd," she said. "I wanted to introduce you to Mary Vining and some of the others."

"Don't worry," he said smiling, "I'm quite content. Isn't this a minuet that's starting?"

"Can you dance it?" she asked eagerly.

"I would like to try."

"It's not hard. My teacher told me to keep thinking, coupé, high step and balance, and then over again. You know about *coupé?*"

"Yes. I've practiced a little. Shall we find our places?"

Mary was grace itself and O'Hara did not do badly. The music rippled and tinkled from the harpsichords; the violins streamed out their delicate melody; and under the glittering chandeliers the dancers swayed and stepped, their powdered heads now and then all but touching, then retreating again in the rhythm of the movements . . .

It was not till midnight that a pause was made for supper. O'Hara had caught sight of Robert Morris' tall form and Mary had spied several of her friends during the dancing, so as they made their way to the dining room where the bountiful collation was spread, they found themselves in the midst of laughing groups. With the confusion of voices it was only possible for O'Hara to talk for a few minutes with Miss Vining but each found surprised pleasure in the *French* of the other. Mary kept bringing more of her friends into the circle until O'Hara had met the Misses Chew and Miss Peggy Shippen and their escorts. He noticed the interested looks of a number of the young men as they turned toward Mary and after supper a little rush of popularity seized upon her. He did his duty by several of the young ladies and then retired to an alcove to chat with Robert Morris. They both found their eyes straying frequently to the figure in white which stood out from the colored satins and brocades about her.

"A new star in the firmament, I see," Morris said thoughtfully after a time. "Do you really mean that is the Carson girl? I thought she was but a child."

"She's thirteen but extremely mature."

"In a city of beautiful girls I would say the others must soon look to their laurels. So, you're ready for your journey?"

"Yes. We set forth the day after tomorrow. My thanks to you again, Mr. Morris. And now I must meet my young charge and have her safely home before it's too late. This is her first ball."

"Your role of guardian must be a pleasant one. And my good wishes to you again. You may have chosen well. Sometimes when the counting-house seems particularly close and musty, I long for a breath of the wilderness myself."

O'Hara waited at the edge of the dancing floor until Mary's partner brought her to him, leaving her with a lovelorn bow.

"I'm afraid we must go, now," O'Hara said. "As it is, your father may not be pleased at the hour."

Mary's lips pouted for an instant and then she smiled. "I know. You promised. Oh, it's been the most *wonderful* evening. Beyond anything I could have imagined. And I could have had plenty of partners, just as you said. But I liked you best. There's one thing I must show you before we leave. It will only take a minute." She drew him into the hall. "It's Anne's *Greenery*. Come this way."

They went to the end of the hall where Mary pushed a half-opened glass door. Inside, the walls of the room were draped with vines, while feathery ferns rose from the floor on all sides! Mary stood against the green background, the pale light from the hall touching her whiteness.

"Isn't it pretty?" she asked.

Suddenly O'Hara moved close, took her in his arms and kissed her with all his strength. For a moment she seemed to melt, yielding, into his embrace. Then she drew back, her eyes wide and frightened.

"Mr. O'Hara! What made you do . . . such a strange thing."

His face was crimson. "I'm ashamed," he said. "I hope you can forgive me. Please forget that it ever happened. We must go now and prepare to leave."

They spoke no more to each other as they made their adieux and descended the marble stairway. But once in the carriage Mary's voice quivered.

"I'm tired," she said. "All at once I'm *so tired.*"

O'Hara put his arm about her gently and drew her close. Her head drooped against his shoulder. It had been the lovely young white line of her throat, like a dove's breast, he thought, that had overcome him.

"I'm so very sorry that I startled you back there," he said. "It was because you looked so beautiful and I . . . like you so much."

Mary raised her head. "It was that?"

"It was that. Will you forgive me?"

She settled again with a little sigh. "I wish you weren't going away."

"But I'll come back again. I promise you."

They found Mr. Carson in the hall in not too good a humor. "You call two o'clock a reasonable hour, Mr. O'Hara?"

"I apologize, sir, but supper was not served until midnight and after that several young men . . ."

"I believe I could have had partners till dawn, Father," Mary broke in. "I'll tell you all about it. . . ."

"Not tonight," Mr. Carson said firmly. "Say goodbye to

Mr. O'Hara and up to bed with you. I'll hear the news tomor-row."

O'Hara bowed over her hand and kissed it. "Thank you for the privilege of escorting you," he said.

"I had a most pleasant time," she answered primly and turned to the stairs. Neither had said goodbye. At the landing she stood for a long moment, looking back. Mr. Carson did not notice, but O'Hara did.

On the second morning after the ball O'Hara stood, dressed for the journey in deerskin leggings and jacket, looking around the small room that had come to seem like home. He had arranged with Hastings that he would keep it for the present, so now his fine clothes were in the chest and closet and certain small treasures like the silver knee buckles were locked in the drawer of the desk. He was ready to go. Sam had carried his packs down to the taproom where Elliott was waiting. The horse, Pitt, and his pack horse were tied at the door. He was taking these few moments to be alone and think of his situation. He was setting forth upon new and probably perilous adventures; drawn to this way of life by an indescribable inner compulsion; within three weeks from the sunny day he had landed, he had made his decision; he had in that short period come in a measure to know this city, met some of its most important business men, danced at one of its most fashionable balls. And strangest of all, he had for the first time in his young life kissed a girl as a man and a lover.

"My God!" he spoke aloud, and in his tone there was only a reverent awe. "Things do move fast in this new country!"

CHAPTER TWO

BUT IN THE shadowy and mysterious forest time did not pass so quickly. Elliott had chosen the southern route for his own reasons, without explaining that there were certain additional hazards along the way, the chief being the more impenetrable forest. So now, after the first two weeks they progressed slowly on the faint road, if road it could be called, occasionally hacking down fresh undergrowth which blurred the trail.

O'Hara, quick-witted, eager to learn, watched the trained woodsman constantly and began to master the secrets of his craft. Elliott conducted himself entirely by the subtle signs of nature: thickened bark on a tree, the direction and length of shadows, the course of the streams, the snapping of a twig or scuffle of leaves which might indicate game, the changes in the sky which foretold the weather, and every variation in the smoke's rise and drift from the fire. Dusk fell early upon the forest floor and then the two men hobbled their own and the two pack horses, chose a wide spreading tree, and settled for the night. They had had dry weather so far which made a fire no problem with plenty of brush wood about.

One thing had surprised and pleased O'Hara; that was his

increasing fondness for the beast, Pitt. It was a new experience to him to own an animal and he knew for the first time that peculiar intimacy that can obtain between a man and the horse he constantly rides. Pitt now responded to his voice, whinnied at his approach, and nuzzled against him as he stroked the soft, starred nose. As to Elliott he could not say his feeling for him was that of a developing affection as with Pitt, but at least there was a growing respect. Two men living together in the wilderness come to know the quality of each other even while they are still strangers. O'Hara soon knew that Elliott in spite of his picturesque profanity was a decent man. One night as they leaned against a tree, smoking their pipes by the fire, the subject of women came up.

"I was in love once," Elliott said, "but I fought it. I'd never bring a woman to the frontier."

Something inside O'Hara felt unaccountably like a stone. "Why not?" he asked. "There must be women there."

"Not mine," said Elliott sharply. "I've seen too much." After a moment's pause he added, "The Injuns won't violate a woman but they'll scalp her or knock her baby's head against a tree in front of her. I've seen that and a lot more. The frontier's no place for women and a man's a damned selfish brute to bring one here."

"But they come, don't they?" O'Hara pursued anxiously.

"Oh, sure they come. Sure they do. God knows why, for no man's worth it, but women are made queer. Well, I guess I'll turn in. Which in this case means turn *over*," he said with a laugh and closed the conversation, by drawing his blanket about him.

But as the nights passed Elliott became more and more willing to talk. O'Hara was especially eager to learn about two subjects: the Indians in general and Fort Pitt in particular.

"You know," he said one night, "I've never laid eyes on an Indian. If we run into some on our way as you say we're going to, I won't know whether they're the kind to shoot at or parley with."

"If we have any luck," Elliott reassured him, "the ones we meet will be as anxious to trade as we are. The Delawares I know are friendly an' if we swing round through Western Virginia as I'd like to, the Cherokees and Catawbas there are pretty easy to deal with."

He paused for a long minute before he went on. "I've been in this business about ten years and I still don't know how to describe Injuns to you. They have a big grievance against the whites, sure. This was all their country. You can understand them for wantin' it back. But it's their treachery, an' their *cruelty* that's beyond belief. You'll find a regular settler won't even talk about it. He just shoots. Course once in a while you run into a good Injun. There's old Logan, the Mingo, an' Cornstalk, he's a Shawnee, an' White Eyes. He's a Delaware an' the best of the lot. I've met him and I'd trust him. But even if Chiefs like them are friendly they can't keep a whole tribe in bounds. So the fightin' goes on and the whites keep on thinkin' the only good Injun's a dead one. An' damned if I blame them."

He eyed O'Hara as though he feared to frighten him with the whole truth and decided to lighten his touch.

"I saw a sight one day, 'pon my soul! Last time I was at Fort Pitt I went out to the Nine Mile Run on an errand an' I stopped in at a Colonel Proctor's. Well, sittin' there by the fireplace was an Injun big as life an' twice as stuck-up, an' handsome as the very devil if I must say it. He was all decked out in scarlet cloth with a hat thing trimmed with gold lace. Never saw such a get-up, leastways not on an Injun. Colonel Proctor says, nice an' polite, 'Guyasuta, this is Mr. Elliott, the trader.' He kinda bowed his head like a king on a throne, an' I mumbled something. He speaks English if he wants to, but he had an interpreter with him, fellah by the name of Simon Girty! An' I'd trust the Injun as quick as I would him, by the way. Never liked the cut of his jib somehow. Eyes too sharp. You'll run into him sometime."

"Well, what else about this Guyasuta?" O'Hara asked eagerly.

"Oh, I haven't seen him since. The Colonel said he was off up New York way to see Sir William Johnson about some treaty or other. Guess that was why he was so fancy. This Sir William is up to the ears in Injun affairs. Has an Injun wife I hear. As to that, George Groghan, the King of the Traders, they call him, married a Mohawk! So, there you are! The whole Injun business is too big an' mixed up to explain all at once. There have been treaties an' treaties an' massacres an' massacres. Well, don't get scared. I've got along with them so far."

"This Guyasuta," O'Hara said, "I believe I'd like to be meeting him."

"Belike you will," Elliott answered, "if you set out to. He's the big chief of the Senecas an' he's around. Always tryin' to make a treaty with somebody or other, an' then stirrin' up bloody hell the next thing. The settlers hate his hide. I've heard though," he ended thoughtfully, "that if he ever takes a man for a friend, he sticks to him. But I wouldn't know about that."

At the end of their third week's travel, the monotony broke. They had been riding through a glory of falling color which Elliott had explained to his woodland novice. Richest of all were the red oaks, while amongst them the beeches sent down showers like yellow arrowheads. Lower came the purple and rose leaves of the pokeberries, and here and there the spice-bushes, yellow and fragrant as incense, with their own dark red berries which Elliott explained the Indians used to cure a fever.

"They work too," he added, "for I've tried them. Got sick once on the trail an' I believe they pulled me through."

The excitement came at the end of a cool day which now had the sharp promise of frost in the air along with the faint hint of the last witch-hazel blooms. The sunset was beginning to die when Elliott, listening sharply, raised his hand and they both reined their horses. A moon had risen and spilled a pale light upon the trail and the encircling mountain ridges. Suddenly from a hillside came a loud bellowing. Elliott turned back beside O'Hara.

"I'll be damned if that ain't a bull-moose after a mate. He's a bad tempered brute at best but when he's ruttin' he's a devil on the loose. He's in a bad way now, the poor bugger. Late in the season for him, too. Listen to that!"

Not two hundred yards away there rose a long mooing call.

"That's the cow," Elliott said softly. "She's answerin' him."

Then he gripped O'Hara's arm and pointed in front of them. A large black bear crossed the trail some distance beyond them, apparently attracted by the lady moose's proximity and the thought of fresh meat. He moved noiselessly into a thicket below the riders, unaware of their presence, as the wind was blowing toward them. But it had served the cow-moose well also for her love-answers ceased and it was evident she had slipped away at the scent of danger. Elliott already had his rifle drawn and bade O'Hara do the same.

"There may be a fight here if the bull-moose comes on. We'll just sit tight unless the wind changes."

The moose came on, lured by the answering love-call which had sounded so enticing and then died away. He reached the edge of the sparse thicket and saw the bear.

"That bear hasn't got a chance," O'Hara whispered, as he peered to see the huge bulk of the moose with its six- or seven-foot spread of antlers.

Elliott only moved his head and kept his rifle at the ready.

The bear, apparently angered at the loss of his prey and feeling himself invaded on his own ground, threw himself back upon his haunches and prepared to fight.

"It's the moose that doesn't know what he's up against," Elliott whispered back.

Even at their distance the two men could see the contest in the moon's white light. With a bellow of rage the moose reared on his hind legs and struck two driving blows with his sharp front hoofs. But just as he did so, the bear slid forward and parried them with his forearm, throwing the moose off balance. For a second he was on his knees but it was long enough. With a coughing roar the bear swung his left paw in one mighty blow to the neck of the moose just back of the cheek-bone. There was a snap and the great beast rolled over, and was still.

"That done it!" said Elliott taking careful aim. His shot rang in the air and the bear, the victor, his triumph short-lived, reared for a moment and then fell.

O'Hara felt his heart turn over. "That was a mean thing to do," he said hotly. "After the fight that bear put up, I think you might have let him get away! Would he have attacked us?"

Elliott laughed. "I doubt it," he said, "if we'd minded our own business, but lad, we can't use *sentiment* in the wilderness an' we can use that bear skin some cold night. The moose is the biggest piece of luck, though. There aren't too many of them around. Just a few straggle down from the north, and their skins are a prize. Stronger an' tougher than deer. Well, I'd better get to work."

He was off his horse, hobbling it and drawing his hunting knife from his belt in a matter of minutes.

"I'd rather do this job by daylight but by then Mother bear or some other animal might have come for a moose meal so I think I'll get on with the skinnin' now."

O'Hara followed him along the trail and finally into the thicket. There was for light an afterglow in the sky and the full moon rising. He felt upset and squeamish and the next half hour increased his discomfort.

Elliott began with the bear, parting the thick pelage and with quick, deft strokes of the knife, cutting from the throat to the tail and then carefully down the inside of each leg to the foot.

"Tell you one thing about a bear," he said conversationally as he worked on, "clumsy gait he's got. But don't ever let that fool you. There's no man livin' can keep ahead of a bear on foot, and many a hunter's found that out to his sorrow. Say, O'Hara," he said later, "go back to my pack, will you, an' bring me that bag of salt. I can't cure these skins, of course, so we'll just have to trade 'em green."

He had begun upon the moose when O'Hara, consciously loitering, came back with the salt.

"Watch it!" Elliott said sharply as the other set the bag down casually. "My God, man, that stuff's more precious than gold in the Back Country. Tell you what. If anybody ever thinks of a cheaper way to get salt out there than by pack horse over the mountains his fortune's made. Hate to use any of this for the skins but I have to. Come on, now. Get your knife out an' I'll give you a lesson."

O'Hara had to turn aside several times but he stuck it through. The two skins were finally spread out and Elliott, carefully, gingerly, took small handfuls of salt and rubbed the crystals into each rawhide. Then, after two slabs of the meat had been secured, the two men carried them and the pelts back to the trail and unhobbled the horses. Elliott had said they'd better ride on for perhaps an hour before they ate and settled for the night.

"There may be a lot of visitors to the thicket an' we might as well be out of the way. We'll throw the skins over the pack horses."

So they moved on through the now quiet forest, leaving the scene of struggle behind them. O'Hara kept swallowing frequently, still with an uneasy stomach. As he had watched the traders in the Philadelphia store handling the pelts he had smelled the wilderness upon them and vaguely sensed conquest, but it had not been acute knowledge. He had not then been an eyewitness to the fury of a lovesick moose, the courage and skill of a bear, and the death of them both.

Elliott was unusually cheerful. When an hour had passed he reined in a small clearing and soon set about making a fire and starting supper, while O'Hara attended to the horses. He was unusually tender with Pitt and felt some easement as the animal waited for his caresses and rubbed his nose against him. All in this evening the whole animal world had changed for O'Hara, and while Pitt was in the upper level, he was still of it. Would he himself, the young man thought, ever be able to skin a fresh kill as casually as had Elliott? Or should his own place have been in the counting-house after all? A little later, he began to feel more normal. They each had two thick strips of flitch with their johnnycake tonight, and after some hot coffee and a pipe the dark world of the wilderness looked brighter.

It was when they were making their way up the first mountain that Elliott sniffed the air. "Snow tonight! I can always smell it. But if it ain't too deep we'll plout through all right. We ought to hit a half-face pretty soon. Huntin' camp," he explained. "I an' another fellah built it once."

The cold sharpened, the snow fell and the men woke chilled in the night to take turns mending the fire. Once O'Hara sneaked an extra stroud from his pack to throw over Pitt's back. In the morning it was a white world and heavy going. But Elliott had been right about the hunting camp; by sundown they reached it, thankfully.

"Look at that!" he said proudly as they drew up to it. "We did a damned good job if I do say it! Even our pile of leaves is still in there!"

O'Hara studied it with interest. A huge log formed the back with stakes set along the sides growing taller toward the front. Cross slabs made the roof, sloping to the back, and moss and bark filled the chinks. The whole front was open but deep inside was shelter. They brushed away the snow, and got a fire going with handfuls of leaves. Then between them they spread the moose skin carefully over the top.

"Now, my lad, we'll lay on the bear skin an' cozy is the word."

It was strange to O'Hara how true Elliott's optimism became. Their wet deerskin clothes dried out quickly by the fire, then moving back after their meal they found themselves surprisingly warm and comfortable.

"Now the way I figure it," Elliott said, "we've been goin'

slow an' steady from daylight till sunset, makin' I'd say about eight mile a day — three weeks, twenty-one days. . . ." He took a dirty almanac from his inner pocket. "I'd say we'd get to Fort Pitt the middle of December at the latest. One thing I always think about crossin' these mountains. You're always goin' *down* on one side of them!"

All at once he grinned kindly at O'Hara. "You've been itchin' to get there an' mebbe when you see it you'll wish you were back in Philadelphia. Not much to look at in a way and yet — them two rivers aren't meetin' there for nothing. That's what this Colonel Washington thought when he was a young fellah. Lieutenant, he was then, from Virginia. He was sent up to meet the French along the Ohio and tell them to get the hell out. An old trader I know was with him then. He said this Washington rode down to the point in what's Pittsburgh now, looked both ways an' said, 'This is the place for a fort.' So these Virginians begun it after he left. He didn't get anywhere with the French."

"So?" O'Hara prompted with interest.

"Well, the French got there, told the Virginians to go back where they come from and then finished the fort themselves an' called it Duquesne. The English kep' tryin' to get it back but it wasn't till old Iron-gut Forbes took hold that they won. My hat's off to that one. Sick unto death all the time he was gettin' the road cut through for his army an' carried on a litter the last of the march, but he had the spirit! They said when he got in sight of the Fort he yelled, 'I'll sleep there tonight or in hell!' An' by God, he did. I mean he took the fort and named it Pitt for the Prime Minister, an' that's the story."

"And there's been no more trouble after that?"

Elliott laughed heartily as he got up to rebuild the fire.

"Listen to him!" he said, returning to the bear skin. "My lad, when you've been out there a while you'll learn there's *always* trouble. When I got there for the first time ten years ago there was plenty. All the Injuns had got up on their hind legs an' were makin' war. Bad. There was a fellah commandin' the Fort then, Captain Ecuyer, his name was. He took to Injun fightin' like a duck to water. He had every cabin in the town burnt so the Injuns couldn't hide in them an' then he brought every livin' soul into the Fort. I just got in in the nick of time."

"I hadn't pictured it as so large," O'Hara said in surprise.

"Pretty good size. Of course it's been added to. Well, this Ecuyer organized everything. Every man an' woman had a job. Lookouts all the time, day an' night. Then he collected all the beaver traps and crowfeet ones too an' put them along the top of the one rampart that wasn't finished! Pretty smart for just an *army officer* to think of!"

Elliott smoked thoughtfully, remembering.

"He tried his best to keep things clean but we had some sickness. Couple cases of smallpox. There's a kind of bridge between the Fort and the stockade. He made a little hospital there under it. One day some Injuns came up under a white shirt flag to parley. What a pack of lies they had to tell! Said all the tribes were comin' at us an' it was just their friendship for the whites that made them come to warn us. They told Ecuyer to take all his people and get out of the Fort as fast as he could and *get away* before they was all massacreed."

"What did he do?"

"Stood there cool as a cucumber and lied right back at 'em. Said we were just fine. Plenty ammunition, plenty to eat and he'd hold the Fort against all the Injuns in the forest. Said three armies were right then on the way to us in three different directions, and they could get right back an' tell their chiefs that. Then he . . ."

Elliott paused, and glanced at O'Hara before continuing. "Then he did the damnedest thing. He told them he'd like to give them a present to show his regards for them, and didn't he take two blankets off the smallpox beds and hand out to them! He just smiled an' told them to get the hell out but when he come back into the fort, he wasn't smiling. 'Hope it works fast,' he said."

O'Hara's face was aghast. "You don't mean that an English army officer did an unspeakable thing like that?"

"Don't get excited," Elliott said. "Mind Ecuyer had seen plenty. There had to be forays sent out, to cut spelt and get game an' so on. We was always covered but still every once in a while the copper skunks would sneak up an' we'd lose a man or two. An' what they did with them wasn't pretty. We'd find them afterwards. An' plenty other reports came in. Ecuyer hated the Injuns something bitter. 'I could watch every one of them roast in hell,' he said once. Well, I didn't mean to give you such a harangue. Things are pretty quiet right now, or were when I left. But that fort has had plenty blood spilled over it. I haven't told you the half."

"But the town? You say this Ecuyer burnt all the houses?"

"Oh, it's all built up again. That was nine — ten years ago. Log cabins ain't hard to raise. There's quite a little town there now. It's a lot nicer in the spring when the King's Orchard's in bloom. That's a bunch of apple trees down toward the Fort. Women bring seeds over the mountains when they come an' make little gardens round their houses too. I always fancy a garden."

And that night for the first time O'Hara dreamed of Mary as

she had driven with him out to John Bartram's in her pink dress and poke bonnet. He was telling her he must leave and he could see tears on her cheeks as she said, "But I like you so!"

Even in the cold morning the dream persisted in his breast like a warm and fragrant flower, so he spoke little to Elliott for fear the reality of words might dispel it. Elliott, noting his silence, was concerned.

"I oughtn't to have gabbed so much last night. I should have held my whisht. But what I told you's past an' gone. Mebbe things will be better from now on. Don't take it too serious."

"I was very much interested," O'Hara told him, but said no more.

There had been a high wind toward morning which had shaken most of the snow from the tree branches and drifted the trail so their progress was slower than usual. It was in the afternoon when O'Hara's tender dream had melted away, and he was riding tensely, peering sharply about him as he had learned to do, that he saw the danger ahead. On a heavy branch under which Elliott must pass in a few seconds there crouched a great tawny beast, ready to spring. There was no time to call out and the sound might be fatal. O'Hara reined Pitt, raised his rifle and fired. The painter fell in the snow so close to Elliott's horse that the animal vaulted and reared in fright. Elliott was overcome with shock and embarrassment.

"Damn my gizzard," he said, "how did I come to miss that! You'd think I'd never been in the woods before! Which limb was he on?"

O'Hara pointed it out. They were both off their horses now, looking at the panther.

"Got him in the head, too," Elliott said admiringly, then he held out his hand. "Thanks. You're a good man to travel with."

O'Hara looked with tremendous pride at the creature before him. Because of his own quickness and skill he had saved Elliott's life. The jaws of the painter were open and the great claws bared. But over and above the ghastly threat of the animal's power was its beauty! The huge cat lay there, its tawny pelage unblemished, the delicacy of the soft yellow-tinted hair within the ears, the gray of the throat and the pale yellow below the neck, contrasting with the darker *tenné* coat.

"Big one," Elliott was saying. "About eight foot from nose to tail tip I'd guess. Well, here's a pelt we weren't expectin'. Would you like to try your hand? You shot him. We can clear away a little snow here an' let you get to work."

"You go ahead," O'Hara said. "I think I'll watch. I'm not too sure of myself yet," he added, allowing his double meaning to go unexplained.

As Elliott's sharp, quick knife stripped away the fur O'Hara steeled himself to look on, his eyes still full of admiration for the animal itself.

"This is the most beautiful creature I've ever seen," he said.

"Reckon it is," Elliott answered. "All of 'em are. But the Injuns think they've got the devil in them. *Dark spirit,* they call it. An' I'll tell you a funny thing about the meat. It's whiter than chicken an' tastier than pork but most hunters an' settlers out here won't eat it unless they're starvin'. It's crazy but I can't myself. I 'spose the Injuns started it with all their devil talk. Well, do you mind if we don't make a supper of it?" he laughed.

"But what about the skin? Will no one want that either?"

"Oh, that's a different story. There's no rug prettier than a painter hide. You'll get a nice trade for this one an' it's all yours."

Before they slept that night Elliott spoke his thanks again. "Good man!" he repeated, "good man! I had my doubts about you but you're shapin' up all right."

And with this praise hugged to him, O'Hara felt his heart warm even though the wind blew cold.

In general, however, the weather favored them by not growing any worse. By early December they were over the last mountain and Elliott had begun to talk about the Indian village at which they would eventually stop, and to explain that the furs most wanted were *beaver* skins. "For the dandies' hats, you know."

"If we get enough there," he decided, "to make the trip worth while, I think we'll head right into Pittsburgh and let Virginia go. Depends of course on how many traders have been there afore us but I've got along pretty well with this clan so they've mebbe saved me some. Wouldn't be surprised if you make out with them too. You've got a good grin when you use it. How about learnin' some of their lingo?"

"Fine," said O'Hara, "I've been thinking about that. I believe," he added modestly, "that I have an ear for languages."

"You may even get a little use out of your French. Some of the older Injuns picked it up when the Frenchies held the fort. Well, now, let's see."

Each evening thereafter, huddled under their blankets on the bear skin with the painter pelt over their knees and that of the moose stretched from a tree to two stakes above them, the lessons went on. Elliott was amazed.

"Damme if you don't do pretty near as good now as I do!" he said one night. "They know some English but it tickles them when you can talk a little Injun." He raised his head and sniffed the air. "I don't like the smell of this," he said. "Snow

again, as sure as a skunk has a stink. If I mind my bearings
there's a settler's cabin about a day's jog ahead of us. I've passed
it before but I never needed to stop. Looks like we might have
to tomorrow."

"Would they take us in?"

Elliott laughed. "Law of the frontier," he said. "Every
traveler welcome, 'specially in a storm. It's give an' take though.
They're lonely as the devil, most of these families, an' a stranger's a gift from heaven. Gives 'em something different to think
about."

"Have they — extra rooms?" O'Hara asked in surprise.

"My God, listen to him?" Elliott laughed again. "Were you
expectin' *beds*? What you're damned glad to do is to lie down
on the floor with your feet to the fire. Well, we can see what
tomorrow brings."

It brought the worst weather they had had. The cold was
bitter and the predicted snow came not as a soft drifting shower,
as before, but as a biting drive of tiny particles with a hard
wind behind them. It did not block the trail but it stung the
face and blinded the eyes and was particularly distressing to the
horses. As O'Hara felt Pitt lag beneath him he tried with every
tone and caress to encourage him. For himself he felt worn out
and utterly miserable. He could see Elliott peering anxiously
through the sleety mist as the day wore on. Suddenly he gave a
yell, as the first dusk seemed imminent.

"There it is! There's the cabin! You can see a light!"

O'Hara saw it too. Hardly a flame, but a dim something that
was not darkness. They both urged the weary horses on to
where a right-hand break between the trees led them to a
clearing and a log dwelling. The men dismounted stiffly
and Elliott pounded at the heavy door. They could hear voices
within and then the sound of a wooden bolt being drawn back

and the latch string pulled out. A heavy-set unshaven man still perhaps in his thirties opened the door enough to look cautiously out.

"Well, strangers," he said.

"Could you give us shelter for the night?" Elliott asked. "We're pretty well tuckered with the weather."

"Aye, it's bad. Come in. Come in."

"What about the horses?" O'Hara asked anxiously. "Would there be shelter for them too?"

"Aye, there's room in the shed. My stable's pretty small. Wait there."

He shut the door and came out again wearing a hunting coat and cap. "Round this way," he said, leading them past the cabin to where a small neat stable stood with a lean-to shed beside it.

"Just about room for my horse an' cow in there, but the shed here will keep the snow off your beasts," he said, beginning to move some rough farm implements to the side.

"Got feed?"

"Yes. Just about enough to last to Pittsburgh."

"I'm glad. Mine's runnin' kinda low. Well, come on into the house when you get them fixed up. Bad night an' no mistake!"

O'Hara blanketed Pitt, wiped his face, patted him and left him to eat his meal. The horses all seemed well and full enough of life now. Even the shed was certainly an improvement over the raw outdoors.

Once in the cabin O'Hara looked around him with interest. Though he was to see many more like it, this was his unforgettable first. One large room served for all needs. Above the big fireplace hung a rifle on elk's horns, while over the fire itself on the great crane a kettle of mush was boiling. Stirring it stood a youngish woman, thin except where the heaviness of her body proclaimed a soon to be born child. As the travelers, exchanging introductions, came up to the fire to warm themselves, the woman burst into tears.

"Now, now," her husband said irritably, "don't start that again! She's been bawlin' so much this last week we might 'a been flooded out. Think shame to yourself now," he added to the woman.

"I'm sorry," she said, struggling for control. "It's just that I'm clean done out. An' when I think of what's ahead of me . . . the little one here," pointing to a baby on the mat, "she can't even walk yet an' . . ."

"Ach," her husband said harshly, "you'd think to hear you, you're the only woman ever raised a passle of young 'uns. Now let's get some mursh an' no more of this bletherin'."

Elliott's voice rose, calmly casual. "Tell you what, Ma'am, the way it is. When a man sets out to make him a place in the wilderness he has to chop down every tree himself, an' get the stumps out before he can plant him a little patch of corn. Then he has to build a cabin an' a stable with his own hands an' he feels done out pretty often. Yes sir. Then he gets him a pretty little wife like you an' she raises him a family an' *she* gets done out. But before you know it these here children will be big enough to help you an' you can sit an' spin like a queen. So don't you worry, Ma'am. Things'll go fine for you."

They ate, crowded on two rough benches at the hewn log table. The wooden noggins held the hot mush and there was milk to go with it.

"I never tasted anything so good in all my life, Ma'am," O'Hara said to the woman. She had brightened a little and her smile showed what a pretty girl she had been.

"It's only mush," she said, "but we've got plenty, so just eat up."

There was a bed at either end of the cabin. The four older children, from the seven-year boy to the two-year-old, were put into one, with a stroud and a couple of coats over them. The present baby was put into the other bed where the parents presumably would sleep on either side of it later. The four adults on the settle and a bench drew near the fire which the man, John Forsythe, had quickened with new logs.

"Well O'Hara," Elliott said, "this feels pretty good, eh?"

"It feels wonderful. I haven't been so comfortable since I left Philadelphia!"

The woman looked at him in wonder. It was frontier custom not to ask too many questions so this was her first knowledge of where they had come from.

"You've been to Philadelphia?" she asked.

"Yes, Ma'am. I was there three weeks after I came from the old country. Do you know the city?"

"But I came from there," she said hardly above her breath. "Tell me how it looks now so I can picture it again."

O'Hara had been moved by the experience of the evening. He had borne the rigors of the weather; he had been a party to the tragedy of animal mortality; but, here was the human element of the wilderness and he was shaken by all the implications of what he had seen. He looked from the woman, her slight form braced against the hard settle, her arms encircling her unborn child, to the other two men, sitting silent as though waiting too. He made a quick decision.

"I'll tell you all about my three weeks there," he said smiling.

It was not for nothing that he had had an excellent classical education. His narrative flowed vividly; his descriptions were dramatic. He began at the wharf itself, then passed to The Crooked Billet with Hastings and the ever-grinning Sam, to his first meeting with Elliott, and then his dinner at the Carsons' with detail upon detail: the rugs, the paintings, the silver-laden dining table. He told of the city streets as he had walked them; of the Garden of Delight and last of all, *of the Ball!* Here he let himself go, and all at once in the rude log cabin in the forest there seemed to be the golden blaze from crystal chandeliers, the sheen of silks and brocades, and powdered heads that bowed and receded and then bowed again in the dance, while the wind moaning over the cockloft became the music of the violins. O'Hara described it all except Anne Bingham's *Greenery*. It and what happened there were for his heart alone. When he had finished no one spoke for a moment, but the woman's eyes shone and a faint color had risen in her cheeks. Her husband's face was softened too.

"I can picture it all to myself now," she said. "Over and over I can think about it. Thank you, Mr. O'Hara."

"Got so interested I forgot to make up the fire," Forsythe said with gruff praise.

Elliott was profanely pleased. "I'll be damned," he said, "if this fellah doesn't keep surprisin' me all the time. Here he's come over three hundred miles with me an' let me do all the talkin' an' now he breaks out, layin' it off like a preacher or a Philadelphia lawyer."

But it was the woman's eyes that gave O'Hara a glow in his heart. He and Elliott went out ostensibly to see the horses while the couple got themselves to bed. Then they returned, bolted the door, drew in the latch string and settled with their blankets on the floor. But O'Hara lay awake for a long time watching the shadows on the wall, considering the drama he had wit-

nessed. "This," he thought, "is the way a new country is settled. There has to be this hardship for the man, this bitter
pain for the woman, this peril for them both and for their children." For the rifle across the elk's horns spoke eloquently of
that. Elliott was snoring comfortably and at last O'Hara too
fell asleep.

In the morning there was early noise and confusion as the
children, tousled and none too clean, milled about the room.
There was also a good smell of frying flitch with strips of cold
mush sputtering in the fat.

"Now eat hearty," Forsythe told them. "We had pigs an'
right now up in the cockloft we've got enough hams and flitches
to run us into summer. So, don't hold back."

They ate the good hot food with zest and then said their
thanks to their hosts. O'Hara had slipped out to the stable as
soon as he woke and opened his pack. He had noted the children's uncombed hair and that of the woman, drawn tightly
back in a braid but otherwise uncared for. Now, after the other
two men had gone out, he drew forth from the folds of his hunting shirt a comb and a small mirror, and held them out to Mrs.
Forsythe.

"Maybe you'd care for these," he said. "It's a small return
for all you've done for us."

She took the comb first in a sort of wonder. "I haven't had
a one for more than six months! The young 'uns broke my last
one. Oh, I don't know anything I'd rather have. I can fix myself up a bit now, and them too. It does raise the spirits. Are
you *sure* . . ." she began anxiously.

"Perfectly sure. And here's something else for you."

She took the small mirror into her hand and slowly, very
slowly and with fear looked into it. The excitement had colored her cheeks, her eyes were blue and her hair still brown,

for youth had not completely left her. She lowered the mirror suddenly.

"I . . . I supposed likely I looked . . . worse," she faltered.

"Every nice-looking woman should have a looking glass," O'Hara said lightly.

She followed him to the door, clasping her treasures.

"I'll make out now," she said. "I thought I was at the end of my string, but I'll make out now, thanks to you, sir."

"And thank you, Ma'am, and good luck to all of you!"

He found Elliott discussing the Indians with Forsythe.

"Didn't want to ask you in front of the Missus. Had any trouble?"

"Been pretty quiet," the settler said. "Course you never know what they may be up to by spring. But as long as the snow lies we're safe enough. The nearest ones to us are a passle of Delawares. They've got a village along the banks of the Allegheny . . ."

"That's just where we're headin' for," Elliott said, "to do a little tradin'."

"Devil of it is we never know what might hit us. Well, we all just hope for the best an' keep goin'. Same as you, I guess."

The two travelers rode side by side from the cabin back to the trail.

"I've got my belly nice an' full an' my feet warm for once so I think I can hold out the rest of the way," Elliott said.

"Me too," O'Hara agreed. Then he added, "Do you know when that woman has her baby she'll have six children *under seven years?* I asked her."

"Yep! He ought to sleep in the stable for a spell, that fellah. Well, you know my views on women out here."

"Will there be a doctor or . . . a midwife or anyone to help her when her time comes?"

"Hell, no. She'll get through or she won't. Chances are with this many she will. But sometimes . . ." He hesitated, then went on.

"Once I helped a man bury his wife. She'd died tryin' to have her seventh. I happened along. The ground was froze an' he needed an extra pair of hands. An' before we were done he asked me if I knew where he could find another woman. It made me sick to my stomach, sort of. I told him he could damned well find his own wives an' kill them off too. Course he was in a hard spot. I guess I shouldn't have said it. But him askin' me right at that time ι . . Well, you gave that little body back there something to keep her cheered up. I felt like I was at that *Ball* myself. Must have been quite a rout."

"It was that," O'Hara answered, and then they reached the road and rode on single file as before, the younger man's face serious and set.

It was a gray, cold afternoon with a sullen sunset reflected in the broad waters of the Allegheny when they reached the Delaware village. The track from the main trail was only roughly broken so they came slowly upon it, giving O'Hara a chance to study it as they approached. There were the clustered tepees as he had expected, with an ordered look of settlement about them. Smoke rose from the top of each with a welcoming suggestion of warmth and cooking. At each side of the dwellings were wide fields with what seemed to O'Hara tall black sticks emerging everywhere from the snow.

"What are the black poles for?" he asked Elliott as they drew rein together.

He laughed. "Don't you know corn stalks, man, when you

see them? Oh, I forgot you don't raise corn in the old country.
You see the settlers cut down the stalks for fodder but the Indians don't go in for horses so they just let them stand after they
gather the ears."

He came closer to O'Hara. "I hardly need remind *you* about
manners an' it sounds crazy but you get on better with these
sons of bitches if you're polite to them."

"I'll remember," O'Hara said smiling. "What do we do now?"

"We wait. They'll have seen us from the time we left the
road, but it will be a while before someone comes out."

It seemed, indeed, to O'Hara a long time. Then, with great
deliberation an old man dressed in a deerskin tunic came from
a tepee and walked, unsmiling, toward them. Elliott dismounted
at once and leading his horse went to meet the Indian. He
bowed and spoke and the old man raised his hand in greeting
and then looked inquiringly at O'Hara.

"Come on," Elliott encouraged him. "Try your French on
him. He's Magataw, the chief here."

O'Hara approached the Indian, bowed deferentially and
said, "Bon soir, Monsieur. Comment allez-vous?"

"Bien, bien," the man replied thickly at once and motioned
them to come in.

It was supper time and only a few Indians were outside, but
these all recognized Elliott and spoke in friendly fashion to
him. Their guide led them to a tepee which he indicated was
his own, bidding one of the young men see to the horses. He
held the deerskin flap while they stooped and entered. O'Hara
blinked hard in the smoke but soon saw an elderly squaw in a
heavily-beaded tunic stirring a pot over the central fire, and another Indian man, tall and remarkably handsome, standing at
the side.

"My God, that's Guyasuta!" Elliott said under his breath.

There were brief introductions and then they all sat down in a circle around the fire while the squaw dipped out the stew and handed them their portions. It was hot and filling but not tasty and O'Hara had difficulty getting his second helping down. Each time he raised his eyes he found those of Guyasuta fixed upon him. When the food was consumed the general silence was broken. In a mixture of English, Indian and bits of French the strangers told of their journey and Elliott inquired about the trading prospects. Their host, now in high good humor after his meal, said they must all sleep first to make their brains sharp for the next day's bargaining. Guyasuta volunteered in a few words that he had just been to see the great Delaware chieftain, White Eyes, and was bringing friendship news to the Delaware brothers here from his own tribe, the Senecas.

"The hell he is," Elliott said softly out of one side of his mouth to O'Hara.

After the men had sat about smoking their pipes for some time, while the squaw finished her work and stretched out on one of the side beds made of boughs and skins, Elliott spoke of their packs and he and O'Hara went outside to fetch them. All was quiet around the village.

"This Guyasuta," O'Hara said, "what a remarkable looking man!"

"You've got your wish about meeting him an' he seems to like you all right for he never takes his eyes off you. I don't know what the devil he's here for but he's usually up to no good. If he's making soft talk to the Delawares, he's got some scheme in mind, sure as shootin'. Well, our packs will be a little safer in with us."

"And . . . and you think we're safe in there ourselves?"

"Oh, sure, sure. They won't harm a man that's broken bread with them an' trusts their hospitality. Besides, they know me. I've never cheated them yet."

When they returned to the tepee Guyasuta and the chief were in earnest conversation which stopped abruptly. Their host pointed to the bed on the other side of the cabin from his own, indicating that Guyasuta preferred to sleep on the floor by the fire. When Elliott protested, there was only a signal of polite finality from the two Indians. It had therefore been arranged.

"It is wise," the chief said in his own tongue, which Elliott interpreted, "that we seek sleep early so that we may be prepared for the new day."

He went to his own side and lay down on the end of the bed, his feet touching those of his wife. There were plenty of blankets and pelts for all to place both under and over them, and cushions of deer hair for further comfort. In a few minutes all were settled, Guyasuta's great length beside the fire.

As in the Forsythes' cabin O'Hara could not go easily to sleep. The air was heavy, for one thing, with the smoke, the odor of cooking, and another new smell which he would learn later was peculiar to the Indians. He lay looking about him, his eyes picking up various features of the dwelling. He stared at the bark lining the tepee, placed with skill; at the weaving frame along with the cooking utensils; at the heavy bunches of dried herbs and grasses hanging from one of the poles; at the fireplace set in a depression in the center and outlined with cobblestones. From this his eyes sought the man who lay beside it. Almost at once Guyasuta turned his head and looked at him. In this mutual gaze they were now for the first time alone, sharing some strange affinity. In an unconscious reaction O'Hara smiled. There was no change of expression on the Indian's face for a second, then he, too, smiled, raised his hand in a slight gesture and turned back to the fire.

"I believe I've got me a new friend," O'Hara thought with surprise as he fell asleep.

The next day began early, before O'Hara was properly awake. There was stir and noise now throughout the village and evidently excitement over the coming of the travelers. In the rough shed where the horses had been tied there were drying shelves around the sides. With the horses turned out there was room for the trading to begin. Elliott and O'Hara spread forth their wares, and one by one the Indians came with their pelts. O'Hara had made his own selection and now discovered it was good. Beads, vermilion, tobacco, neck ornaments for the women, combs, three more looking glasses . . . He soon discovered these latter were the most valuable. He watched Elliott making his own trades and copied his technique.

"Beaver," Elliott would say firmly when presented with fox. "I have to have beaver!"

The Indians stared with greedy eyes at the bright array of trinkets, then slowly went back to their wigwams and returned with the beaver skins. Elliott accepted a few fox and lynx along with them but when the trading was over both men had a good bundle of the popular pelts.

At the very end, Elliott produced the moose skin and with a dignified speech of thanks, presented it solemnly to their host.

"We thank great Magataw for food, for beds, and always we will be his friends."

O'Hara's quick ear had already caught on to more of the Indian patois so he added a thank you and farewell of his own. There was an almost jovial leave-taking as the old man was apparently overcome with pleasure at his gift. Before the travelers left Elliott inquired about Guyasuta who had not been seen all morning.

"He leave before sun," Magataw explained.

With final reciprocal gestures of good will the travelers set off, their packs now built up high upon the pack horses.

"Well, that was a good haul," Elliott announced with satisfaction. "We'll just make a bee-line now right into Pittsburgh. I hated to part with that moose skin but it always pays to leave them thinking they got the best of it. Either of us will be welcome another time."

It was four o'clock on a cold, sunny day when they reached their journey's end. O'Hara, tensely excited, scanned the towering white hills that rose to the south and west, and then fixed his eyes upon the little town itself as they rode slowly through it. He had prepared himself for disappointment but he felt none. This was indeed the frontier, but there was evident everywhere the strong, determined business of living: the smoke from more than half a hundred chimneys, the men and women going about their errands from house to house along the snowy tracks, the Fort and its imposing Bastions, with the broad, rolling rivers half glimpsed at its feet; this town, he felt, was the habitation of people who had come to stay.

"We'll go first to the tavern," Elliott was saying, "an' get ourselves fixed up. Semple's. He's a good soul but his wife has a sharp tongue. Never see much of her, though. Sticks to the kitchen. He keeps a very good house, considering. Has to be for pretty often a bigwig from Philadelphia or somewhere comes through on business. It's up here on the hill. Doesn't look too bad, does it?"

"It looks very good to me," O'Hara answered. And indeed

it did. A large, spreading log structure on a slight eminence overlooked the rest of the town. There were plenty of stumps at the front with rings for tethering the horses, so the men tied up their beasts, unfastened their packs, stamped off the snow and entered by the heavy front door. The big room O'Hara saw did not have the polished look of The Crooked Billet tap-room but it did have the same comfort: the great, blazing fire, the chairs and tables for the guests, a good smell of cooking food, and a well stocked bar at one side. A short stout man with red apple cheeks and longish white hair around a bald crown greeted them.

"Mr. Semple, this is James O'Hara fresh from Ireland, try-ing his hand at a little Indian tradin'. Can you put us up?"

"Aye, aye, aye. I've got rooms. From Ireland, you say?" turn-ing to O'Hara.

"Originally. I've been two years working in Liverpool just before I came over."

"Well, well! I came from Scotland myself when I was a younker. You'll find the place here full of Scotch-Irish. Tough as hickory knots. Made for the frontier. Give them a psalm-book in one hand and a rifle in the other an' the devil himself couldn't beat them. So now, I'll wager you could do with a quick meal, couldn't you?"

"All we've had today is a bit of jerk for our breakfast. I got some from the Delawares back yonder. But we're hungry enough now to eat a live polecat!"

"Right. I'll tell Sally in the kitchen to set you up something. Would you like a wee drop to wet your thrapples first?"

The men drank the whiskey neat, standing close to the fire, the warmth within and without slowly thawing their chilled bodies. Then they sat down to a hot dish of fowl and dumplings which Sally, broad, weathered and full of talk, ladled out to them. When she had left them, Elliott leaned over to his companion, and spoke in a low tone.

"I just thought of something. Tonight if you'd like . . . I mean if you'd want. . . . Oh hell, you know what I mean. I can tell you the best place to go."

O'Hara colored. "No thanks, I believe not," he said.

"No offense. Just thought I'd mention it. Tell you what *I'm* going to do tonight. I'm going to toast myself, rump an' stump, in front of that fire an' 'wet my thrapple,' as our friend Semple puts it, a good few times an' then go up to a *real bed* an' sleep till the last trump or thereabouts."

"I suppose they have quarters for the horses too?" O'Hara asked.

"Oh, sure. Semple has a big stable an' plenty of fodder an' feed. He has a boy here who attends to the beasts."

"I'll look in on Pitt," said O'Hara, "after I take a walk. I'd like to see the Fort before dark."

"Well, look your fill tonight if you want to but you can see it all better tomorrow."

O'Hara's room was small and very chill. There was a bed, however, with a big feather tick and decent sheets and it seemed to the young man fit for a king's palace. He opened one pack, hung up his few clothes on hooks along the wall, pushed the pelts into a corner, and then putting inside his shirt a quill pen and some paper, he went down again and out into the cold. It was the delicate hour of the winter's day when sunset drifts into twilight. The stars hung now purely shining for all lovers, above a gold and rose afterglow in the sky, and the moon-blue snow below. In the air was the faint sound of rolling waters.

O'Hara hurried down the little rise of ground, past log cabins with a poor light coming through their greased paper panes and on impetuously to the Point where he slowed up and looked intently about him. There on the side of the Allegheny with their tracery of bare branches stood the trees of what must be the King's Orchard; there was the main Fort itself, plainly to be seen along the banks of the Monongahela. It had not been for naught that Elliott had drawn a rough diagram in the half-face cabin by the firelight. O'Hara knew his lesson well: left the Monongahela, right the Allegheny, while at their meeting stretched the broad waters of the Ohio, the *Beautiful River,* Elliott said the Indians called it.

He went nearer the Fort. Pitt, named for the Prime Minister, fourteen years old this month, he had been told, strong looking, bastioned like a star with its lookouts and gun holes, could hold a guard of over two hundred men, Elliott said. There must be a good many there now for O'Hara could see lights and hear shouts, and suddenly a song! About four hundred yards away, he estimated, stood the older fort, Duquesne, finished and manned at last, as he had heard, by the English. Wooden palisades now surrounded it and between it and the other stood a small redoubt.

O'Hara felt a pricking of the skin as he looked at the scene. More even than in the settler's cabin in the forest he felt the mortal struggle, the spilt lifeblood, and the stubborn courage by which this new country was being born. And now he, a stranger from hoary cities three thousand miles away, caught up mysteriously in the web of fate, was to be a part of it! He turned slowly about, his eyes on the little town lying for the moment at peace.

"I'm not sorry I came," he thought. "I don't believe I'll ever be sorry."

Once back in the tavern after assuring himself that his horse was comfortable, he spoke to Mr. Semple.

"Would you be having any ink I could either buy or borrow?"

"Aye, I've got a bit ink though not too many call for it. It's dear though. A wee bit bottle will cost you a shilling."

"I'll take a one," said O'Hara. "Is there a post or a messenger going back to Philadelphia any time soon?"

"One in the morning. Give me your letter, laddie, and I'll see he gets it. That will be two shillings more. For the Post."

O'Hara with his small container of ink went to one of the farthest tables. There were a number of men including Elliott in the tavern now eating or drinking but he felt entirely removed from them all as he spread out the paper, dipped his quill and sat in thought. Then in his best hand he wrote: *Mistress Mary Carson, Honored Madam:*

When he had finished he read it all over, consideringly. He *had* to tell about shooting the painter, for when the skin was properly cured he intended to send it to her for a rug. The description of their night with the Indians would relieve her from the dread she had voiced concerning them. He had written more or less lightly about the visit at the settler's cabin. She would like the part about the comb and the looking glass. It was his last sentence which he questioned. *During the nights on the journey when we had to endure the severe cold I thought of my hours with you and felt warmed in spite of the weather.* Was this too much to say? Should he rewrite the whole missive, leaving this out? He sat there, thinking.

Then suddenly with what was almost a gust of passion he signed himself, *Your most obedient and humble servant, James O'Hara,* folded the letter and sealed it.

CHAPTER THREE

IF THE NEW WORLD's sunshine in October had been startling to O'Hara, that which greeted him this December morning in Pittsburgh was much more so. The snow lay deeply upon the town, covering the roofs of the raw log cabins and warehouses with curving windrows and topping the sharp posts here and there with tufts like tow; the icicles hung glittering and unbroken from the eaves; the cold was intense, yet over it all the sun shone strongly, steadily benign. The young man, stepping out on the tavern porch for a moment before breakfast, liked the thought of this. A bright day had met him at Philadelphia, another welcomed him now to the frontier. With expectancy strong within him he went in again to the roaring fire and the smiling face of his host.

"Well," said Mr. Semple, "and how did you sleep, laddie?"

"Like a top. This is good air here."

"And plenty of it! We're about ten below zero this morning. Well, draw up to the table and get some breakfast under your belt. Elliott still asleep?"

"I guess so. I didn't disturb him."

"Aye. Best not. He don't like to be roused. Works hard and rests hard, that fellah."

He sat down opposite as Sally set a plate of bacon and eggs before O'Hara, smiling archly at him as she did so.

"Don't mind her," Semple said, when she had left. "She's forty if she's a day but she makes sheep's eyes at every man that comes in. Have you any definite plans for yourself now that you've got here?"

To his surprise O'Hara spoke confidently. "First of all," he said, "I'm interested in this Fort. I'm astonished at its size. Last night I had only a twilight glimpse of it. Now I'd like to see it all. Then I want to get to know the proprietors of a trading store. Learn what I can about the business and as soon as possible, set out for myself."

"Good!" said Semple. "At least you know what you're after. And I 'spose Elliott's warned you it's no soft job, the trading?"

"Yes, but I'm prepared to face it."

"Aye. If a man wants eggs he must put up with the cackling. About the Fort now. I watched it being built. Captain Harry Gordon, he was the engineer, stayed with me at my old place. Oh, it was a beautiful sight that fort when it was just finished. Aye, but it was! Ready for a garrison of a thousand men and officers. That was the day of its glory. Never been quite the same since."

"What happened? War?"

"Floods," he said. "The one in '62 was the worst. Even the oldest Injun couldn't remember one as bad. When these two rivers out here go into spate there's a watery rampage for sure. So, a good deal of the earth works were washed out and considerable damage done one way or another. But it's still a mighty fine strong spot anybody would find if he had a mind to tamper with it."

From the smaller room behind the main one there came the

sound of loud voices rising to a pitch of anger. Mr. Semple drew a prodigious sigh as he rose from his chair.

"Trouble again," he said, "and it looks to me as if we're in for plenty more. Come along. I may need an extra fist."

O'Hara followed him curiously. At one side of a billiard table two men were arguing with violence.

"Why you blasphemous, treasonous dog!" the one was yelling. "The king's the king! We're bound to support him! In the old country you'd hang for this kind of talk!"

"But we're not in the old country, I tell you. We've got one of our own and nearly tore our livers out to get it. And the king has no right to tax us to pay for his damned dirty war in Europe that we'd nothing to do with. I say to hell with the King and let's get on with our own business here."

"Nobody in my presence will say that, and me a loyal subject of the Crown!" the heavier of the two men shouted as he lunged out at the other's jaw.

It was a matter of seconds before the two were embroiled in deadly earnest. O'Hara, in spite of the seriousness of the fight he was watching, was filled with amusement at Semple's tactics.

"Gentlemen, gentlemen!" the latter cried, landing a skillful blow first at one man and then the other, "Gentlemen, I beg of you, *stop, desist!* (Two more well aimed punches which found their mark.) "This is a peaceful house!" (*Right, left!*) "I will allow no fighting . . . Give the big fellow a good one O'Hara," he said finally in an aside when it was evident the two fighters were growing winded. "I'll take care of this one."

O'Hara gave his best which was good indeed to the man indicated while Semple landed a *coup de grâce* on the other. After a few minutes the two men, dazed, bloody and groggy, regarded each other from the chairs where Semple managed to install them after he had gotten them up from the floor.

"Good, gentlemen!" he said. "Good! You were wise to stop. Now you've had it out, you can be friends. But just remember there must be no fighting in my tavern. Tell Sally to fetch a basin of cold water, son," he said in a low voice, following O'Hara to the door, "then you go and take a nice walk. I'll swab them up and give them a good dram of whiskey and they'll never be clear that we were in on it at all. That's the only way to handle the thing though. If they're both knocked out soon, there's not likely to be trouble after. Thank ye, laddie!"

O'Hara did as he was bid and then walked out into the crisp bright air. Now in full day he could see the town clearly, and the great spreading pentagon which was the Fort. Tremendous! Amazing! England must have expected a long and bitter fight with the French to have caused her to build such a bulwark here in the wilderness. And then her ancient enemy had fired their old stronghold at General Forbes' approach, as Elliott had told him, and in the light of its ruins marched away and never came back! Strange. But, O'Hara mused, governments had misjudged situations before and poured out money needlessly, and probably would again. He wished his father could see this masterpiece of defense, though. For floods or no floods, it still stood a supreme achievement for any country, let alone a backwoods colony, and he was determined to see it all as soon as possible. He could then write a full account back.

He walked to the edge of the great ditch where he had stood the night before, reasoning that in all likelihood someone would come along to cross the bridge into the fort enclosure and perhaps be willing to act as guide. In this plan as in everything, O'Hara felt a compulsion for prompt action. He waited for an hour and then his reward came. An officer, perhaps in his late

thirties, with a height above his own, broad shoulders and a
friendly countenance, came up to the bridge from the town.
He nodded pleasantly and was starting across when O'Hara
spoke.

"If you please, sir, would it be possible for me to go into the
Fort? I'm new here and I'm very much interested. My name's
James O'Hara," he added, "a couple of months over from the
old country."

The other reached his hand.

"Captain William Grant, at your service. We're not very
busy here, just now, as you may have heard and I'll be glad to
show you around. I'm pretty proud of the Fort, some parts of it,
especially," he smiled. "So take a good look from here and then
we'll go inside."

"The man I traveled with coming from Philadelphia told me
a bit of the history of it but I wasn't prepared for anything so
large."

"Biggest the British have built anywhere on the frontier.
Covers seventeen acres here at the Point. Of course that's including the outworks. Inside the ramparts it's about two. Well
now! You get a good view here of the Bastions and the walls
between. These next the town as you can see are faced with
brick, but the whole thing is what we call a *dirt* fort. Earth
works are easier to keep up and the best protection you can get
from gunfire."

The Captain paused to laugh.

"We've got one figure about that which always gets an argu-
ment from strangers. The dirt for this fort was dug out of this
ditch you see before you, and it amounted to 66,000 cubic yards!
I've had plenty officers come out here and say it couldn't be done
with picks, shovels and wheelbarrows. And I always say you're

damned right it couldn't, only it *was* done. Well, let's go on in."

They crossed the bridge over the ditch and the drawbridge beyond.

"We still take this up at night," Grant explained. "We've had no trouble with the French this long time but the Indians, like the Biblical poor, are always with us. Blast their hides."

Inside the gate the Captain led the way to the center of the open space from which he could point in all directions.

"You see," he said, "the simplest way to explain this to you is that we start here with a five-sided parade ground bordered by five rows of buildings which in turn are protected by the five high mounds of earth shaped like ramparts. These long buildings are the barracks for the officers and men. The little log one where we came in is the storehouse for flour, by the way. The brick house here to the right is the Commandant's home. Underground are storage supplies, casemates for powder, the guard house, and so on."

"My father's a soldier with the Irish Brigade in France and I'll be writing him of this. I wish he could see it."

"Be sure to note the brick pavements by the barracks," the Captain laughed. "They were my idea. Now, for the Bastions — they have different names but they're all alike so you need see only one. We'll go into the *Monongahela* to give you a good view of the rivers."

He led the way up a narrow ramped access which brought them out at the top of the defense. O'Hara drew a long breath and for a moment could not speak. He could feel the Captain's eyes on him.

"Quite a spot, eh?" the latter said.

At their feet rolled the deep, still waters of the Monongahela, white-spotted now with patches of ice. Across from it rose a steep sheer mountain of snow. To the right between low-lying banks rushed the swifter Allegheny, shaking off its ice as a dog sheds water, hastening on to its marriage with its neighbor river and the great consummation at the Point itself. Then on and on after their union flowed La Belle Rivière, the Ohio, on and on widely bending, sweeping into the far wilderness!

"I've never seen anything like this," O'Hara said at last. "And I've seen many rivers."

"There *isn't* anything else like it," the Captain agreed. "It's unique. And I often think that long after this fort is gone and forgotten there will be something else important here . . ."

"I was thinking that myself," O'Hara said quietly.

"At the tip of the Point itself is where the old Fort Duquesne stood. Right below us here you can see a small redoubt we built about eight years ago. A blockhouse.* Good tight little structure with plenty of rifle holes. But if you'll look clear back over the fort, you'll see my special pride, the King's Gardens! Of course I can point out only the location now under the snow but the trees outline the walks and the thick block of them there along the Allegheny are the fruit trees — The King's Orchard."

"I spotted that last night from what Elliott told me."

"Of course the floods did a lot of hurt but we've come back pretty well these last years. We don't need so many vegetables now since the garrison's small, but I've seen the time we set out ten thousand cabbage plants! Our worst trouble after the floods and the Injuns have been the grasshoppers. They're a curse and no mistake. You know a gardener's always hoping for *next season,* and I can't wait. I want to plant more flowers this spring if the seeds come through. Well, I hope this has given you a little idea of the Fort. Come again any time you like. There

* This blockhouse still stands.

aren't many parades to see this weather. The men just hole up in their barracks."

"You've been more than kind and I thank you for your time and your courtesy. Captain Grant?"

"Yes."

"I'd like to ask you a question. Just before I came here this morning there was a fight at Semple's Tavern where I'm staying . . ."

Captain Grant interrupted with a chuckle. "Did Semple stop it in his usual fashion?"

"He did."

"I watched him at it once. Funniest thing I ever saw. It always seems to work, though."

"It's the cause of this quarrel I wanted to ask you about. One man was for the King and the other was against him. Something about taxation. I heard a bit about this on shipboard. Is it serious?"

Captain Grant's face lengthened. "I'm damned if I know," he said. "We hoist the Union Jack every Sunday over this Fort on the Flag Bastion. I'm a British officer," pointing to his uniform, "and I've never thought over the years that I could be anything else. But now . . ."

He paused and looked out over the river. "Two years ago a Colonel Washington was out here. Stayed at Semple's, by the way. He was interested in buying some land. He came to the Fort and we had a long talk. He's a good man and a fine soldier. He's been round here different times when there was trouble. He was with Braddock when he was sent out to take Fort Duquesne from the French and then later with Forbes. This Braddock was an excellent general, by the way, but he didn't know anything more about Indian fighting than a rabbit, so his army was about wiped out except for what this young Washington saved. The Indians were on the French side, you see. When Forbes came out, he knew what he was doing. But you've maybe heard all this. Well, Colonel Washington told me there's a lot of restlessness along the Atlantic coast — at Boston especially, over this taxation business. But he trusts it will calm down. Said he was going back to his place in Virginia and farm and hope for the best. *But* he added something that I've thought over pretty often since, for I admire the man. He said if it came to the pinch he'd certainly stand with the Colonies. So I don't know. Guess we'll all have to cross that bridge when we come to it. *If* we come."

As O'Hara turned to go, the Captain spoke again.

"The queer thing is that in spite of all the hardships and dangers the people *like this country!* Maybe they're just land hungry and there's plenty of it here, God knows. But no, I think it's more than that. Take me, now. When I was first sent over to America I fairly prayed to get back to England. Then little by little I began to feel at home. Even out here on the edge of the wilderness there's something in the air . . . something that makes you feel an inch or two higher than you are. And of course there's adventure and excitement. Odd thing, though, you know. Well, keep your ears open. You're likely to hear more about all this, I imagine, rather than less."

As O'Hara walked back to the tavern, the sun was higher and the snow glistened. On the rough, rutted tracks through the town there was now plenty of activity: a rider who looked as though he might have crossed the mountains; a pair of hunters evidently setting forth for game; some straggling Indians in their beaded skins; a settler's wagon rattling over the bumps; and here and there a woman in full linsey skirt and shawl mak-

ing her plodding way with a basket on her arm. He noted now
particularly the squat warehouses along the Allegheny. These
would likely be the trading stores. The cabins, comprising what
Elliott last night had called the High Town, were more on the
Monongahela side above the fort. To south and west toward
the white hills, and on and on beyond them stretched the un-
claimed wilderness.

All at once he felt shaken by a realization of the country's
immensity. He thought of the neat gardens, the farms, the es-
tates even, which he had known in the old world. They now
seemed, in memory, puny, niggardly, limited, *pent,* in contrast to the unimaginable vastness here. Even the rough settlement partook of the freedom of the wild. And a desire for
ownership rose in him like a lust.

"I'll buy some land soon," he decided. Then with his quick
smile he added aloud, "And I've an idea I'll keep on buying
it!"

When he re-entered the tavern he saw a small crowd gathered
before the fire where a man was talking in frightened tones.

"That's what my brother said it must have been. A mad wolf.
He's down with pleurisy, my brother is, so I came here to get
help. We just landed there about two mile back a few days ago,
me an' my family. Come from Philadelphy. My brother says
there's only one cure he knows of for me. It's one of *these pills.*
He says he's heard there's a Doctor Marchand, a furriner, over
on Sewickley Crick that has them. I got to get one. I *can't die*
an' leave my family just when I've brought them out here. If
someone would just ride there with me an' show me the
way . . ."

The speaker turned his white face and saw O'Hara on the
edge of the group. Recognition struck them both at once.

O'Hara remembered him as the man storing his wagon at the market.

"It's you, then!" the stricken man exclaimed. "I'm Silas Porter an' I told you in Philadelphy we couldn't fail to meet out here. I'm glad to see a face I know even if I don't mind your name."

"O'Hara!"

"That's right. I'm in bad trouble. You mebbe heard . . ."

A man spoke. "About this pill he talks about, Mr. Semple. Have you heard of it? Is it any good?"

Semple chose his words carefully. "We've all heard of it out here and I've known two men who took it and didn't . . . didn't get . . . I mean they got well. Far as I'm concerned if I was bit by a mad wolf I'd take anything I ever heard tell of, so I would. And they do say this pill has some power, some way."

"I'm nice an' rested now so a ride won't hurt me, I guess, an' I know the way to Sewickley Crick. I'll go for your pill, Mr. Porter. You just show me the road to your brother's cabin so I'll know how to get back to it. Then you get right in there an' keep warm an' comfortable." It was Elliott who spoke.

There were tears in Porter's eyes.

"I can't ever thank you. You see I feel all right so far but they say the . . . the effects come on sudden after a few days. Would you be ready to start now?"

"Have a bite to eat first," Semple broke in. "That'll be my contribution. Sit you down, Mr. Porter, and you, Mr. Elliott. You can't set forth on an empty stomach."

"I think I'll be going with you," O'Hara said to Elliott quietly.

Elliott was not a smiling man but he smiled now.

"Well now, a little companionship along the way might be real nice. It isn't too far. About twenty mile or better, I'd judge. We'll strike out along the Monongahela till we hit the Yonghigheny and the Sewickley branches off it. You're sure you want to come?"

"Of course I'm sure," and this time O'Hara smiled.

They ate quickly, with Semple interrupting several gruesome tales of mad wolf bites and preventing other incipient ones by a steady flow of loud conversation about the weather, the chance of floods, the coming dance at the Commandant's house and the latest perfidy of the Indians.

When the men had finished eating, Elliott and O'Hara went to their rooms to put extra clothing under their hunting shirts and breeches, collect their rifles and two blankets apiece. The stable boy brought round the horses, O'Hara making sure Pitt had been fed. Provisions for themselves and the beasts were fastened behind the saddles and the three set off with all the men in the tavern waving them good luck from the porch.

They allowed Porter to lead the three miles to his brother's cabin. As he dismounted there he thanked them again, his lip trembling.

"Did anyone get the wolf?" Elliott asked a little hesitantly.

"No, it got away. That's what's worryin' my brother. The boys have to go out to the stable to feed the stock . . ."

"Can they shoot?"

"Aye, can they! Both of them."

"Good. Tell them not to go out without a rifle. And you keep yours handy and a hunting knife too. Well, don't worry now. We'll be back soon."

"You think the wolf might still be around?" O'Hara asked as they rode on.

"Could be. We'll keep our eyes skinned. I'll pick out the trail an' watch ahead. You keep looking round. And be ready. This is one of the worst things that can happen out here and to think that poor cuss ran into it almost as soon as he landed."

"Is it like a mad dog?"

"Only worse. No one knows why, but just once in a while a wolf goes mad. Then he seems to make straight for human habitation. Over on Chartier's Crick once there was one tried to jump right into a cabin. It don't happen often so everyone gets sort of careless. Out here you have to forget about lots of possibilities or you'd go crazy, I guess."

"But this pill. Do you believe in it?"

"Danged if I know. Some say it's not worth a swallow, but I met up with one man who swore he was cured by it. He was bit by a mad dog an' he never got rabies. So, that's why I had to make this trip. Give poor Porter there any chance there is. The doctors, what few we've got on the frontier, don't seem to know anything but bleedin' for a mad bite, an' that never helps. Well, we'll see."

Near sundown they ate from the food Sally had given them and fed the horses. The moon was bright and the Indian trail they were following beside the river recognizable from recent tracks.

"We'll keep on as long as we can," Elliott decided. "We can't get lost and the doctor's cabin, I've heard, is the first one on the Crick. Thank God there's no wind."

The horses plouted patiently on through the snow, no sound above their movements except a soft flow of water and an occasional breaking twig in the frost. They stopped now and then for a few minutes during which O'Hara dismounted, patted Pitt's nose, stroked his flanks and rubbed his knee joints. It

was, Elliott figured, about nine o'clock when they sighted the
light of a cabin.

"This must be it," he said as he directed his horse toward it.

In response to a knock on the door a bearded, past middle-
aged man holding a candle opened it a little way and peered
out.

"Yes, what is it?" he inquired with a heavy accent.

Elliott told him briefly of their errand. He did not open the
door further.

"I'll get a mat for you to stand on," he said, "my wife is particular about her house. Wait."

In a few moments he was back, opened the door and spread
a worn mat just inside. Elliott and O'Hara placed their snowy
shoe packs carefully upon it.

"Now you say a mad wolf, yes? That makes the worst hydro-
phobia of all. I will get you the pill."

"You think it will cure him, Doctor?"

He nodded and then shook his head. "That is the answer.
Yes — no. I got these from an old doctor in Switzerland. I
bring them with me to this country. Not many times I have
reason to give them. When I do mostly they help. Sometimes
not. But there is nothing else I know to do for a mad bite. So I
give the pill and hope to God. I get it for you."

It was a very large pill, brown in color. The doctor wrapped
it very carefully in a bit of linen cloth.

"Take care," he said to Elliott. "Where will you carry it for
safety?"

"Next my skin," he said, "and I'll tighten my belt you can
be sure."

"There is one thing you must tell this man with all your
strength. He must take no liquor, *none,* for two weeks. If he

does the pill will not work. I cannot tell you why. I only know it is true. Will you start back at once mebbe?"

"Our horses are tired. We'll rest till near daylight if . . . if you . . ."

The doctor shook his head as they all three looked about the room. There were woven rugs on the floor, there were cushions on the settle; the table had been rubbed smooth, on the mantel was a pewter candelabra and a vase — this was not a settler's cabin.

"I . . . I have no place, I am sorry. My wife . . . but in the stable is a big pile of hay and in it is almost like feathers . . ."

"We have blankets and thank you very much. What is the fee for the pill?"

He glanced over his shoulder and then spoke low. "For this, one pound *if the man gets well*. If not, there is no fee. That is fair, yes? A pound is not too much for a life. If not, nothing."

"You will trust us to bring you the money if the man gets over this?" Elliott asked wonderingly.

"My friend, when two men ride through this weather to help another, I'm sure they can be trusted."

They thanked him and went back into the night. The stable stood clear in the moonlight and in a few minutes they had the horses in the shed and they were burrowing into the hay.

"If I just don't roll over an' squash the damned pill," Elliott said as he touched it carefully through his shirts. "I'll sleep on my back to be sure. But if this Porter gets well he'll never have a pound to pay for it."

"I can manage it," said O'Hara.

"We can go halvers. You know that doctor fellow's scared

to death of his wife. If I had one I'd be good to her but I can tell you I wouldn't let her boss me."

For answer strangely enough O'Hara laughed. "Oh, I guess there could be women who would wind their husbands round their little fingers and the men would like it!"

"Speak for yourself," Elliott rejoined. "Ugh, it's cold! As between hay an' feathers I'll stick to the feathers. Punch me when you wake, will you? We ought to start off early as we can."

They reached the cabin of Porter's brother about two hours past noon the next day. A young boy answered their knock and motioned them to enter, but inside they stopped, transfixed. The whole family of perhaps a dozen people of all ages were kneeling upon the floor. Even the sick man in the bed lay with his hands clasped above him. A woman with a rather beautiful face, now fixed and white, spoke.

"We are at prayer . . ."

"Did you get the pill?" Porter broke in hoarsely.

Elliott drew it from his bosom, removed it from its wrappings and held it out to him.

"Careful with it! Swallow it right away."

"Hand me the whiskey bottle, Abigail," Porter said taking the large pill nervously into his hand.

"No," Elliott ordered sharply. "You're not to touch a drop of liquor for two weeks or the pill won't work!"

"I'll be damned," came from the man on the bed, "the cure's worse than the disease!"

"He will take no liquor," the white-faced woman said quietly, bringing him a noggin of water. Then she resumed her position on the floor. "Will you both join us in prayer, gentlemen?"

O'Hara fell at once upon accustomed knees. Elliott stood for a moment and then awkwardly assumed the same position. Through the sudden silence the voice of the woman rose in an agony of supplication.

"O Lord God we come to Thee in our time of peril. Save Jonas, oh, spare him! Grant that the poison in his veins may be driven out. O Lord God, hear our prayer . . ."

O'Hara looked up. The woman's white face was raised as she went on, straining, beseeching, imploring, compelling the very heavens to bend to her need. At last, apparently at the limit of her strength, she opened her eyes and rose as if exhausted. The rest got up at once and the wife of the cabin set some food on the table before the strangers. Then with what cheerful heartiness they could muster Elliott and O'Hara said their goodbyes.

"You'll be fine," Elliott said to Porter. "That pill will do the job. As to the wolf, if he hasn't come back again by now, don't worry. He's off to hell an' gone. And don't think this thing happens often. The folks here will tell you it don't."

O'Hara shook hands quietly with the man on the bed who reported he was feeling better every day.

Porter followed them to the door. "I can't ever thank you," he kept repeating, with tears in his eyes.

When the men were out on the trail again Elliott spoke.

"I never heard the beat of that! If Porter gets well I'll never know whether it was the prayer or the pill cured him! You'd have thought the Lord was right in the room the way that woman talked to Him. Do you take much stock in this prayin' business, O'Hara?"

"I've always been taught to," he said.

"I wouldn't know how to go about it, myself. Course once or twice when I've been in a pretty tight spot I guess I said *some-thing* but I doubt if the Lord would pay much attention to a greenhorn. But that woman back yonder! She was on pretty close terms with the Almighty, I'd say."

They got back to the tavern in time for supper. Tired and cold they stood by the roaring fire and gave Semple the news. He had a bit for them also.

"The Indian agent got in just a little while ago — I mean McGill."

Elliott was surprised and pleased. "Now that's fine," he said. "I'd like O'Hara to meet him. I didn't think it was time for him to be round here again."

"It ain't but he says he got wind the Senecas have their backs up about something and he wants to talk to Girty about it before he goes out among them."

"What's an *Indian agent?*" O'Hara asked curiously as they climbed the stairs to their rooms.

"Just about what it sounds like. The government appoints men to try to keep the peace between the Injuns and the whites. The big agent for all these parts is George Croghan. King of the Traders, they used to call him. But McGill is sort of Assistant. Younger, you know. He's a good fellah but I think he's pretty sick of his job. He's a family man an' this business keeps him stravagin' all over the wilderness about as bad as a trader. We'll have a talk with him."

As a matter of fact they all ate their supper together. McGill was a mild-mannered, stocky man with a pair of shrewd eyes. He seemed glad to see Elliott and eager for a chance to talk.

"I can see," Elliott said after the conversation had been general for some time and O'Hara had listened with interest and answered the stranger's questions, "I can see," Elliott repeated, looking at McGill, "that you've got something in your craw. Out with it, man!"

"I've got plenty," he said. "I'm about ready to give up the whole job. You can listen to this and tear your hair."

He drew an official looking letter from his inner pocket.

"These are our latest instructions from the honorable members of the Assembly:

Resolved: That it be recommended to the inhabitants of the frontiers and to the officers at all the posts there to treat the Indians who behave peaceably and inoffensively, with kindness and civility and not to suffer them to be ill-used or insulted."

"Oh, my God!" Elliott groaned. "So you're to go to a man whose wife was scalped last year while she was out weeding her flax, and whose boy was captivated by them and say, 'Be kind to the Injun. He meant no harm.'"

McGill drew a long sigh and went on.

"The trouble is, as you very well know, that you can't tell how soon a *peaceable* Indian is going to put his tomahawk through your skull. But listen to this. This riled me even worse:

Employ for a reasonable salary a minister of the Gospel to reside among the Delawares and instruct them in the Christian religion.

Now that I will not do and Croghan agrees with me. And I'll tell you why. There was a young fellah just graduated from the New Jersey College at Princeton, a preacher. He was bound he was going to convert the Indians. It was his *mission,* he said. He went to a camp of them in the Kittochtinney Valley. A friend of mine is agent there and he told me about it . . ."

"How's your supper, gentlemen?" Semple broke in as he approached their table.

"Fine," the men chorused at once.

"You need to fill your bellies after your cold rides," he admonished as he passed on.

"Well, this young fellah I was speaking of preached to them and they listened like they believed every word. Sat like they were spellbound, drinking it in, he said. He'd studied up on their dialect and they all knew some English. And at the last he *baptized* them, every last one of them. Yes, sir. He came to report to my friend, just walking on air. 'I've been given souls for my hire,' he said. 'The Lord has used me as his instrument to save these poor savages from hell-fire and bring them into the kingdom.' He was beside himself with joy. And you know what those God-damned Injuns did two weeks after? Rose up and massacreed every white for miles around and the young preacher into the bargain!"

He took a long drink of whiskey. "So, I'm not hiring any minister to go among the Delawares. If any one wants to go, his blood won't be on my head."

"You're right," Elliott said, "but what will you say to Congress?"

"Nothing. Those men sit back there safe and comfortable on their fat arses and they don't know any more about the real situation out here than a babe unborn. They *pity* the Indians. Well so do I in lots of ways. A good many settlers have taken their lands and not paid the Indians a cent nor has the government. It's a shame and I've tried my best to remedy it. But the trouble is you can't *trust* an Injun. You pity him today and tomorrow he scalps you. I'm going to get out of the whole business by another year if I can."

Both men suddenly turned and looked at O'Hara. McGill seemed really concerned.

"You're new here and going out to trade. I shouldn't have talked like this in front of you. But this I'll say and Elliott here will bear me out. The traders are almost always safe. The Indians are glad to see them. They want the wares and if you're *honest* with them they'll do you no harm. That right, Elliott?"

"That's what I've found, like I told O'Hara. An' he's got a big thing in his favor. He can pick up their lingo like anything."

"Good! That's what they like. And you see, it's the settlers they attack mostly. Bitter about losing their lands, you know, and they don't discriminate much on who paid them and who didn't. And as to that, most of the settlers feel the land's as much theirs as anybody's. So it goes."

"What's up with the Senecas?" Elliott inquired.

"I'm not sure. That's what I want to talk to Girty about. Run into him since you got here?"

"No, an' I don't care if I never do."

"Why, what's bitin' you at Girty?"

"Oh, I dunno. He's got an Injun look to me. Mebbe he lived amongst them too long."

"Who's Girty?" O'Hara asked with interest.

"He's a chap that got captivated by the Senecas when he was just a shaver and he grew up with them. Then about eight years ago at the end of Pontiac's war he was released as a hostage."

"Yes, an' he tried to get back to the Injuns," Elliott put in.

"Well, he'd got used to living with them. He's helped me out as interpreter more than once these last years. He lives near Pittsburgh now. What about a game, gentlemen? I could do with a little diversion. Billiards or cards, eh?"

"Play billiards?" Elliott asked O'Hara.

"A little."

"Go ahead you two while I toast my toes. Sometimes I think

I'm gettin' old. When you're done I'll give you a game of cards. No exercise for the legs in that."

O'Hara liked McGill. They played with about the same skill and were beaten cheerfully by the other two men who joined them. They stood then in the back room going on with their conversation before returning to Elliott.

"When do you start out?" asked McGill.

"I'm not sure. I've only just come and I must get to know a trading firm first." He smiled. "And Elliott tells me I have some school work to do!"

McGill laughed. "Oh, I know what that is. I had to learn it myself once so I could settle disputes.

1 Fall Buck	a Buck
2 Does	a Buck
4 Foxes	a Buck

and so on. You see I still know my trader's arithmetic. Well, best of luck to you, and don't take my harangue in there too much to heart. We're in different lines of the Indian business, and you're in a very profitable one. Shall we settle for cards now if Elliott's ready?" As they neared the door he added thoughtfully, "The thing about the Indians is that they can neither be ignored nor wished away."

The next day O'Hara met the heads of the biggest trading firm in Pittsburgh: Simon & Campbell. Simon was tall and lean, Campbell, tall and stout, both Scotchmen. The big warehouse made the one in Philadelphia look small, but it had the same wild smell of pelts pervading it, and on the long tables at one side a bewildering variety of objects for the traders' use in their bartering. O'Hara moved slowly along, studying the assortment, for Elliott had left him after a word of introduction and at the moment both Simon and Campbell were busy. Here in great numbers were kettles, broaches, mirrors, ribbons, penknives, coat buttons, vermilion, crosses, jews'-harps and countless trinkets which he could not name. On one table clothing was piled : shirts, stockings, caps; on another strouds and blankets. This building in which he found himself was, he knew, the center of an enormous industry which extended into the depths of the dark forests of the new world on the one hand and far across the sea to the old one on the other, where a beaver skin might make a rich and shiny hat for a young man of fashion. He had seen those beaver hats and admired them, without dreaming that one day he himself would be trading in strange and dangerous places to secure the skins to make them.

When the proprietors were free he went to speak with them. They sized him up with practiced eyes and apparently were satisfied with what they saw.

"How soon do you want to set out?" Campbell asked.

"As soon as you think I'm ready," O'Hara smiled. "Mr. Elliott suggested I should wait till after Christmas."

"A good job too," Campbell went on. His face was round and suggestive of plenty of meat and drink. "We have a bit of old country good cheer at the season. The woods are full of wild turkeys and they make fine dinners. We have some singing through the street and the Commandant always has a dance in the Fort Christmas Eve. You're young. You'd better have a bit pleasure before you tackle the forest, eh?"

"What I would like to do if I may is to come here every day for a little while to observe and listen. I might learn a good deal from other traders as they come and go."

"There's nothing to stop you," Simon said in his more serious voice. "Just keep from under foot and you can watch what goes on as much as you like. And meanwhile learn the *Buck* table. We've got an extra copy here, haven't we? We keep making them for our traders."

He dived among the papers on a desk behind the counter and produced a sheet, which he handed to O'Hara. "You study that till you know it by heart. You can't hesitate in front of an Indian or he'll get the best of you."

"Thank you very much," O'Hara said, "and I can assure you I'll learn it."

"Come in again whenever you want to," they called after him as he left.

Once in the tavern he sat down in a far corner and opened the paper on which he saw what McGill, the agent, had called the "Trader's Arithmetic." He read the careful, spidery writing slowly: It began:

1	Fall Buck*	a Buck
2	Does	a Buck
2	Spring Bucks	a Buck
1	Large Buck Beaver	a Buck
2	Doe Beavers	a Buck
6	Raccoons	a Buck
4	Foxes	a Buck
2	Otters	a Buck
2	Summer Does	a Buck

With a fierce concentration O'Hara studied his lesson only to find at the end of an hour that he was not yet perfect. This was going to take practice. Below this list was an even longer and perhaps more important one for the trader, for it dealt with the prices for trade goods:

* This is the origin of our slang expression "a buck" as the equivalent of a dollar.

1 stroud	4 Bucks
1 Blanket	4 Bucks
Brass Kittles	1-10 Bucks

He stopped a little dazed. This would demand quick thinking. It would take *sixteen foxes*, then, to buy a stroud or *eight otters* to buy a blanket. As to the kittles! A faint uneasiness swept over him which even the rigors of the wilderness had not produced. But he dismissed it. Other men had mastered this equivalence. Certainly he could also. But he decided with Christmas now only two weeks away he would wait until after that to set forth.

A few nights later a dark, thickset young man entered the tavern and sat down with a mug of ale opposite O'Hara who was waiting for Elliott. There was a certain magnetism about the stranger's eyes and a power, half friendly, half malevolent about the large striking head which now raised suddenly.

"Stranger here?" he inquired.

"Yes."

"My name's Girty."

"Mine's O'Hara."

"Irisher?"

"Yes."

"My father was an Irishman. A trader an' a devil for drink he was. He got killed by an Injun back at Paxtang . . . Oh, so here's Mr. McGill and our fine friend Elliott. He thinks he's better than God, that one. Elliott, I mean."

The two men had come from the back room, stopped to speak to Mr. Semple and then advanced toward the table. McGill's greeting was hearty.

"Well Girty! I've been trying to get my sights on you. How are you?"

"Pretty fair. How's yourself? And Mr. Elliott?"

Elliott mumbled something and sat down next to O'Hara. McGill began at once on his business.

"I'm on my way out to the Senecas and I felt I'd like to see you first. Know how things are out there?"

"Oh, so-so. Guyasuta's got the wind up I guess. An Indian I know was in town last week and he stopped to see me."

"What's wrong with Guyasuta?"

Girty shrugged. "Oh, same old story. He feels the whites have cheated them. So they have. He's off now to see Sir William Johnson up in New York State but he'll be back soon. You know the way *he* covers the ground. Then you'll have to do some smoothing down, I reckon."

"I only wish I knew how."

"Well, a little money, a few presents, a little soft talk . . . it all helps."

O'Hara leaned forward. "You know Guyasuta, then?" he said to Girty.

"I ought to. I lived ten years with the Senecas."

"What is he like?"

"Why are *you* interested?"

O'Hara glanced at Elliott, but the latter spoke for himself.

"We stopped at the Delaware town as we were coming in. The old chief there has always been friendly to me so he kept us the night with him and Guyasuta was there too. O'Hara here took a fancy to him," he added with a short laugh.

"Guyasuta was *there?*" The words sprang from Girty automatically.

"Don't ask me why," Elliott rejoined.

Girty collected himself at once. "Oh, he gets together with them once in a while I guess. So you liked the Chief," he said to O'Hara. "There ain't many that do I can tell you."

"Well, I did," O'Hara maintained. "I felt I would like to know him better. He's got a strong face," he added.

Girty looked at the other young man with interest.

"I'll tell you one thing," he said. "If he likes you an' takes you for a friend he'll keep you for life. If he's your enemy it ain't so good for you. He never changes one way or the other."

"Does he speak English?"

"Fine!" Girty answered, "but he don't like to. Usually takes me along to the conferences to interpret. It looks big, an' besides he an I can chew things over in Injun without the rest knowin' what we say."

"Girty," McGill said, "could you come out along with me to the Senecas? I would appreciate it and of course I'll pay you. Your presence would be a big help. I think I'll have a talk with some of their half-chiefs before Guyasuta gets back. Maybe I can soften them up a bit. But I'd like to have you along. How about it?"

"Why, I guess mebbe I could go. I'm just doin' a little tradin'. Just when the maggot bites me. When do you want to start?"

"The sooner the better."

"Except that you can't be sure everything's settled until you've seen Guyasuta."

McGill considered. "Maybe you're right at that. How soon do you suppose he'll be back?"

"Oh, the way he goes, I'd say if you set out in a couple weeks by the time you'd get to their town he'd likely be there too. He'll cut across like the crow flies."

"It wouldn't spite me to be keeping comfortable here at Semple's for a bit longer. And I can make the rounds of the Delawares while I wait. So maybe I'll do that. That would bring us till after Christmas. I can count on you, then, Girty?"

"Sure, I'll go. I won't take any sides, mind, but I'll interpret if you ever need any help. What are *you* plannin' to do, young feller?" he suddenly asked O'Hara.

"Trading, when I think I'm ready," he answered.

Girty laughed. "There'll soon be more traders than Injuns in the woods," he said. "Course it's about the best you can do out here unless you take up land. Well, since I've wet my whistle I guess I'll be gettin' along. Good night, gentlemen."

During the next two weeks O'Hara went daily to the trading store and at night studied his "Trader's Arithmetic" until he was letter perfect. With Elliott to put him sharply through his paces, trying his best to entangle him, O'Hara became confidently expert. Meanwhile he was growing more and more familiar with the life of the town. He went back several times to see Captain Grant at the Fort, young Pittsburgh's crown and reason for being, realizing now that, paradoxically enough, it was because of the bristling cannon and rearing Bastions that a few gentler aspects of life were present in the stormy triangle. For, as Captain Grant told him, there *were* a few satin petticoats lifted above the mud and snow of the streets just as there was an occasional bright waistcoat or well queued wig in the tavern. O'Hara himself had overheard two men one night over their bowl of rum argue as to the merits of Johnson or Hume; and travelers of consequence came and went.

For the most part, though, he saw this outpost of the Back Country for what it was: a dirty, dangerous, exciting mixture of muddy bordering waters and snowy streets, of ill-clad soldiers, rough traders, Indians and storekeepers; of express riders flinging wearily from their horses; of fighting wagoners; of messengers fraught with evil report or good; but most important, of a few steady stalwart pioneer citizens who had put their roots down firmly as they built their log cabins and in so doing had simply and unconsciously planted a city.

During his conversations with Captain Grant, as they stood on the Monongahela Bastion or sat in his small office in the barracks, more of the Fort's history unfolded before him.

One day Grant slowly filled his pipe. "I guess you know the story of our siege here under Captain Ecuyer."

"Yes. Elliott told me that."

"Good man he was, Ecuyer, but there came a week when we knew we couldn't last much longer. Supplies were practically gone. Unless help came from the east soon . . ."

He paused until O'Hara prompted him.

"Well," he went on, "we were in despair. If we had to surrender it would be torture and death. Then, early one morning before daybreak . . . you know at that hour in the forest there is a great silence. We've no song birds west of the mountains. It's what you could call a 'breathless hush.' At that moment one of our sentries heard, faintly, away off, the sound of *drums*."

There was a catch in the Captain's throat as he went on. "If I live to be a hundred I won't forget that sound. Every man, woman and child in the Fort were soon awake and listening, standing like statues. We all knew what it was. It was Colonel Bouquet drumming his way through the forest to our rescue."

"And he saved the Fort?"

"Oh, yes. The Indians had heard the drums before we did, of course, with *their* ears. They got all the force they could muster and went out and met Bouquet about twenty miles east of here at Bushy Run. He had a strong little army. Two Scotch regiments. The Black Watch for one. You know the fighters they are!"

"I do, indeed."

"Then he had a battalion of Royal Americans and about four hundred or more Rangers. Even so, it was a battle! But at the end the Indians broke and ran. A regular rout. You know what the Scotchmen said when they got here? What they minded more than the Injuns was the *heat*. It was fearsome that day and of course they'd never known anything like it in the old country. Well, there's a story for you. As a matter of fact the ground here's soaked with them. Come back when you want another."

As the Yuletide approached new emotions and old memories thronged upon O'Hara. He thought of the Christmases he had known in Paris as a schoolboy and most tenderly of the older ones in Tyrawley, Ireland, when his mother was alive. What happy days! How carefree his heart! For the first time a bitter sweep of homesickness overcame him as he wondered how he came to be here at all in this wilderness of a strange land! And then all at once he knew that the real longing within him was not for either Paris or Tyrawley. It was for Philadelphia. For the Carson home hung with holly and pine. For the mistletoe in the hall and the fire blazing, and the table spread, as he knew it would all be. And for *Mary!*

He had received no reply to his letter, but there had not yet been time. The worst of it was that he might have to start off before an answer came. Then it would be many weeks, indeed perhaps months before his eye could see the precious communication, for he was sure she would write. And of course he would send her another letter before he left. He had already dispatched the precious panther skin, now all shining beauty, by a special express rider with a brief note fastened within the bundle:

For Mistress Mary Carson

Merry Christmas though this may come late.
I hope the rug will feel soft to your feet
on cold nights, with best wishes from your
most obedient servant, James O'Hara.

He wondered if his phrasing might seem indelicate as though
he were thinking of the skin beside her bed. For he was. He
liked thinking of it there. Well, he hoped she would take no
offense.

The tavern now took on an atmosphere of near gaiety. Even
Mrs. Semple relaxed her customary grimness and helped put up
the pine around the walls. A tremendous supply of logs for the
fire promised warmth aplenty, and as Mr. Semple supervised
the stacking of it inside and out, his cheeks quivered with excitement and good will. Odors of cooking and baking filled the
rooms and covered the pungent reek of soaking spilt liquor
from the heavy oaken tables and the kegs along the wall. There
was even a *tree,* dragged in by Hatch the stable boy and set
up, with much loud suggestion and jesting, near Semple's
counter-desk. Sally came with a basket full of strings of corn
to toss over the boughs and a few little ornaments she'd made
of old newspapers which she stuck on the ends of the sprays, as
Hatch stood on a stool to help with the high ones. Everyone
pronounced the effect quite fine, and O'Hara, as he praised, felt
the past returning. Especially he found himself thinking of his
mother. She had been dead now six years but she was vivid in
his memory. She had been small and quick and pretty with
smooth dark hair, Irish eyes and lips that laughed easily. She
had called him *Shamus* with soft teasing, and managed without
pressure to hear his confidences as he sat on a sofa in her bedroom before she went asleep. She had questioned a little but
mostly listened, weighed and offered practical advice on many

subjects, some of which he would not have discussed with his father. Once when he had confessed even then that he had a longing to go to the New World she had paled. Even he, a teen-age boy, could see the color ebb in her cheeks. But after a moment she had spoken in her usual voice.

"Shamus," she said, "my old grandmother used to say that if a man didn't follow the deep driving desire of his heart when he was young he was no good for anything ever after. If there comes a time when you feel you must cross the sea, then go you must, and even if it breaks my heart, I'll bless you."

She had not been there to give her blessing but somehow he had felt it just the same. So now as the Yule approached his mind kept glancing from Paris to Tyrawley, to Philadelphia, and back to the busy tavern with its increasing holiday custom and its atmosphere of lusty zest for living that seemed to belong to the raw new town and warm it under its drifted snow. He had already received an invitation to the dance at the Commandant's house on Christmas Eve. Elliott and McGill also. Captain Grant had evidently taken care of that. And while it would be a far cry from the Binghams' ball and while he would not have any emotional interest in any ladies present, he was young with an occasional bored moment and so was looking forward to the event.

The day before Christmas a man and a boy entered the tavern with an air of excitement, their faces beaming. They edged through the group of talkers to Semple's desk, whereupon that gentleman gave one look and uttered a yell.

"It's worked!" he called out. "The pill! It's cured you! Damned if it hasn't!"

Jonas Porter joined in the shout. "That's right," he said. "I'm a well man. They say after two weeks you're safe and it's past that. I came to see the men that fetched me the pill."

Mr. Semple was already looking about the room.

"Elliott! O'Hara! Come here!" he shouted. "They're around somewhere. Just hold on a minute."

Elliott appeared from the back room and O'Hara from upstairs where he had been considering what he would wear to the dance. As they recognized Porter they fell upon him, making him tell his story over and over. How he had waited, hardly daring to sleep for fear . . . how he had thought the two weeks would never end, but now, look at him! Fine and fit as a man could be. He drew his benefactors a little to one side.

"I was so scared that day you left me the pill I never thought to say did it cost anything or how much? I thought me an' the boy here would ride over to this doctor's an' thank him an' if there was a charge . . . Just one pill you'd think wouldn't be much . . ." He looked at them anxiously and Elliott cleared his throat.

"Well, now, his fee is sort of queer, you might say. He said if you . . . if you didn't get well it would be nothing. If you came through all right it would be a pound."

"A . . . a *pound!*" Porter's face blanched.

O'Hara spoke quickly. "I have a little money I'm not needing at the moment. I'll lend you a pound and give you five years to pay it back. Agreed?"

The color came slowly back to Porter's face. He drew a long breath. "You really mean five years to pay?"

"That's right. I expect to be round here that long. As to the big fee you see it was for your *life,* actually. So you mustn't begrudge it, or," he added shrewdly, "spend it on anything else. We guaranteed to take the money back to the doctor if you got well."

"I'll take it. I give you my word. Just tell me the way and the boy an' me, we'll set off early in the morning with it."

He left with the pound in his pocket, his thanks multiplied by the loan.

"I'll never be sure," Elliott said, "whether it was pill or prayer. But I guess they could work together. Anyway, we did a good job, O'Hara. Let's have a drink on the head of it."

As he dressed for the dance that night in the second-best shirt and knee breeches he had brought with him, O'Hara mentally checked his preparations for setting out the day after the morrow. Pitt was in fine fettle and also the pack horse he had bought in Philadelphia. In his room at this moment was the large bundle of trading wares he had selected with care. Since most of them were small articles he figured he had enough for several months' trading. He had picked up much information from his days at Simon & Campbell's, and even learned more dialect from Girty who seemed to have taken a fancy to him. Indeed it had been decided that he would start out with Girty and McGill but part from them before they reached the first Seneca encampment since their business and his would not mix well. He glanced toward the corner where his rifle and hunting knife lay ready. His stomach still felt queasy as he thought of skinning an animal, but if he was hungry enough . . . He would have a good supply of jerk in any case and the men said the Indian villages were not too far apart. As far as he could prepare himself he was now ready.

When he reached the Fort that night in company with Elliott and McGill he was surprised at the general stir all about them. Men and women, most of them singing at the top of their voices, were crossing the drawbridge into the Pentagon where Captain Grant met them in the Parade Ground and directed them toward the Commandant's house. Here there was a blaze of candlelight, a roaring fire, and a hearty greeting from their host, a tall man in his sixties with piercing black eyes. There was apparently no mistress for the home and the large room had the rather bare air of a bachelor's headquarters. Most of the furniture, in any case, was now moved toward the walls to leave dancing space.

O'Hara surveyed the scene with keen interest. As to dress, there was variety. Red, gold, and white uniforms on the officers, deerskin shirts and pants in predominance among the other men, with a few knee breeches like his own and McGill's. The women, he noted, were mostly of early middle-age with only a few young girls and a handful of smaller ones. Most of them were dressed in linsey-woolsey skirts and basques, with a white kerchief crossed at the neck, but as the Captain had said, here and there was evident a fine silk petticoat!

The room was soon well filled and alive with talk and laughter. Suddenly the Commandant gave a signal for quiet.

"Ladies and gentlemen, guests, I wish to welcome you and to say we will now start the first dance. Pick your partners, please, and make up your sets. Mr. Craig here, will call the figures. All right, you musicians, get ready to strike up."

O'Hara then noticed three older men in the corner, one with a fiddle, one in uniform with a fife, and one with what looked like a battered wooden flute. The latter and the violin had probably been brought across the mountains with sacrificial care, and he guessed the fifer might belong to the fort's band. There was a stirring mêlée now as the men and women paired off and formed small groups, into one of which O'Hara was propelled by Elliott. He found himself partnered with a buxom woman in her forties perhaps, who grabbed his hand and smiled delightedly at him.

"This is a big night for us," she said. "We don't often get a dance except at weddin's and house raisin's and then there ain't room like this."

"But I don't know how to do this," O'Hara demurred. "I'll maybe spoil your fun."

"Not a bit," she said cheerfully. "You'll learn quick. Just listen to the calls and follow me."

All at once the music started with a shrill, rollicking tune and Mr. Craig on a chair began to shout his commands.

> *"First couple out to the right!*
> *Around that couple and take a little peek.*
> *Back to the center and swing your sweet.*
> *Around that couple and peek once more,*
> *Back to the center and circle up four.*
> *Right and left through and lead right on. . . ."*

O'Hara floundered through the steps guided by his partner who though far from slim was surprisingly light on her feet and bounced her way through the dance with a contagious enjoyment which began to touch O'Hara too. It was a far cry from the minuet and the waltz but there was here a reckless abandon in the shrill rhythm of the music, the beat of the feet, the clasp of the hands, and the violent swinging of warm body pressed to warm body . . .

"This set's just about over now, listen!" his partner whispered as Mr. Craig's voice grew louder.

> *"Home you are with a balance all,*
> *Swing around eight and swing around all,*
> *Go up the river and cross the lake,*
> *A grand Allemande and a grand chain eight!*
> *Hurry up gents and don't go slow*
> *And meet your honey with a promeno!"*

When everyone stopped for breath the men mopped their faces and the women sought the chairs to rest between dances.

Everyone was gay, hilarious even, as though lifted completely above the harsh rigor of daily living by the exhilaration they had just experienced. O'Hara was sensitively aware of this, and a mingled pity and respect touched him as he watched. The guests at Mrs. Bingham's ball with the powdered wigs, lace jabots and brocaded satin were not subduing a wilderness and making the far reaches of the new world fit for habitation. *These* were the men and women, these upon whom his gaze now brooded! These had met peril and steeled themselves against it; but in so doing had not lost sight of the fact that happiness is an integral ingredient of the human heart. So when the opportunity came, they could fling their shoulders high and stamp and swing and revel in their evening's pleasure, even though the men's faces were beaten and weathered by the elements and those of the women older than their years from hardship.

Elliott seemed to be amusing himself with one of the younger women but McGill came over.

"Well, how do you like the backwoods dancing?"

"It rather took my breath away at first but I caught on to it a little. By the end I was beginning to enjoy it."

"Here comes Captain Grant to check on you!" he said after some minutes.

"You got on first rate," the latter began when he came up. "I was watching you. Quite a contrast from a ballroom, but I can tell you it stirs up the blood better than a minuet. Or is that an advantage for us bachelors?" he added laughing. "Oh, here we go for the next dance. Come on. Grab a partner!"

It was one of the little girls this time but O'Hara was pleased. She was younger than Mary but that same light of early innocence on the face reminded him of her.

"You'll have to help me," he whispered smiling.

"Oh, I *will*," she said, taking his hand.

The musicians struck up again, Mr. Craig shouted from his chair vantage and a delirious wave of sound and flying movements swept the room.

"Stand up straight and simmer down eight,
Swing on the corner like swingin' on a gate,
And then your own if you ain't too late!"

When the third dance ended the Commandant invited his guests into the dining room where great bowls of spicy negus waited. No one minded that noggins were often passed from lip to lip. The main thing was that there seemed no end to the bounty. Their host and Captain Grant dipped and dipped and even the women kept coming back, though apologetically, for more. The lemons which gave the delicious and unaccustomed tang had been brought, they knew, over the mountains from the east and before that in ships from Spain! This was the treat of the year and thirsty throats made the most of it.

When all had well drunk and they had returned to the main room a shout above the general clamor rose from one of the men.

"How about a few kissin' games now?"

Bedlam followed with the men's heavy voices seconding the suggestion and the women's half-hearted disclaimers all but drowned in the general confusion. The fiddler settled it.

"Here we go!" he called. "Make up your rounds for 'Oh, Sister Phoebe.'" And he began to play.

Quickly the men started pulling the women and girls into the circle amid much coy and feigned reluctance on their part. McGill spoke to O'Hara.

"I don't feel like kissing games. As a matter of fact I'm sort of homesick tonight. I think I'll make my manners to the Commandant and go back to bed."

"I'll go with you," O'Hara said promptly.

"Why, you're a young blade," McGill looked at him in surprise. "Why not stay and have the fun? . . . Well, we can watch the first round, anyway."

The two circles were moving now with everyone singing including the man in the center of each. The words and plaintive cadence of the old English folk song had been borne without loss across the stormy Atlantic; carried indestructible over the mountains to be heard now in the western wilderness and then to be borne along the Monongahela, the Allegheny, the Ohio, south and north and still on into the deeper unknown; for the frail echo of a song's lilt, the fragile memory of a rhyme were among the settlers' few imperishables.

So, now they sang:

> *"Oh, Sister Phoebe, how merry were we*
> *The night we sat under the juniper tree,*
> *The juniper tree, I, oh!*
>
> *Take this hat on your head and keep your head warm,*
> *And take a sweet kiss, it will do you no harm,*
> *But a great deal of good, I know."*

Each center man grabbed a woman and brought her into the middle of the ring where he kissed her with quick heartiness. Then she stood there alone waiting to choose a partner for the next kiss while round and round flew the linsey-woolsey skirts and the buckskin breeches as the rhythm quickened. Some of the older women sat along the walls, watching, but the men of all ages had joined the circles.

"Well, that's the way it goes. They'll keep this up for a good

while and then go back to the dancing till morning. You're
sure you want to leave now?" McGill asked.

"Yes. I'll go with you to the Commandant. I think Elliott
must be going to stay it out."

"Oh, him! He won't leave till the last dog's shot! When he
gets started there's a surprising amount of ginger in him."

When the two men emerged from the Fort the little town was
quiet and dark, except for the faint candle glow behind the
tavern windows. O'Hara glancing behind him was surprised
to see sentinels with their rifles ranged around the Bastions.

"Why, they have lookouts posted!" he exclaimed.

"Ah, yes," McGill agreed. "This would be a fine night for
an Indian raid with nearly every able-bodied man at the dance.
There's something you have to get used to, O'Hara. Out here
there is *always* danger!"

On Christmas day O'Hara slept till past noon, missing his
breakfast, but appearing in his white shirt and breeches when
Mrs. Semple pounded the gong for dinner. There was small
variety possible in the daily fare, but now the table groaned
with platters of venison, wild turkey and dumplings, corn pone
and a pudding for dessert! And all this with plenty from the
kegs along the wall to wash it down. Gradually an air of robust
well-being filled the room and toasts were drunk indiscrimi-
nately to the King, the colonies, the Prime Minister and Benjamin Franklin! Suddenly O'Hara found himself on his feet.

"To Pittsburgh!" he cried. "And may a great city stand one
day where we are now!"

A roaring outburst followed the toast, both from those whose
interests were in agreement with it and from those who were
now mellow enough to drink to anything.

As the afternoon wore on toward the sunset, O'Hara sat at

the farthest table where the western colors could be seen through one of the two glass windows in the town, and wrote his second letter to Mary. When he had finished, he dusted and sealed it, and then sat with it in his hand as though by the prolonged contact it might carry more of his love. For he knew with every passing day that love it was. He sat now, planning the future with the wholly illogical and unreasoning confidence of youth. He must of course wait a few years for Mary to grow up. It need not be many. She had spoken herself of girls she knew who had married at sixteen! Now, as with everything, his determination had been swiftly and strongly made. He would build a house for her in *The King's Orchard*. No other place would be fair enough. While he had not yet seen the trees with their springtime bloom and autumn fruit, even the bare boughs now were to him a frame for the bridal home! Somehow he would bend events to his will so that he would own a portion of this plot, the name of which delighted him. And the town would grow, even as his toast implied. *Their* town, his and Mary's. They would help build it.

So he mused, watching the rose and gold of the winter sky burn with beauty above the hills of snow. And again, strangely, he thought of his mother. When he was a small boy he had watched and listened as *she* sat at a west window in the sunset, playing sentimental old songs on the small pianoforte. There was one which he had particularly loved without knowing why. He could still hear her laughter as he begged for it.

"Oh, Shamus! You are the funny lad! Why do you like that song? You can't understand it. You're not old enough!" But of course she always sang it for him.

The melody now ran clearly through his mind, but most of all, the words.

Have you seen a white lily grow
Before rude hands had touched it?
Have you marked but the fall of the snow
Before the earth hath smutched it?
Have you felt of the wool of the beaver,
Or swan's down ever?
Or have smelt of the bud of the brier,
Or the nard in the fire?
Or have tasted the bag of the bee?
O so white, O so soft, O so sweet, so sweet,
  so sweet is she!

He sat on, smiling to himself. He was old enough to understand it now.

CHAPTER FOUR

IT WAS BREAKING SPRING when O'Hara returned to Pittsburgh. He had not expected the trip to last so long, but
while there had been delaying hardships aplenty and some
dangers, in the main it had been successful. The pack-horse and
Pitt, too, were laden with skins and within himself there was a
feeling of buoyancy. He was now a seasoned trader. His particular gifts had stood him in good stead. His quick ear had
picked up enough of the dialects to assist greatly in the conversations and he had found that many of the older Indians remembered some French from the days when France held the lake
forts.

He did not know that his wide smile showing the rare com-
plement of strong white teeth had all but bewitched the Indians. Because they warmed to his friendliness O'Hara had
felt no fear. He had eaten with them, slept with them, listened
by the fire to their tales of hunting and war, making out what
he could; traded honestly with them and honestly sympathized
with their complaints. Their lands, their hunting grounds
were going. More and more the white man was taking them.
What would be left for the red man? Ah, what indeed, he
thought, as he made his way through the depths of the forest

between villages, the tales of Indian massacres receding from his mind as his heart kindled toward his new friends.

There had been some touching incidents. Once when he was snowed in at a Delaware settlement for nearly three weeks the Chief, who had evidently taken a strong fancy to him, had suggested that he remain and be adopted into the tribe. If he would do so they would give him a maiden to wife. She was brought in, before O'Hara in his embarrassment could reply. He had hated himself for his fleeting thought of desire, for the girl was beautiful, like a slim, bronzed flower. She stood meek and yielding with the faintest smile, as though beneath her impassive façade there lay a warmth of eagerness.

The Chief dismissed her and O'Hara mustering all his diplomacy explained that however much he was honored by the proposal, and admired the lovely maiden, he must pursue his work as a white man just as the Chief continued his as an Indian. Also he added shyly that there was a girl of his own race whom some day he hoped to marry. The Chief had accepted the explanation with composure and without rancor, and they had pledged friendship in any case.

Indeed O'Hara had wondered as he had first set out whether the Indians might have the embarrassing custom of some primitive tribes of offering their women to passing guests as a courtesy. But he soon learned that the red man guarded his wife and daughters as jealously as the white man. Indeed more carefully if anything.

It had been in the Shawnees that O'Hara had taken the deepest interest. In the first place the great chief, Cornstalk, was in their village when he reached it and while he had heard of the man briefly from Elliott he was entirely unprepared for the actual encounter. Cornstalk was taller than Guyasuta though not as handsome, with features less finely cut; but his bearing was one of such regal dignity that O'Hara was amazed. Besides this, his English was fairly good and he seemed glad of a chance to speak it; there was from the start a fine rapport between them since their ideas could be freely interchanged. A dozen questions in O'Hara's mind could now be broached.

"If it is not impolite," he had said, "I would like to know all I can learn about your way of life, the small things as well as the big."

And the Chief was pleased. "Not many white men care to learn of us," he said.

So he displayed his war bonnet made with eagle feathers, symbols of power; he produced two wampum belts, red for war, white for peace; he showed him how they made their colors; red from what O'Hara knew was red iron oxide, ground in small mortars and mixed with grease; black from charcoal, white from gypsum, yellow from clay. He explained how the inner bark of the swamp ash was made into string and how the women powdered Indian corn so fine it became a powder to heal sores. He told how a hunter prepared for a real hunt. Here his English failed him, but O'Hara gathered from highly descriptive gestures that he drank purges, took emetics, had a sweat and then bathed in water to which sweet fern had been added. Cornstalk broke some of this from a great bunch hanging from the roof, and handed it to O'Hara. Even when dry there was in the fronds a woodsy perfume.

"By this means," Cornstalk went on, "the animals do not smell the hunter as he comes. They smell forest."

One set of burning questions in O'Hara's mind he forebore to ask. These dealt with the scalps hanging like a grisly frieze around the Chieftain's wigwam. Cornstalk saw the young man's eyes fastened upon them one night and spoke slowly.

"You would like to know more of this custom?" he asked.

"Yes," said O'Hara, "if you care to tell me."

Cornstalk smoked for a few minutes in silence then waved an arm toward the trophies.

"Not all from white men," he said. "Many from Indian enemies," and he smoked a while longer. Then he began carefully to speak.

"This," he said, touching his own scalp lock with its decorative feathers, "has man's power in it. Everything the man is, what he will do and what he will be is all in the scalp lock. When I take one from an enemy that power all comes into me. You see?"

O'Hara nodded.

"So — many scalps, much power."

"They are not all the same size," O'Hara commented hesitantly.

Cornstalk touched his own head, clipped close except for the scalp lock.

"With most Indians it is easy to get. With white men's heads covered with hair we take all to make sure."

That night O'Hara's sleep was not as sound as usual.

The Shawnees were slow, deliberate traders and O'Hara did not hurry them. Instead he waited, observed and listened and, he hoped, became their friend. His reward at the end of his stay was more than beaver skins. By Cornstalk's own invitation he witnessed an adoption ceremony which had to him remarkable overtones. A young Mohawk was being taken into the tribe, for what reason O'Hara could not discover though it became plain the custom of adoption was a familiar one. He had taken his place with the group of onlookers with pleasant anticipation, a feeling soon dispelled.

Between two rows of warriors armed with wooden bats,

sharply pointed sticks and knives the young brave ran the gauntlet, while O'Hara, whose stomach had perforce grown stronger, again found himself sickened. The Mohawk stood finally and with difficulty at the end of the lines, his face impassive, his eyes like steel and his body battered and bruised, the flesh hanging here and there in strips. The warriors nodded approval and proceeded to the bloodletting which was not pretty to watch but not as painful certainly for the young man as the gauntlet. Then the whole group raised their voices in a chant that thrilled O'Hara to the bone. He could make out only occasional words, but when the new young Shawnee had been led away by the squaws afterward to receive, as he was given to understand, rest and care (Egad, he needs it! thought O'Hara) he made bold to ask Cornstalk if he would translate the Adoption Song.

Once again the request for information pleased the Chief. He began to intone the words slowly to which O'Hara listened in amazement.

> "Ho! Ye sun, moon, stars, all ye that move in
>   the heavens, I bid you hear me!
> Ye Winds, Clouds, Rain and Mist,
> Ye Hills, Valleys, Rivers, Lakes, Trees and Grasses,
> Ye Birds, Animals and Insects,
> Ho! All ye of the Heavens, All ye of the Air,
> All ye of the earth,
> I bid ye all to hear me!"

O'Hara had been brought up in a religious atmosphere. The small Book of Common Prayer which his mother had given him on his twelfth birthday had crossed the sea with him, and now, the paths of the wilderness. He had not read from it on this trip, indeed had brought it along, he feared, as a sort of talisman, but now he hurried to his pack to look up what he was sure was there. With the small volume in his hand he leafed through the Order of Morning Prayer and stopped at one of the Canticles. The various sentences leaped from the page:

> *O ye Sun and Moon,*
> *O ye Stars of Heaven, O ye Showers and Dew,*
> *O ye Winds of God, O ye Dews and Frosts,*
> *O ye Mountains and Hills,*
> *O all ye Green Things upon the earth,*
> *O ye Fowls of the Air, O ye Beasts and Cattle . . .*
> *Bless ye the Lord.*

Strange, strange that the words he had heard sung from a child in quiet Christian churches should have been so nearly duplicated in the savage rite he had just witnessed! What vital affinity with the universe ran through the spirits of all men, savage or civilized, whether they were calling on the forces of nature alone or through them to God himself!

He was, as a matter of fact, thinking of this now as he rode on his last lap through the budding greenery of the trees on his return to Pittsburgh, intensely conscious of the beauty about him; the afternoon sun brought out the soft blush running up the stems of the sassafras and sumac and lighted the springing Sweet Fern with which he had already become acquainted, and the thick dark tangle of bushes he did not know by name. There was lonely silence, there was always danger, but there was a curious peace also, for now he felt at home in the forest. So he rode on confidently into the little town, wondering first if a letter awaited him, and second whether The King's Orchard would be in leaf.

Pittsburgh looked very different from his last memory of it.

The snow was gone as though it had never been, the buildings looked more crude than they had with their white covering but the trees were burgeoning and would soon soften the general outlines even more than the snow had done. He stopped first before the warehouse of Simon & Campbell, tied the horses and went inside, keeping a wary eye meanwhile upon his skins. Only Simon was there but he gave a hearty welcome.

"Well, well, how did you make out?"

"Not too badly, I think. Would you be kind enough to give me a hand with the pelts?"

Between them they carried the packs into the counter, the piles being greater even than O'Hara had thought.

"Well, well," Simon said again, "you have got a good few. Of course we can't tell much until we weigh them."

He concentrated then on the scales while O'Hara watched carefully and waited. All at once Simon looked up.

"I'll tell you," he said, "this will take a while and my partner will check when he comes in. Why don't you get along to Semple's and get some supper. I'll wager Sally's cooking will set pretty well after your trip. How long have you been gone now?"

"Nearly three months."

"Oh, you'll need a bit rest-up. Trading's hard work. Come in, then, in the morning and we'll settle accounts."

O'Hara didn't feel entirely easy but he had his own list of the skins and supposed all would be well. Besides he had a consuming desire to get to Semple's desk as fast as he could. As he rode up the slope to the tavern his heart lifted, for The King's Orchard was, indeed, in leaf!

Semple received him like a returning son.

"My word, laddie, I'm glad to see you! There's no way to

know whether a trader's alive or dead while he's out on his rounds. Why you look braw enough, that's sure. Did you have good hagglin'?"

"Pretty fair, I think. It's good to be back. Would there . . . would there be a letter for me?"

Semple grinned widely. "I've smelt it many's the time since it come. Lavender. My guess is it's not from *your father!* Off with you then, up to your room now and see what she says."

O'Hara, scarlet, took the little missive, tried to smile and hurried off as he was bid. Once in his room his fingers were clumsy on the seal. It was not only that they were work hardened but there was a tremor in all his frame. Finally the paper with its delicate writing lay open to his eyes.

DEAR MR. O'HARA:
    The rug is the most beautiful present I have ever received.
I have it beside my bed and each time my feet touch it I think
of you. (And sometimes in between.)

He had to stop here to ease the pounding of his heart. Then he read it all through and then again . . . and yet again! He could not see the words often enough. She described the two fine routs she had been at with no lack of partners but wished withal that he had been there. One had been given by Peggy Shippen and was most elegant. Her sister Elizabeth and her husband had come for Christmas. They had decorated the rooms with greens and lud, but they looked lovely. There was mistletoe, in the hall and she got kissed betimes but she paid small attention. There were different kinds of kisses. Father was well but he and all the men were always talking politics now about how badly the ministry in London was acting toward the Colonies and she supposed they meant the King. She was going to Miss Jayne's Young Ladies Academy and was learning French and would he please be very careful about the Indians and send a letter when he could? She signed herself, *Your sincere friend and well-wisher, Mary Carson.*

O'Hara smiled tenderly, his face alight. Then it clouded. The trouble with him and his *Dear Delight* as he had begun to call his love to himself, thinking of their visit to the Garden, was that the distance between them not only separated them physically but made even the exchange of letters so infrequent. He would write tonight and hope for a speedy express. He raised the letter to his lips, smelled the delicate lavender fragrance again and then put it next his heart.

The following weeks were quiet compared to the ones he had just passed. He realized now that he was more tired than he had ever been in his life. Semple explained that this weariness was common to even the most experienced traders; so comforted by this O'Hara slept for days, coming down only for dinner. His settlement with Simon & Campbell had been satisfactory, and yet he had a slight feeling of uneasiness, especially as they had pressed him to take part credit instead of money. It was only after insistence that he received cash in full for his skins. He determined to visit the other warehouse before he set off again. Elliott was still out and McGill had returned to the East on his own errands. Simon Girty dropped in often of an evening, professing real admiration for O'Hara's new proficiency in the Indian dialects and his general attitude toward the "Red Brethren" as he termed them.

"They ain't bad, the Indians, when you get to know them. Take me, now. I'd as lieve live with them as with white men. I'd have stayed on with the Senecas if Bouquet hadn't made them give up all their hostages after Pontiac's war. That was about nine year ago. Before that we'd roamed all over the wilderness northwest of the Ohio. Good life, when you're used to it." His black eyes looked far away.

One evening as they sat together over their noggins Girty began to speak only in dialect. O'Hara, eager to learn, listened hard and replied as he could. Girty explained the similarities and the differences, corrected O'Hara's mistakes and after a couple of hours, grinned at his pupil.

"By God, you've got the twist of it!" he said. "I'll tell you something. I know McGill is stepping out soon. You'd make a damned good Indian agent."

"*Agent?*" O'Hara echoed, amazed.

"That's what I said. If you go out again, don't stay too long. Something might come up."

"Who would recommend me?"

"McGill and I get on pretty well. I'll put a flea in his ear next time he's back about the dialects. But I know he likes you and he wants to get shed of the job."

O'Hara went one day to the other big trading store to meet its proprietor, Devereux Smith, and was at once drawn to the man. Simon & Campbell were both pleasant enough if *canny* but Smith was a man of parts with a good mind and a breadth of vision. His interests went beyond the financial. He too, O'Hara found, expected Pittsburgh to grow and wanted to be a witness to, a partner even, in this development. They talked for hours, Smith, slender and graying, yet with a youthful face listening attentively to all the younger man had to say.

"My interest has always been in business," O'Hara told him. "I refused an Ensign's Commission that my cousin Lord Tyrawley would have got for me in the old country, and went into a ship broker's office instead when I was through school. I wanted to learn business methods. I don't know what I'll be doing here later on, but . . ."

Devereux Smith looked shrewdly into O'Hara's eyes.

"I know," he said. "You'll be Pittsburgh's first captain of industry!"

Then they laughed together and somehow the friendship was sealed.

"You get on with the Indians?"

"Fine," said O'Hara. "And I've got the hang of their dialects. I seem to have an ear for them."

"Wonderful! So you'll go out this next time for us? Ephraim Douglas is my partner."

"I will that, and thank you. I'm all cleared up with the other firm."

"You know," Smith said meditatively one day, "I see a good many men from the East as they drop in here. They bring disquieting reports. One of my best friends here, John Ormsby, goes as far as to say we're going to have war. Next year or the next. He's an old soldier — he was out here with Forbes — and he's sure it's coming."

"Are you?"

"Afraid so. But we live a day at a time and there's always room to hope. I mention this because you're new and hardly had a chance yet to become a real American."

O'Hara smiled. "It doesn't take long."

"Good! When would you like to make your next trip?"

"As soon as my horses and I are completely rested."

"I need a man to go out to Kaskusky for a few months. It's a good sized Indian town near the junction of the Mahoning and Shenango rivers and a proper place to work out from and keep an eye on our affairs. How does that strike you?"

"Sounds interesting. I could stay the summer, but I want to be back by late fall. I have some business east at Philadelphia then." He hoped his cheeks did not redden.

"You may need a little different articles of trade out there," Smith went on. "More traps, files, knives of all kinds and brass wire, for instance. And plenty of Jews'-harps, whistles and bells. The Jews'-harps have taken the Indians by storm. But I'll fix you up."

The next week O'Hara set out on his second trading trip but not before he had walked in The King's Orchard breathing deep of the sweetness which filled the air like a light drifting incense. *It's a bridal fragrance,* he said to himself. *And one day I shall bring my bride to this very spot when the apple trees are in bloom.*

Then he started again through the dark impenetrable forest which covered the hills and banks, crossed by occasional paths, touched humanly here and there by a band of Indians, a settler's cabin, or a canoe on the silent rivers, as he journeyed to Kaskusky.

It was early November when he returned with the sumac and sassafras now bright red, laden again with peltry and alive with his accomplishment. Smith was congratulatory in the extreme as he heard the full report and looked over the skins.

"I'd hate to lose you as a trader," he said, "but you'd make a fine Indian agent. It's pretty good pay. I'll speak up for you if I have a chance."

Elliott was now back at Semple's and the two men met with hearty pleasure. When O'Hara said he intended soon to leave for Philadelphia Elliott scratched his head and opined he wouldn't mind going along.

"Got a little business there," he said. "Ought to see to."

"So have I," O'Hara replied casually.

They traveled this time without the pack horses and by Forbes Road which, built of military necessity, ran along the high ground to avoid alike ambush and swamps.

"Why the devil didn't we take this route going out to Pittsburgh?" O'Hara asked irritably one day.

Elliott gave him a shrewd sidewise glance. "You'll always be a better man for going on the trail I took you," he said.

"So! You were proving me then?"

"Might be. An' you stood up pretty damned well, I must say. In our business you can't know too much about the forest an' there ain't always a Forbes Road to travel on when you're a trader."

It was late afternoon on a mild December day when they reined their horses and tied them in front of The Crooked Billet. Everything inside was just the same: the comfortable taproom, the friendly Hastings, Sam's grin. O'Hara hurried up to his old room and penned a note:

MR. WILLIAM CARSON, HONORED SIR:
Within the hour I have arrived in Philadelphia, lodging at The Crooked Billet as before. I should like to pay my respects to you and Mistress Mary if I may at your earliest convenience. Would it be possible for me to call upon you this evening? I shall eagerly await the kindness of your reply.

Your most obedient servant,
JAMES O'HARA

When Sam had been dispatched with the missive O'Hara nervously laid out his best clothes, checked on his knee buckles, and brushed his thick blond hair vigorously, wondering how he would look with a queue. It would not be practical of course for the wilderness, and he had stopped short of powdering up till now. But he longed to be at his best tonight if . . . A tap at the door made his heart jump in his breast. Sam grinned with pleasure as he presented a note and received a benefaction for the same. O'Hara opened it hurriedly.

DEAR MR. O'HARA:

My daughter and I will be at home this evening and would be pleased to have you sup with us at eight of the clock if you care to do so.

My best compliments, sir:
WILLIAM CARSON

When he reached the house, he felt that he had never been away except for a certain strength and assurance within him which he had not known before. He shook hands with the old serving man and was shown into the library where Mr. Carson rose to greet him warmly.

"Welcome back to Philadelphia!" he said. "Have you decided the East is best after all?"

"I'm afraid not exactly that, sir, but I'm delighted to be here."

"It's a year isn't it since you left? Well, we must hear all the news of your wanderings. Ah, here is Mary!"

She stood in the doorway, dressed again in rose, but changed by the twelve-month into new beauty. Fourteen now and a woman in her form at least. O'Hara felt himself trembling as he went to meet her and bow over her hand. She smiled sweetly upon him.

"You've *grown,*" she said. "Isn't he taller, Father? Could that be?"

"I knew a young man that grew out of his wedding suit,"

Carson said. "In height, that is. I guess most men grow out of theirs in the other direction."

Then they all laughed together and sat down before the brightly burning logs. At first O'Hara listened to their news, gently deflecting questions about his own affairs. When supper was announced Mary looked up at him archly.

"You can't put us off all evening, Mr. O'Hara. After we sup you must tell about shooting the panther and all the rest of it, Indians too. I promise to be brave as I listen but hear it I must."

So, when they were back again in the library, O'Hara spoke of the strange year that he had lived since seeing them. His powers of description were good and his listeners' eyes, especially Mary's, encouraged him. He told of the trip out, the Fort, the town of Pittsburgh and the months of trading. He found himself presenting the Indians as a completely friendly and hospitable race in spite of the large question on Mr. Carson's countenance!

"Then you really weren't in any danger after all?" Mary exclaimed delightedly. "Unless it was from the panther," she added.

"I managed pretty well," he answered, and she didn't seem to notice any evasion.

The problem of seeing Mary alone loomed large in O'Hara's mind. He was constantly made welcome at the Carson home, to tea or supper when he feasted his eyes upon his Delight, but found that by accident or design her father was always present. The weather had changed, snow had fallen and the suggestion of either a walk or a drive would seem rather ridiculous, so O'Hara chafed as he got through the days, filling them with what small business he could, hoping always for the opportunity he craved. He did his banking, renewing acquaintance with Morris, roamed the streets, or sat restlessly in the tavern.

One day the taproom door flew open and a rider entered. His whole bearing indicated news.

"Well boys," he shouted, "the fat's in the fire now!"

"What's up?" came from all sides.

"Give me a dram to warm me up an' I'll tell you . . . Well, here it is," he went on when Sam had rushed him a noggin. "The English have had three shiploads of tea in Boston harbor for weeks. The authorities there tried to get it sent back on account of the tax. When they got nowhere with their petitions, a crowd of Bostoners fixed themselves up like Indians, got on the boats and pitched all the tea into the harbor! Now, can anyone say we're not in for trouble? I'm on my way to give Mr. Franklin the message. Just stopped for a drink." He threw some money on the counter and was gone.

O'Hara left the uproar of the taproom at once though it was an hour before tea time at the Carsons'. Once there, he told Mr. Carson what he had heard and the two sat with grave faces, discussing the matter.

"It's bad, this," Mr. Carson said. "You see it's been one long series of irritations and when at last there's one too many . . ."

"Surely there will be reasonable men both here and in England."

"When troubles edge toward the breaking point it seems as though reason disappears. Oh, I haven't lost faith. I hope and I pray, but sometimes in the dead of night . . ."

His face suddenly looked old.

"I think of Philadelphia if . . . if war should actually come. I know half the best families here would stick with the Crown. God help the rest of us."

"Mr. Carson," O'Hara said, "I wish to speak to you upon an entirely different matter when I have this opportunity. There is something as an honorable man I must tell you. I love your daughter."

Mr. Carson's jaw dropped as he started upright in his chair. "I cannot believe I heard you aright!"

"You did, sir. I have loved her from the first time I saw her. It happens that way sometimes to a man. It was so with my own father, he said. I am asking your permission to tell her."

"She is still but a child! I cannot have her burdened by any such declaration at her age!" His voice was sharp.

O'Hara spoke slowly, considering each word.

"You do, I think, know something already of my character. I have ambition. I believe Pittsburgh because of its location will grow into a city as time goes on. I intend to grow with it. I hope one day to be a man of ample means. Right now I do not know whether I can return to Philadelphia even as often as once a year. I will do my best, you may be sure. But my own work and the times are both uncertain. This is why I wish to tell Mistress Mary now of my feeling for her. I cannot go back for another year or perhaps more without doing this. Surely it cannot harm any girl of any age, sir, to know that a man loves her."

"You would not of course," Mr. Carson said slowly, "try to exact any promise from her?"

"I will not," O'Hara said. "Much as I should want to. But I would like your permission to see her alone. You may be certain I shall in no way abuse the privilege."

For what seemed an unconscionable length of time Mr. Carson sat in thought. At last he spoke.

"You have been manly and honest, O'Hara, and for that I respect you. I will not try to disguise from you the fact that if you were planning to remain in Philadelphia or anywhere in the East rather than in the western wilderness, I would view your suit with more favor. Indeed the very thought of Mary's ever going to live under the rigors of the frontier makes me shudder. Surely you can understand that."

"But it will not always remain the frontier, sir. And if Mary should ever later on . . . become mine, I would guard her happiness with my very life. As I have told you I greatly desire your permission to speak to her of what is in my heart. But it is only fair to add that I intend to do so anyway."

The faintest smile crossed Carson's sober face. "You are a young man of determination, but I can't say I care much for any other kind. So, since I have little choice, go ahead and talk to her. But remember, I shall do the same."

"That is a father's right. But I thank you for your kindness, sir. Perhaps after supper tonight? Since Mary was gracious enough to ask me to stay on the evening."

"I'll leave you alone then. Only be sure you are not importunate. I will not have her disturbed. Please remember she's but fourteen."

O so white, oh so soft, oh so sweet is she! ran through O'Hara's mind.

"I will remember."

They heard the reverberation of the heavy knocker on the front door, voices, and then the butler appeared with a business-like envelope in his hand.

"Sam brought this over from The Crooked Billet, if you please, sir. He said it was marked 'Important' and mebbe Mr. O'Hara ought to have it at once."

"For you, then," Carson looked surprised.

"If you will excuse me," O'Hara said, as he opened the seal.

He read, and read again, his face flushing with pleasure.

"Good news, I should say?"

"Very, I think, and startling at that. It's my appointment as an Indian Agent."

"Well, well, *well!*" Carson said. "Why that's quite a job, I know. Your first recognition then! I congratulate you. How did it come about?"

"I'm a bit puzzled myself, but I think it was like this. A Mr. McGill, who has been an Agent and wanting to give up the job, was out at Semple's Tavern in Pittsburgh a year ago and I got to know him. I've had a little luck learning the Indian dialects and I think he heard about this after my first trading trip perhaps and recommended me. I must say I am very pleased."

"Where did the letter come from?"

"It's from a Mr. Duncan, a member of the Assembly. It was sent out to Semple's. It must have got there just after I left and Mr. Semple sent it right on by express rider."

Mr. Carson rose and shook hands. "This calls for something stronger than tea to celebrate," he said. "I am amazed and delighted that you have achieved a real office so soon. This will mean travel?"

"Yes, a great deal. A trader can pick his tribes. A Government Agent must go about among them all. I will have part of the Pennsylvania and Ohio area, as this states."

"There will be danger?"

O'Hara smiled. "There is a certain peril in crossing the ocean and yet one does not hesitate to board ship. I'll take a chance on the danger."

Mary had been out at an afternoon party and now came with a small rush into the library, her cheeks as crimson from the frosty air as her bonnet and cloth muff. She was excited.

"Oh Father and Mr. O'Hara, have you heard the news of what happened up in Boston? Some men dressed up like . . ."

"We've heard, my dear."

"Everyone's talking about it, even on the streets! They're calling it the *Boston Tea Party* and that's very funny, isn't it?" She giggled delightedly.

"I'm afraid not," her father said, "but run along and get ready for our own tea. We'll speak of this further."

It was nine-thirty when Mr. Carson, with an odd look upon his face, excused himself on the plea of letters and left the young people to themselves. Mary was surprised.

"He always does his letters at the office," she said.

"I asked him as a favor if I could have a little time with you, alone."

"You did?" A soft blush slowly rose in her cheeks and deepened as she saw O'Hara's eyes full ablaze fixed upon her.

"W . . . why, Mr. O'Hara?"

"Because," he said gently, "I have something to tell you."

"A secret?" she smiled.

"If you wish. Do you remember the day last year when we visited Mr. Bartram's *Garden of Delight?*"

"Of course."

"Ever since to myself I have called you my *Dear Delight.*"

"Oh, I like that," Mary exclaimed. "Is that the secret?"

"No, I want to tell you that I . . . love you."

"After being away so long?"

"I loved you before I left and every minute since I've been gone. I expect to love you all my life."

She raised her beautiful eyes to his and her face was covered with light.

"Oh Mr. O'Hara, I'm so surprised, but I'm *so* glad. I'm sure I must love you too. I think about you so much and when I

first saw you here when you came back, I felt so queer and so
. . . *quite* different from the way I feel toward Father."

"That is as it should be," O'Hara said, smiling with tender
assurance.

He crossed over to her wing chair, sat down on the arm and
drew her close. His head bent to hers.

"May I kiss you?"

"As you did that night in the Greenery?"

"Yes."

"Oh, please do. I won't be startled now."

It was a long time before he released her. His face was one
burst of joy.

"And now," he said, "we must talk about our marriage —
not for a while of course — but it will be wonderful to plan for
it!"

"*Marriage?*" Mary's eyes were filled with a frightened surprise. "Oh, I wasn't thinking of marriage, Mr. O'Hara."

He was gently tolerant. "We must wait a year or two but
when two people love each other as we do, they eventually
marry, of course. So let us speak of it anyway."

Mary looked up at him piteously.

"Mr. O'Hara, are you coming back to live in Philadelphia?"

His face paled a little. "No," he said. "I have cast my lot in
with Pittsburgh and I must be staying there."

"But don't you see? I *couldn't* go out to the frontier. I
couldn't leave all this," sketching a motion toward the luxuri-
ous comfort around her. "And my father and my friends and
the city here. I would be terrified of the Indians and . . . and
all the wild life there."

She went on, plaiting and then smoothing a fold of her satin
skirt.

"What I was thinking of was that we would go on loving each

other and writing letters and being together — like this — when you would come back. Would that not be . . . enough?"

He looked into her innocent young face and felt a mist in his eyes. "Yes," he said gently. "That will be enough for several years perhaps. And then we can talk it all over again. Just to know you care for me will warm my heart wherever I am."

"Oh, I'm so glad!" she said. "You frightened me a little. But you must remember, Mr. O'Hara, that I could never go west and live in Pittsburgh."

His assurance was a little dimmed but in the breathless joy of the caresses he put his doubts behind him. He told her of his new appointment and explained that his duties might keep him away for more than a year. He could not be sure.

"But you will write often and tell me everything you are doing?"

"Of course and you must also."

"Aren't you proud of being an Indian Agent so soon?"

"I am! I've never felt so proud over anything except . . . that you love me. There's one matter though I must prepare you for."

"What is that?"

"I'm going to see the member of the Assembly tomorrow who sent me my papers. He may tell me I have to get back to Pittsburgh at once."

"Oh, no! Not before Christmas . . . *and the holiday rout?*"

"I hope not. But my Dear Delight, a man must go where and when his business takes him. If he put a ball before his work he wouldn't be much of a man, would he?"

"I suppose not," she said slowly, "but how can I bear you to leave so soon?"

"We'll make the most of every minute. Will you come for a

walk with me tomorrow, even in the snow? The paths are clearing wonderfully."

"Oh, yes, Mr. O'Hara. I'll go anywhere with you!"

"*Anywhere?*"

"In Philadelphia," she amended, smiling a bit roguishly. "You mustn't catch me up like that."

O'Hara's fears were justified. He was urged to return to Pittsburgh immediately and take up his new duties. There was always unrest among the Indians here or there and he was told that the reports coming east in regard to his success with the dialects as well as his friendliness with the red men made it advisable that he should start work at once. The possibility of coming war with the British made this unusually important, for the Colonies must make every effort to keep as many of the tribes as allies as possible. One question Mr. Duncan, the Assembly member, asked him.

"We have judged from various sources that you as of the present wish to become an American. In case of a conflict with the Crown, may I ask for a frank statement of your position?"

"My allegiance will be to the Colonies. I pledge it."

"Good!" said his questioner. "Then get out west as fast as you can and try to make the savages feel the same way. Have you met Croghan?"

"Not yet, but I've heard of him of course. An Irishman like myself," he smiled.

"Amazing man. Getting on a bit now and more interested in his large land holdings than anything, so you may not run into him. But as a trader he was King and as Deputy Indian Agent he got closer to the Indians, especially the Iroquois, than any other man except Sir William Johnson up in New York State. They've worked a good deal together. Both have Indian wives, by the way. You will be in a general way under Alexander McKee who is taking over Croghan's Deputyship. Hope you get on, and all success to you! The times are ticklish."

Before he left Philadelphia O'Hara went to a silversmith's and purchased a delicate gold brooch in the shape of a heart. There was a diamond in the center and on the back he had the jeweler engrave J. O'H. to M. C. He would have liked to add *with love* but feared her father would object. At the end of his last evening at the Carsons' he gave it to Mary before his final goodbye. Her surprise and joy in the gift put an end to her imminent tears.

"It's *so* beautiful," she kept repeating, turning it this way and that, looking at the initials and exclaiming over the diamond. "And oh, Mr. O'Hara, I like . . . love you so!"

"Would you not say James, or perhaps Shamus which is the Irish for the name? My mother called me that."

"It sounds a little strange to me but I'll say *James* if you would like me to and you must say *Mary*. I *wish* you didn't have to go!"

"Not half as much as I do, but it must be, I fear. Goodbye, my Dear Delight."

A last kiss on the soft young lips and he was gone out into the winter street to make his way to The Crooked Billet and complete his preparations for the journey. Elliott had been greatly pleased over the appointment and insisted that he had finished his business and would return along to Pittsburgh; so once again they set forth together.

As O'Hara rode on he felt upon himself the hand of destiny even more than on his first trip. While of an intensely practical nature he had also, in his Irish blood, something of the mystic and the philosopher. His thinking was mature beyond his years, just as was the depth and certainty of his love. He pondered now on a thought that had come to him before. He believed that in the greater matters of life the mind must fling itself forward beyond the present data and grasp as a possession that which lay beyond. Surely this was the only way to success. So as the dusk of the forest finally closed in again upon the travelers, O'Hara felt the premonitory challenge of eventful years lying just ahead and the up-leaping of his own powers to meet them.

CHAPTER FIVE

O N A BRIGHT AFTERNOON in early May 1775, a weary rider flung himself from his horse at Semple's Tavern and brought the news that the farmers of Massachusetts had surrounded the British red coats in Boston! The war, then, had begun.

O'Hara had arrived in Pittsburgh the day before after a long stretch in the wilderness. He had come back this time with a limited sense of accomplishment. The Delawares and the Mingoes and perhaps the Cherokees he felt would stick with the colonies or remain neutral. Of the Shawnees in spite of his own friendly relations with Cornstalk, he was not so sure. There had been constant warfare the last two years between them and the settlers who had been pouring into the rich Kentucky region which the Shawnees regarded as their own. A delegation of them had even come to Pittsburgh to remind Alexander McKee, the present Deputy Superintendent, that this white encroachment below the Kanawha River was a flagrant violation of solemn treaties. O'Hara had been present and listened. So did McKee; but the latter was powerless to offer redress. He could only condole with the Indians and counsel patience.

This local war then had continued until at last the Shawnees were beaten back. For something had gradually happened to the settlers. Instead of scattered, anxious men, each prepared to defend his own cabin and family, there had developed a common courage, a kind of determined cohesion which increased their fighting strength. This, while they did not know it then, was to help render them more nearly invulnerable in the great revolutionary struggle yet to come. But while they had actually bested the Shawnees for the time being, the deep bitterness on both sides remained.

O'Hara at his various listening posts had heard tragic if isolated stories. The son of Daniel Boone, whose fame he knew, had been killed by the Shawnees. On the other hand the family of Logan the Mingo, the unfaltering friend of the whites, had been cruelly murdered, and Logan with a number of ardent young Shawnee warriors had wreaked a terrible vengeance. So it had run. O'Hara knew now that on the fringes of any so-called *conventional* war, if there could be such a thing, there would be the blot of unspeakable savagery.

With all this in the back of his mind he listened to the tumult of voices in the tavern for it was but a short time after the arrival of the express rider until the room was filled. When he could be heard, Samuel Semple spoke.

"There must be a meeting called! We've got to prepare resolutions as to where we stand."

"There's no two places to stand," a man shouted. "We're all on our side, ain't we?" he ended somewhat ambiguously.

A roar of approval went up.

"We've still got to have a meeting and get things organized. It's all very well to cry *liberty* an' such but mind you there will be fightin' too."

"Let 'er come! We've got rifles."

Devereux Smith raised his hand to be heard.

"I suggest we hold a mass meeting of all citizens for the expression of public opinion. How about next Tuesday, that's May the 16th. That ought to give time to send the word round. If we have too big a crowd for here we can meet in the meadow."

"How about the Fort?" someone cried.

"That's British, you fool. We can't talk free there," another answered.

There was continued shouting and arguing, much drinking and even laughter, in spite of the serious matter under consideration; then the day was agreed upon for the general meeting and gradually the group thinned out. O'Hara sat at one of the tables with Devereux Smith and his friend, John Ormsby. The latter kept shaking his head sadly.

"A sorry business, this! A sorry business. I knew they'd been getting itchy up Boston way, and hell might break loose any time. The fact about Pittsburgh itself is that we haven't had too much cause to complain. England's been pretty decent about sending us help when we asked for it. But we've started a new country and we'll all have to stick by it. How about you, my boy?" he asked O'Hara.

"I'm with you," he said. "I can't quite explain it to myself, but I'm here and I intend to stay. At whatever cost," he added.

"Good," said Ormsby. "And I think, Smith, that it would be a good idea to have a few Resolutions ready *before* the meeting. We might get Hugh Brackenridge on to it. He's a lawyer. We'll get nowhere if we wait for the crowd to put forth suggestions."

"I think you're right. Tell Semple how you feel and I'll talk to Brackenridge. By the way, O'Hara, you and Brackenridge ought to be pretty congenial. He's just lately come to settle here and hang out his shingle. Quite a scholar. Graduated from New Jersey College back at Princeton about four years ago. You'll be sure to be running into him soon."

After supper O'Hara walked out in the May evening. The King's Orchard was in bloom and a gentle breeze blew from the rivers, but in spite of the beauty around him his heart was sad. There had been a number of letters awaiting him when he returned yesterday. One had been from an Irish solicitor with the news that his elderly cousin, Lady Mary Tyrawley, had died and left him a legacy. Of course he would appreciate the money, but he felt real grief. Lady Mary had come next to his mother in his heart. He had visited her from his small boyhood on, and had loved the big country house, the stabling where the riding horses lived, the big hound Nicanor with the long silken ears who sat close to his mistress at meals and watched with melting eyes for the tidbits handed him. The room where O'Hara had always slept had had a sloping ceiling that seemed somehow to enfold and caress him; out of the dormer window could be seen the lovely ragged water meadows and a bit of the river beyond. Over her domain as over her young relative Lady Mary, tall, handsome and reserved, had exercised firmness mingled with kindness. Now, the thought that stabbed O'Hara through his memories was that during his years in America he had written her so seldom! And to her, old and lonely, letters would have meant much. Why had he not sent them? It was an anguished question which he could not answer.

But there was another and sharper ache in his heart. There had been three letters from Mary, each moving him with the charm of her recounted days, and her words of affection. But in each she had managed to mention her fear of the frontier. While this was in relation to himself it meant also that she shrank from even the thought of its dangers and hardships. With almost superhuman effort he had managed to get back to Philadelphia the year before, only to find Mary a little older, a little more beautiful, and himself more hopelessly in love. Even without Mr. Carson's frank talk with him then, he could not fail to be aware that Mary was fast reaching the stage when many admirers would besiege the Carson home. Would her feeling for him be wiped out by the ardor of other present lovers while he was far away? He was afraid he could not get back east now for he was sure he would be sent out at once to deal with the Indians as best he could since war had really begun.

The War. On top of everything else, the war. While he knew he was no coward he had no stomach for fighting. If there was only some other way he might serve the Colonies! Well, he came of a soldier line and he must carry on as best he could.

Through the gathering dusk he looked at the Fort. Even that depressed him. For in the three years and a half that he had been in Pittsburgh the great fortress had fallen into a mild disrepair. Its first brilliant glory had departed. The earthworks here and there were crumbling, the Bastions had breaches, the drawbridge looked rusty and unsafe. He thought of going in to see Captain Grant but in the light of the present news he decided against it. So he continued walking along the paths in The King's Gardens while the darkness which suited his mood closed in. When he made a sudden turn about he all but ran into another man.

"I'm sorry, sir. I was thinking and didn't know there was anyone near."

The other man had a pleasant voice. "No harm done," he said. "I was doing a little thinking myself. Sometimes it comes easier while you walk. My name's Hugh Brackenridge."

"Why, this is a coincidence. I heard you mentioned only an hour or so ago by Devereux Smith! He said I'd soon be running into you but I didn't expect to, literally. I'm James O'Hara."

"Well, I've heard of you too and from the same source. That ought to be a proper introduction. I've just come to Pittsburgh within the last months and I gather you've been away during that time. I've got me a cabin along the Monongahela. Would you care to come with me there and continue our thinking out loud?"

"I would like nothing better. I'm depressed tonight and I dreaded going back to the tavern. Thank you for the invitation."

The young men made their way to the group of log cabins above the river at one of which Brackenridge stopped. The door was open and a large candle burning on the table.

"I only went out for a breath of air. I've been working all evening. Sit down and let's take stock of each other. My word, I'm glad to meet a young man who can handle the King's English!"

O'Hara sized up his host with pleasure. A tall, slender chap with a broad scholarly brow and serious eyes but a mouth mobile and friendly.

"Well, now, O'Hara, tell me about yourself first. When I start they say it's hard stopping me!"

O'Hara laughed and sketched his background briefly as well as his years in the new world. Brackenridge listened intently.

"I had an upbringing as different from that as day from night. Pioneer farm boy beyond the mountains, dead set to go to college. I got my first Latin and Greek from a minister in return for doing chores. Walked thirty miles to do it."

He paused and smiled. "I'll tell you one of my darkest hours.
Just to give you an idea. I had borrowed a copy of *Horace*
from this Reverend Blair and one morning when I went out
early to milk I took it along intending to read a little in the
quiet when I'd finished, so I laid it on a stump. When my pail
was full I heard a yellow-breasted chat I'd been listening for,
so I set down the milk and went looking for it. When I came
back the cow had chewed up Horace! *There* was a tragedy."

O'Hara's face was more compassionate than he realized.

"But," Brackenridge went on, "I managed. I taught school
when I was fifteen and finally got to New Jersey College and oh,
it was like heaven to be there. The studies and the friends!
One of my classmates was a chap named James Madison; we all
feel he'll be a statesman one day. And Philip Freneau was another. He's a poet already but he'll be a better one. I think
you'll be hearing about these two, at least, as time goes on.
We had a little Whig literary club and we amused ourselves
writing satires against the Tories. Philip and I wrote a long
poem we called *The Rising Glory of America.*" Hugh laughed.
"We didn't leave much out. Discovery, settlement, growth, the
future. I read it at the commencement exercises and the people
seemed to like it."

"Could you repeat some?" O'Hara asked eagerly.

Brackenridge looked abashed. "There," he said ruefully,
"I knew I'd talk too much. It's the lawyer in me, I guess."

"No, please. I really want very much to hear the poem. Even
a little."

Brackenridge still looked embarrassed but finally stood up.
"I'll say a few lines from the end. Can do it better standing."
He declaimed in a strong voice:

"Tis but the morning of the world with us
And Science yet but sheds her orient rays.
I see the age, the happy age, roll on
Bright with the splendours of the midday beams,
I see a Homer and a Milton rise
In all the pomp and majesty of song,
Which gives immortal vigour to the deeds
Achieved by Heroes in the field of fame."

O'Hara clapped loudly. "That's fine!" he said. "That's real poetry. I congratulate you! And thanks for saying it for me."

"It sounds different, somehow, here than in Princeton. Rather young and bumptious, but we meant it when we wrote it. And," he said, leaning forward, his dark eyes intense, "it *is* the morning of the world for us here in America. Everything is before us! Only we've got to be free."

They talked then of the war that had really begun, of the part they might have to play in it and of the meeting set for the next Tuesday.

"Smith came right over to see me about that and I've been working this evening on the Resolutions. You see, one of the men can have them tucked in his shirt tail all the time and after the Committee confers, can bring them out and no one in the crowd will know that they aren't spur of the moment proceedings. You know why I didn't go east to practice law?" he added suddenly.

"Why?"

"Because I think there's a big future for this little Pittsburgh."

"So do I. That's why I came myself. Business is what I foresee."

"Well, once the war's over you can go ahead with your indus-

try and I'll dream of something better than coon-skin acade-
mies. A university some day. Why not? You know what my
life's motto is? *Liberty and Learning.*"

When the young men finally parted, it was with a warm
handshake and O'Hara went back to the tavern strangely comforted.

The next Tuesday was fair and warm and a surprising number of men gathered in the meadow above the Monongahela.
Amidst the noise and confusion a Committee was finally
named: John Ormsby, John Campbell, Edward Ward, Samuel
Semple, Thomas Smallman and Devereux Smith. And after a
short conference the latter read out to the crowd the *Resolutions.*

"Resolved unanimously that this Committee have the highest
sense of the spirited behavior of their brethren in New England
and do most cordially approve of their opposing the invaders
of American rights and privileges to the utmost extreme."

"Yea! Hurray! Hurrah!" yelled the crowd.

There was a further Resolution that the Standing Committee should secure such arms and ammunition as were not employed in the actual service and deliver them to any captains of
independent companies who would apply for them.

More cheering, more speeches, more cheering, and then gradually the meadow cleared. But the excitement was far from
over. From back in the woods a dozen or more men carried a
thirty foot pine tree, stripped of its branches. This they set up
in the center of the village and proclaimed it the *Liberty Pole.*
Whiskey was rolled by the barrel from Suke's Run and when
night fell a huge bonfire was built to light the scene. Excited
pandemonium reigned. People joined hands and danced

around the pole, singing, shouting, swearing. The pent-up emotions of restricted lives now found expression. O'Hara and Brackenridge were in the circle which constantly grew and heaved in the glow of the bonfire.

When at last they agreed they had had enough, they dropped out and went into the tavern where the older men were toasting "liberty" and once in a while, confusingly enough, "His Majesty King George the Third, God Bless Him."

"A thought struck me when the Resolutions were being read," O'Hara told his new friend. "That was the suggestion of the *Independent Companies.* I've just inherited a bit of money and I wondered if perhaps I could fit out a company with it when the right time comes. The legacy was from an old cousin I was fond of. She was a spirited old lady and I have an idea she would like it to go to the cause of liberty and independence."

"I haven't an extra sixpence to bless myself with," Hugh said mournfully. "I'll have to give my help some other way."

They talked till late, glad of the congeniality of their youth and ideals. But in the morning the message O'Hara expected came. He was to set out again at once for the Shawnee territory, by way of the Delawares, giving the latter encouragement and support as he went. It would be his longest and most important trip. He wrote to Mary, more ardently than he had ever done before, explaining his difficulties, lamenting his separation from her and begging her to keep the most dear and special place in her affections for him even though other young men desired her friendship. It was all he could say, he decided, as he sanded the words torn from his heart, and sealed the letter ready to send by the next express rider.

He had been five days out on his new journey when he reined

Pitt suddenly one afternoon. He noticed with the keen eyes he had developed a small pile of sticks, the kind of smokeless fire the Indians built. An Indian or a group of them was therefore near. He sat motionless looking sharply about in all directions. Suddenly he saw the figure of a man leaning against a tree, his glazed eyes looking back at him. It was Guyasuta! He jumped from his horse, and holding the bridle advanced quickly to the Indian who looked up at him wonderingly.

"O'Hara," he muttered through swollen lips.

"You are sick. What is it?" O'Hara asked quickly.

"Snakebite," the old man said. "Rattler, very bad. Water. I can hear stream."

So could O'Hara. He tethered his horse, got one of his cooking pots and hurried in the direction of the sound. When he returned Guyasuta drank with great parched swallowings. O'Hara then wet a large handkerchief and placed it on the sick man's head.

"Now let's look at the bite," he said. "On the leg?"

He had not far to search. Under the loosed deerskin legging the leg was swollen to twice its size. The small tragic red marks were plainly visible. He had received some instructions from Elliott on snakebites. If possible and in time the wound should be sucked. He asked Guyasuta, knowing he himself could not have reached the spot, making his lips form a sucking sound.

"Mebbe too late. You're not afraid?"

"No," said O'Hara. "I'll try."

"You have food?"

"Yes."

"Bring some. Wash poison out of mouth first with water, then eat food and spit out."

O'Hara provided for his own safety, then applied his lips to

the wound though he feared the poison had now spread. A
faint shudder went through him but he persisted without hesitation, spitting out the venom if he had caught any, then the
water, then the chewed food.

Guyasuta looked on him with yearning eyes between the
retchings that shook him. The strange bond established in the
Delaware chief's wigwam that far away night seemed now indis-
soluble.

"Brave man. Good man," muttered the Indian. "You know
pocoon? Bloodroot?"

"I think so."

"Find some." The words were faint.

O'Hara searched with an anxious heart. He was afraid the
Indian was dying, and he himself for the first time was feeling
the horrible danger of rattlers. He watched his every step for
fear he would see the flashing loop of a black and yellow neck.
After a short time he came upon a clump of bloodroot which
Elliott had once told him was an Indian cure. He pulled it up,
root and all and went back to Guyasuta. The heavy perspira-
tion still dripped from him and he was retching desperately.
Weakly, as he could get breath he directed O'Hara.

"Mash root and . . . lay . . . on . . . bite."

It was not difficult to do, and in a few seconds a moist mass
was spread on the leg.

"Mash leaves. Put water on. I drink. . . ."

This too was done. O'Hara kept bringing fresh
water from the stream, bathing the hot face and hands, and
finally persuading the Indian to lie down with a rolled blanket
for a pillow. The soft, sifted afternoon light finally began to
fade. O'Hara ate his supper of jerk and water, and as the night
fell, spread his other blanket on the ground beside Guyasuta

and sat close. The Indian had stopped retching now and seemed drowsy. Whether this was a good sign or not O'Hara did not know. He kept feeling the improvised poultice of bloodroot and when it became hot from the fever he placed a new, cooling one on the wound. Once Guyasuta spoke in his own tongue but O'Hara knew the words.

"My son. My son," he said.

Toward morning O'Hara too fell asleep. When he woke at daylight with a start Guyasuta's eyes were open and watching him. It was evident that the fever was down.

"I get well now," the Indian said simply.

O'Hara remembered that with a snakebite the outcome was not long in the balance. He felt an almost unwarranted sense of thankfulness and pleasure.

"Good! Wonderful!" he said smiling at his companion.

He examined the leg. The swelling had gone down quite appreciably. The clean blood of the victim and his own ministrations had evidently overcome the poison. He felt happier than he had for weeks, and Guyasuta's words of the night before made a warmth in his lonely heart.

It was the work of a few minutes to shoot a squirrel. The skinning and cleaning took longer but he had become expert. The fire had been built first and now the pieces were soon bubbling in the pot. With a pinch of the precious salt he carried and a bit of jerk to dip in the broth, there was soon a tasty breakfast. Guyasuta ate ravenously. O'Hara guessed he had not done so for some days. After the meal was over the facts all came out. The Chief had been making his way on foot alone through the forest as he liked to do when he was overtaken by a sudden sickness. His head was heavy, he said, his stomach full of pain. He had made a fire but had not strength to hunt or to cook. While in this dazed weakness he had trodden on the rattler. He seemed greatly ashamed of the happening for to him it was an evidence of carelessness — a quality which Indians did not tolerate in the woods especially. All he was able then to do was to sink down under the tree where O'Hara had found him.

When he urged O'Hara to go on and leave him there to gain some strength, the young man flatly refused. So, the two through the pleasant days and the more quiet nights were close together, the strange tie which neither could explain growing stronger. Each in their conversations tried honestly to present the problems of his race. O'Hara told of the war and Guyasuta shook his head sadly.

"If the white men fight even their *King* for this country, they will want it all. Then what will the poor Indian do? My heart is heavy."

"Could you not make your Mingoes and Senecas help the Colonies in this war? The white men would repay you!"

Guyasuta shook his wise head again.

"I have made many treaties. They have been broken like rotten sticks. But what I can do to keep the peace, I will do."

When O'Hara found he would not be more specific he dismissed the subject and turned to forest and Indian lore. He spoke once of Simon Girty and Guyasuta looked off through the trees.

"Sometimes with a man you need eyes here," he said pointing to his forehead, "and eyes here," he added, touching the back of his head.

"So!" O'Hara said in surprise.

When at last travel was possible O'Hara put the Indian on his own horse and walked beside him to the nearest friendly village some ten miles away. Their parting was touching in the extreme to O'Hara, for Guyasuta said again half under his breath, "My son. My son!" And the young man wrung the Chief's hand as he would have his dearest white friend's.

As he went on his way to fulfill his newest commission, O'Hara thought to himself, *No matter what happens after this, I have now had what is probably the biggest experience of my journey.*

There had been, however, near the end of his homeward trip an incident that shook him more than he liked to admit. He had stopped at a little Indian settlement on the Muskingum to stay the night with John Heckwelder, the Moravian missionary whom he had met once at Fort Pitt. Just after they had gone to bed an Indian runner arrived with a message for Heckwelder. O'Hara overheard the words in amazement.

"Get our friend O'Hara out of town immediately as eleven warriors from Sandusky are well on their way to take or murder him."

"I can't believe this," O'Hara burst out. "Why would any Indians want to murder *me?* I've been friends with them."

"I'll get you a guide as fast as I can, but there's no answer to your question," Heckwelder said, adding, "And I've lived among them for a long time."

When the guide, a handsome young Indian named Anthony, stood before them he looked O'Hara in the eye.

"Do you trust me?" he asked.

"I do," O'Hara said. "So let's be off."

They walked through the woods toward the Ohio along devious paths, O'Hara leading Pitt. When daylight broke Anthony stole to the river at intervals until at last he spied two white men cleaning out a canoe on the opposite shore.

"Here," he said, "you had better cross. We daren't call to them. Can you swim it?"

"I think so. If my horse can."

"Oh, they can always swim, the horses."

When he had thanked his guide O'Hara spoke to Pitt, stroked his nose affectionately and led him into the stream. The river was quiet and not too wide at this point, but still it was a chill and exhausted man and horse that reached the other side. The men they had seen so intent upon their work had finished it and gone into the house during the crossing and after a few muffled shouts as he neared the shore, O'Hara had thought best to save his breath for swimming. Once at the house there was a pioneer welcome and after a hot breakfast and a drying out before the fire he went on his way but with knitted brows.

"Maybe it's not well to be overconfident," he muttered to himself.

So it was April, almost two years after he had left it, when he was again at Fort Pitt. He made prompt report of his travels to Alexander McKee and also to General Hand, then Commandant at the Fort which was now considered Colonial property. He found that some time earlier Guyasuta along with Captain Pipe, a Delaware chief, The Shade, a Shawnee, and several others, had been there for a Conference and had promised neutrality at least; O'Hara hoped that his influence had helped bring this about.

But there was so much important news of the war itself to catch up on that for days he talked of little else to Semple, Smith and Brackenridge. Colonel George Washington of Virginia, they said, had been appointed Commander in Chief of the Army by the Congress and all agreed he was the best man.

"He stayed here once, mind, at my very tavern. Well, well, you never know what any traveler will turn out to be!" said Semple complacently.

There had been a dispiriting first winter for the Continental Army up at Cambridge, by all reports; then that next spring while General Howe was holed up in Boston watching as a cat does a mouse, a lot of heavy guns had been miraculously brought down from Ticonderoga through three hundred miles of blizzard and thaw and mounted on Dorchester heights overlooking the city. This had turned the score. Boston became untenable and Howe had taken to his ships. But of course he'd try to strike elsewhere. New York maybe? Or Philadelphia.

From then on though things had gone badly for General Washington. Mostly defeat or withdrawal: Long Island, Manhattan, White Plains. He had ferried his army to New Jersey and finally had reached the Delaware. As the tellers went on with the story at this point, each man broke in excitedly upon the other's version of how on a cold snowy night the General had taken his army over the river amid the ice and captured Trenton! If only, they all lamented, he could have followed up this victory with another at once! But, report had it, his men were poorly fed and more poorly clad — many of them without shoes in the snow — and General Howe was pressing hard upon them. At last word they were quartering in a place in New Jersey called Morristown.

But the greatest piece of news was in connection with what was called *The Declaration of Independence*, written and approved the summer before. The newspapers which the express riders had brought over the mountains at the time had carried copies, and this first night after O'Hara's return, he and Hugh Brackenridge pored over one in the latter's cabin.

"It's the best writing I've ever read," Hugh said. "There's some question yet who was responsible but one rider said people in Philadelphia were sure it was a young Virginian by the name of Thomas Jefferson. It's a wonder to me they didn't let Franklin do it. But," he added thoughtfully, "he'd have put a joke or a quip in somewhere and Congress couldn't take a chance on any levity with this. Read it! I want to listen."

O'Hara read it slowly aloud:

"When in the course of human events it becomes necessary for one people to dissolve the political bonds which have connected them with another and to assume among the powers of the earth . . ."

He read it through, but on the last sentence his voice caught. The eyes of the two young men were misty.

"And for the support of this Declaration we mutually pledge our lives, our fortunes and our sacred honor."

"You see that cut the tie forever," Brackenridge said. "There's a sadness about it but we daren't think of that now. You know Congress and General Washington were still trying for peace with the King when something happened last spring a year they hadn't bargained for. Ever hear of Fort Ticonderoga?"

"Just the name."

"Well, it's pretty strategic. Stands on the border of New York and Vermont, dominating the water route to Canada. Without orders or a by-your-leave two American officers, an Ethan Allen for one and a Colonel Benedict Arnold, pushed right up to it and captured it! That showed the King that the

Colonies meant business, you see, and things went on from there in earnest."

"Benedict Arnold?" O'Hara repeated in surprise.

"Yes. Know anything about him?"

"I had a letter just yesterday from a girl I know in Philadelphia. She mentioned that one of her older friends was — well — very much interested in this Colonel Arnold."

"Yes? Did she mention her name?"

"Peggy Shippen."

"Prominent people, I hear, the Shippens. Devereux Smith told me they're one of the families there that lean to the Tory side. And there are a good many more, I guess. Well, what are you going to do now?"

"Raise my company, I hope. Unless . . ." he hesitated, "unless I should go back to Philadelphia first."

"Ah," Hugh smiled, "so that's the way the wind blows, eh?" O'Hara nodded.

"I've got my own girl picked out from back home, but I have to earn a little more before I can think of marriage. Well, good luck to us both, and to the girls, as well. It's not an easy life for a woman out here."

At the sharp spasm of pain that passed over O'Hara's face Brackenridge looked concerned.

"Is that the trouble?"

"The most of it."

"I'm sorry. I always talk too much. Don't worry, though. Love breaks down all barriers."

"I hope so," O'Hara answered.

As a matter of fact he was desperately unhappy. Along with the letter from Mary which awaited him had been one from her father. It was kindly but very firm. Mary, he said, was now seventeen. It was right and natural that many eligible young men should frequent their house and constitute her escorts in the social life of the city. He had talked again with her and found that she felt she could never go to live on the frontier. If then, O'Hara was still determined to make Pittsburgh his home it would seem advisable for him not to see Mary again. While it was true that she now cared for him, it was inevitable (with no disrespect to O'Hara) that she would get over it and eventually marry within the sphere in which she had been brought up. After each of O'Hara's visits, she had been for some time unsettled and unhappy. So, from the standpoint of a father, he felt that the visits should cease. He would always have the greatest interest in Mr. O'Hara's career and with all good wishes, etc. . . .

O'Hara sat in his room and read this over with something like physical pain in his heart. He was a reasonable man and so could understand Mr. Carson's attitude. His one hope during the last two years had been that the strength of his own love and an increasing warmth of feeling upon Mary's part would overcome her reluctance to the thought of the frontier and, as Hugh had put it, break down all barriers. He had now but two choices. One was to go to Philadelphia and against Mr. Carson's wishes storm his home and Mary's heart, thereby perhaps bringing unhappiness to her and anger to her father. The other was to pour out his longings to her in his letters as he had been doing — fortunately they had not been forbidden — and *wait*. Oh, hardest, most unbearable of all human burdens! To wait. And in his love to compel her by the very power of the thoughts he would send out to her, to remember him and hold him dear.

There was of course one other course which strangely enough he did not even consider seriously. This was to leave Pittsburgh for good and return to the East. When the idea passed fleetingly through his mind, he spoke aloud to himself.

"It's one of the laws of love that a wife's place is with her husband wherever that is. So it will have to be with me."

But at the same time he clenched his hands. *I will not despair and I'll never give up,* he thought.

He wrote to Mr. Carson, making no reference to the matter of his letter, merely stating that he regretted greatly that since he was about to raise and captain a company for frontier service it would be impossible for him to return to Philadelphia at this time. With kindest remembrances to him and to Mistress Mary, he remained his most respectful and obedient . . .

The next day after a more or less sleepless night he made the rounds of the most important men in the village including General Hand, who was now out of British uniform. With a determined expression on his lips and a strange light in his eyes O'Hara explained that he wished to purchase a section of The King's Orchard. At first he met with surprised resistance but he persevered. He had money, *hard money* and it was scarce. By the end of the third day he was the possessor of a plot of land along the Allegheny, in the midst of the apple trees. Devereux Smith who had been appointed to consummate the deal was curious.

"What the devil do you want this particular spot for?" he asked. "You've got all that other property."

"I intend to build a house here when the war lets up a little."

"Ah, hah! If you're getting a nest ready you must have the bird picked out!"

"Perhaps," O'Hara replied, but with such reserve that there were no further questions. At least he felt he had in this instance thrown his dreams and intentions forward far beyond the data in hand, as a strong man should do. There was a power, he believed, in this active faith.

The matter of raising a company took more time than he had imagined. The problem of the settlers round about was that in enlisting for general service they were leaving their homes unguarded. O'Hara felt their position keenly. It was to him a marvel that *any* man under existing conditions would volunteer for new perils while his family was left to face alone the constant old ones. But their love of liberty was a fire in their bones and with it an incurable thirst for adventure.

"You'll get your men," Semple encouraged O'Hara. "There's a good few enlisting now in the Eighth Pennsylvania for the regular army. It's the Scotch-Irish hereabouts you can count on. I'll tell you about them, laddie. As I always say, give a Scotch-Irishman a Bible, a bottle of whiskey and a rifle and he'd beat down the gates of hell itself."

By the first of October a company of forty men had been formed and outfitted. For frontier fighting there was no uniform, only the regular hunting shirt and deerskin breeches. There were, however, two other necessities: ammunition and boats. For the assignment given O'Hara by General Hand was to proceed with his company down the Ohio to Fort Randolph on the Kanawha River at the Virginia border, there to protect the countryside, to hold the Indians in check and to prevent them from making any contact with British forces.

Ammunition was not too plentiful but with his money and business acumen O'Hara managed to secure a goodly amount. So much that after the party had left, General Hand and Captain Grant wondered uncomfortably how this had been achieved. There were a few good boat builders in Pittsburgh and samples of their workmanship were always moored along the rivers. O'Hara bought two large, stout "flatboats," laded them with the food supply, goods for Indian trading, ammunition, and finally his men.

Through the bright, early haze of an October morning the boats pushed off, heading down the Ohio, with a friendly group of interested well-wishers on the shore waving them farewell. One of these was Hugh Brackenridge. He had said his real goodbye the night before almost with tears.

"I'm no woodsman, O'Hara," he lamented. "I'm not physically strong. What little I have to recommend me is up here," touching his forehead. "I'd be worse than useless in frontier fighting and I hate myself for it. They might use me as a chaplain. I guess I didn't tell you I started out for the ministry before I changed to the law."

O'Hara had comforted him. "Don't forget," he said, "that brains are better than brawn. You'll find your work and do it well. Just be here when I get back. Don't forget!"

As the boats moved slowly down the great Ohio O'Hara was overcome with the unimaginable loveliness of the new scenes. The great river wound among wooded hills, each bend bringing a more striking panorama into view. Herds of buffalo, elk and other deer could often be seen standing in the shallows and upon the shining water itself here and there were fleets of ducks, geese or snowy swans. The men had soon discovered also the riches beneath the water and had caught large perch and bass.

One never-ending pleasure to O'Hara was the quick flame-like flashes among the already coloring forests: the scarlet green and gold plumage of flocks, apparently, of parakeets! And once pigeons flew overhead in such numbers as to darken the sun! Everywhere the impression was first of incredible and primeval fecundity, and second of unutterable loneliness. For there were no towns along the banks, no settlers' cabins, no Indian villages. All had withdrawn to less exposed sites. So the flatboats moved on in the great silences until it seemed as though the men were lost in the lush and unbelievable beauty of an empty world.

At night as O'Hara lay looking up at the stars he thought of Mary's last letter which he carried next his heart. The scraps of war news in it were discouraging as had been the fuller reports brought to Pittsburgh by the express riders. Mary wrote that her father thought people in general were not concerned enough over the war. Peggy Shippen, of all her friends, talked most about it for she still was interested in Colonel Benedict Arnold. He had had the only real victory lately. They said he had built a fleet of ships from raw timber up at Lake Champlain and with them had checked an invasion from Canada. Peggy bragged about him all the time and it looked as though she might be in love, but the way she flirted, even with General Washington himself when he had been there, was a caution. Of course she would flirt with anybody. Over the last lines of the letter O'Hara pored though he knew it well by heart.

> I am wondering what you will be doing in the war and what danger you may be in. I say a prayer for you every night.
>
> Your true friend,
> MARY CARSON

This said so much and yet so distressingly little. Only *his friend* after all that had passed between them? How much restraint her father had already put upon her he had no way of knowing. She would before long have his last letter telling of his new title — for a *Captaincy* had been automatically accorded him — and of the proposed trip to Fort Randolph.

How long he would have to stay there he could not say. But if there should be any way of sending a letter, he told her, he would surely write. And then he sent his love, as he put it, unchanged and unchanging.

When at last the boats reached the mouth of the Great Kanawha river they moved up to the fort itself. And a sorry looking place it was! No one, least of all O'Hara, had been prepared for its general decrepitude. A half dozen men in worn frontier dress greeted them with subdued cheers.

"We could yell louder all right, but we don't want to stir up any trouble."

"Have you had much?" O'Hara asked.

"Plenty," one of the men said. "You see most of the fellahs round here have gone off to join the Ninth Virginia an' that leaves the families pretty unprotected. We'll get back a-kitin' to ours, now you're all here. We've been prayin', I tell you, that help would come for we'd been told Governor Pat Henry had sent for it. Well, you can bet your boots you're welcome."

And so the months of the company's duty began to roll. They all fell to at once to rebuild the fort and establish themselves in what semblance of comfort was possible. Patrols went out daily in all directions to scout for Indians. O'Hara knew the necessity for this. It was indeed what they had been sent here for, but as he explained one night to his men, he himself had always had peaceful relations with the Indians both as trader and agent. He had never killed a red man and only once had felt his own life was in danger from them. He urged his men to go slow, to be sure any Indians they caught sight of were indeed enemies. But in two weeks time three of his men had been killed. From then on the eyes of the recruits were like steel and their lips shut tight. They shot first thereafter and O'Hara

said no more. He did decide, however, to do some trading himself. He found a half dozen men, bored sufficiently to be willing to take one of the boats down a little further and across the
river. Then with a white cloth fastened to the top of his rifle
and a big trader's sack over his arm he advanced alone into the
forest. As he had surmised, they had not been unobserved.
Very soon a group of Shawnees were around him. He talked
to them in their own tongue, urged them to stop their forays
on the other side, and then set forth his wares.

When the time for actual barter came he was adamant: he
didn't want furs; he wanted *powder*. By what devious means
the Indians got powder no one was ever sure, but they usually
had it. There was now heated and angry discussion while the
tempting array of goods lay spread before their eyes. When
they made their refusal, O'Hara nodded and quietly began
putting the gay strouds, the trinkets, the jews'-harps, the ver-
million and the rest back into his sack. At once there was an
outcry and more consultation. In the end the trade was consum-
mated and when the boatload returned safely to the Kanawha
with a goodly supply of powder O'Hara could sense the rising
respect among his company.

"But why wouldn't they just shoot you or tomahawk you and
keep the goods and the powder both?" one man asked.

"I honestly don't know," O'Hara answered. "They are used
to trading for one thing and though you won't believe it, they
have certain principles that govern their actions."

"Principles!" The men shouted in derision, but O'Hara
stood firm.

"I mean that. Besides, some of them may have recognized
me or my name. I've been around among the Shawnees a good
deal."

"An' what sort of principles makes them come across here an' plunder an' kill every family they can find?"

"They were once promised this land by a treaty, down through Kentucky, and the whites didn't keep their word."

"By God, that's news to me," one man said. "What'll we do now, then? Just sit here an' let them swarm over the country-side?"

"No," said O'Hara, "I've warned them now and told them to pass the word. As to us, we'll have to go on doing what we're here for."

One day in late December they had a visitor, a tall young man with bright red hair. O'Hara brought him up to the fire with eager hospitality. Whatever his reason for coming he presented a welcome diversion. Besides, O'Hara liked the man on sight.

"Clark," the stranger was saying. "George Rogers Clark is my name. I just thought I'd have a look at your fort here."

"I'm James O'Hara. Captain," he added, laughing a little at the incongruity.

Clark joined him. "Oh, I can beat that, as of the last weeks. I got promoted to Lieutenant Colonel! But . . . you're not native here are you, Captain?"

"Irish once. American now."

"Fine! Well, I guess you've been round enough to know titles don't do you a damned bit of good in wilderness fight-ing, eh, men? Nice to have at soirees and things like that."

There was an engaging mixture of hard strength and friend-liness about the stranger, with humor thrown in.

"Well, I suppose you'd all like to hear the latest war news," he said.

The men who were there at the moment gathered close.

"I'm just fresh from Williamsburg with the Governor so I got it straight. And some of it's good for a change, Dad Drabit! Burgoyne has surrendered to our General Gates up at Saratoga!"

There was a wild burst of cheers.

"The rest isn't quite so fine. General Washington and his army are at a place called Valley Forge in Pennsylvania and they're in the devil of a bad way. Not enough clothes for half of them in this weather, and short rations. And why in the name of God should this be? They're not too far from Philadelphia. People there have enough and why can't they share it? Hasn't Washington got a Quartermaster that's worth his salt? I can't understand it, but all the messages that get through say the men are suffering something terrible. Howe's in Philadelphia. The Congress has moved out to a place called York, to be safe. Hah! Well, I guess that's about all I know."

O'Hara could see Clark's eyes upon him with an intentness that was disconcerting. When the men present had gone out on their various duties Clark spoke.

"I'd like to talk with you where we'd be sure to be alone. Other scouts likely to be returning here?"

"Yes."

"Could we go out and find a nice soft log anywhere to sit on?"

They went out laughing, and into the deep wood behind the fort, where they finally settled on a fallen tree.

"I'll try to be as brief as I can," Clark began.

"I've got an idea and it's burning a hole in me. This is it. As I see it, we've got to capture Kaskaskia and Vincennes or the British may come smack down between them from the north and then all the Kentucky area and Virginia too would be wide open for them. See? If we can take Kaskaskia we'd cut off some of Detroit's provisions and get command of the two big rivers. It would help control the Indians and might even win them over to the American side. Then," he added, "Vincennes later."

"I wish I knew the geography of this better," O'Hara said regretfully.

"Oh, I can help you on that." Clark took a bit of pencil and paper from his pocket and quickly drew a rough triangle of south-flowing rivers with Kaskaskia on the lower Missouri at the left and Vincennes on the Wabash to the right. He sketched in the Ohio flowing toward and joining the Wabash and then the uniting of all the waters at the point of the triangle where they became the Mississippi.

"Do you get the picture?"

"Very clearly. But why not Vincennes first?"

"Has to be the other way," Clark said. "Now. I've just been with Governor Patrick Henry and told my plan. He approved of it but he didn't like the idea of sending a force a thousand miles from their eastern base. But luckily for me Tom Jefferson was there at the time and he and two others spoke up for me."

"You know Thomas Jefferson?" O'Hara asked with interest.

"I've known him since I was born," Clark said. "Our plantations join. He's some older than I am. Another redhead, by the way. Say, how old are you?"

"Born in 1752."

"Why, Dad Drabit, so was I!"

They slapped each other's shoulders in a kind of jubilation.

"I thought when I met you there was a kinship between us," O'Hara said.

"Me too. And now for the most solemn promise you've ever made. Can you keep what I've told you locked inside you? Not a word to any man?"

"I can and I will."

"Good. I trust you and I'll need you and your men. Will you join me?"

"When?"

"Probably not till spring. I'm going north, up round Fort Pitt now to do some recruiting. It'll be tough work in any case but I daren't let the men know all they're getting in for. On the face of it, it's for the defense of Kentucky. That's what the Governor told the Assembly or they wouldn't have approved it."

"But it's not true."

"True as far as it goes. True enough for wartime. We are going to defend Kentucky but we're going to do it by invading the enemy's country and smashing him there. Are you really interested in the expedition and in any case will you keep the secret on your honor?"

"Yes, to both," O'Hara said slowly as they rose and shook hands. "The only thing is that we were supposed to go on down toward the Ozark in the spring."

"Just hold on here till I come. You're pretty much on your own, aren't you?"

"Oh, yes," O'Hara smiled. "Not much supervision possible here."

"Then wait for me and don't let an Injun pick you off in the meantime."

"Eh bien," O'Hara said without thinking, as he smiled.

The effect of the words on Clark was electric. He grabbed O'Hara's shoulders.

"Don't tell me you know some French!"

"I was educated in Paris."

Clark's face was a study of amazement and delight.

"The Lord sent you," he said. "I know about as much French as you could wad a gun with and my men don't know that much. Kaskaskia and Vincennes are full of Frenchies, so you see what it'll mean to have you along."

"And you would have gone on with this without anyone who spoke French?"

A wide and most infectious grin spread over Clark's face.

"I'll tell you how I have things figured out. In any big project like this there's seventy-five per cent damned hard work, twenty per cent bluff and five per cent luck! I take chances. When I have to. Only now for the love of heaven, stay alive till I get back here to meet you!"

Before he left O'Hara asked a favor.

"When you finally leave Pittsburgh would you bring any letters for me that may be there? At Semple's Tavern."

Clark looked at him keenly.

"This undertaking I'm interested in is going to be hard as the devil and plenty dangerous. I'll not think ill of you if you go about your own affairs instead of joining."

"But you feel it's going to be important in helping win the war?"

"I do, by God!"

"I'll be with you, then. But," he smiled, "don't forget the letters."

They parted with something like affection: two strong handsome young men, the same age, and nearly the same height, but more important, with much the same qualities of courage and determination.

At Fort Randolph winter crawled its way to spring, monotony punctuated by rifle shots and death. O'Hara developed the habit of watching the sky at night, naming the stars he knew, noting the silvery vapor of light in the Milky Way, the splendor of Orion, and most of all, the unimaginable remoteness and energy of Sirius, the Dog Star. All this beauty brought some comfort and even occasional exaltation to his lonely heart. For in addition to his desperate longing for his love he brooded often upon the death of Cornstalk who had been murdered early that fall in this very place. He remembered the Indian's kindness; the days and nights they had spent together; and he grieved for his friend. As to his men, he had the feeling that they, like himself, would welcome any change and ask few questions when Clark's boats finally reached the Kanawha to pick them up.

This came to pass on the 18th of May. Clark had succeeded in raising a force of 150 frontiersmen, and twenty settlers' families had joined for protection on the river journey. O'Hara's flatboats fell into line with the others and they all floated down stream. Clark had sent orders ahead for as many men as Kentucky could send to meet him at Dennon's Lick but there were, alas, very few when they got there. However, to make up, among them was Simon Kenton, known all through the Back Country as the most expert scout of them all. He, as their pilot, now guided the little fleet to the Falls of the Ohio, after they had dropped the settlers at a spot called Corn Island. It was the day after they had shot the rapids at the Falls that Clark suddenly began feeling inside his shirt as he and O'Hara were talking.

"Dad Drabit, I forgot your letter! Here, take it. If the inside's as sweet as the outside smells you'll be all right."

There was, then, only one. But while it carried the perfume of lavender as usual, O'Hara's heart felt like lead as he read it. For it was a cool little note, telling briefly of Philadelphia in wartime and ending with the statement that since she could not know where he was she felt it might be better if she did not write again. For the present. And she returned to the formal "Mr. O'Hara" in her salutation. His despair this time was absolute. She had accepted her father's dictum then without a struggle, and his own great love had been of no avail. One fact rose at once to his mind. On this wild and desperately dangerous adventure upon which he was embarking he would now have no fears. The fatalism of the frontier enveloped him. If death came, what did it matter when life had lost its sweetness and its hope. Under cover of darkness that night he tore up the letter and dropped it into the river, his heart drowning with it.

The little fleet of boats went on without mishap while Clark cheered his men and planned his strategy. Suddenly as they neared Massac where he intended to leave the boats and march overland to Kaskaskia they spied a canoe gliding toward them with one man in it. As he drew near they recognized him as one of the settlers, William Linn. He handed Clark a dispatch which he said had reached Corn Island soon after the boats left: *France had signed an alliance with the United States.* Here was unbelievable bolstering to the morale of the little force before their plunge into the wilderness! Clark's idea was to take the fort at Kaskaskia when he got there, frighten the French including the acting Governor Rocheblave, out of their wits, and then gradually show leniency. Now with this trump card up his sleeve he had something with which to dazzle them when he was ready.

They left the boats in a little gut near Massac and began to march single file through the forest, treading soft as Indians. O'Hara, his heart still heavy, found a certain comfort in the comradeship of these intrepid men, calm and casual in what he felt must be extreme danger.

"Aren't there Indians around here?" he asked Clark one day.

Clark grinned. "They're *all* around. Tribes of them. But I've got to take the chance. We'll get through," he added cheerfully. "The worst trouble now is that by another day we'll have nothing to put in our bellies."

It was true. They had to travel light and supplies were soon exhausted. There was, however, one saving fact. This was the berry season in Illinois: dew berries, blackberries, and wild raspberries hung in ripe plentitude and the men fell upon them with zest.

"Why can't we shoot a deer or some game?" O'Hara asked softly one night, with hungry curiosity as he and Clark talked together.

Clark explained patiently. On the frontier, especially through the Virginia and Kentucky areas, almost anyone could tell the sound of one rifle from another. The Indians were good at this. If they heard shots now they would know they were from white rifles and get the little company's location at once.

"I'll tell you a story," Clark said. "Back in Kentucky there was a girl that thought her husband was dead. Been gone two years. Indians got him. Well, on just the day she was going to marry again a shot was heard in the woods and she screamed, 'That's John's rifle.' And by God, it was. These fellahs here . . ." He stopped and looked over his sleeping men, sleeping that light sleep of those in danger whom a mere breath can arouse. "These fellahs know their rifles like their own souls and they can shoot them like . . . well, the ones from Virginia and Kentucky have a saying that they never shoot a squirrel except *in the left eye.* That tells you!"

O'Hara became more and more convinced as they proceeded that although Clark acted as though he had started upon this expedition with a sort of debonair casualness, he had in effect prepared the way before hand with all the skill of an intelligence officer. There must have been scouts and "spies" sent out earlier to make maps and advise on the route; and when they finally came to the Kaskaskia river there were in care of a French farmer enough boats to take the men across.

"These boats just *happened* to be here, I assume?" O'Hara asked with a twinkle.

"Guess so," Clark answered, unperturbed.

The farmer was helpful. He spoke to O'Hara who translated. Yes, Kaskaskia had been keeping spies out but had learned nothing, he believed. There were a great number of men there but the Indians had generally left. The largest house inside the fort was that of Lieutenant Governor Rocheblave.

They ferried across the narrow river and waited for night. Clark's decision was to attack at once, leading part of his men to take the fort, the rest waiting for a signal to attack the town.

As midnight neared, Clark with Simon Kenton, O'Hara and a small group slipped up to the fort. To their amazement they met with no resistance at the gates. They found Rocheblave's house and got in. When the Lieutenant Governor woke it was to see himself surrounded. On one side of his bed stood a young man six feet tall with bright red hair. This was George Rogers Clark. On the other stood a second red-haired six-footer. This was Simon Kenton. At the foot stood several more husky, dirty bearded men with rifles ready.

It was easy to take Rocheblave into custody but the gallant Virginians left Mme. Rocheblave undisturbed in her chamber only to find next day that most of the official British papers were missing!

"Dad Drabit," Clark said then, "we shouldn't have been so damned polite."

As soon as the fort was secured that night, Clark gave the order that he wanted all hell to break loose in the town. O'Hara, at the head of the few Virginians who knew a little French, tore through the streets in the van of the company, shouting that Kaskaskia was now taken and anyone leaving his house would be shot down. As a matter of fact no shot was fired but the Americans kept up a fiendish uproar all night long, seizing all the village arms, setting patrols, demanding food, and otherwise behaving like conquerors.

And so Kaskaskia fell to Clark and the nearby town of Cahokia mildly surrendered soon after. Within the fort the officers relaxed a little. The one whom O'Hara liked best was Captain Leonhard Helm, probably sixty but sound as a nut. He was a jolly man with Rabelaisian humor and a good education, as learning went, known amongst all the company for his favorite drink of apple toddy. Now during this brief military hiatus, Helm sat by the fire and prepared his drink, expounding on the recipe as he did so.

"To a gallon of apple brandy or whiskey you add one and a half gallons of well-sweetened hot water, a dozen large apples, nutmeg, allspice, cloves, a pinch of mace and a half pint of *good rum*."

As he spoke he drew from his inmost shirt little papers of spices and a small bottle of rum.

"I was afraid I might be killed for this on the march but the

Lord preserved me. I got the whiskey and apples here in the town," he added. "Now we'll let this stand three days, then heat it up with a hot poker and you'll taste a drink that has, shall we say, some *authority*."

O'Hara had a question and he decided to ask Helm.

"This capture of Kaskaskia," he said quietly. "It was so *easy*."

Helm turned around and stared at him. "Easy!" he said, and then he laughed. "I doubt if there's another man in the whole Continental Army that would have dared to do what Clark did. At any minute on that march we could have been surrounded by Indians and killed or tortured, every man Jack of us. We made it, and we had luck at the fort here, of course, but don't ever call the whole thing *easy*."

Clark came in and grinned at Helm as he stirred his brew.

"Well," he said, "I've got the inhabitants scared of my very shadow. Now I'll begin being gradually lenient and they'll think we're pretty good fellahs. There'll be some tough work ahead with the Indians, though, as they come in. I'll have to bamboozle them some way. Then . . ." his red hair seemed to bristle as his mouth set grimly . . . "the big trip."

"To Vincennes?" asked O'Hara.

"To Vincennes. Are you sticking with us? There's not much else you can do now, is there, Dad Drabit."

"In any case, I'm sticking," said O'Hara.

CHAPTER SIX

ALL HIS LIFE through, though it contained other dangers and hardships, O'Hara was to shudder as he thought of that march to Vincennes! Then along with this tremor of memory there would come a grin of amazement and satisfaction. It had been incredible; it had been impossible; but Dad Drabit, as Clark would say, they had done it!

The moment Kaskaskia was under complete control Clark began his preparations for the larger enterprise. It was most necessary for him and his small army to remain there while he dealt with the surrounding Indians; but he must find at once what the situation was at Fort Sackville in Vincennes. For this latter information he sent Simon Kenton, the intrepid scout, with Shadrach Bond, another expert woodsman, to cover the 240 miles that lay between. They left on July 6th, just two days after Kaskaskia had been captured. While waiting for their return Clark began his great game of bluff with the Indians, which O'Hara watched with fascinated interest and took part in whenever possible. Kaskaskia was surrounded by tribes on good enough terms with the French but unfriendly to the Americans. Clark had a ridiculously small force compared with the number of his adversaries, so concealing this fact as best he could he put on his show. With an air of utter confidence, almost indifference, he met the chiefs as they came in like a conqueror not to be trifled with. He let slip amongst the French the delightful lie that a huge army was even now at the Falls of the Ohio on their way to join him before he attacked Vincennes. This rumor was soon passed on to the Indians.

When Bond returned he reported that Kenton had joined up with Daniel Boone and gone on to raid the Indian country to the northwest, but as to Vincennes itself they had, dressed in blankets, looked the place well over, been undiscovered, and decided that no alarm of Clark's proximity had reached it. There were no regular troops there and no concentration of Indians.

"Why don't we start off then at once?" O'Hara asked Clark one night.

"Can't do it," Clark said. "Not till I get these Injuns here under my thumb. If we leave now, as likely as not they'd swarm up behind us on the march and that would be the end of us. I'll get them," he added. "I'll scare the hides off them yet!"

The next day the village priest, Father Gibault, now completely won over to the Americans, came with a proposition. He was accustomed to going once or twice a year to Vincennes, to shrive his flock there. Dr. Laffont, the physician, also made an annual trip. Why could they not go now together and by judicious diplomacy, win the French populace over to the Americans without the need of marching troops? To Clark and his officers this sounded only too fine, considering the few troops they had! The good Father, while emphasizing that he would indulge in no secular manipulations himself, yet hinted delicately that in his spiritual conversations with his parishioners he could give strong suggestions, while Dr. Laffont could pursue his efforts in the open. The Indians on the outskirts of Vincennes knew them both and were friendly to them. The plan seemed at least reasonable so Clark bought them two horses and on July 14th they set off into the wilderness with two friends who might be useful and one of Clark's own men added as a spy to see that no double-dealing went on.

"Looks too good to be true," Clark said to O'Hara, "but Dad Drabit it just might work. Luck's been with us this far, anyway. And we can't take a chance on *missing* a chance."

In the stillness of the nights, sometimes under the luminous stars, sometimes alone by the fire in Rocheblave's former house, the two young men talked together as young men will, lightly of life and death, seriously of adventure and ambition and occasionally hesitantly when stars or fires burned low — of love. Clark so far was emotionally untouched though his feeling was intense as to what the right wife could mean to a man.

"Now take my mother," he said once. "She married my father when she was fifteen, went to housekeeping in a little cabin he built himself right on the frontier and had ten children. She's got five officer-sons in the war this minute and as proud as the devil over it. Now if I could ever find a girl like her!"

O'Hara, his heart torn with his love and his despair, longing for the release of a shared confidence, still found himself unable to speak of Mary. And somehow as he tried to picture her delicate beauty in a log cabin, her slender body worn by birth pains and hard work as a frontier woman's must, his heart failed him. Who was he, *what* was he, to steal her away from comfort and safety? So, he, too, in these talks spoke of love only in the abstract and if Clark's discerning eye sometimes watched his tense face curiously, there was no question asked.

Early in August, Father Gibault, Dr. Laffont and their companions returned with good news. Their diplomacy, secular and spiritual, had been crowned with success! The people of Vincennes, with no strong attachment for either side, had agreed to cast their lot with the Americans. A few were holding the ramshackle fort and it only remained for Clark to take over. A handful of men would be enough, they declared jubilantly.

"It looks all right so far," the Colonel said somewhat dubiously to his officers that night as he scanned them. "If old Hamilton just keeps his ass on his seat out at Detroit."

A growl went up from the men, a fierceness of anger, a consuming hatred the like of which O'Hara had never seen before.

"I'd give my life to capture the Hair-Buyer," a man said.

"So would we all. Do you think he's up to something now?" It was Helm who spoke.

"Don't know," Clark said. "I've had a spy or two out there and they got the idea he's planning to set off to attack Fort Pitt."

"*Fort Pitt?*" O'Hara echoed, more moved than he would have believed possible.

"Well, they couldn't be too sure. They were damned smart to get there and back with their lives. Williams and Hurley went."

The men made no comment. They had learned that Clark with all his casualness had his feelers out everywhere. So when a man or two were suddenly missing for a time no one questioned the absence.

"I want the best officer among you to take twenty-five men and go to Vincennes and hold the fort. I'll come on if I have to, but if I don't it's all to the good. I've got plenty to keep me busy here. For this job I'll pick you, Helm."

There was a murmur of approval. Everyone liked the jovial Helm and respected him. He was a trained Indian fighter and a soldier of resource.

"Select your own men, Captain, from the enlisted," Clark went on. "You'll know what to do when you get there. Have a sharp eye out for the British, keep the populace happy, smooth down the Indians, and see that the guns all work. They've got one field gun at least, Gibault says."

So the force set off with Captain Helm putting the little papers containing his remaining spices carefully next to his skin. The ground then was not swampy, the rivers not flooded, for it was still August. It was felt that the trip would be easy.

Meanwhile the work at Kaskaskia went on. O'Hara had not only become official interpreter but also in a sense "quartermaster." With his shrewd business ability he procured in divers ways the supplies needed by the troops. On Clark's part there were two great problems: always the Indians, who were gradually being won over. Clark amazed them and in a sense delighted them with his cool courage. *The Big Knife,* as they called him, was a man they could understand. As his stories grew in magnitude and bravado the chiefs became more and more respectful. With his own men Clark faced trouble. They had enlisted for a short term, now up; they were far away in strange country; they were sick and tired of everything; they wanted to go home. Like a juggler Clark tossed up for them a dozen good reasons why they should stay on. So, as winter advanced the original troops were still there. However, a new and great anxiety had developed. The encouraging messages from Helm had stopped. Because of this Clark sat up till all hours with O'Hara, walking the floor, talking, pondering.

"It's Hamilton I'm afraid of, and if Helm can't get a man through to me, I won't try a messenger from this end. He wouldn't have a chance. At least I'll wait a little longer. Listen to that goddamned rain!"

For it was falling, falling, now, constantly, often mingled with snow and sleet upon the flat and all too receptive Indian lands.

"Now, this fellah, Hamilton . . ." O'Hara began.

"One of the Crown's fine officers," Clark said through his teeth, "and Dad Drabit, he may be a gentleman from the skin out, but he's connived with the Indians and given them presents if they brought in white scalps ever since he's commanded Detroit. That's why he's called the *Hair Buyer* and there isn't a man on the frontier that doesn't hate him like . . . like . . . oh, the devil's too nice a word."

"*A British officer!* Are you *sure?*"

"My fine young friend, in this country you have to learn to swallow a lot without choking."

"But this Hair-Buyer business makes me sick at my stomach! I don't believe I'll sleep too well tonight."

"I can't sleep *any* night just now."

It was not until the end of January when the tension was becoming unbearable, that the news came in a most unusual and circuitous way by the arrival of one Francis Vigo, a St. Louis merchant, thoroughly pro American. He had gone to Vincennes in the interest of his business and found the fort and the town itself taken over by General Hamilton and his troops! Captain Helm had had only a few faithful men with him in the fort at the last, it appeared, and the British had seized it without firing a shot.

"And what about Helm now?" Clark asked anxiously.

A smile broke over Vigo's swarthy countenance.

"He's on his parole not to leave his quarters or try to send word to you. And in the meanwhile it would seem the Governor's taken a great fancy to him and they drink a kind of *toddy* together."

In spite of the grievous news a roar of laughter went up from all the men listening.

Vigo went on with his report. He would guess that Hamilton must have close to five hundred men, and the fort had three field guns and two swivels.

"He thought I was so innocent, he told me his plans even. The season now is too bad, he says, but next spring he will attack Kaskaskia. When I left he made me swear a solemn oath I would not communicate with you *on my way home to St. Louis!* And I didn't, by God! I went there first and came right back!"

Again the throaty laughter rose and Clark slapped Vigo warmly on the back. "Good man!" he cried. "Smart man! We can't even try to thank you. But we'll give you the best we have for your supper and a bed to sleep in tonight."

When Vigo was gone in the morning Clark and his officers held a council of war. The situation could not have been blacker. The prairie from Kaskaskia to Vincennes was now either freezing water or half frozen mud all the way; the weather, winter cold; their force small; the whole idea of making the march under present conditions, fantastic.

As against this there were these other facts; Hamilton would never dream of suspecting an attack now, which was mightily in their favor, while by spring if he united the northern and southern Indians and came upon them here in full strength he would be irresistible. Then not only would Kaskaskia fall but there would go Kentucky and Virginia too! This was the threat that sharpened the decision of the men as they listened to their leader.

"I tell you," Clark said, "we have only one course. We've got to attack Hamilton in his own quarters and at once. For," he added, "if we don't take him, he'll take us as sure as you have a gut in your belly."

"Oh no, he won't," yelled one fellow. And a chorus of angry shouts joined him.

O'Hara, listening, said nothing. The plan seemed suicidal, and his heart was very heavy. Clark, catching sight of his sober face, winked, and the unquenchable optimism of his friend raised O'Hara's spirits a little. After all, why should they *not* gamble upon this last and wildest chance of all? If he could be certain that a letter awaited him back at Semple's Tavern, perhaps he would now know more fear for his own safety. But Fort Pitt itself seemed a limitless distance away, and Philadelphia as far removed as heaven.

That night as they had their usual talk O'Hara knew the young Colonel was serious enough in spite of his insouciant wink.

"I've got to play-act this time," he said, "if I ever did. So if you see me struttin' round like a turkey cock you'll know the reason. All the same," he said half under his breath, "I'd bind myself seven years a slave to have five hundred troops!"

"What do you really think of the situation then?"

Clark eyed him shrewdly. "Can you take it straight?" he asked.

"I wouldn't be surprised."

"Well, it's about as bad as anything could be this side of hell. But we've got no alternative. And," he added flinging up his head, "the whole business somehow suits me to a T. I like danger. I like taking a chance when I have to. It brings out all the . . ."

"Red in your hair," O'Hara finished, grinning.

"Right!" They laughed together.

"One thing all this campaign has done for me, is to give me a friend," O'Hara said seriously. "I've meant to speak of this before."

"Same with me. Well, we're one year's children, as the old women say, maybe that's why we've kind of stuck together. You've helped me in more ways than your French, O'Hara."

They shook hands in a rare display of affection, then each turned somewhat shamefacedly to his bed.

The play acting went on gloriously. To see Clark's superb confidence no one would have guessed there was a difficulty in the way. Hamilton, from his swagger, was as good as captured. The troops braced to it; the local women thrilled to it when a detachment came from Cahokia to join up; Kaskaskia raised its company too, and there was a feast to celebrate the general leave-taking. On February 5th Clark with his force of a hundred and thirty men and a dozen pack horses set out. Each man had his own normal material equipment: a rifle, a knife and a tomahawk; and on the spiritual side the friendly Father Gibault had graciously granted absolution to Catholics and Protestants alike! Thus caparisoned in body and soul as it were, the men plunged into the rain and the mud.

It was soon evident that the march was going to be worse than anyone had dreamed. The inundation was so deep in places that the men were often up to their arm-pits in water, trying desperately to keep their powder and rifles out of the wet as they slogged along. Day or night they were never dry and never warm. The things that kept them going were that first they were physically hard as nails, and second, that Clark's high spirits and invention never failed to raise the morale. The men were allowed to shoot at game as they passed, since they were too far from Vincennes for the sound to matter and there were no Indians in that immediate vicinity. This meant that there was a feast of good hot meat every night in the pots even though the camp was on wet ground. There was also entertainment in the way of games and imitated Indian war dances. In addition to this enlivening by night Clark and his officers kept going about amongst the men by day, shouting and encouraging them and running as much through the mud and water as any of them.

On the 13th they reached the bank of the Little Wabash and here the difficulties just past seemed small by comparison with those facing them. Ordinarily the Little Wabash was narrow with a good strip of land between it and the Main Wabash river. Now, because of torrential rains the two streams had joined higher up, submerged the ground between and now presented a wide turbid expanse to the gaze of the wet, cold, weary men. O'Hara eyed his friend, the young Colonel, inquiringly.

"Now what?" he asked.

"Well, this might be enough to stop any set of men not in the temper we are, but Dad Drabit, we're pretty tough!"

He sent most of the men to camp on the higher ground above the river while a small group built a pirogue. When it was finished several men paddled out in it with instructions, somewhat the same as Noah's dove, to find some dry land, but in their case *to report it anyway!* They did, but oddly enough it was the truth! A tiny island reared itself in the midst of the wide morass. As they all started for it an unusual incident proved inspiriting. A drummer boy from Cohokia found the water too deep for his short legs and began to float the drum with himself upon it! As the laughter spread he started singing comic songs, as the men propelled his strange craft for him. When O'Hara called Clark's attention to this the Colonel laughed loudest of all.

"Just what we needed!" he said. "Any diversion is welcome, by God!"

The next morning on their tiny island the men heard the distant boom of the gun at Fort Sackville; by two o'clock they were on the banks of the big Wabash, nine miles below Vincennes, wet and cold as usual but now hungry into the bargain. This river could not be waded and they had but two boats. To divide the men as would be necessary with part on one side during the ferrying and part on the other was dangerous to the point of extremity but there was no other way. One more chance had to be taken. By evening they were all over the river but as the red morning sun rose they saw, still ahead of them a flooded plain! Morale was cracking for the men's stomachs were empty. Clark went out himself and measured the water. "Only up to my neck," he whispered to O'Hara and Bowman, one of his best officers, when he came back.

"But we're six feet or over," O'Hara said anxiously. "What about the shorter men?"

"God help them. We've got to go on. Every one of you here around me do just what I do."

He wet his hands, poured a little powder on them and blackened his face like an Indian in war paint, then giving the Indian war whoop which they all knew only too well, he plunged into the water. Without a word the troops followed him.

Of the whole ghastly trip the last stretches were the worst.

Weak, cold and starved, the men, trying again with desperation to hold their rifles and powder horns above the water, waded up to their chins, clung to trees as they appeared or floated on occasional logs. The two canoes picked up those sinking from utter exhaustion. Finally, more dead than alive, they landed, some dropping half in and half out of the water, on a dry woodsy spot of about ten acres in plain sight of Vincennes! The great march was over. All they had to do now was to give battle to a force probably four times the size of their own!

But as they thawed out at the carefully screened fires, or, in the case of the weakest ones, were walked up and down until the numbness went out of their legs, something like spirit returned to them. Nothing to come could be as bad as that which they had passed through. The sun shone, and at this very moment a canoe load of squaws on their way to Vincennes was captured quietly along with nearly a quarter of buffalo meat, corn, tallow and kettles. The men soon drank broth on their empty stomachs and were once again invincible.

"The holy angels must be just swarmin' around you," one solemn soldier told Clark.

"When I get time, I'll thank them," he grinned.

In the ponds near the town they could see ducks swimming and a few hunters out shooting at them. The thought of roast duck sent the saliva trickling over many a bearded chin. O'Hara with three Frenchies was dispatched to capture one of these hunters and bring him back. It did not prove hard. The man was evidently impressed with O'Hara's manner and elegant Parisian French and came peaceably.

"We've got to put the fear of God in him now," Clark said to O'Hara. "You do the translating. He seems to listen to you."

The orders were quickly given. The man was to go back

to Vincennes, pass the word quietly that the Illinois army was
here to take the fort. The people were to stay in their houses.
The women were to have food ready to feed the soldiers. Did
he know a man named Captain Bosseron? He did. Good! Better than best! He was to tell Bosseron, who was really anti-
British and a friend, to find some way to get a message to Captain Helm that the Virginians were here. And if he, the hunter,
warned Hamilton, he would be executed.

"Make that strong!" Clark told O'Hara.

"*Exécuté*," O'Hara repeated.

The villagers were to remain tranquil and Bosseron was to
bring to Clark any extra powder he had. By a careless wave of
his hand toward the woods back of them Clark conveyed the
impression that it too was full of troops. So the hunter set off
and the men waited. Anxiously. But not for long. Bosseron
himself came with powder and good news. Hamilton suspected
nothing. He and Helm were having their nightly game of pic-
quet. The message to Helm had been taken by a Mrs. Henry
whose husband was also a prisoner. The garrison had been
working hard all day on repairs and were now resting. What
more could Clark want? What indeed, Dad Drabit!

Bosseron went back to his anomalous position and Clark's
little army moved up to Vincennes, seized the main street si-
lently and put out guards. There was nothing conspicuous
about those who entered the town. After they had washed the
black from their faces they looked like any other woodsmen or
French Canadians who were always moving about. Even with
the first burst of firing the fort remained quiet, Hamilton no
doubt blaming it on one of the shooting sprees that the Indians
or the French often engaged in.

It was at this point that a few of the enlisted men approached

Clark with a request. It was practically certain that as Helm sat at the game, his toddy was simmering on the hearth. Couldn't they fire into the chimney, knocking the clay and plaster down the flue into the mug? For the sport of it? It was exactly the type of thing that tickled Clark's fancy; also although it would waste some ammunition it would send troop morale soaring and he wasn't sure just then how much might be needed before they were through. He gave consent. Some time later when Hamilton realized he had an enemy at his gates, a volley hit the chimney and the anguished voice of Captain Helm rose above the noise of battle.

"You rascals! You've ruined my toddy!"

Clark's men, all expert riflemen, were ordered to pour in the hottest fire possible from different directions, then cease and indulge in great laughter, shouting and noise to bewilder the enemy and make him think fresh troops were constantly being brought up. Between the gaps in the log fort the Virginians could pick any form that showed itself, and from the trench where Bowman had managed to install himself and a fair number of men, it had been possible to knock out the British big guns in the first hour. All through the night the noise, shouting and firing of the Virginians gave the impression of a large army. By four o'clock Clark sensed that the number of Hamilton's force while several times larger than his own, had still been exaggerated and that the complete security felt before had not added to its effectiveness now. Clark also knew that his own boldness, bluff and ingenious pretenses were once again going to work.

About nine o'clock he told his officers he was going to ask for surrender. Some writing equipment was secured and Clark settled on a stump behind a wide tree to his task.

"Can you spell, O'Hara?" he asked.

"Pretty well," O'Hara smiled.

"Watch me then, for I can't. And I'll bet the old Hair-Buyer can spell like the devil. All right, let him, Dad Drabit!"

When the message was completed after corrections it read as follows:

SIR:

In order to save yourself from the impending storm which now threatens you I order you to immediately surrender yourself up with all your Garrison Stores Etc. Etc. for if I am obliged to storm you may depend upon such treatment justly due to a Murderer beware of destroying Stores of any kind or any papers or letters that is in your possession or hurting one house in the Town for by heavens if you do there shall be no Mercy shewn you.

G. R. CLARK

This, under a white flag of truce, was sent into the fort, and at once all firing ceased. During the lull the Virginians went in groups for a hot breakfast in the town, the first real meal they had had in days. The Governor's answer was brief and elegant.

Gov. Hamilton begs leave to acquaint Col. Clark that he and his Garrison are not disposed to be awed into any action Unworthy of British subjects.

H. HAMILTON

When hostilities began again they were heavy. Clark's men refreshed by their good meal were ready for action in earnest. Some of the crack Virginia riflemen began shooting into the fort from two directions with a hot cross-fire. By noon the fort was quiet. The great gate was unbarred and a man emerged under a white flag who wore what could only be described as a grin. It was jolly Captain Helm himself! He brought the news that Hamilton was ready to give up if the terms were acceptable.

When the two companies of the Illinois regiment finally drew up to the fort gate to receive the surrender of the British garrison, Hamilton eyed them in bewilderment.

"But where is your army, Colonel?" he asked in a strange voice.

"This is it, Governor," Clark said, smiling.

The men talked the moment over that night, Clark, Helm, O'Hara and Bowman. They all agreed that when Hamilton turned his head aside there were tears in his eyes.

"And why mightn't there be?" Helm said. "He had enough men to take you if he had only known how small your force was. He's swallowed a bitter pill, yon one, but he's still got his hair on, that's more than he deserves."

"I don't know whether he could have won anyway," O'Hara said. "The British aren't used to fighting men who shoot a squirrel only through the left eye!"

There was laughter and jollity and many a recounting both of all that had gone on upon the ghastly and incredible march and inside the fort itself as Helm waited and hoped. Of one thing they were all convinced. Vincennes could have been captured in no other way.

The men were quartered in the town after the fort was garrisoned, and O'Hara, in a house where the French flowed pleasantly around him, slept for two days from utter exhuastion. When he finally woke and stretched with vigor in spite of sore muscles he knew that he was more of a man than he had ever been even after his Indian journeys. He was now hardened, seasoned, *toughened* not only in body but also in mind. He collected his original company of whom there were now but twenty-nine and prepared to go back at least to Fort Randolph, or, as he hoped, to Fort Pitt. He had done what he had promised Clark he would do and could now leave honorably. The Indians around Vincennes, quick to sense change of masters, kept pouring in and had to be dealt with. O'Hara stayed on a little longer to be of what service he could with the dialects, and then on a bright March morning set off overland with his men.

He and Clark had had strangely little to say on their last night together.

"Your best bet is to head for Corn Island and pick up some boats there," the Colonel said. "I wish you felt like coming on to Detroit with me. That'll be my next move."

O'Hara shook his head. "Sorry, but I must get back now. I'm not really a soldier of fortune, you know."

"You've made a damned good try at it, I'd say. I'm going to need more men. I may have to go back to Fort Pitt myself later to recruit."

They stood as they had at their first meeting: two strong young men, their eyes on a level, born the same year on opposite sides of the Atlantic and thrown together by fate to help work out a new nation's destiny in the American wilderness. They wrung each other's hands hard and said no more.

The journey back by contrast to the one just past was uneventful in the extreme and when they reached Fort Randolph there was a letter for O'Hara left by some traveler giving instructions from General Brodhead, now commandant at Fort Pitt.

"Another new one," O'Hara muttered but he smiled over the

message. Since his force by now must be small, the General wrote, he was to check on the Indian situation around the countryside and if satisfactory, he was to return with his men to Fort Pitt by the end of the summer.

October was in full flame when they finally reached the last waters of the Ohio. The men were eager to scatter to their various homes before a new order sent them off to join the Eighth Pennsylvania or perhaps the Ninth Virginia. Their joy in their return was natural, but O'Hara was surprised at the quick anticipation of his own heart. He sharply quelled the thought of a letter and concentrated upon the dubious pleasure of being again in the only home he had. He looked over the rolling rivers, the fort, the bright-colored wooded hills, the little town itself. Nothing was changed except that now no red coats showed among the deerskin suits. He hurried from the wharf along the dusty street to Semple's, but before entering the tavern he went to the stable to see Pitt. The horse whinnied with joy and nuzzled against him. O'Hara laying his cheek to the soft velvet nose, spoke to him tenderly. There were worse friends than a horse.

Samuel Semple was in his usual place behind his desk-counter, but at sight of O'Hara came forward with both hands outstretched.

"Bless my stars and garters!" he shouted. "We get so damned much bad news in here that I can't believe the good when I see it with my own eyes. Welcome back, laddie. We've lost track of you altogether. Where all have you been?"

"It's a long story but a pretty important one, I think. Suppose I wait . . ."

"Right. I'll pass the word to Devereux Smith and young Brackenridge and a few and we'll hear it all tonight. Agreed?"

"Gladly. It's good to be here. Is . . . are there any letters for me?"

Semple looked embarrassed and made a show of fumbling about his desk. "Now come to think of it, I don't believe there is. Everything gets held up in wartime."

"Right!" said O'Hara. "I'll have a look at my room now."

He had thought he was prepared for this blow, but he was not. Deep down below all his determined sophistry, he knew now that he had not given up. That, indeed, it was this slim but unquenchable hope rather than the blackness of despair which had steeled him through the sufferings of the Vincennes march. He had lied when he told himself he believed he had lost Mary forever. That was only that the contradiction might eventually be the more sweet. Now, the lie had become the bitter and desperate truth. If after these long months she had not written then she had indeed meant what she implied in her last letter.

He looked about the familiar room and then flung himself upon the bed. His body was tired enough, but it was his heart that was more spent. Over and over like a throbbing in his brain came a line from Spenser which he had read as a schoolboy and which had persistently come to him as he struggled through the freezing waters.

When shall this long weary day have done,
And lend me leave to come unto my love?

He fell at last into a troubled sleep and woke startled from a dream of drowning as the great gong was beat for supper. He tidied himself quickly and went downstairs. Here was Hugh Brackenridge waiting for him, one great smile of welcome. Smith came in soon and John Ormsby and they settled to eat.

"Semple says you're to save your story till later so everyone can hear it together. We've had a bare hint of it from a scout who came through and we're pretty eager to get the whole of it. My word, man, you look thinner but very fit, I must say," Brackenridge appraised.

Hugh looked thin himself. His brow seemed higher and whiter and his eyes more dark. O'Hara guessed that his lack of fighting strength still was a bitterness to him.

"But what about news from the east?" O'Hara questioned. "Tell me what's been happening in the war. I'm away behind. The last I heard was over a year ago about General Gates capturing Ticonderoga. Wherever that is," he added laughing.

They all began at once and then settled to more intelligible turns. O'Hara knew of the terrible winter at the Valley Forge, but had not known that the British General Howe had all that time been comfortably ensconced in Philadelphia, feted and dined by the Tory families; that he had resigned a year ago in May, been replaced by Sir Henry Clinton who had orders to evacuate the city and get his forces to New York.

"Of course," Smith said, "they're smart enough to see that's the best harbor on the coast and they can bottle up the Hudson River from there. On his way across New Jersey Washington's army fell on him, Clinton, that is, and there was a pretty hot battle from all reports at a place called Monmouth. But we won."

"And what's happened since then?" O'Hara asked eagerly.

"Well, you know how a war drags on. A wearisome business, it is."

"There's *Stony Point* this summer," Hugh put in eagerly. "We must tell him about that."

"Go ahead," said Smith, "though I doubt if that fight did

much more than give a general a nick-name. When we didn't hold on to the Fort what the devil did we take it for? Well, go on. Tell him."

Stony Point, Hugh explained, was on the west side of the Hudson, held first by the Americans, then taken over by the British in May. One night in July a General Anthony Wayne who hailed from somewhere in the Philadelphia area attacked the fort with about thirteen hundred picked troops and the garrison surrendered.

"And it seems, the way he stormed the place as if he wouldn't stop at hell itself, made his men call him *Mad Anthony*, and now I guess everybody's saying it. Must be quite a man."

"But I still don't understand the whole thing. He took that fort the 16th of July with all this flourish and then evacuated it two days after. That doesn't make sense to me. But who can make sense out of a war? You heard about the alliance with France last year?" Smith questioned.

O'Hara told them the way the news had been brought to them on the river by the man in the canoe.

"But you haven't likely heard of the young Frenchman that's come over to help us. Just in the spirit of liberty. No other reason. Quite a young fellah with a title too. Marquis, isn't it? Name's La Fayette. He was in this battle of Monmouth we were speaking of and we hear General Washington's quite taken with him. Well, I guess that brings you about up to date."

"Of course the Indian wars in New York State had been bad, bad," Ormsby put in. "All the Iroquois except the Oneidas and part of the Tuscaroras have sided with the British and murdered and plundered like mad. This August a General Sullivan, we hear, went up with a big force and just about wiped them out. For once the whites give as good as they got, I guess. A bloody business! The worst they say there's ever been. You heard about Girty?"

"No. What about him?"

The men all spoke at once.

"Defected! A year ago this spring! Went over to the British! Lock, stock and barrel, and been doing the devil's own work with the Indians ever since. Everyone now calls him the *White Savage*."

"I can't believe it!" O'Hara burst out.

"I can," said Smith. "I never liked the cut of his jib. He had an Injun look to him. Well, he's with them again now, and up to all their dirty tricks."

O'Hara was speechless. Somehow this news of Girty which Clark had either not known or not thought of repeating hit him very hard. He had been friendly with the man and had not thought ill of him.

"Congress is back in Philadelphia," Hugh went on, "and they've voted half pay for seven years after the war to all officers and a bounty of eighty dollars to each soldier. I guess," he added, his face falling, "it's helped enlistment."

"So, Philadelphia is free now?" O'Hara asked from a tight throat.

"Oh yes," Smith said. "General Washington put a General Arnold in charge there just after Clinton left. Benedict Arnold his name is. He cuts quite a dash, we hear. Drives round the city with a carriage and four, dines out when not entertaining himself and just this last spring married a Philadelphia girl about twenty years younger, they tell me. A Miss Shippen. Of course her family are Tories but I guess in society they all mix! From what I can hear that was the case even when the British were there. Well, I guess that's about all the news, O'Hara. Things are sort of quiet this fall but there can be a flare up any time. What we want now is to hear your story. Eat up, fellahs and let's get to it."

O'Hara hadn't counted on so large an audience but Semple had passed the word amongst the other tables so when supper was ended fifteen men drew their chairs and benches forward to listen. He was embarrassed but he felt an obligation upon him to tell them all, for Clark's sake. Also because of the old feud between Western Pennsylvania and Virginia over their border line, he must tell now of the courage of the Virginians and Kentuckians as well as of those who had been recruited from around these very parts.

"Stand up where we can all see you," someone shouted.

So O'Hara stood and hesitantly at first, then in full confidence, told the main story while the listening men scarcely breathed. It was a long recital but the men sat motionless until it was done, then to O'Hara's surprise they each came forward to shake his hand. He had never felt so much an American as in that moment.

He went back with Brackenridge to his cabin later and they drew close again.

"How's the law going, Hugh?"

"Not too badly. It's unbelievable how many little jobs come along. There's the matter of wills, for example. These times make men think of them. Not much money in that but it all counts up. Of course when I can help a poor man out in any way there's no charge. What are you going to do next?"

O'Hara shook his head. "Haven't an idea. I'll report to Brodhead tomorrow. He sent for me to come back."

"Good man, I hear. They change commandants here every

time the wind blows. I wish you could stay in Pittsburgh, but where honor calls . . ."

"There's one thing I find I can do better than shooting a gun, though I've mastered that fairly well. At Kaskaskia I took over the job of getting supplies for the men. I thought I might just mention that to Brodhead."

"By all means. Quartermastering, isn't it? From all I hear they can do with some good ones. Our army's had pretty slim pickings. How . . . how are things on the personal side?"

O'Hara shook his head. "I've never felt so lost," he said.

"Don't give up, man. *Amor omnia vincit.*"

"I wish I could think so," O'Hara said.

The next day he went to the Fort to call upon General Brodhead, whom he found businesslike but pleasant and eager to hear his tale.

"You *did* take off with Clark without special orders but I guess results justified it," he said when O'Hara finished.

"Colonel Clark is a difficult man to say *no* to, General."

Brodhead laughed. "I know only too well for I've tried it. Now, what I want you to do is to go back east to Headquarters with papers to General Washington. We need clothing and supplies desperately for our soldiers out here. Reports say this is going to be the coldest winter in years. I know His Excellency will be eager to hear of the Vincennes campaign and who better to tell him than you who were on it? When you get through your recital I've an idea our requests will be granted. Not," he added hastily, "that Washington doesn't do his best all the time, but he's got the hardest job in the world. A *mortal* hard job," he added.

"When should I start?" O'Hara asked.

Brodhead stroked his chin. "Right now," he said, "our army's up around West Point, Washington and Clinton sort of eyeing each other across the Hudson but both apparently afraid to move. My sources of information are good. Have to be. Toward the end of November Washington intends to bring his troops down to a place called Morristown, where he wintered last year. Why don't we say you will leave in about two weeks time."

"Right, sir. But where is this Morristown?"

"In New Jersey. If you go straight to Philadelphia, you can get directions there."

When O'Hara set forth once again, his face toward the east, his feelings were mixed. He was greatly honored by his commission, and thrilled at the thought of meeting the Commander-in-Chief. He was now rested and physically alive and the feel of Pitt under him once more was inexpressibly good. But on the other hand, his heartache increased as the miles were covered on the now familiar Forbes road over the mountains. If he were only in truth going unto his love as the poem said! He had decided to see her if this was possible even though he realized that the very sight, if that were all, would be the torture of a knife in the wound.

He rode through the glory of the last days of Indian summer, the brilliance of the foliage still a surprise to his old-world eyes, stopping occasionally to gather some of the late grapes which grew luxuriantly where there was fallen timber, or beside the smaller water courses, where the crab apples turned golden and fragrant on the ground amongst the autumn leaves. These varied his meals of game or the eternal jerk and water and made him think of the Carson dinner table with its great bowl of fruit and glow of candle light. In his nightly camps he pondered upon the vulnerability of the human heart. As to his own body it had endured unimaginable suffering of strain, cold, hunger and distress, and had survived and triumphed. But the heart. O God, the heart! It could not be hardened or *seasoned* as the body in its anguish. According to the immutable law by which Nature had ordained the mystery of love for her own vast purpose of continuance, the heart must remain tender, violate, susceptible to deadly wounds. Unhealing.

He had much else to think upon as the days passed for the mildness of Indian summer left in a sudden bitter wind and the first snow began to fall. There had been rumors in Pittsburgh of a hard winter and the present discomforts tended to support the prophesy. He had blankets and now a trained woodsman's skill, so he built his fires, rubbed Pitt's knees and endured the cold. Often he mused upon Girty and his shocking defection. He thought of Guyasuta and wondered what part he was taking now in the war. Girty knew him well. Could the *White Savage* have persuaded the *Red* to follow him? He wished ardently that he could have seen his Indian friend before he left Pittsburgh, but in these times that would have been difficult. He wondered, too, if he could locate Elliott while he was in the east. His old traveling companion, according to Semple, had left for Philadelphia as soon as they heard it was evacuated.

So, the miles were finally covered and he drew rein again at the familiar Crooked Billet. One way to secure directions to Morristown had occurred to him. As Philadelphia was now, he must tread carefully between the Revolutionist sympathizers and the Tories. One man he knew he could trust. This was the Mark Bird he had met on shipboard who was even then in 1772 making cannonballs at his foundry "just in case." He had not seen him since, but he intended to see him now.

In the old taproom he was given a hearty welcome before the

big fireplace. Hastings looked older and a bit haggard and let
no word slip as to his own leanings, probably for business pur-
poses. Sam was the same, friendly, grinning and eager to talk,
but O'Hara was cautious even though at the moment there
were no other customers present.

"And what have you been up to since we saw you?" Hastings
inquired.

"Oh, a little of this and that. There's plenty to keep a man
busy in and around Pittsburgh. It's good to get back to civilized
life for a change, though. What all has been going on here?"

"Plenty. And yet it's surprising how much we've gone our
own way at that. We had General Howe for a while running
things as though the war was only meant for balls and routs,
then Clinton a short time and now the English are gone and
our own General Arnold is in charge. He and Miss Peggy Shippen were married in the spring. That set the town by the ears."

"So?"

"Oh, yes. Quite a whirlwind courtship. He's a widower,
much older, but they tell me he's got a way with him. Must
have, to catch a belle like Miss Peggy."

"Could you direct me to the Bird Iron Works at Birdsboro?"
O'Hara said abruptly.

Hastings looked surprised. "I can. That's at Hay Creek just
up along the Schuylkill a little way. Have you decided to come
east for a job?"

O'Hara laughed. "No, I'm a fixture on the frontier, I guess,
but while I'm here this time I want to make a long-delayed call
on Mr. Bird. He was very kind to me on the ship coming over."

He could not relax in his room as he did before. He longed
to ask for news of the Carsons but the words would not come.
Instead he had supper with Hastings and Sam and filled his

talk with Indian tales to which they listened avidly. The next
day he set out for Birdsboro and reached it by early afternoon.
There before him were the great foundries, there the little
town of workmen and on the hill beyond, the spreading manor
of the owner.

Like Hastings, Mr. Bird seemed older by more than the intervening years and for a moment, looking sharply at his guest
who had been shown into the drawing room, he did not recognize him. Then as O'Hara introduced himself recollection
returned in a rush, and there was a warm greeting. O'Hara did
not wait but told him quickly the purpose of his call, apologizing as he did so for not accepting the kindness of his invitation
long before.

"Of course I can direct you to Morristown," Mr. Bird said,
"and you'll find the roads pretty fair. However, I suggest that
you spend the night here and in the morning I can send one of
my grooms to ride with you. He knows the way and it will save
you time as well as give him something to do. He's lame and
couldn't go into the army. Have you got a good horse?"

"The best," O'Hara smiled. "Pitt and I are real friends."

"*Pitt!*" Mr. Bird's eyebrows went up. "I assume, though,
you've broken your British ties?"

"Absolutely."

In the quiet of the library after dinner O'Hara summarized
in brief for the older man all that he had done since his landing in the country on that bright autumn day seven years before. Touching the highlights, helped by Mr. Bird's perceptive
questions, he gave a good résumé, climaxed with a quick account of Clark's exploit. Mr. Bird drank it in and his face
lightened.

"This is good news," he said. "I'm on the edge of things,

too old to fight, more's the pity. But we make the balls for the soldiers to shoot. It's something anyway."

"A tremendous something, I should say."

"At any rate, O'Hara, your visit is heaven-sent. I've been low in spirits. I've been discouraged and you have been like a bracing gust of cold air to blow away the vapors. We've had some bad times." He shuddered. "That winter our army spent at the Valley Forge was enough to make every man desert! But General Washington! There's the main reason we still have a chance. I envy you your interview with him."

They talked on till midnight.

Very early the next morning O'Hara said goodbye to his host with something like affection, and with the young groom beside him rode off by way of Trenton and Newark for Morristown. Once there they spent the night at Arnold's Tavern (where mine host at once boasted of the fact that it had been the General's Headquarters the year before) and at the earliest hour next day which he deemed suitable O'Hara dismissed the groom with thanks and a benefaction and then made his way past The Green, now snowed over, to the substantial, widespreading white house on the edge of the little town, now the temporary home of His Excellency. Just across the road was a group of log huts inhabited, Arnold had told him, by the General's Life Guards. He approached the front door, noting as he did so the beauty of the curving fanlight and the narrow, corniced windows bordering the entrance, and stated his business to the sentry. The door was at last opened to him by a handsome young man of perhaps twenty who looked carefully at O'Hara's papers and then conducted him through to the great kitchen-living room at the back.

"His Excellency is busy in his study just now so you may

have to wait a little, and this is the warmest place in the house. I am Colonel Alexander Hamilton," he added, "Aide to the General. And glad to meet you, Captain O'Hara."

When he withdrew, O'Hara looked about him with delight. He had not seen such a kitchen since he left the old country: the great fireplace with pots and cranes and skillets; the spinning wheel and reel at the side; the grandfather's clock, the work tables and rush-bottomed chairs all about. There were servants attending to their work, paying no attention to him. Probably many such messengers as he, waited there. Once a pretty, plump, brown-haired little woman came in, gave a few firm orders and left with a half smile in his direction. He wondered if this might be Mrs. Washington.

When he was finally shown into the General's study, O'Hara found his knees weak as water and his heart beating fast. The man at the tall secretary rose with true Virginia courtesy.

"Captain O'Hara, sir, you have made a long journey. Will you be seated?"

"Your Excellency, sir," O'Hara managed as he bowed, "I thank you."

His immediate impression was of the General's great height — about six feet three, he would judge — then the broad shoulders beneath the gold epaulets, the strong steady face with its high brow, large nose and wide, firm mouth. He had anticipated much and was not disappointed.

"I had word from General Brodhead that I might expect you. I gather you come with certain requests but in return are prepared to recount to me some news I very much desire. Is this correct?"

"Substantially so, I believe, your Excellency."

"Well," said the General, "suppose we let the requests wait

until you have told your story. I know the mere fact of the capture of Vincennes. You can imagine how much I will relish complete details. Will you proceed, Captain?"

"It's a long story, General."

A faint bitterness crossed the older man's face. "I have time to hear it all. Unfortunately *too* much time just now."

As O'Hara plunged once more into his account he realized he was telling it this time with a difference. There was now no need for selectivity. Because of the intent interest in the face before him he omitted nothing. As he had lived it, so he told it, fluently, descriptively, pouring it all out now to the one who most needed to hear it. Only once did his voice break a little: when he told of the point at which they had had to abandon the horses to their fate and go on without them. The General spoke.

"You are fond of horses, Captain?"

"Very, sir."

"So am I. My mare Betsy and my gelding Nelson . . . like a part of my own body when under me."

"I understand that." The two looked at each other with quick sympathy.

"Go on, Captain, if you please."

There was a lightening of the tension occasionally when the General smiled. Over the young drummer boy and Captain Helm's toddy, in particular.

At the end O'Hara said, "I wish I could present Colonel Clark to you more clearly, sir."

"I think you have done so, Captain." Adding, with a twinkle, "Dad Drabit."

For what seemed like a considerable time Washington sat quiet. O'Hara, watching him, thought to himself, *this man would always be good company, even if he said nothing.* But at last the General spoke.

"I can't thank you sufficiently for this clear, dramatic account of a remarkable campaign. My spirits have been lifted so much more by it — so immeasurably much more — than by the incomplete and conventional reports I would otherwise have received. Now I wish to inquire into a remark you made concerning the time spent at Kaskaskia. You said you managed to secure provisions for the troops while there?"

"I did, your Excellency."

"You found this work congenial?"

"Very much so. More than soldiering. My interest has always run to business."

The General was threading his large boned fingers together as he considered.

"We've had serious problems everywhere with our provisioning. Just now I badly need a quartermaster for our hospital at Carlisle, Pennsylvania. A good day's ride from Philadelphia. Will you take this position, Captain?"

"I will, your Excellency."

The lack of hesitation seemed to please the General. "Good! My only orders are to secure what the men need there by lawful purchase if possible, if not — by any other means. This is war. Do you understand?"

"I do, your Excellency," O'Hara smiled.

"I will do what I can about money. It is tight, very tight. And now, about the requests from General Brodhead?"

O'Hara presented them, adding details from his own observation. The General's face fell into heavy lines as he sighed.

"The trouble is that most of our own men here need clothing. My army camped now in Jockey Hollow just a little to the west of here are many of them in a bad way. But I'll write General Brodhead that I'll do what I can. No man can do more. I'll notify him, also, of your new assignment and you, too, must have your orders with you."

He turned quickly to the secretary and wrote for some moments, then he rose and handed the papers to O'Hara.

"My thanks again for the Vincennes account which has not only interested me but encouraged me. Can you go soon to Carlisle?"

"Within a few days, your Excellency."

"Good. It's bad enough for well men to suffer, but harder still for the sick. My best wishes go with you."

O'Hara bowed again as he said goodbye to the Commander-in-Chief, but not from the routine courtesy of soldier to general. He knew he was in the presence of a great man and his soul made obeisance too. He spoke of this as he talked for a moment with Colonel Hamilton before he left.

"He's so strong, so utterly good, he seems more than human."

Hamilton smiled. "He's all you say, but he's human enough too. He's got a temper and how he can swear! When occasion demands," he added.

"So?"

The Colonel looked both ways. No one was near. "At Monmouth one of the generals disobeyed orders and nearly lost the battle. I was there. Well, His Excellency just cut loose and the air was blue! It did the men a lot of good, too, I guess. In any case he's the greatest man we've got and I'm proud to serve him."

O'Hara rode directly back to Philadelphia as the bitter cold continued, and on the evening he reached The Crooked Billet again, he supped quickly and then in his room dressed with the greatest care in spite of a pounding heart and unsteady fingers. He brushed his hair almost with violence, since the life he had recently lived had not improved its texture, and fastened it at the back with a rich black bow. He chose his finest white stock with the lace ruffles, his plum-colored satin waistcoat, his silver knee buckles! In all the details of his dress, at least, he could do his love no more honor. Then, clothed for the street, he started on the familiar walk to the Carson house.

In spite of the alleged inuring of his body he felt an actual weakness overtake him as he climbed the steps. He bit his lips hard as he sounded the great knocker. The old man servant opened the door, looked startled and then smiled as he ushered the guest into the hall and took his hat and cloak. It was this smile that steadied O'Hara as he waited to be received. Suddenly he saw Mary at the upper landing! She had evidently heard nothing and was descending slowly, her face sober, her eyes downcast. All at once she looked up, stopped, and then gave a cry.

"Mr. O'Hara! James!"

She started down precipitously while O'Hara rushed forward and caught her into his outstretched arms as she tripped at the last stairs. They stood then, her head pressed to his breast as sobs shook her, his face against her hair.

"My darling! My darling! My dear Delight!"

There was a sound behind them and they both looked up. Mr. Carson stood there in the library doorway.

"Father!" Mary cried. "I did my best to please you. I tried, oh I tried so hard! But I couldn't forget him!"

"So I see," Mr. Carson said quietly.

Then because he was a gentleman as well as a father he came forward and held out his hand to O'Hara.

"I see," he repeated, "that a mere parent cannot stop the course of true love. Come in, come into the room, my children."

But once there, he did not stay long. After the briefest questions and answers he left them to themselves.

"I'll be in the drawing room, O'Hara, when you go."

"It may be quite late, Father," Mary put in.

"Very likely," he said with a smile. "Very likely."

There was so much to tell of all that had happened during the cruel intervening months but for a long time they said nothing but words of love as he held her close. Then with a strange joy they poured out to each other the anguish of their former fears.

"I thought never to see you again!"

"I was sure you didn't care!"

At last when their hearts were absolved they began upon the events which they had not shared. O'Hara gave a highly expurgated account of his exploits, emphasizing the lighter incidents and the crowning success at the end. He told her, too, of his interview with General Washington and his new appointment.

"Carlisle?" she said incredulously. "Oh, that's not so far away. You can come to see me, often perhaps?"

"What could hold me away, now?"

And then it was Mary's turn to tell about Philadelphia in the war years.

"There was such gaiety while General Howe and all his officers were here, you wouldn't believe it," she began, "but last winter I didn't go to the routs. It seemed wrong when our men were in such dreadful straits at the Valley Forge. Then last May the biggest affair of all was held, the *Meschianza,* and Father felt I should go to that. The army was not really suffering at the time and he thought I would never have a chance to see the like again. And I never will," she added.

"What was it like?"

Mary drew a long breath. "I wish I *could* describe it. You see it was a sort of farewell to General Howe, and his young officers paid for it. I guess most of them are very rich young men. One of them, whom everybody liked even though he was a Britisher, was Major André. He planned it. I went with Becky Franks and her brother. Oh, *everybody* in society was there. It was on May 18th, and I'll never forget that date. First of all, everyone went up the river on barges with flags and decorations and bands playing like a water pageant, until we came to 'Walnut Grove,' that's the Whartons' estate. Then we got out and walked through files of troops to the jousting field."

"To the *what?*"

"I knew you wouldn't believe that but it's the truth! There was a real jousting field with grandstands and marquees all around. Then the Knights came riding out. Seven *Knights of the Blended Rose* with red and white favors and seven *Knights of the Burning Mountain* with yellow and black."

"And they actually jousted?"

"It was mock, of course, for their lances were blunt, but every now and then a horseman was unseated. At the last a herald announced that the honors were even and everyone went into the ballroom and danced. Then at ten there were fireworks on the lawn. Oh, I *loved* that! And at midnight the supper was served. *Four hundred and thirty covers laid.*"

O'Hara whistled softly.

"It was like a dream! Pier glasses around the walls with all the candelabras and hundreds of tapers reflecting in them. And the costumes! And the colors! Do you know," she added,

"Father heard that the silks alone for the Meschianza cost *fifty thousand pounds.*"

"Incredible! Wicked!" he said, his face stern. "And some of our men with no shoes for their feet."

"I know. There was strong feeling, but no one could do anything. Except Allan McLane," she laughed. "He was so mad about it that he got his dragoons together and they made bombs out of iron pots filled with powder and rode round the British outposts and threw them every which way at dawn. We danced until four, and everyone was just getting home then."

"Good man, McLane!"

"I know the Meschianza was all wrong and yet, you won't think ill of me?"

"As if I could!"

"Well, I'm so glad I was there. It is something to remember always. Like a vision. I'm glad that Major André planned it."

"He's the young officer you said everyone liked?"

"Oh, yes. No one could help it. He's so charming and friendly and gay. Do you know, he painted all the scenery for the Southwark Theater last winter? Some young Tory helped him. And I really think he's in love with Peggy Chew."

"And she?"

"I know she likes him very much. Before he left he wrote her a little poem. It's not actually a love poem so she read it to a few of us. I remember the last verse. Would you like to hear it?"

"Of course."

"He said that when the war was over if he got back to 'Cliveden,' that's the name of the Chew place . . .

> Say, wilt thou then receive again
> And welcome to thy sight,

The youth who bids with stifled pain
His sad farewells tonight.

"It sounds so pathetic somehow, doesn't it?"

"War is always tragic," O'Hara said, and then asked about the Arnold-Shippen wedding.

Mary did not approve of it. General Arnold was too old for his bride, was a widower and lame from a wound.

"Not that I would hold the lameness against him, it just all seems unsuitable. But I'm more worried about another of my friends. Do you remember Mary Vining? The girl who speaks French so well?"

"Yes, I do remember her. We talked in French quite a little at the Bingham ball. What about her?"

"She's so clever and witty and beautiful and admired and . . . I think she and General Anthony Wayne are in love, *and he's married!*"

O'Hara was serious. "That's not good. Not good at all. You're probably mistaken. Why do you think such a thing?"

"Because," she said slowly, "because they look at each other the same way you and I do."

Finally even by lovers' time O'Hara felt he must leave. After the last long kiss Mary stood with him by the library door and gently fingered the gold buttons on his waistcoat, her eyes downcast.

"In all this evening," she said, "there is something you have not asked me."

"I know," he answered.

"Why not?"

"I've been afraid."

"I think perhaps it would be safe to ask me now."

"Mary!" His voice broke on the words. "Will you marry me when the war is over and come to live with me in Pittsburgh?"

She raised her eyes then and the shining glory in them made his own mist over.

"Mr. O'Hara," she said, "I will go with you to the world's end."

CHAPTER SEVEN

THE LITTLE TOWN of Carlisle lay cozily asleep under its Cumberland Valley snow when O'Hara reached it early one afternoon after his hundred and twenty mile ride from Philadelphia. He had an immediate feeling of satisfaction as he looked about him. This had not the raw frontier aspect of Pittsburgh nor yet the civilized urbanity of Philadelphia. Rather it reminded him in the modest comfort of its stone cottages blocked around the open square, of villages he had seen in the old country. His quick eyes noted the quarry on the hill beyond, where evidently most of the building material came from; he could see a small church spire, a brick edifice that looked as though the law might be administered there; two unmistakable taverns, and on the edge of the town a long low barracks turned hospital. He rode there at once to present his credentials and look the place over.

The physician in command was a Colonel White, a harried looking man of perhaps sixty who grasped O'Hara's hand in relief.

"I had word you were coming," he said, "and if you can help us here you're as welcome as spring. Sit down," he indicated his bare office, "and I'll give you the picture. We need everything and I guess I needn't tell you that to apply to Congress and wait till they vote on it and then *get* it here . . . well, I've given up on that. We'll have to depend on local supplies."

"I surmised that from General Washington's orders," O'Hara smiled.

"The thing I must tell you at the start is that this is a good little town. Patriotic to the core, but it's been about bled white. When the war broke, nearly every man in it enlisted. Take the Butler family. He was a gunsmith and when all his five sons joined up he did too. When the neighbors tried to remonstrate his wife said, 'Let him alone. Every man that can shoulder a musket ought to be in this war. I'll make out somehow.' That's their spirit. Brigadier General Richard Butler is one of their boys. He's with General Wayne right now and of course General Irvine hails from here."

"I've heard of them."

"Oh, you'll find fine folks in Carlisle, but they're all hard up. They can't help us. And the farmers . . . well, it's winter and they need their stock. So, you'll have a hard job. Come along now, though, and I'll show you the place."

O'Hara had seen death and danger but his tour of the so-called wards left him shaken. This, then, was the aftermath of war; these were the men who had not escaped cleanly for either life or death. They looked up at him with anguished eyes and he looked back at them with a grim determination. Here was a job to do, a big one, and he meant to do it.

In the first place the building was cold. While most men had beds of a sort there were still many on the floor on straw pallets, and the straw under the coarse covering was thin. There were not enough blankets; there was not enough nourishing food; there were not enough medical supplies; and of course, as Colonel White told him, not enough help. O'Hara sat down again in the office and concentrated upon the problem, his heart working with his head.

"I'll begin today," he said at the end of their conversation, "where I can. I'll get a load of straw somehow. And I'll get some beef killed at once. You must need a lot of broth."

"My God, yes," the Colonel said.

"I'll work with you," O'Hara said, getting up. "I'll do my best. I went to see Dr. Benjamin Rush before I left Philadelphia and he helped me get a few medicines. . . ."

The other gripped his arm. "Any chloroform?"

"Two bottles."

A long sigh escaped White. "I'm a merciful man by nature, I think, but we've had to do some pretty bad things without chloroform. I've been delaying some operations. Now they can come tomorrow."

O'Hara went out to where Pitt was tied and brought in the box he had carried in his blanket roll. The doctor accepted it as more precious than gold.

Back in the town proper O'Hara worked fast as was his wont. He arranged for lodgings at the Green Tree Inn and after explaining his mission to the owner secured the names of a dozen farmers in the neighborhood. Though it was now mid-afternoon he was bent upon getting at least a load of straw to the hospital before night. As he came out again on the steps he stopped short. *Elliott* was just tying his horse at one of the stumps! He looked up and nodded as though they had met the day before.

"My word, but I'm glad to see you!" O'Hara exclaimed. "Where under heaven did you come from?"

"Well, I've been here and there," Elliott said with his usual

bland evasiveness. "Fact is, I heard you had been around Philadelphia and Hastings told me you had this new job so I decided
mebbe I could be of some use." He looked straight at the question in the other's eye. "I'm a fairly good man as long as I'm on
a horse but I've got a leg that would give out in half a day's
march. That's why I'm not in the army. Single man an' all, I
know it looks bad. But that's how it is. Could I give you a lift in
your quartermastering?"

"*Could* you!" O'Hara responded. "You're heaven-sent, my
friend."

He poured out the needs of the hospital and his plans for the
rest of the day and they rode off together when Elliott insisted
he didn't need food for a few more hours. The first farmer was
hesitant. He had his own problems; he could hardly make a
living; he had been in favor of the war but felt when men enlisted they ought to be prepared to take whatever . . .

O'Hara broke in coldly. "I want the load of straw now, immediately. And tomorrow I want you to kill a beef. If you co-
operate you'll be paid. If you don't I'll take them anyway. Order of General Washington. Now let's get at the straw. We'll
help you load it." The man who spoke was young but the authority in his voice was mature enough, and the farmer knew
when he was bested. Besides, the word *Washington* held
magic. O'Hara talked as they worked, but now ingratiatingly,
entertainingly.

"It's good you have an Irish tongue in your head," Elliott
remarked on the side.

When the straw was ready the farmer accepted his pay, and
promised, if grudgingly, to kill a beef next day. His son drove
the load and Elliott and O'Hara rode ahead. The sunset sky
was now a cold pale violet and the wind was bitter.

"I've got to get some more heat in that place," O'Hara said. "There's just one fireplace in each of the big rooms . . . you'll see, and the poor devils at the opposite ends don't get any warmth at all. And I'm going to get more blankets if I have to strip the town," he added grimly.

When they reached the hospital it was almost dark. An orderly came out, looked at them in amazement, told them to unload the straw in the shed, then went to call his superior. When White appeared in a cloak, a lantern in his hand, he, too, stared, astonished.

"Well, you do work fast, Captain. I hadn't expected any results so soon. Some of these fellows have their bones sticking into the floor and they'll bless you for this. The last Q.M. here didn't bother much about anything."

"I intend to bother, Colonel, and if you'll direct us a little we'll build up the pallets right away. Of course this straw will be cold. How about that?"

"Straw warms in a hurry and we'll put the fresh next the floor. We'll all lend a hand here. Tell the cook and his boy to come out," he said to the orderly.

They worked fast, all of them, carrying in great armfuls of the straw from which they had shaken the dust as much as possible. O'Hara and Elliott helped lift the men to the side on their blankets as the pallets were piled high with the fresh bedding. In every case there were relaxed and grateful moans of relief as the patients finally felt the new softness under them. O'Hara studied each fireplace and the wood beside it.

"Enough here to keep good fires all night?" he questioned.

"We're often short of wood too," the Colonel said.

"Why, the country round here is full of timber!"

"It's not the trees, it's the choppers. We have to ease along as best we can."

"You've plenty for tonight and tomorrow?"

"Oh, yes."

"Then use it freely. I'll get some choppers and Elliott here and I can swing an axe, too, if need be. This is a bitter cold night, Colonel, so don't skimp the fire."

"I've got the sickest men and all my chest cases in the warmest places but the cold does come in the cracks and no mistake."

"I'll try for more blankets tomorrow but now we'd better get along."

He saw the men's eyes following him as though they realized a new force was working for them. O'Hara smiled and raised a hand as he left the wards; the efforts in return touched his heart. He asked the Colonel as he left what his next most pressing need was after the meat.

"Flour," he said, "*flour,* for God's sake!"

"Is there a mill near here?"

"Over the hill there only a couple of miles but the miller won't sell to us."

"We'll see," said O'Hara, as he said goodnight.

Once back at the inn he and Elliott had a late supper, then stretched their cold legs to the fire and settled to talk. There was much to catch up on. When their main events had been sketched in, Elliott's mind proved full of the defection of Pittsburgh's renegades.

"That somehow cut deep with me," he said. "Girty I always mistrusted some but I never thought of anything like this. A queer cuss, though. But Matthew Elliott, no relation of mine, thank God. For him to be a turncoat seems hard to believe. They can do us plenty damage, too. Girty most, of course, damn his hide."

"Have you heard anything about Guyasuta?"

"Not lately. Saw him a few months back. He was upset. He

told me he had meant to side with the Americans, but too many things had happened." Elliott drew a heavy sigh. "If the whites only had a clean conscience, but God A'mighty, after all they've suffered you can't blame them if they do a little killing for themselves. You like the old fox, do you? Guyasuta?"

O'Hara hesitated. "You may wonder at it, but I do." He told then the story of the snakebite and the days in the forest.

"Every man to his taste," Elliott said. "Of course some of these fellahs like the great Sir William Johnston himself are married to Indians. Could you marry one, O'Hara?" he asked curiously.

O'Hara laughed and shook his head. "I'll tell you a secret, though. Mistress Mary Carson of Philadelphia has just done me the honor of promising to marry me when the war's over."

Elliott stared, dumfounded, and then clapped his thigh. "Well, I'm a dirty, stinkin' weasel if I ever suspected a thing! All the times I've been with you, too. You're a close-mouthed one, you are. So you're to marry *pretty Polly Carson!* That's what they call her, I hear, in Philadelphia. Do you call her Polly?"

"No."

"What then? *Mary?*"

"When I name her."

Elliott laughed. "I see. I won't quiz you on the pet words. What does she call you?"

"Mr. O'Hara, usually."

"Well, I'm damned pleased for you!" He held out his hand. "Congratulations, old fellah. Stick to quartermastering and you ought to have a whole skin when the war's over. It'll be back to Pittsburgh then, eh?"

"Right. I want to get a house started soon in The King's Orchard. Well, I see mine host is looking at us as though he doesn't want to set out fresh candles. We've worn these about to the stick. Shall we go up?"

As they climbed the stairs Elliott still kept muttering: "Pretty Polly Carson! Well, I'll be damned!"

The next days were full from dawn till dark. O'Hara had made his plans with businesslike acumen. Once he remedied the worst features of the immediate situation he would be free to pursue a normal routine of supply. Now, however, there had to be quick measures taken for there were too many avoidable deaths, the Colonel told him, at the hospital. It was the worst winter in years and the ice and snow not only doubled the hazards of the sick but also the problems of the quartermaster. He and Elliott had first of all checked with the farmer about the beef. The latter had been as good as his word. The animal was killed, skinned and quartered. They left it to freeze for a day and went on, a hard, plodding ride to the mill. Here there was trouble. The miller, a short stout man named Cox, met them with a stare as cold as the weather. He had his regular customers, he was running a bit slack anyway, and *he had no flour to sell to the government!* O'Hara sized him up and decided blandishment might work. He looked around with interest.

"Quite a little difference between mills here and the ones in France," he said consideringly.

"How so? *France?* What do you know about France?"

"Oh, I used to live there. We boys often went out to a mill in the country to get ourselves weighed and look around. Now *there*, the bands came down like this . . ."

In a few minutes time Cox was watching and listening. O'Hara moved over the big, dusty floor, commenting and asking questions as he went. In another fifteen minutes he had skill-fully switched to the war and the Vincennes campaign. Cox was eating it up and at the end he said slowly, "Course, I might mebbe let you have a couple sacks. That any help?"

"Very much," said O'Hara. "If you could make it three . . ."

They finally left with four, carefully carried in front of them.

"It's been a great pleasure to meet you, Mr. Cox. We don't always run into a man so interested in events," O'Hara had said solemnly, as he offered his hand in parting.

"Well, you talk pretty good. Ain't hard to listen to you. Mebbe I can let you have a little more flour from time to time. That Clark must be quite a fellah!"

"I haven't told you the half yet."

As they rode back Elliott chuckled. "My lord, you buffaloed that one, all right. Good as a show to watch you."

"I thought from the look in his eye he couldn't be threat-ened, but there's always more than one way to skin a cat!"

In two days there was meat in the great pots and fresh bread in the oven. The flour on hand had been scant and moldy at that.

"You see," the Colonel explained glowingly, "if we can give the weakest men a good noggin of broth with decent bread broken in it, they've got a meal. And meat of course for the stronger ones."

"Have you salt?" O'Hara asked.

"Very little. Just enough to take the flat off. Congress bought it all up and Cumberland County's share for the duration was eighty bushels! So you can guess how much we have here."

"It's one of our big problems in Pittsburgh too," O'Hara said. "It's all brought over the mountains by pack horse and it's worth its weight in gold when it gets there. Have you had any eggs for the men?"

"*Eggs!*" the Colonel echoed. "What are eggs? We've never seen them here."

"There ought to be quite a few hens round these parts waiting to do their duty for their country," O'Hara said, grinning. "We'll see."

He bought a farm sled and a work horse, feeling Pitt should not be subject to the indignity of *hauling*, and with Elliott and himself on the seat, proceeded to comb the town for blankets. He greeted the women at their doors courteously, explained his errand, and at the end smiled, showing his wide white teeth. In most cases it worked. One blanket from a family and here and there a pillow. O'Hara had noted that many of the men now had only their worn uniforms rolled under their heads. At one door the woman did not return his smile.

"My only son died at Valley Forge. They were cold there, too." She gave him two coverlets.

They made the rounds of the countryside as the weeks passed, buying when the farmers would sell, stealing when they wouldn't. Quietly over the snow the sled often made its way in the dark of night. The horse was hitched to a tree near to a barn. Elliott and O'Hara with a covered lantern moved to the pig pen or the byre. Elliott did the sticking with his sharp hunter's knife and between them they dragged a calf, a pig, or a sheep back to the sled. They found surprisingly little outcry from the beasts. As hunters they came upon their prey softly; the kill was swift; the leave-taking was cautious and the animals drowsed again.

Back of the hospital Elliott dexterously did the skinning, then there was a change of meat in the pots while the Colonel and his aides gloried in the fact that the patients had never been so well fed.

"Gumption," Elliott kept repeating. *"Gumption!* That's what you've got, O'Hara."

Meanwhile O'Hara began to enjoy the town itself. As Colonel White had told him there were good people here, distinguished people, and while most of the men were away in the service, the women brought them close in their conversation. Little by little he grew familiar with the names of Irvine, Wilson, Armstrong, Blaine, Montgomery, and Denny. Of all the women, he most admired Agnes Denny. She was not young but she was still beautiful with her fair complexion, bright sandy hair and blue eyes which reflected the energy and intelligence of her mind. Her favorite topic when O'Hara sometimes paused for a chat was her son Ebenezer who was with the Pennsylvania line. When she told of his being a dispatch bearer to Fort Pitt when he was only thirteen — six years ago — O'Hara gave a startled exclamation.

"What does he look like?" he asked.

"Like me," his mother laughed, "only his hair is redder."

"Why, I saw that boy out there! More than once. He was so young to be crossing the mountains alone. Everyone spoke of it."

"He shipped out for the West Indies after that and went to sea until he got an Ensign's commission in the army and joined the First Pennsylvania. To think that you've seen him!"

"It's a pleasant coincidence to me. I hope to see him again."

"He wrote me a joke about himself. He's a good boy to write. When he joined his company he wasn't used to marching. All the walking he'd done for several years was pacing a quarter deck. So one day when he was just about ready to drop,

Captain Montgomery — he's from here too — came up and whispered to him, 'Listen, Eb, for the honor of old Carlisle don't disgrace yourself!' That kept him going. He's with friends for sure. Colonel Dicky Butler comes from round here. We've always known him. But the man Ebenezer is always writing about is his general, Anthony Wayne. He worships that man."

"I keep hearing about him," O'Hara said. "I'd like to meet him, myself."

The most important stories heard, some of them over and over in the Green Tree Inn, from the farmers or from the women as he met them, were written back to Mary as he penned his loving missives to her three times a week. He wrote the most prideful tale with relish for it was about a woman. Carlisle had a heroine and no one would be long in the town without knowing it. This was *Molly "Pitcher."* She had been living in the family of General Irvine here until she left to join her husband, John Hays, with Revolutionary troops in New Jersey. When he was wounded at the battle of Monmouth she fired his gun and then did an even greater service by carrying water on that hottest of June days to the wounded and dying. She had found a pitcher by the spring and this she filled over and over in full view of the British and held to the poor parched lips. "Molly, *pitcher!*" the men kept calling, and the name had stuck. Oh, O'Hara wrote Mary, the townsfolk would never forget this. Indeed everyone, hearing of it, should remember, he added.

But the tenderest of all the Carlisle stories he saved to tell her in person. This was of Regina, the Indian captive. Something deep in his heart turned over as he thought of it. A dozen mothers in the town had made sure he heard it, and Mrs. Denny had taken from her Bible a bit of paper on which she had written the famous hymn and allowed him to copy the verse.

When the worst needs of the hospital had been met and some sort of routine established for the supplies O'Hara left Elliott in charge and made a hurried trip to Philadelphia. In addition to the joy of again seeing his love, he wanted to consult her about the plans that he had worked on night after night for the house to be built in the King's Orchard. And when they finally pored over these together they were closer than they had ever been.

"This first house will have to be logs, but just wait! One day you'll have the finest home in Pittsburgh," he promised gaily.

Mary called her father to look at the design and O'Hara went over it again.

"I thought a good sized parlor with a dining table where we could eat when we had guests and then a very large kitchen-living room with the cooking fireplace. You've no idea how comfortable and pleasant such a room can be! I modeled this a bit after the one I was in at General Washington's headquarters at Morristown. Then three bedrooms upstairs. Does it seem . . . I mean, sir, do you think this would be . . . be adequate for a start?"

Mr. Carson looked at their love-lit faces. "I think it sounds very commodious and I expect to come to visit you."

"And I can take all kinds of furnishings with me. Mr. O'Hara said we can have two wagons when we make the trip!" Mary said eagerly.

It was so sweet, so intimate to dwell upon the rooms which would contain their life together. After Mr. Carson had left them and O'Hara had put the plans back in his pocket Mary must needs see them all over once again.

"If only the war was finished!" she sighed as their one precious evening was finally drawing to an end. "Father says it may drag on for years yet. And you'll have to be in it somehow, won't you?"

"I'm afraid so. But now when we're sure of each other everything seems so much easier. We must try to be patient. Oh, I almost forgot the story I saved to tell you."

Mary brightened. "I love stories. Is this one true?"

"Absolutely. Have you heard the name of General Bouquet?"

"I . . . think so."

"He won the battle of Bushy Run and saved Fort Pitt when the French and Indians were making trouble. Then he forced the Indians to return all their captives to Pittsburgh."

"Their what?"

"Their captives. The people they had taken back to live with them. Most of these were claimed by their families there but the rest Bouquet brought on to Carlisle. There's a square in the middle of the town and after sending the word around the countryside he had all the captives stand in the square . . ."

Mary had been sitting on a hassock at his feet. Something in her face made him reach down suddenly and draw her up to his knee, holding her close.

"There was a Mrs. Hartmann who had lost her little girl, Regina, when she was only seven and now eight years had passed. The poor mother could hardly wait to get to the square. She looked at each person there but couldn't see a trace of her child, and no one recognized her."

"Oh, Mr. O'Hara, I don't think I like this story."

"You will at the end. Mrs. Hartmann went to General Bouquet with the tears running down her cheeks and told him of her terrible disappointment. He thought for a minute and then asked if there was any song she had sung to her little girl that she might remember. 'There is one,' Mrs. Hartmann said, 'that I used to sing to her every night when I put her to bed.' 'Sing it,' the General said."

O'Hara drew a slip of paper from his pocket. "I copied this to read to you. Mrs. Hartmann stood there while everybody stayed perfectly quiet. Many people in Carlisle still remember all this, you see, and here is what she sang:

> *Alone yet not alone am I,*
> *Within this wilderness so drear;*
> *I feel my Saviour always nigh,*
> *He comes my weary hours to cheer.*
> *I am with Him and He with me,*
> *I cannot solitary be.*

"And all at once a tall girl with her skin tanned like an Indian and her long hair hanging down her back rushed to Mrs. Hartmann and flung herself into her arms. It was Regina!"

O'Hara waited eagerly for Mary's comment. He could see she was moved for there were tears in her eyes. But when she spoke the words were not what he had expected.

"They don't still do that, do they?"

"What . . ." he began.

"The Indians. They don't still carry people off, do they?"

He made his voice very strong. "Why dear Delight, this happened *sixteen years ago!*"

She seemed content, though even during their most tender farewell he fancied there was a shadow in her eyes. And all the way back to Carlisle he kept wishing that he had not told her the story of Regina, the captive maid.

The winter ended at last and spring flooded the valley; the Judas trees turned the woods to rose and the distant circling mountains were as blue as the skies above them. O'Hara took satisfaction in what he had accomplished. The sick men had been warmed and fed, and besides this, Colonel White said he had sent a letter to General Washington, commending the services of his Commissary. The war seemed to be shifting to the south and as the summer advanced O'Hara kept wondering what his next assignment would be. While he had grown fond of Carlisle his work here had lost something of its challenge and he found himself hoping for a larger post. Meanwhile he was eager to get back to Fort Pitt and arrange for the building of his house.

It was August before he went, leaving Elliott in charge again. It was an easy journey this time of year and at the end he felt once more as though he had come home. Nothing had changed except for a few new houses along the Monongahela. He went about his plans promptly after an evening of good talk in the tavern with Semple, Hugh Brackenridge and Devereux Smith. They were all interested in his affairs and when they heard the log house was eventually to hold a bride they became excitedly eager to help. So, the next morning they all joined to pace off the ground and drive the stakes at the corners. Four apple trees would have to be sacrificed but the rest would form the bower which O'Hara had particularly wanted for Mary's home.

Two elderly boat builders who he knew to be good general carpenters were engaged to put up the building, working on it as they could find time, and a copy of the carefully drawn plans was given to Devereux Smith who agreed to keep an eye on the work as it progressed.

O'Hara found his friends discouraged about the course of the war, Brackenridge most of all.

"It seems to me to be running slack, as far as we can learn.

And it's hard to watch the women and children round the country here trying to get in their bit of harvest while their men are away. If only we were winning! The last we heard of a real engagement was when this Colonel Tarleton's cavalry cut ours to pieces down in Virginia. That was back in April. I guess Cornwallis has settled himself in the South and it will likely be hard to dislodge him. They say he's called 'the modern Hannibal.' "

"All right. Hannibal was beaten, wasn't he? I pin my faith on General Washington. If you could meet him, you would too."

"Hope you're right," Hugh said. "At least I'm glad your personal affairs are pointing toward a happy head. The war! The war! If there's ever any end to it."

"You're keeping busy, aren't you?"

"Oh, so-so. I'm doing some writing. I'd like to author a book some day on pioneer life. I guess it would turn out to be a kind of social satire. Then I still make a few verses." He laughed.

"I'll tell you my latest. I get so wrought up over this business of *duels*. We keep hearing about them every now and then from back east especially. I think it's the damnedest silliest performance I ever heard of for two men to stand up and pot at each other over some trifle for their *honor!* Fiddlesticks! Well, anyway, here's my rhyme. I think I'll send it to one of the Philadelphia papers.

> *To fight a duel!*
> *I'd live ten years on water gruel,*
> *Rather than stand up and be shot at,*
> *Like a raccoon that can't be got at."*

So the young men laughed together as they said goodbye while agreeing that dueling should be outlawed. And O'Hara made his way back to Carlisle over the road that had now become familiar to both Pitt and himself.

He had been there barely a month before the news came that stunned the whole town and for a time shattered his own heart. The post rider told it first at the Green Tree Inn and then in the Square where a crowd was not long in gathering. The word was that within a week's time General Benedict Arnold, hero and friend of General Washington himself, had turned traitor and gone to the British and his liaison man, Major John André, had been caught, unfortunately out of uniform, and hanged as a spy. So, the news.

O'Hara when he heard it could not speak. Voices were voluble enough all around him, exclaiming, lamenting, vilifying, questioning, but he made no answer to anyone. He went up to his room and shut the door. A shudder ran through him as he sat. Benedict Arnold, a *traitor!* The trusted general who had been given charge of West Point at his own request had been guilty of this black, this dastardly betrayal, and was safe now, the post had said, on a British ship lying in the Hudson! It was unbelievable. It was too ugly to be true.

And Major André! O'Hara felt the smart of tears in his eyes. Only a year older than he, himself, for Mary had told him so. The gay, the gallant, the friendly young man who had won all hearts, had painted the scenery for the Philadelphia theater, had arranged for the Meschianza, had written the tender farewell verse to Peggy Chew which Mary had read to him, *hanged.* Oh, what would Mary's heart feel about all this, for Arnold's wife was her friend! Had Peggy been a party to the plot? The Shippens had always had strong Tory leanings, he knew. What would become of her now? And Major André. . . .

He could eat nothing at supper for the food choked him. Elliott was silent too. Oddly enough when they did speak it was to say the same words at once.

"Who can you trust?" And the saying of it together brought something like a smile to their faces.

Mary's letter when it came was almost incoherent in its distress. She longed for O'Hara so they could talk of it all together. She had no relief in speaking with her father for he was so bitter. He even said the Major deserved hanging! But as the girls talked it all over among themselves their sympathies went out to Peggy Arnold with her new baby and their tears were for John André. Oh, war was so cruel. And how long would it last? And what dangers might he, O'Hara, still have to face?

More bad news came belatedly on the heels of that of Arnold and André. Two thousand men under General Gates had been utterly routed by Cornwallis at Camden, South Carolina! The modern Hannibal, indeed. Perhaps Brackenridge had been right. At least Gates was now ousted and General Nathaniel Greene, who stood next to Washington himself, was in charge of the southern campaign. O'Hara for the first time felt a vague discouragement. And the next word of a mutiny in the Pennsylvania line did not lift his spirits.

"Poor devils," he said to Elliott. "The wonder is there hasn't been mutiny before this, considering what the men have borne, and for the most part without pay."

"Congress ought to be made up of ex-soldiers," Elliott said savagely. "Then we might get some action."

And another winter passed, lightened for O'Hara only by the brief occasional trips to Philadelphia which were to him as cold water to a thirsty soul. Then with spring came the new appointment for which he had been hoping. In its character, however,

it was an enormous surprise. Chosen by Washington, ratified
by Congress, he was now Quartermaster to the Army in the
south! He was to join General Anthony Wayne and his companies at York in May and proceed with them to Virginia, seeing to their provisioning from the point of contact on. A letter
from Robert Morris came also, a friendly one, congratulating
him upon his good work at Carlisle and explaining the financial details in connection with his new job. He might need
warehouses for certain supplies though in the main he imagined the army would have to "live off the land." But, he
added, and this cheered O'Hara, he had the feeling that they
were entering upon the last and winning stage of the war. He
would lay his bets on Mad Anthony every time!

One thing O'Hara decided at once when he had recovered
from the pleasurable shock of the news: he must have Elliott
with him.

"We know how to work together," he said. "There's a new
Commissary due here and since you insist on serving without
pay, there's no appointment necessary. Will you come?"

So it was settled and early in May after leaving hospital affairs in good order they rode off once more together. Aside
from the prospect of a big and challenging job, O'Hara's great
anticipation was the meeting with Anthony Wayne. On his
last tender trip to say farewell to Mary she had told him more
about the general: his dash, his courage, his constant solicitude
for his men, and of course . . . his love. Everyone in Philadelphia, that is in their social group, knew of this now, she said.
The blaze in his eyes and the answering yearning in Mary Vining's whenever they met, simply could not be hidden. While
his home was near Paoli and Mary's was in Delaware, they were
both well known in Philadelphia. Mary came up for all the

balls, and Wayne had been a member of the Colonial Committee for Safety before the war. The odd thing was they had never met until just before Stony Point. From then on their secret was all too manifest.

O'Hara's plan was to reach York well before the army and have some supplies ready when the men came. Using his tried methods of simple purchase, threat and cajolery he was able to secure a great quantity of smoked meats, cheese, flour and vats of lard from the wide and rich countryside. York itself reminded him of the old country even as Carlisle had done and the farms around it were beautifully fertile. He made the purchase of a warehouse of sorts and into this he and Elliott, working tirelessly with their helpers arranged the stores in neat order.

"They'll have wagons with them," O'Hara said, "so we had better not buy more until we're sure how many we'll need. Do you feel nervous, Elliott?"

"Like a cat."

"So do I. I was a little too puffed up, I think, when my appointment came. Pretty sure of myself. And the devil always gets a kick in at you for pride. Now, I'm scared. It's a big jump from being Commissary at a hospital to feeding an *army*."

Elliott grinned at him and slapped his back. "You've been in tight places before. Don't worry. Your gumption will see you through."

One afternoon toward the end of May they heard the drums! In the moment O'Hara realized the difference between regular troops and the frontier sharp shooters of the Vincennes campaign. The sound came nearer, rhythmic and compelling. Then in view on the dusty road came the officers on horseback and the soldiers in companies rank upon rank behind them.

O'Hara made a quick decision. He and Elliott should be on horseback too, not standing in the dust like a pair of schoolboys when the officers approached. It was a matter of minutes until he was on Pitt, and Elliott mounted beside him. When the commanding officer drew up he knew at once that it was Mad Anthony Wayne. The General sat as well in the saddle as any man he had ever seen, with a fine figure and an easy grace. His gray eyes had a reckless light in them even here on the quiet road. Spirit, vigor, endurance were written upon his handsome face, vanity too, perhaps, but even more clearly, honesty. He wore a bright blue coat with red lining and creaseless lambskin breeches, and he smiled as he spoke.

"Captain O'Hara, I take it?"

"The same, sir. Quartermaster at your service, with my helper, Mr. Elliott."

After the greetings the General looked keenly at O'Hara.

"I've heard of your good work in Carlisle, that you can even *steal* upon occasion. That cheered me up no end. We've had a bad time about provisions all through this war. My men are hungry right now. I suppose you haven't . . ."

O'Hara nodded. "We came on ahead and pretty well stripped the countryside. We have a sort of warehouse here. What about fried ham and slapjack for the men's supper?"

Wayne stared. "Do you mean that? Good God, the boys will be sure they got shot on the way and have gone to heaven! Just a minute, and then I'll go and see your stores."

It ended with the soldiers camping in the open field south of the town. The fires were started, the great skillets brought out, the cooks making use of the long trestle tables O'Hara and Elliott had built, and before long there was a smell in the air that made the men cheer.

When night fell the soldiers settled for sleep on the ground, their stomachs for once warmed and filled. There was plenty of sassafras in the woods and O'Hara had hired all the small boys in town to dig roots of it, so there had been sassafras tea with a bit of milk along with the supper. Even without sugar it was a palatable drink and one which the men would have had in their own homes. They gulped it greedily.

Elliott slept at once but O'Hara could not. As he walked to the edge of the encampment he saw another figure pacing under the stars. It was Anthony Wayne. When he saw O'Hara he signed to him and together they moved farther away.

"I wanted to talk to you when all was quiet," the general began, "but I didn't like to wake you up. My thanks again for that meal. It's put new spirit into the men . . . and me too."

"I'm glad. Of course you understand I can't manage one like that *every* night, but I'll do my best. I'm having some beeves killed tomorrow morning and dressed. Even though the meat will be fresh it ought to taste pretty good. How long before we leave here, General?"

"Let's see. This is the 21st. I plan to beat at daybreak on the 26th. Will that give you time to load your provisions?"

"Oh, yes."

"We have a nasty job to do tomorrow. I wanted to tell you this so you and your friend would be prepared."

"So?"

"Let's sit down," Wayne said. "I guess I should lead up to it. You heard, of course, about the mutiny in our line?"

"Yes."

"That was bad, bad. I did my best to dissuade the men. *I* knew what they had suffered. *I* knew their grievances were legitimate. But even granting that you can't have mutiny in the

army. It threw a scare into all of us." His voice had been quiet
but now it seemed to catch fire.

"And I maintain if it hadn't been for *Arnold,* the whole thing
would never have happened. Damn him to hell! Did you know
he's been in the South with the British *fighting against us?*"

"No. Oh, no!"

"Well, he is even now. I've known the man for years. Never
liked him much, but I respected him as a brave officer. He was
always in and out of quarrels though, making enemies. Of
course while he was commanding in Philadelphia he spent
money like water, and there was plenty of criticism. And at last
somebody brought a lot of more or less trivial charges against
him to Congress and there was a court-martial. He was
acquitted but with the order that Washington should reprimand
him. That, I guess, was the last straw, for he's proud and touchy
as the devil. Even though I heard that the reprimand was almost praise, he couldn't stand it. But, *treason!*"

Wayne only paused for a second and then went on.

"*I've* been bitter myself. Congress passed me over once in
favor of General St. Clair. He comes from round your Pittsburgh way, doesn't he?"

"A little to the east. Ligonier, I believe. I've never met him."

"Well, he's the old-fashioned kind of general who leads his
troops *from the rear.* And that's not my way."

"So I've gathered," O'Hara said, a smile in his voice.

"The trouble with St. Clair is that he's got too much Scotch
caution. Oh, well, the point is any man in the soldiering business has to take the bitter pills that come, swallow them and
keep his mouth shut. But *Arnold . . .*"

He was quiet until O'Hara reminded him.

"You said something about a job to do tomorrow?"

"Yes. In a way it's all bound up with what I've been talking about. After the mutiny the troops were warned again that any deserter would be shot. Every man understood it but . . . we've got five back there now under guard to be executed at sunset tomorrow."

O'Hara could not speak.

"I ought to be hardened," Wayne went on. "I am, to death in battle. I've seen soldiers fall round me and it didn't faze me, for I was right there with them and knew I could be the next one, myself. But to line five decent men up and shoot them down like dogs . . . God, I have to watch it. *Order* it! One's just a young chap. Shouldn't wonder if he was running off to see his girl. Well, I thought I'd tell you, so you and Elliott could keep out of the way, if you want to."

"Thank you, General. I . . . I appreciate your telling me."

"It's a hard necessity," Wayne answered and then the two sat on in silence with the Maytime night all about them. There was an almost full moon showering its white light; there was the scent of blossoms like a whisper, and the distilled essence of spring itself rising from the waking earth; there was a little warm wind moving amongst the new leaves like a caress. Were the five men who were appointed to die, now awake? O'Hara wondered. Were they watching their last moonlit night? Did the beauty of this their last springtime lie upon them now like an agony?

At length Wayne stood up and so did O'Hara. The General hesitated and then spoke in a low voice.

"I believe," he said, "that you and I have mutual friends."

"I believe we have," O'Hara answered.

Then, without saying more the two men made their way back to their own quarters.

The troops were subdued the morning after the executions and the noisy jollity of their first evening in York did not return before they got under way at daybreak on the 26th. From then on they skirted down along the Blue Ridge Mountains toward Fredericksburg. The plan, as O'Hara learned it, was to march to Virginia and join the Marquis de La Fayette whom Wayne described out of the corner of his mouth as "a statue looking for a pedestal." He admitted, however, that the young nobleman along with his intense ambition and love of liberty had the qualities of a good officer and would probably acquit himself well in this campaign.

"I can work with him, all right," he said.

O'Hara found his own duties discouraging as the weeks went on. The men were marching hard and were always hungry. The supplies in the wagons dwindled and the countryside through which they were passing was very different from the fertile farms around York. For this had been ravaged by the British with Arnold in the lead, and he had not spared the torch. Fields and barns were blackened ruins. The best cattle had been slaughtered or driven off and every good horse apparently impressed. Elliott was still his cheerful self but sometimes O'Hara in his desperation did not appreciate his friend's humor.

"Did you kill those two cows you said you found?" he asked Elliott one morning.

"Yes, we managed it. But I'll tell you how it was. It took four men to hold up each cow while we knocked it on the head."

They searched henhouses, taking all the chickens and eggs they could get their hands on, despite the owners' protests. This was small provender but better than nothing. With the helpers allowed him, he and Elliott shot hares and squirrels and every turkey buzzard they could bring down for the northerners didn't know they were scavengers and they helped fill the pots.

In addition to the burdens of his work something else bothered O'Hara. He smiled grimly sometimes as he considered the contrast between this march and the one to Vincennes, for in this army there were women and a good many of them. A very few like "Molly Pitcher" were brave wives, but the majority were those who plied their ancient profession as casually here as anywhere else. One large, blowzy girl apparently had marked O'Hara for her own and gave him no peace. One night he woke to find her snuggled cozily against him. He shook her to her feet and gave her several resounding whacks upon her seat. She went off, he hoped in pain, crying, "O Captain, you hain't got no heart."

The next day he spoke to Elliott.

"I've got another job for you."

"Not another hen roost, for God's sake," Elliott groaned. "It's taken me two days to get the lice out of me from the last one."

"No. This is serious. From now on you've got to sleep with me."

Elliott gazed at him and then grinned.

"Me lad, I'd as lieve sleep with a wet dog as with another man!"

"So would I. But listen."

He told his problem and Elliott found it amusing. "So, you're afraid of her, eh?"

"No, I'm not afraid, but I'm a decent man and I intend to remain so. And I won't have that filthy trollop hanging around me."

"All right. I s'pose I'll have to protect you. I'll lie near you but I won't get close."

"You'd better not," O'Hara said, and they both laughed.

One pleasant feature of the march to O'Hara was making the acquaintance of Ensign Ebenezer Denny of whom his mother had spoken so often. He was a friendly youth with a good sense of humor and when there was a chance he and O'Hara swapped yarns of both Carlisle and Pittsburgh. There were nights, too, when the camp was asleep, that Wayne seemed eager again to talk to O'Hara. Though they still avoided the intimate disclosures bound to come ultimately, there grew with each meeting a feeling of mutual respect and friendship. Moreover, Wayne told him many interesting bits of army news. Alexander Hamilton, for instance, whom O'Hara had met in Morristown, had hardly spoken to General Washington after the hanging of André, so he was no longer on the staff but again an officer of the line. Well, everybody had felt badly about André. Nathaniel Greene? *There* was a general for you! Quaker, too, believe it or not. He had a nice sort of slow grin but by God, he wasn't slow about anything else. The report was that when he couldn't get Cornwallis to stand and face him down here, he went after him, snapping at his heels. Good man, Greene.

Whenever Wayne spoke of Arnold his voice became hard as stone. "I'll tell you a pretty piece of gossip about him. He sent a letter to La Fayette about an exchange of prisoners or something and La Fayette wouldn't even open it. Sent the aide back with it. Arnold was second in command then to a General Phillips. Next day the aide came back with the letter and said Arnold was now commanding officer of the force as Phillips had just died. La Fayette still wouldn't touch the letter but the rumor went like wildfire that Arnold had poisoned Phillips to get the command! And I wouldn't put it past him."

"How do you hear all this?"

Wayne laughed. "Oh," he said, "that's the easiest thing in the business. We have couriers, scouts, runners. And spies. La Fayette has the best of those for he pays them out of his own pocket. He outfitted his men, too. I wish to heaven I could. Our men look like scarecrows. Nothing but rags to their backs."

"And I wish I could feed them better!" O'Hara said regretfully.

Wayne clapped him on the shoulder. "It may not seem such good pickings to you but let me tell you they've had a damned sight worse. You're doing wonders in a hard job. I've an idea things may get better a little farther south. By the way, I hear La Fayette has picked up English fairly well, but still you may be able . . ." He paused. "I mean . . . I understand your French is pretty fluent if we should need it."

"It's at your service. I'll be very honored to meet the Marquis."

They met him just outside Fredericksburg where, with his gracious courtesy, he had ridden with a few troops in their fresh suits behind him, to greet General Wayne. It seemed a happy meeting and while the soldiers all rested the two generals talked. O'Hara stayed near to help with the language difficulties when he could. He liked the Marquis with his young, eager face and aura of unquenchable optimism. The news he brought was that Cornwallis was encamped around Richmond with his supply base at Williamsburg toward the sea, while the cocky little Colonel Banastre Tarleton (whom the Continentals hated almost as much as Arnold) was using his flashy cavalry to beat up the banks of the James River for forage. With Wayne's troops the Marquis said their own forces would now number over four thousand; Cornwallis had about five.

But the great news was that the French Admiral de Grasse was on his way from the West Indies with ships and almost an army of men. *That* ought to turn the tide! If he just got there, the Marquis added ruefully.

When the talk was over and La Fayette gone O'Hara said to Wayne, "I like that man. Maybe he's a bit vain but aren't we all?"

"True," said Wayne. "And we ought to forgive him anything because of what he's got the French to do for us. Well, it's on to Richmond now and for myself I'm red hot for a fight."

But Cornwallis had left when they got there, and the days ran on until the 4th of July, the nation's fifth Independence anniversary. It was wet in the morning but cleared by noon and the men celebrated with a regular *feu de joie,* extra rum rations, and the best supper O'Hara could scare up. The provisioning was becoming a little easier now, but even so O'Hara was still discouraged and very tired. For one thing there had been no exchange of letters between him and Mary. The army messengers did not carry personal mail and there was no other means of communication. This was hard. He found that something of the energy and drive he had felt on the Vincennes campaign had gone out of him. Perhaps to be in the army and not of it was dispiriting. Like Wayne he might be unconsciously eager for action.

It came, for the soldiers at least, two days after the celebration. They had moved to a place called Greenspring where they discovered Cornwallis was already. Wayne ahead with his eight hundred picked Pennsylvanians mistook the van of the British for the rear and set upon them. Young Denny, who was close to him, reported it all later to O'Hara.

"A bullet went right through the plume of the General's

infantry cap and I swear to you he just looked at the feather falling and then at the enemy and *seemed amused!*"

The hero worship on the young man's face was dazzling. "And when we could see we were in a trap with the British closing in on both sides what do you suppose the General did?"

"Ordered an attack," O'Hara smiled.

"How did you know, back here?"

"I know the man."

"Well that's what he did. All at once he yelled, *Forward . . . charge . . . bayonets!* So we did and the British evidently were surprised and thought the whole army was behind us. They drew back to reform and we retreated then in good order. It was getting dark anyway. But imagine a man who wasn't able either to hold his ground then or fall back, saving himself by driving into the enemy with his bayonets! Well, that's Mad Anthony for you."

The hot weeks passed slowly. Watermelon season came and the men feasted. The country generally was more fruitful and O'Hara was less put to it to find provisions. He was still restless, however, and often longed to talk to someone of what lay nearest his heart. The opportunity came one Sunday in late August. They were camping along the James River near the Byrd mansion. There had been divine service that morning under the elegant shade of the great trees; now it was night and he found himself alone with Wayne, looking up at the stars.

"Let's sit down," the General said, as he had that night in York. "Let's talk. You've never told me about your plans. I mean with Mary Carson. Is everything . . . settled?"

O'Hara's voice was full of happiness. "Yes," he said. "It is now, but I had a long time on tenterhooks. We expect to marry as soon as the war's over."

"Live in Pittsburgh?"

"Yes."

"Will she be contented there? It's still pretty rough frontier, isn't it?"

"That was the trouble at first but now she's willing to go and I feel sure I can make her happy. I'm having a house built there in the King's Orchard. It's really a lovely spot. A big grove of apple trees along the river. And there will be a few women she can be friends with. Her own kind, you know. With it all, sometimes I'm anxious."

Something in the words made Wayne reach over and lay a hand on his shoulder.

"Don't worry," he said. "When you're free to love each other everything else will smoothen before you. Now with me . . ."

Even in the darkness O'Hara could feel a gathering of tension, of anguish in the other. He thought of this man, smiling at his falling plume in battle which meant he had missed death by a hair's breadth; ordering the bayonet charge when defeat was upon him. He who sat next to him now, he knew, was not Mad Anthony, the intrepid general, but Anthony, the lover.

"It will ease me to talk about my own problem," Wayne went on. "You've probably heard it all anyway from your Mary. You see, I'm married. We were too young when it happened. Neither of us knew what we were doing. For years now we haven't been close. I never knew what love was until I looked into Miss Vining's eyes. Then we both knew."

He was silent and O'Hara waited, suffering with him.

"The thing is," Wayne finally said, "I'm a gentleman, I hope. I haven't much stomach for low compromise in morals. But I tell you as a mere man I would stoop to it because of the fire in me, but I couldn't ever ask it of her. So there we stand. Absolutely without hope." A terrible sigh was wrenched from him.

"What can I say to you?" O'Hara burst out. "Only that I feel for you from my heart. I had my own time of despair, you know. I wish I could . . ."

"There is nothing anyone can do. The reason we can't even *hope* is because the circumstances under which I would be free are those I could never wish for. Well, tell me about your plans with 'pretty Polly Carson.' She's a sweet young thing. How did you get to know her?"

So O'Hara told him of that first meeting, of the Garden of Delight, the Bingham Ball and the years since. It comforted him to go over it all and strangely enough it seemed to interest Wayne without arousing envy.

"Yes, yes," he said. "That's the way it should be. Thanks for telling me. It's sweetened my own thoughts, somehow."

It was only a few nights later that the accident happened. A message came to Wayne from La Fayette, rather an excited message. Would the General have the kindness to come at once to discuss important strategic matters? De Grasse with his whole fleet and his men were arrived at the Chesapeake Bay. General Washington was on his way south to Williamsburg with his own army. The British had gone to Yorktown. It looked as though the end was in sight.

Wayne was immeasurably elated. At eight o'clock he bowed good night to Mrs. Byrd on the great portico. Shaved and powdered and handsome, wearing his cocked hat and dress sword he joined two officers and O'Hara who had been invited to go along to help with any language problems. They all mounted and rode off into the night, reaching the outskirts of La Fayette's encampment two hours later.

Out of the darkness came the challenge of a picket whose

voice sounded frightened. Wayne answered with the counter-
sign and prepared to ride on. But the sentry was evidently
thinking of Cornwallis, Tarleton and the British raiders for he
doubted Wayne's reply and fired. O'Hara saw a streak of red
go past him and then saw the General sway in the saddle. They
all called out then to save themselves from being riddled and
rushed to help Wayne. They got him to La Fayette's quarters
where a surgeon was called. He found the ball had struck the
thigh bone and was evidently lodged behind it, though the
agony of pain was all in the foot.

The following day the General professed himself able to talk
plans, then insisted on getting back to his own quarters in the
Byrd mansion. From then on he lay in bed, fuming and cursing.
Of all humiliating accidents to be shot by one of their own sentries! Of all intolerable times to be laid up now with General
Washington coming and three thousand French troops just
landing! But one evening when O'Hara was visiting him in
his room his mood was quiet and somber.

"I don't like this, O'Hara," he said. "It's as if someone had
stepped across my grave, as the old women say."

"Oh, nonsense!" O'Hara said. "If you'd gotten that wound in
battle you'd have taken it as a matter of course and not tried to
find an *omen* in it. You're really over the worst now."

And he was, for on the 12th day after the shot he got dressed
again in his best and limped to a carriage when he rode off to
an elegant supper of welcome for the Commander-in-Chief.
The next day he reported that things were really on the move
at last. Cornwallis in Yorktown, the French fleet shutting him
off from the sea, and all the Continental troops, it was hoped,
soon to reach ground just in front of him. An electric thrill ran
through officers and men alike as the march began.

The siege of Yorktown was to O'Hara the most thrilling experience of his life, more even than Vincennes, for here was not a backwoods battle but a conflict in which two large and trained armies confronted each other in a last desperate struggle which was to decide the destiny of a country, the country he himself had elected to make his own.

Between his arduous labors behind the lines when he, with Elliott and his helpers foraged for food to feed Wayne's troops, O'Hara watched keenly the preparations that went on. The first thing to be done as young Ensign Denny had reported to him was the building of a long line of trenches right before the enemy position, the first parallel it was called. Already over a thousand men were at work making breastwork baskets and filling them with soil, while as many more guarded them from sudden attack. In the main, things were quiet. The British fired a field piece now and then but the Continentals did not reply. For one thing all their artillery was not yet in position. The British regulars had full regimental bands and now often they could be heard playing; and when the wind was right the sound of singing came also. To O'Hara it had an eerie effect.

"Isn't Cornwallis scared? Doesn't he know this is *serious?*" he asked Wayne one day as the music was borne upon the air.

Wayne grinned. "We think my lord expects relief. He's just planning to sit tight until Clinton can get here and then all will be well. Of course that's not quite General Washington's idea."

The night of October the 6th was picked for the opening of the first parallel. It was just past full moon and if the sky was clear the men with their picks and shovels, only eight hundred yards from the British inner defenses, would be easy to hit. But the clouds were kind, the firing did little damage and by dawn the trench was finished. Three days later with the artillery in place the Allied bombardment began and from then on never ceased. A second trench was dug still nearer the enemy; there were sorties by the British; a capture of redoubts by the Allies; but always, steadily, mercilessly, day after day, in light and in darkness, the endless pounding from the French and the Continental guns.

On the bright morning of the 17th, a drummer boy was seen mounted on a British parapet. Above the firing the sound was lost but everyone knew what it meant. The guns all grew quiet and then they could hear the drummer. He was beating the *chamade,* the call to parley, the sweetest music in the world to the ears of the Allied soldiers.

The surrender was carried out with dignity on both sides. On Hampton Road south of Yorktown the victorious armies lined up: the French in their white gaiters and coats, their epaulets and gold braid; and opposite them those glorious ragged scarecrows (as Wayne had called them), the men of the Continental Army of the United States of America! The British general's sword was offered and returned; the British regiments came out, bands playing but colors cased, as they left their guns in a meadow nearby. The great war was won and O'Hara as he watched the ceremony felt a lump in his throat even as his heart rejoiced.

One episode of the day had brought bitter disappointment to young Ensign Denny. He told O'Hara about it that evening. A fort on the bank of York River was to be formally given over and the new standard raised.

"Dicky Butler . . . I mean General Butler from Carlisle but I've always known him . . . well, Dicky was given the standard but he passed it to me. He said, 'Eb, I'm short and you're tall and besides this will be something nice for you to remember.' Well, I took it as proud as you please but just when we got inside the fort General Steuben grabbed it from me and raised it himself. I could have kicked him!"

"Come on, Eb," O'Hara said sympathetically. "Let's go celebrate a little and forget our troubles."

It was several days before he could talk to Wayne, then O'Hara began jubilantly, "Well, so we've won!"

"Damned if we haven't," Wayne agreed, but without enough enthusiasm.

"How soon do you think we can start back?" O'Hara asked eagerly.

Wayne looked at him with a strange expression.

"I don't know. General Washington has asked me to stay on . . . put it in a way I couldn't refuse as a soldier. I think you may get the same orders."

"Stay *on!*" O'Hara said, his voice unsteady. "Why should we have to stay on when the war's over?"

"The war's won but it's not over. There's a difference. General Greene's still down south and he may need some help before he clears things up. Besides we've got nearly eight thousand troops here even after the French that came up with de Grasse have gone back to their ships. You can't just say *scat* to an army that size and go off and leave it."

O'Hara turned his back. In all his life he had never known such a stab of disappointment as he felt at this moment. Ever since the drummer boy beat his *chamade,* he had been busy reckoning the time — in weeks and days until he would again hold Mary in his arms and plan definitely for their wedding. And now . . .

Wayne was speaking slowly. "After this we may be able to get letters through. That will be a help."

And all at once O'Hara felt ashamed. For him no matter when he got back, the heaven of his marriage lay before him; for Anthony Wayne there would be no such consummation of love. He turned suddenly and looked into the other man's eyes from which the reckless light had disappeared.

"Of course," he said, forcing a cheerfulness he was far from feeling. "We have to do out our duty. And time passes. And there's one thing sure. When we finally get back to Philadelphia we'll both get a welcome that will be . . ."

"Worth waiting for," Wayne ended for him.

And even with an effort, the two men smiled at each other.

CHAPTER EIGHT

I T WAS the month of May. The month of Mary! And the
wedding day itself with sunshine, new verdure, and soft
airs was as freshly beautiful as though just dropped from the
hand of God. In a front room at The Crooked Billet with Sam
to assist him O'Hara arranged his newly powdered hair, tied
it with a black satin bow, fastened his elegant lace stock, but-
toned his rose satin waistcoat, and finally in knee breeches and
long coat, gave a last fastening to the silver knee buckles with
hands that trembled. For it seemed past belief that time's slow
march had actually brought him to this moment! He thought
of that far-off conversation with Wayne when they had discussed the possibility of their being detained in the South.
O'Hara then had considered the delay in terms of months. As
a matter of fact it was more than two years and a half since the
night when — as Mary had told him — the Philadelphia watch-
man making his rounds had called out upon the hour: *Past one
o'clock and Cornwallis is taken! Past two o'clock and Cornwallis is taken! Past three o'clock* . . . For Colonel Tench
Tilghman who had carried the great news had ridden well.
Mary had been awakened by this shout and had not slept at all
after, as she said, her mind chanting its own paean: *Now he will
come back soon, soon!*

But the weary wait had dragged on with only letters to solace their hearts, until at long last the duty was done and Wayne and O'Hara returned to Philadelphia together with the last of the troops. After the first rapturous reunion with his love, O'Hara had gone back at once to Pittsburgh to check upon the house. He had been more than satisfied. It stood, strong and not unpleasing in its simple design, in the midst of the apple trees. He had bought some necessary furniture to supplement that which Mary was bringing: an oak trestle table, straight chairs and two rockers for the kitchen, and a four-poster bed for the room upstairs. The great fireplace delighted him for the mason had done a fine job even to a decorative row of flat cemented stones below the mantel! The workmen had all apparently put forth special effort, which was touching, as was the welcome from his old friends, and their eagerness to be of help. Devereux and Mrs. Smith had found, they thought, the perfect cook-housekeeper for Mary, whom O'Hara at once interviewed and engaged. In addition to the middle-aged Prudence Bond, he had acquired a young indentured Negro youth by the fascinating Irish name of McGrady, which amused O'Hara out of all reason. They had looked each other in the eye and liked what they saw. It was McGrady who knew the exact answer to his question as to when the apple trees would be in bloom, for O'Hara had planned over the years that he would bring Mary to the King's Orchard when the perfumed blossoms would surround her. And it was McGrady who promised to get the cooking utensils for the fireplace and later to purchase the food supplies which O'Hara listed for him. It was then early March so they reckoned the time carefully.

"The young lady, suh, ain't mebbe used to the frontier?"

"No. She comes from Philadelphia."

"We all gonna try to make her comfortable, suh. I looken out for her very special myself, suh." His speech still was richly southern.

His new master clapped him on the shoulder.

"I'm glad I found you, McGrady."

One thing lay heavily upon his heart as he started back again over the long but now familiar route. This was the news of the burning of Hannastown the July before! The little village about twenty miles from Pittsburgh had been important, with its law courts held in Robert Hanna's big tavern, its neat log houses and general air of respectability. There were prominent citizens, too: Colonel Procter belonged there, so did Archibald Lochry, names known both east and west. On a sunny afternoon, so the report went, while most of the men were helping a neighbor harvest, the Indians had stolen upon the town. The women and children got to the fort and the men, fighting as they went, hurried there when the alarm reached them. By courage and by ruse they held the small stronghold so that there were only a few deaths and a few captivities. But at the end the pleasant little village with all it held of patient building lay in ashes. All this was tragic enough but the part that distressed O'Hara immeasurably was that the leader of the raid had been *Guyasuta!*

"I can't understand that!" O'Hara had lamented to Devereux Smith. "I thought *Guyasuta* was a good Indian."

"There's just one good Indian, my friend," Smith said between his teeth. "That's a dead one."

So O'Hara had to hide his hurt and his questions until a later day.

Now, back in Philadelphia as he stood in the last hour of his bachelorhood, dressed for the greatest event of his life, his busy mind kept checking over the details of the last weeks here in the city when the preparations for the trip were in progress. Had he forgotten anything that would add to Mary's comfort? It had been his concern waking and sleeping. One wagon was already gone with the heavier furnishings in it; the second wagon, with its sturdy oxen, was standing now on the side street just beyond the Carson home. The hard seat had been upholstered with cushions. Under it were boxes and traveling bags, while in the back of the wagon were the Oriental rugs which Mr. Carson had insisted upon giving, and on top of them three feather ticks with pillows, sheets and covers. Over this O'Hara had spread a waterproof tarpaulin for use if needed but chiefly to keep curious eyes from looking upon what would be the marriage bed.

There was the clatter of hoofs below on the cobblestones and the sound of wheels.

"There you are, Mr. O'Hara! Carriage is waitin'. You're mighty handsome, I tell you. Anybody know you was a bridegroom just by lookin' at you."

"Thanks, Sam." He peered from the window. Christian Febiger, Mary's brother-in-law who was to stand with him at the ceremony, was looking up and waving. His wife Elizabeth, whom O'Hara had never met until this spring due to his short and infrequent visits at the Carson home, was to be Mary's matron of honor. He wrung Sam's hand now and looked his last at the house that had first sheltered him in the new country; then having already made his farewell to Hastings, he ran down the stairs and out into the bright sunshine. Febiger stood by the carriage handing him in as though he were royalty.

"To the Locust Street Presbyterian Church," O'Hara said to the driver.

"Don't you suppose I've already told him that?" Febiger asked.

O'Hara grinned. "On an occasion as important as this, it's best to leave nothing to chance." There had been one immediate bond between the two young men for Febiger had served under Anthony Wayne at Stony Point and admired him greatly.

"We're to sit up front," Christian was saying now, "until Mary and her father come into the church. Parson Brown has given me all the directions. He says bridegrooms are too nervous to be trusted. Do you want to keep the ring or let me have it till the proper time?"

"I'll keep it if you don't mind. I have a feeling I'd rather no other hand touched it till I put it on her finger."

"All right. Relieves me of responsibility. O'Hara . . . ?"

"Yes?"

"You know I wish you and Mary all the best in the world, even if . . . even though Elizabeth and I have been anxious about the match . . . afraid it's too big a step for Mary to take after the way she's been brought up and all that. But I do want to tell you now . . ."

"Yes?" O'Hara prompted again, his face grave.

"Well, since we've met you we feel better. If anyone can take care of her, I'm sure you will." He reached his hand and O'Hara grasped it without speaking.

Inside the church everything at first was quiet for the young men were early, then there began the sound of footsteps and rustle of stiff silks as the guests walked up the aisle and settled in the pews. Parson Brown sat solemnly upon the pulpit dais, his face ruddy above his white Geneva bands, his eyes fixed upon the door. O'Hara's heart was beating thunderously. Christian Febiger's words had struck him deeply. He knew Mary's family were concerned about her marriage to him;

when he allowed himself to be objective, so was he. Her happiness, her very life was soon to be in his keeping, and while the most desperate perils of the frontier were now past there were still dangers . . . had he been honest enough about these? O God, had he because of the strength of his love in any way deceived her?

At last there were sudden movements in the back of the church, Parson Brown was coming down from his high chair to stand before the pulpit, Febiger was nudging him and rising, they were out in the aisle moving to join the minister . . . Then O'Hara looked back and all his doubts and fears vanished as a mist before the sun! For Mary in white ribbed satin, and a little veil of cloudy lace was coming toward him, a smile upon her lips! He went, in his eagerness, more than the proscribed steps to meet her, then, her small hand clasped tightly in his strong one, they stood together repeating after Parson Brown the vows which made their union sacred and eternal.

The reception at the Carson home later was both elegant and gay. There were flowers everywhere and in the dining room where an elaborate collation was spread, the silver gleamed and the crystal sparkled. To make up for Mary's disappointment at the lack of music at the wedding (Parson Brown felt it savored of Episcopacy) three violinists in the wide hall sent waves of melody through the rooms, where an elite group of Philadelphians were gathered to do honor to the young couple. There was a constant flow of guests at once up the stairs to the front room where some of the wedding gifts were on display for an hour longer before they were packed according to prearranged plan and put into the wagon. The gift causing the most comment was the dozen cut champagne glasses from General Washington!

Judge Bingham spoke to O'Hara in the drawing room about

it. "Quite a signal honor for His Excellency to remember you in this way. May I ask how you became so close to him?"

"I hardly know," O'Hara admitted. "Of course he couldn't help but feel my strong admiration for him. Then he professed himself . . . satisfied with the work I did in the South."

"No special bond?" the Judge kept pressing.

"Well, we found out we're both very fond of *horses*."

"Ah, could be that. Very likely. What about your own horse. Mary told my wife about him. Thinking of changing his name now?" The Judge laughed.

"No more than Pittsburgh is thinking of changing its name," O'Hara replied smiling. "Pitt has been with me everywhere I've gone and he's to travel with us now, tied to the back of the wagon."

At the moment a tall, handsome man appeared in the doorway, his eyes searching the room. It was Anthony Wayne! Alone. O'Hara went quickly to meet him, and the two shook hands without speaking. What was there to say that they had not said to each other already?

"If you'll come to the library I think Mary is there at the moment . . . and some other old friends."

Mary Vining, beautiful in yellow silk that set off her dark hair and eyes to perfection, was in a small group by the window. She turned as if drawn, saw Wayne and colored until her face was rose. So, thought O'Hara, no wonder everybody can tell what's going on. Wayne spoke to the bride, bowing low over her hand, greeted a few others and then made his way with great attempt at casualness toward the group in the corner.

When it was time for O'Hara and Mary to change from their wedding to their traveling attire, Christian Febiger with perhaps a little too much champagne signaled for all to keep quiet while he gave, as he put it, his last instructions to the groom. O'Hara felt a moment's uneasiness but when Febiger's voice rang out it was in the old rhyme which he already knew.

Lead her like a pigeon,
Bed her like a dove,
Whisper when you're near her,
"You're my only love."

There was general applause and laughter and raising of glasses which O'Hara and Mary acknowledged smiling, then she started upstairs with her sister Elizabeth, and O'Hara followed with Christian. Not, however, before he had seen Wayne and Mary Vining quietly slip out the front door. Poor Anthony! he thought.

When they came down again O'Hara was in his uniform and Mary was all in dove gray with a tiny bonnet of the same material edged with white ruching. Practical, but oh, so becoming! There were exclamations from the ladies, admiring glances from the men, and then the goodbyes at the doorway with good wishes floating after them as they reached the wagon now drawn up before the house. O'Hara lifted Mary to her place, sprang up beside her, taking the lines in his hand, and amid a chorus from the steps they drove off, with O'Hara's last glance for Mr. Carson. He had had a long talk with his father-in-law the night before, and now he raised his hand in what to the rest would seem merely a gesture, but which was really the expression of a vow; then the wagon rattled over the cobblestones and on out to the Lancaster road.

"I may cry a little," Mary said brokenly.

"I don't wonder. You've been so brave all day. Put your

head on my shoulder and cry all you want. You'll feel better."

But in a short time she sat up again. "It was a beautiful wedding, wasn't it?"

"Absolutely perfect!"

From then on they went over all the details of the day including their own emotions, until suddenly they realized they were both very, very hungry.

"I was too excited to eat any of the lunch," Mary said.

"I too."

"And, I really don't believe I had much breakfast."

"Same with me!"

They laughed and brought forth the big basket packed in the Carson kitchen which they fell upon with healthy young appetites.

At dusk O'Hara took off the big tarpaulin and folded it. Mary looking back, saw the soft blankets and the linen sheets and pillow cases from her own bed!

"You've thought of *everything* for my comfort, James," she said later, when darkness enfolded them and they were ready to settle between the white linens.

"I tried to," he said.

As a matter of fact he had discussed with her in detail the arrangements for this night. They could, by leaving earlier, reach a tavern of sorts, but he had tested it, found it noisy and none too clean. If they slept in the wagon now, as they would have to do many times later, they would actually have more comfort and certainly more quiet. Mary had voted for the wagon. O'Hara had explained that they would stop at the larger places as they came to them for hot meals and over night if she wished. Also for supplies to carry them to the next inn. Between times there were cooking utensils, dry groceries and smoked meats slung underneath the wagon and he was an experienced wilderness cook.

Now, they lay together and by the time the first half hour had passed O'Hara had made love. But Mary was tense and distressed. "I wish there were some other way," she said with tears.

He gathered her to him, repentant. "I was too eager, too impetuous. You must forgive me, darling. I should have waited. I should have talked with you first. Please try to understand. I was swept away."

He began to talk to her then, gently, of many intimate things. Little by little she voiced shy questions and he answered them. Overhead the moon, almost to the full, rolled in splendor, while sweet fragrances stole upon their senses from the woods.

"*On such a night as this,*" O'Hara quoted once and Mary went on with the lines. They could not sleep as the hours passed. Perhaps it was because of the excitements of the day; perhaps it was because of an unconscious anticipation. For now O'Hara caressed her in new and tender ways until the tension all went out of her body and she moved closer as though seeking.

Before the darkness ended a strange and wonderful thing happened. Suddenly, softly, without apparent volition, they drew together; for him the desire of love rekindled; for her the hesitant, the fearful became all in the moment as a familiar warmth that stirred the pulses and flowed with yearning through every vein. She yielded now in utter giving until at the last she was overtaken by a tremulous rapture . . .

As the kiss ended, Mary lay breathing quickly, holding her lover as though she would never let him go.

"James," she whispered, "I didn't know . . . I didn't dream . . ."

"But this is what I've been trying to tell you, darling."

"I'm so glad it ended like this on our wedding night, aren't you, instead of . . . the other way?"

His cheek touched hers and now it was his tears that lay upon it.

"What is it?" she asked in alarm.

"It's the happiness," he said, "after all the long, long waiting . . . I feel as though I could hardly bear it."

"And now I'm truly your wife?"

"Truly, my dearest Delight. My wife! My own!"

With their bodies fulfilled and relaxed and a peace like heaven upon their hearts they fell asleep at moonset, just before the dawn.

As the days passed they became aware of pleasant surprises. For one thing, for the first time they found *fun* in each other's company. Before, their visits together had been so brief, so fraught with doubts and fears and the shadow of coming separations that their conversations had of necessity been mostly serious. Now in the freedom and intimacy of their new estate, O'Hara's native wit rose to its full flower and Mary's own delightful humor answered it. The woods echoed with their laughter. Sometimes of an afternoon he let the oxen rest for a little, and Mary then donned a blue wrapper which he particularly admired and lay down for a nap in the back of the wagon. One day she roused to find O'Hara near, an eager question in his eyes.

"In the daytime?" she demurred. "I don't think that seems quite . . . *delicate*."

He was immediately grave.

"You are right. Look at Pitt. His eyes are definitely disapproving. And that squirrel over there. He's been watching us with a very shocked expression. We must conduct ourselves with the greatest propriety, *especially* in the forest."

And then Mary's delicious laugh rang out, as her hand reached his.

There was so much to fill in from their backgrounds and neither could ever tire of hearing details of the other's life.

"One thing I want from my old home is a table," O'Hara said one day. "I've already written my sister, Katherine, and sent money for its shipment."

"Your *sister?*" Mary said in surprise. "Why you never mentioned having one!"

"Maybe I didn't. But you see I never was much with her. She was in Ireland with relatives while I was years in France. At any rate I hope she sends the table. I tried to make it worth her while."

"What's it like?"

"It's lovely, as I remember it. Round, with an inlaid edge and *the feet are shamrocks!* I want it for our living room. We could use it for special dining . . . I'm sure it would seat six. I'll keep after it until I get it," he added.

"Don't you ever give up on anything?"

He looked deeply into her eyes. "Not easily," he said. And they laughed again.

They were blessed by the weather. The days followed each other with dappled sunshine on their faces and around them the beauty of dogwood and Judas trees amongst the green. The nights were balmy with a fresh breeze carrying in it the breath of wild flowers: the Mayapples, sky rockets, trilliums and sweet fern. They could watch the stars through the opening above the road. The Milky Way was a silvery vapor. All of this was more than O'Hara had dared hope for and more

than Mary had known to hope for. One thing only had disturbed her and this was the fact that O'Hara's rifle was always
close beside him.

"Is there really danger then?" she asked anxiously.

He had tossed off the question.

"Why I'm a frontiersman and a soldier. How would I feel
without my rifle?"

What she did not know was that his keen eyes constantly
watched the road and the woods beside them. One thing he
feared was that a rattler would bite an ox's leg. A rider could
usually circumvent this danger, but with these dumb, stupid
beasts, as O'Hara always called them, it could be a threat. And
one day it was. Mary was drowsing with her head against
his shoulder and he himself was sitting relaxed, his feet
braced against the wagon front board, when suddenly he caught
sight of a yellow and black looping neck close, too close to the
plodding oxen. The snake had evidently been concealed by
the leaves that still lay on the cart track or he would have seen
it before. He pulled on the lines; then throwing them to the
floor, put one foot hard upon the ends, raised his rifle and took
more careful aim than he ever had done before in his life. The
snake, sensing its own danger had coiled now. He fired and hit
the coils; then as fast as he could he fired again, this time hit-
ting the head. The oxen, frightened, were backing wildly with
imminent threat of overturning the wagon. O'Hara used the
whip until they moved forward again and passed over the rat-
ler's body with Pitt and the pack horse whinnying behind, and
Mary sitting up straight, her face pale.

"Will you hold the lines now for a few minutes?" O'Hara
asked her. "The oxen will behave but I want to keep a sharp
lookout for a possible mate to that varmint."

They drove along quietly until O'Hara finally put his

rifle down, took the reins, and leaned over to kiss her.

"Thank you," he said. "I think most girls would have screamed which wouldn't have helped matters much."

"In all the times I was planning for this trip . . . I don't know why . . . but I never once thought of snakes. Now I'll be terrified ever to get out of the wagon again!"

"No," he said. "I'll tell you something. You have never been out of the wagon that I didn't watch you every single minute. So you've nothing to worry about."

"Oh James!" she said, embarrassment in her tone.

"It's necessary, dearest. And as to . . . well, nothing matters between us now, does it?"

"I suppose not," she said slowly.

But a little later he felt her hand slip through his arm.

"I do feel safe with you, *Mr. O'Hara!*"

They stopped over night in Carlisle and he had to show her all the places familiar to him and take her to call on Agnes Denny, who mothered her at once and insisted upon giving her a lovely pewter plate as a gift for her new home.

"I've got another just like it for Eb's wife when he gets one. I wish he was here now. Do you know he seems to have his eye on Pittsburgh too. What's so special about it, I ask him. Isn't Carlisle good enough?"

"It would be for me," Mary said. "I could be happy here."

"God grant you may be happy wherever you are. The main thing for a woman, though, isn't the *place,* dearie, it's the *man,* and I think you've got a good one."

She poked O'Hara's ribs playfully. "Just see you deserve her for I can tell you have a treasure."

"I'm the one knows that better than anyone else," O'Hara said, "and I'll do my best."

As they left, Mary hugging her plate, Mrs. Denny called

after her. "If you ever need any advice, dearie, on cooking or husbands or any woman matters just write me a letter."

"I will," Mary promised laughing, not knowing how often over the years she was to keep her word.

The traveling grew more difficult as they reached the mountains and the oxen floundered slowly up the stony trails of Tuscarora, Sideling Hill, and Allegheny. There had to be frequent rest periods for the beasts and O'Hara fretted within himself, chiefly because Mary was growing tired. The constant jolting was wearing and she spent a good part of each day now, resting on the feather ticks in the back of the wagon. Once refreshed by this, however, she resumed her place on the high seat and eagerly went on with their endless conversations.

"About church now," she said one day. "You were good to be married in mine when you have a partly Catholic background."

He smiled. "I guess that description fits me. I don't go as far as Tom Paine but I do believe in freedom of religious thinking. Then you see, I had an Anglican mother."

He told her then about the little Prayer-book he always carried and how he had found an Indian rite almost duplicated in it. He would show it to her, he said, when they unpacked.

"There isn't a Presbyterian church in Pittsburgh yet, is there?" she asked.

"Not yet, but they're talking about building one. I imagine it won't be long."

"And you'll go with me to it, then?"

"Of course. And you won't mind if I lend a hand to the Catholics sometimes, will you? For my father's sake."

So their religious problems were settled on the back of the Laurel Mountain, the worst of the lot, "that Bugbear" as Gen-

eral Forbes himself had called it as his men had toiled fear-
somely in making the road over it twenty-five years before. But
there was beauty enough in all conscience to offset the precipi-
tous ascent, for the bushes that had given the ridge its name
were now in full bloom. Masses, as far as the eye could see, of
shiny oval-pointed leaves bearing the clusters of heavenly pink
flowers, each tiny frilled cup a miracle of design. O'Hara
plucked some for her day by day so she could enjoy them in her
hand; and once when her bonnet was off, he tucked a bunch in
her hair with overwhelming effect, for he all but forgot to guide
the oxen as he kissed her again and again.

Most of all now, though, in their talks he tried to prepare
her for the Pittsburgh scene, the house itself, and the people
she might care to know.

"I suppose Hugh Brackenridge is my best friend, at least
nearest my own age. He has a brilliant mind and is an interesting talker and I fancy after his own bachelor cooking he'll
be pleased to have a dinner with us occasionally. Then there
are the Smiths, older but very nice and the Craigs and the Nevilles . . . oh, I don't think you'll be lonely."

As to his own plans he had to answer a direct question from
Mary.

"But what are you going to *do*, James, when we get there?"

He had hesitated, a strange thing for him. "I don't wonder
you ask that but I have talked it over with your father. The
government owes me quite a good deal of money and I suppose I'll have to wait for that awhile. But one way or another
from my trading and a little legacy and so on, I have some
money in the Philadelphia bank, enough to keep us comfortably for some time. I intend to buy more lots. Pittsburgh is
going to grow — I've always been sure of that — but you can't

tell now in what direction, so I'm going to buy in *every* direction to make sure. Land is cheap now. Then I might have a store for a while. People are going to be coming west in great numbers for the soldiers are being paid off in land and they'll probably all come by way of Pittsburgh, so a store might be a good thing for a start, but I'll wait and see. Just trust me, Mary. Shall I tell you a secret?"

"Oh, yes."

He leaned close. "I intend to be a rich man some day."

"I wouldn't be surprised," she answered, "since you've made up your mind to it."

It was at the top of the last, the Chestnut Ridge, that O'Hara stopped the oxen and allowed Mary to look upon the magnificent panorama spread before them. The sun was just setting and a peculiar ambient light flooded the wide scene. The primeval forest still held place over much of it, but scattered here and there were small rolling fields of brown plowed earth and the rising smoke of frontier cabins. Slowly, slowly, nature was being tamed to man's intent and this earnest of the future softened the wildness and touched the hearts of the two young people who looked upon it with hope.

"Oh, it's beautiful!" Mary exclaimed. And even as she spoke the western sky became an intolerable glory while luminous clouds spread toward them until the watchers became part of an Apocalypse, an opening heaven of gold that enfolded them.

Mary's eyes were wet with the wonder of it, and neither she nor O'Hara spoke much during their evening meal and the usual preparations for darkness. But they both knew without words that this night perhaps more than any since their first one, was made for love.

When Fort Ligonier was passed and then Greensburg,

O'Hara realized that the end was only about six hours away and his heart grew anxious. Nothing he had told her could possibly prepare Mary for the actual sight of the place to which she was coming to live. Her own face was somewhat drawn as the last miles passed and when they reached the edge of the town it was white.

What she saw at first was a sprawling pioneer village of fifty or sixty log houses, some of them ramshackle, most of them unpainted; dirty streets in which here and there a drunken Indian snored beside a hog in a mud puddle; evidence round about of the all too primitive sanitary conditions; and facing them the muddy, irregular bank of the Monongahela!

O'Hara didn't speak. He could not, for never in his life had he felt such deathly fear. He drove on. The great Fort came into clearer view with its old moat now a tiny lake in which ducks were disporting themselves. The King's Gardens were green and the apple orchard? His eager eyes sought for the blooms and his spirit fell still lower for there were only, he could see, the empty clusters from which the petals had fallen. He knew their journey had taken longer than he had foreseen but still he had hoped against hope that the blossoms would last. He turned into the narrow track that led to the house, and there it stood, sturdy and strong and all white from the many applications of limewash. He drew the oxen to a stop at the kitchen door, and still neither of them had spoken. Then he saw Mary raise her head and draw deep breaths. He had been too lost in his terrified absorption before to notice the overpowering fragrance upon the air, not that of the apple blossoms but something stronger, more sensuously sweet.

"*Locusts!*" Mary said in wonder. "We've a street lined with them in Philadelphia and I always walked back and forth on it every day to smell the perfume. Oh, James, you didn't tell me we would have *locusts*."

"I never thought of it," he said, his voice uneven in his sudden relief. "But there they are, a whole row of them along the river and just beyond them is the Allegheny itself. Hugh Brackenridge calls it 'the loveliest stream that ever glistened to the moon!' He's a poet, you know."

He had jumped from the wagon and was at her side ready to lift her down.

"We're here, darling. This is home," he said as his arms went round her.

The door which had been closed upon the coolness of the day was flung open now and Prudence Bond in a neat neckerchief and full apron stood smiling at them. She moved aside as O'Hara carried Mary over the threshold and set her down in the big kitchen. And all at once as they stood there together it *was* home. There was the great fireplace glowing before them like a happy heart! The pot simmered on the crane and good baking smells came from the side oven. Prudence had braided a rag rug during her weeks of waiting and it lay brightly in front of the big rocking chair. And against the long wall that had been bare when O'Hara last saw it stood a big walnut dresser, polished to satin, waiting for the bride's dishes. A paper lay on the lower shelf, and O'Hara hurried to read it.

> Congratulations and good wishes from
> your old cronies of Semple's Tavern.

The names followed: Smith, Campbell, Craig, Neville, Brackenridge, Ormsby and of course Samuel Semple himself.

O'Hara was incredulous and deeply moved, and Mary exultant as she smoothed the beautiful wood.

"Was it really made here, in Pittsburgh, do you think?"

"Oh, we have some good craftsmen here, but wasn't it wonderful of my old friends to do this? And doesn't it give a *tone* to the kitchen, though? What about the other wagon, Prudence? Did it get here all right?"

"Aye, sir, and I had the things all set in the other room awaitin' you, all except the bedstids."

O'Hara drew Mary with him to see the big room, now safely and happily cluttered with the precious pieces of furniture.

"It wouldn't be large for Philadelphia but for here . . . it's not bad, is it? We can call it the parlor or drawing room without stretching a point, can't we? And when McGrady comes . . . Oh, Prudence, where *is* McGrady?"

"He's sure to be here on the quick, sir, for everyone, most, has been watchin' for you. There's him now I'll warrant, runnin' like a killdeer."

McGrady entered breathless evidently chagrined that he had not been on hand to greet them.

"I was up Grant's Hill, suh, but I taken the short way back."

"This is your mistress, McGrady, see you take good care of her."

McGrady's eyes were rolling white with admiration.

"Yes, ma'am. Yes, suh. I sure to, suh."

"Now," said O'Hara, with boyish exuberance, "you and I, McGrady, are going to clear out this room, then unpack the wagon out there, lay a rug down and get things back in place where Mrs. O'Hara . . ."

He stopped and looked at Mary and she looked back at him. Then he motioned the servants out and closed the door.

"That's the first time I've said it!"

"I wondered how long I'd have to wait," she answered demurely.

He held her close. "Do you like the sound of it?"

"It's very sweet," she said.

While the two men moved chairs and tables out of the parlor and then unloaded the wagon until they reached the rugs Mary sat in the kitchen listening as Prudence expatiated upon the merits of the new dwelling. O'Hara, overhearing her at one point, grinned.

"It's the finest in the town by far, that little privy is. As snug an' nice built as anybody could wish an' whitewashed to match the house even. There's not another to touch it. Most of them are poor contraptions and . . . I think shame to say it . . . some folks don't have none at all. You'd ought to go out, an' see for yourself, Ma'am, how tidy a treat it is."

O'Hara kept busy at the far side of the wagon until he had seen Mary end her tour of inspection and come up the path again chuckling to herself. He knew the cause of her mirth. When he had seen the small edifice in March he had noticed that one of the workmen had carved two hearts joined with a piercing arrow on one of the walls. Now, he met Mary and asked in a low voice, "Did you like the decorations?"

"Oh, *you!*" she said roguishly and laughed aloud.

The most welcome sound in all the world, he thought, after her white face when they had driven into town.

By supper time the beautiful rose Oriental filled the parlor and Mary had directed the placing of the furniture. The wing chairs at either side of the fireplace, the small haircloth sofa along one wall with candle stands at either end of it, and opposite, a side table with a drop leaf and two rush-bottomed chairs.

"Over here," O'Hara said gaily, standing at the empty wall, "we can put my shamrock table when it gets here. Doesn't it all look homelike already? And tomorrow we'll bring in your boxes and you can unpack your little pretties and set them around."

Prudence, her voice full of awe, spoke from the doorway before Mary could answer.

"You *step* on that?" she asked, pointing to the rug. "You *walk* on it?"

O'Hara and Mary laughed together. "Of course. That's what it's made for!"

She shook her head. "Never seen nothin' like that before. You'd better explain careful to anybody comin' in or they'll never set foot on it, never! I'm afeared to even now when you say so."

They ate supper at the trestle table in the kitchen, with ravenous appetites for the good plain food: boiled flitch and potatoes with scraped horse radish root, hot baked raised cakes and berry jam.

"McGrady he's a great one to scrimmage round in the woods. That's where he got the radish roots. An' he picked the berries up round Grant's hill. I used a bit of the sugar you left, sir, to do them up. I hope it's all right with you," Prudence said a little fearfully.

"I couldn't be better pleased," O'Hara said, helping Mary again to the jam.

When they had finished he and McGrady again began work upon the wagon for there was still much to unload. Mary, according to a gleeful command, stayed below so that the eventual surprise might be the greater. There was endless laboring up the stairs and the noise of moving and settling in the room above the parlor until dusk had fallen. Then O'Hara ran down and proudly escorted Mary to her chamber. She stood in the doorway and gave a cry of pleasure, for the room was large like the one below it with the floor filled richly now with the second Oriental in which blue, her favorite color, predominated. The four-poster bed stood handsomely in place already made up to Mary's amazement; opposite, her own dressing table with the candle holders, and the small mirror miraculously intact!

"But look at this, Mary!"

In one corner stood a three-sided wash stand with tin bowl and pitcher!

"I had it made, and here, you see . . ."

He opened the small door below to exhibit an article for her comfort.

Mary suddenly dissolved in tears and leaned against him.

"It's all so much nicer than I expected. When we drove in and I saw the town first I thought my heart would break but now the house is so lovely, and to think it's mine, my very own! I mean *ours*," she added hastily.

O'Hara smiled. "It is yours, my dear Delight. I'm just going to live in it with you!"

She sank down on the side of the bed. "But I'm *so tired!*"

He was all solicitude. "Of course you are! You must get to bed at once. I'm about worn out myself and what must you be. Let's get settled soon for a good night's sleep for tomorrow will be an exciting day, I imagine. But first, come here to the window." He opened it, apologizing as he did so for the glazed paper panes.

"I'm so very sorry I couldn't get glass for all the windows! I had a hard enough time to get it for the parlor ones alone. But some day . . . Look, darling!"

Through the May twilight they could see the wide, swift-flowing Allegheny, with a glimpse of the great Ohio beyond at the Point. Upon the air hung the heady-sweet fragrance of the locust blooms.

"Isn't it beautiful, the view?" he asked eagerly.

"To think," Mary said wonderingly, "I can see this every day instead of just roofs of houses! Can we leave the window open?"

"Of course. I'll run down and get a candle lighted and we'll be to bed in no time."

He had been struck by the anxious thought of a possibility. So he asked McGrady to sleep on a blanket on the kitchen floor that night and he agreed with his usual alacrity. He had already taken Pitt and the pack horse to Semple's stable during supper, and later the oxen to be tied in the open space behind it.

"You fed the beasts well, as I told you?" O'Hara asked now.

"Yes suh. I done everything you say. All the men round Semple's talkin' 'bout you gettin' here today with the Missus."

"I'll warrant they were," O'Hara said under his breath as he carefully drew in the latch string on the door and ran the bolt. When he got back upstairs with his candle, Mary was already in bed and half asleep. He undressed quickly, blew out the light, kissed her gently and then lay, listening. If what he feared took place there would be no doubt of his waking but he preferred to hear the first sign. He was glad McGrady was in the house; just in case, Prudence, too, was there, in one of the small back rooms. He lay, wondering if he should have stayed up. But then, most likely nothing would happen tonight.

But an hour later it began. First, shouts and yells he judged from the front of the tavern, then the earsplitting, nerve-rending noise of rifle butts on pans, iron pots, and implements banged against each other, a weird cacophony of jangling, shattering sound. He leaned over and touched Mary.

"Darling, can you wake up?"

She roused, heard the noise and clung to him.

"Is it Indians?" she whispered, terrified.

"No, no, dear. Nothing to harm us. It's just a shivaree!"

"A . . . a what?"

"A shivaree. A crazy serenade they give newly married couples. But we'll have to get something on in a hurry for they always want to see the bride and groom. Just throw your dress on over your bedgown and I'll do the same. We'll go out on the front stoop for a minute and that will satisfy them. Then I'll have to give them a treat . . ."

McGrady was at their door with a candle even as O'Hara was pulling on his trousers and they could hear Prudence speaking her mind below.

"Hurry, dear. We want to get rid of them as fast as we can."

They waited beside the parlor front door until the noise was all around them, then O'Hara put the latch string out and slid the bolt. Holding the candle in one hand and Mary's in the other, he drew her out before the yelling crowd. He had, he supposed, seen as sinister looking a group before but certainly Mary had not. In the light of the few wavering pine torches the rough faces and clothing of the frontiersmen must look as alarming to her as Indians. But there were other men scattered through the crowd also, he spotted at once. Even to him these were dangerous looking, for he knew they were keelboatmen just off the river and they usually made trouble. Pressing close to the stoop were some of his own friends, Brackenridge apparently leading them.

"Smile at them, Mary, and wave," O'Hara urged her.

At once there was whistling and catcalls and some shouted remarks he hoped Mary hadn't caught. He held up his hand for quiet and Brackenridge hammered out a tattoo to support him.

"Thank you, men, for this fine shivaree! My wife and I . . ."

"My God," yelled a man, "looks like the bridegroom wears a *nightshirt!* Can you beat that? Seems like we ought to take it off him. We don't wear no *nightshirts* on the frontier!"

There were ribald shouts, but once again Brackenridge pounded and O'Hara called at the top of his voice: "Hey, men, what we all want is a good drink of whiskey right from Suke's Run. Get back to Semple's and I'll treat you all."

"Back to Semple's!" Hugh yelled and the other men of the town joined him. The crowd began to turn.

"Bring me my hunting shirt quick, McGrady. I'll have to go to the tavern, Mary, and treat them, but I'll be back as soon as I can, and you are perfectly safe. Just go to bed, and tomorrow we'll laugh over this. Prudence, see Mrs. O'Hara upstairs and McGrady, bolt the doors. Don't worry, darling, I'll be with you shortly."

He jumped from the stoop and overtook Brackenridge and the others who were plainly concerned.

"We're sorry about this, O'Hara. We were just going to have a bit of fun like we always do when these keel-boaters joined up. They're always out to raise hell. I think if they get enough to drink they'll stick at the tavern, though," Hugh said.

"You've got a beautiful bride, O'Hara," Smith added, "if this hasn't scared her to death. There are a few rough customers in from trading, too. Well, hope we can hold them down."

Inside Semple's there was milling about with noise and shouting. O'Hara ordered the drinks and when the men had found places either beside the tables or on them with their noggins, there was a slight cessation.

"This fellah must be feelin' pretty good," one man yelled. Loud laughter followed. "Wonder why he's feelin' so good?"

"Another drink, men?" O'Hara called above the uproar. "Another round, Mr. Semple!"

It was when this was nearly drunk that one frontiersman, a stranger, shouted, "What about puttin' the bridegroom to bed? Say, don't you think we ought to put him to bed now?"

A wild chorus of assent followed while O'Hara's blood froze in his veins. He had heard of this custom. He saw his friends slowly move closer but he raised his arm and managed to be heard.

"Not yet, fellahs. We got to have a little more whiskey. Isn't this good stuff? Right here from our own distillery at Suke's Run. Come on, Mr. Semple, fill 'em up again."

Anything to gain time, he thought, even as he realized in desperation that he and the townsmen would never be a match for the lewd element of the crowd.

"Hi, O'Hara, give me a hand here, will you?" It was Semple calling.

When he was close enough, Semple said under his breath, "I'm goin' to start a fight an' by God this is one I won't stop. When things get goin' you sneak out the back room here an' leg it for home as fast as you can. That's it," he added in full voice, "just carry one of these jugs around. I've got plenty whiskey, boys, so drink up now!"

It was only a few minutes until he stepped from behind his bar-counter and scanned the crowd carefully.

"I s'pose none of you keel-boaters would happen to be *Mike Fink*," he said.

One strapping man rose slowly, put down his noggin and shook himself.

"An' what would you be knowin' about Mike Fink?" he growled.

"Oh, no offense, no offense," Semple said amiably. "I just heard he was the best fighter on the river an' there wasn't a man could match him an' we haven't seen a good fight here for so long . . ."

The boatman came forward and pranced a few steps like a gamecock, then he took off his shirt and threw it behind him.

"Who's Mike Fink? I'll tell you I'm the best keeler that ever pushed a pole on the old Massassip! I'm a ring-tailed roarer! I'm half horse an' half cockeyed alligator an' the rest of me is red hot snappin' turkle! Whoop! I kin out-fight, no holts barred, ary man on both sides the river from Pittsburgh to N'Awlins an' back ag'in to St. Louiee. Come on, you damned greasy b'ar hunters. Is there a one of you that'll stand up to me? I'm spilin' for exercise."

One huge frontiersman, as broad as the boatman, got up and stripped off his shirt.

"Come along, boys," Semple called. "Push the tables an' the chairs out of the way. Make room for the fight . . . make room now."

Brackenridge, Smith and the others had caught the significance of the ruse at once. With a great show of moving the furniture they managed with loud talking to form a protective screen in front of the door to the back room. O'Hara weaved in and out among them, apparently intent only on preparing for the coming fight, then dexterously slipped unnoticed between them and on through the back room and out the window, not even waiting for the usual exit by way of the kitchen. He ran as for his life, never stopping until, breathless, he tapped at his own back door. McGrady opened it instantly and locked it carefully after him.

"No trouble here?" O'Hara asked him, panting.

"No suh. You had trouble where you was, suh?"

"A little. Think it's all right now. Just stay here, McGrady, and call me at the slightest noise. I don't need a candle."

He took his rifle from its hooks on the way. He would certainly not harm anyone but — if necessary a few shots might scare danger away. On the top stair he found Prudence crouching in the darkness.

"Thought I'd just wait till you was safe back, sir. She cried some after you left — just scared out of her wits, she was. She ain't used to the rough ways out here. But she went off to sleep like a baby at the last. Clean wore out, pore little soul."

"Thank you, Prudence, for staying with her. Everything will be safe now."

He went into the bedroom, closed the door, stripped to his nightshirt, laid his rifle on the floor by the bed and crept in between the sheets. Mary did not waken. He moved his hand to touch her hair and felt that her pillow was wet. His heart ached within him. This, on her first night in their new home! He was not exactly a praying man but he prayed then with a craving intensity that life would not be hard for her and that naught would affright her again for a long, long time.

He lay tensely listening. Once in a while came the echo of shouting voices. Then after the best of an hour there was silence. The quiet was all enveloping so that he could hear the deep, throaty flow of the Allegheny. He drew a long breath, blessing Samuel Semple! At least Mary had been saved from intolerable embarrassment which to her sensitive soul would have been shame. He turned carefully, put an arm around his bride, and he, too, fell asleep.

In the morning the events of the night were like a bad dream when it is past. The sun poured effulgently, a gentle Maytime breeze was blowing with the breath of the trees along the river stronger than it had been in the darkness. Mary and

O'Hara slept late and laughed from sheer happiness as they woke and looked at each other. After all they were young and in love and a bright new day was before them.

"I'm so sorry you were frightened last night at that crazy shivaree!" He tried to speak lightly.

"I guess it was because I was so tired and they *did* look so wild to me. But," she added, "as I think of it now it was a little bit funny too."

"Wasn't it?" he agreed quickly.

"Especially about your *nightshirt,*" she giggled.

"Oh, they may have rough manners, these frontiersmen, but most of them are good fellows."

"Did you treat them all?" she asked.

"Oh, yes. I had to spend quite a little, but it was worth it." He looked at her as she drew her shift over her white shoulders. "Yes," he added. "*Well* worth it."

Before they had finished breakfast they had a caller. Hugh Brackenridge came in, was properly presented and urged to have something to eat. He sat down, curbing his eagerness and ate heartily, his eyes resting admiringly upon Mary as he did so.

"Do you know, Mistress O'Hara, this husband of yours was in such a hurry to get home last night he didn't wait to see the fight!"

"Ah," said O'Hara blandly, "there was a fight, then?"

"My word," Hugh echoed, "was there a fight! The biggest I'll warrant ever seen in Pittsburgh!"

"How did it come out?" O'Hara asked.

"Well you see, Mistress O'Hara, there was this enormous keel-boater who gave the challenge and a fellah from the backwoods who's been out trading, about as big, took him up. We moved the furniture back," he glanced here at O'Hara who

winked in return, "and then they were at it. Never saw anything like it in all my life."

"And who won?"

"Well, you won't believe me but at the end the trader did.
The keel-boater was laid out flat. Semple threw a bucket of
water on him and even that didn't bring him to. The other
boaters carried him upstairs. Took four to do it. Everything
got quiet after that. We'd all had enough for one night."

"Oh," Mary said with a small shudder, "I think a fight like
that must be *terrible!*"

"Yes," said Hugh, "and yet I can think of certain occasions
when it might be — well — useful, can't you, O'Hara?"

"It's possible," O'Hara rejoined calmly. "But now if we're
all finished we'll have to show our things off, Mary. First of all,
the dresser!"

"You approve of it?" Hugh asked eagerly.

"Oh, we love it," she said. "How wonderfully kind of you
men to have it made for us. Mr. O'Hara is going to get my boxes
in from the wagon this morning and then I'll unpack the dishes
and set them in it. Shouldn't we take him into the parlor now?"

"By all means," O'Hara agreed. "We're really pretty proud
of ourselves, Hugh. Mr. Carson, Mary's father, gave us two
beautiful rugs and some furniture . . ."

He opened the door and Hugh stood looking with astonishment into the elegance before him.

"Great Heavens above!" he burst out. "Why, it looks like a
room back east! Isn't this what they call an Oriental?" pointing to the floor.

"Yes," Mary told him. "We have one in our bedroom too.
My father's a merchant so he has the chance to get good ones.
You really like it?"

"Whew!" he said for answer. "You'll have to expect the whole town to come to call when people hear about this. Only I'll warrant a good many will be afraid to step on the rug."

"Why, that's just what Prudence said." Mary laughed. "Won't you sit down now and be our first caller?"

"I'll come back another time if I may. I know you're both busy now. I just ran over early to tell O'Hara here about the fight. Since he didn't stay for it," he added with a side look. He held out his hand and bowed in a courtly way over Mary's. "It is the greatest pleasure to welcome you to Pittsburgh, ma'am, and I congratulate my friend here with all my heart."

"You are a bachelor, Mr. O'Hara tells me," she said.

"Unfortunately so."

"Then when you tire of your own cooking you must come and dine with us, mustn't he, James?"

"My dear lady, that is a most dangerous invitation — for you, I mean — but I'll try not to presume too much upon it. Thank you, though, very much indeed!"

O'Hara walked to the end of the lane with him, getting a few more details of the night before. But Hugh on the whole was grave.

"You're the very button on Fortune's cap, O'Hara," he said. "She's unbelievably pretty but it's more than that. Her manner, her charm! Her spirit shines out of her eyes. Well, you're one of the few men I know who deserves such a woman."

"No, no," O'Hara disclaimed violently. "Far from it. All you can say of me is that I *know* my good luck . . ." His voice was a bit unsteady. "And appreciate it to the full," he added. And then, "How are things with you?"

"Personal or professional?"

"Well, both."

"Personal couldn't be worse. I made an ass of myself a while back and will have to pay for it. Professionally I have hopes. I'm glad I settled for the law. I think there's a chance for a career here one day, though just to look at the place now nobody would believe it."

"Well, there have always been two of us who have had faith in Pittsburgh. Goodbye, Hugh. Come over often."

When the boxes were set into the kitchen, Mary in an enchanting ruffled apron (which was the cause of many private delays in the other room) began to unpack her "pretties" as O'Hara called them. There was a noble pair of brass candlesticks, two little lustre bowls and a Wedgwood teapot for the parlor mantel; and delicately embroidered cushions for the sofa. But to crown it all there were draperies for the two windows which had real panes of glass! O'Hara had given her the measure long before, and now when he with McGrady's help had put up the fixtures Mr. Carson had thoughtfully added, the soft folds of rose China silk fell on either side of the framework to the floor, in bright contrast to the white plastered logs. O'Hara himself was overcome by this last touch of luxury.

"Hugh is right, Mary. We're going to have plenty of callers when the word gets around. Of course I'll be proud as Punch to show off the house, but most of all my wife! You won't mind a deluge of visitors?"

"I'll love it," she said, her eyes sparkling. "To be hostess in my very own house! Oh, there I go again."

"That's right," he said. "I like to hear you say that. First and last it is *your* house. Now, I must get back to work."

They all worked to such good end that by supper it seemed as though the log dwelling had been occupied for years! Enough dishes to make a showing were ranged on the dresser shelves with the rest in the cupboard opposite; the napery was in the drawers; two turkey red cushions sat bright and inviting upon the rockers; clothes and bedding were unpacked and put in the closets upstairs; while all sorts of oddments and treasures were set in their places. These included a Bible and a volume of Shakespeare on the side table in the parlor! At the last and making a small ceremony of it, Mary set Agnes Denny's pewter plate upright in the center of the kitchen mantel.

"I think she would like it here where we'll be most of the time," she said. "I'll write and tell her."

The next morning O'Hara set out early on his own business. With him there was always the conviction that a relation existed between immediacy of action and ultimate success. He paid his bill at Semple's first of all, thanking him again for his inspiration for the fight, then went to the big trading store of Devereux Smith. There he leaned upon the counter, drew in the familiar, heavy smells of forest and fur and got the news of the town after they, too, had gone over the details of the night before.

"Still interested in real estate, O'Hara?"

"I am indeed. What's the latest on that?"

"Well, Isaac Craig and Stephen Bayard, you know, were, up till lately, officers at the Fort but now they've sort of gone into partnership for the mercantile business though really I think to deal in land and lots. They first bought three acres down at the Point between the rivers from the Penns and the last word I got was that they own the land now that the Fort stands on!"

"The devil they do," O'Hara ejaculated.

"But," Smith went on, "we understand they're actually working for a Philadelphia firm, Turnbull, Marmie & Company is the name. They've all got their sights set on Fort Pitt. I reckon the whole place will have to be sold eventually but I'll hate to see it go."

"General Irvine still in charge?"

"Going back to Carlisle in the fall, I hear. Good man, though. Kept order, kept everything in repair, and such gardens! Well, anyway there's a bit more to this real estate business. The Penns hired George Woods from Bedford to come over and survey the town and what a pretty sight it is on paper! You wouldn't believe it! Streets marked out and named for the old settlers. *Smithfield* is one. Now put that in your pipe and smoke it!"

O'Hara laughed. "I'm impressed no end, especially since you deserve it."

"The lots look as neat as a checkerboard. You'd never guess there was a loose hog on any of them. And Craig told me he and Bayard have bought up thirty-seven!"

O'Hara whistled. "Where can I see this plan?"

"Oh, there are several copies around. As a matter of fact, *I've* got one myself. I was just waiting to bring it out!"

They pored over it together, discussing locations. "I'll be writing to the Penns tonight," O'Hara said. "Could I be borrowing this, just until morning? And then I've another matter I want your advice upon."

"Shoot! Advice is the cheapest of all commodities!"

"I've decided to set up in a store."

"A *store!* My word, man, won't that be quite a comedown from all your other activities?"

"A little, perhaps. But I like any kind of trade, any form of business. And the point is I must do something at once. My idea would be to sell necessities, of course, but work in some luxuries too. I believe people would buy them. And there's migration out here now that the

lown to be a storekeeper the rest

st for the present. I expect some-

o. At least I have a feeling . . .

y be able to turn a fairly pretty

cghed, "I wouldn't be surprised.

ant spots if either of them appeal

e."

tch?"

has always been mostly with the

ive the river a fling. He sold out

and he's gone on the old *Massas-*

ight called it. Oh, and Billy, the

ot homesick and they went back

bigger but not in as good a loca-

added another request with his

mily over soon to see Mary. The

few more may wait a while. You

t — but I don't want her to get

"I can hardly hold my women-

D'Hara turned again.

about Guyasuta? Where he is?"

care. That's where he ought to

ss hit me hard. Mike Huffnagle

VERDES NEWS — Rolling H

e Home Refle
on's Art Colle

between the tiles. Excess ce-
ment is washed from the
surface and, after drying, the
section is permanently affixed.

An amateur mosaicist, Dr.
Davis researched his project at
UCLA. He likes to reserve an
hour a day for work on it and to
complete one section a week
when time permits, along with
other projects in the uncomple-
ted home.

Other high points of interest
in the Davis home are the red
tiled family room with its
cathedral ceiling, eight and
one-half by seven foot stone
fireplace, the original of which
is in the Uguccioni palazzo in
Florence; and the Adam living
room. Here the senior Davis
departed from the Mediterr-
anean influence to create an
18th Century setting for the
white marble Adam fireplace
which, according to Davis, dates
circa 1776.

The room is round and features five paried Ionic pilasters
set against wood panelling in
a soft walnut tone. The ceiling is
a gold dome with a white cor-
nice displaying a della robbia
carved frieze of fruits and
flowers. The fireplace, with
classical figures and motifs in
high relief, holds a marble bust
of a Roman woman reflected in
a gold leaf, carved frame

was in the other day. It was in his field, you know, that the men were harvesting when it all happened. He says some of the folks went back east and of course I know some have gone through here on their way to the Ohio country. A pretty heart-sick business, the whole thing. Even *for the frontier,* it was bad. And if I were you I wouldn't make too many inquiries about Guyasuta."

By the end of the week O'Hara had rented the ropewalk. It was a long, low narrow building, but with a new floor and shelves along either side it would make an unusual but to him perfect store. His shrewd sense had at once informed him that by the time a customer had walked the length of it, her eye would have been caught up by many articles she had never set out to buy. I believe, he thought with a twinkle, I'll put the *necessities* at the back. He got hold of a carpenter and with his own help and that of McGrady the store room was ready in a month. There was even some merchandise on the shelves, se-cured by O'Hara's own miraculous (and bordering upon the devious) methods: some things from a storekeeper in Greens-burg who was hard pushed to meet his creditors; a load from Bedford where there had been a fire; and some choice bits from other Pittsburgh stores which had been bought up by O'Hara's emissaries and then set up on his own shelves to the annoyance of their original owners. Orders of course had gone off to Philadelphia and also to New Orleans.

But while the store became a going concern as the summer weeks passed, the house in the King's Orchard had grown so rapidly in popularity it was like to die of it! They came, the rich (comparatively speaking) and the poor; the aristocrats of the town and the shabby, toil-hardened women, starved for beauty. These latter appeared shyly at the kitchen at all sorts of odd hours, were received with warm kindness by Mary, taken to the door of the parlor where they feasted their tired eyes upon its elegance, though, as had been predicted, could not be persuaded to set foot upon the wonder of the carpet. Afterward they were urged to have a cup of tea at the trestle table or perhaps in a red cushioned rocking chair where their tongues became loosed and they told Mary the problems of their lives and begged hungrily for details of her own, back in Philadelphia.

One element of such visits afforded Mary and O'Hara riotous merriment.

"All of these women," she told him, "ask if they can go out and see the . . ." She pointed toward the small whitewashed edifice at the back. "I do believe they're more impressed by that than by the Oriental!"

"They'd probably rather have it," he laughed.

But at the other end of the scale came Pittsburgh's elite, to the parlor door, at four o'clock in the afternoon. These Mary received with dignity in one of her trousseau gowns, sat at the side table and poured tea into thin cups which Prudence in a white apron passed. It was not Philadelphia, but oh, it was close enough to make it apparent that a new young hostess had come to town who must be treated with respect. And Mary on her part reached eagerly out to these women who she knew would be her closest friends as time went on: Margaret Neville, Rachel Craig, Elizabeth Smith, Jessie Brison, the nearest to her in age, wife of the personable would-be young politician who like O'Hara and Brackenridge had a fixed faith in Pittsburgh. These and more she tried to remember carefully and think of when the sight of the village itself dampened her spirits.

One night she and O'Hara sat in the wing chairs facing each

other, he with tablet and pencil, she with a sock on the needles. He was making out a new order and had found already that Mary's advice was excellent. Indeed, he had been more and more amazed by her good judgment in their daily affairs. So now he read over to her what he had written as a beginning:

    2 barrels sugar
    6 casks sherry wine
    1 keg allspice
    6 half gallon coffee pots
    12 blankets
    Soap and candles — amount to be filled in later.
    12 wash basins
    12 sets knives and forks

"And what now do you suggest, Mary?"

"Well," she said thoughtfully, "I would add one dozen best Bibles, some thread, sewing silk, shoe buckles, writing paper, looking glasses if you can get them, some playing cards, and *six dozen finger bowls!*"

"Darling, are you mad? *Finger bowls* out here?"

"Just what we need," she said. "You want some luxuries to put on your shelves. These will give all the women who can't use them something to talk about. And after I've had a dinner party and used mine you'll find you have a rush sale on, from the others. I know women! Oh, *do* order the finger bowls! It will be fun!"

O'Hara laughed. "Well, that's one article I would have felt we could do nicely without, but you may be right at that. It will certainly make talk and that in turn makes business. Well, let's finish the list tomorrow. I'm tired tonight."

He sat watching her. She had changed subtly during the

summer. Her beauty seemed enhanced, and there was added a new poise, a gentle assurance, a trace of maturity.

"Oh, Mary," he burst out suddenly, "don't grow up too soon!"

She looked at him, her eyes bright with laughter. "*Grow up!* Why, Mr. O'Hara, I'm a married woman, with a husband and a house and a household and . . . and everything!"

The dark lashes rested on her cheeks which were now pure rose. "*And everything!*" she repeated softly.

For one second he sat as though stunned, then he crossed to her, knelt down and put his arms about her waist.

"Oh, my dear Delight . . . I can't believe . . ."

She cupped his startled face with her hands.

"Considering . . . I mean, in view of . . . I mean I don't think you should be *too* surprised if what I suspect is true!"

CHAPTER NINE

I T WAS strange, Mary often remarked, that time passed more quickly here in Pittsburgh than it had back in Philadelphia. The days flowed into weeks and even the months were caught in the same swift current.

"It's because so much is happening, I guess," she said once, "and we always seem to be in the middle of it, somehow."

"Don't you like that?" O'Hara asked quickly.

"You know I do," she replied, laughing. "I never dreamed I would feel so important. Do you remember the night we sat on the bench under the locust trees beside the river and planned that the motto for our home was to be *hospitality?* It was just before little William was born."

"Yes," O'Hara said gravely. "I remember."

As a matter of fact his recollection of that evening and of the day and night that followed was still all too clear in his mind, for the primeval curse of Eve had fallen heavily then upon Mary's slender body. During the months before she had been completely well and happier than he had ever seen her, teasing him gently about his solicitude.

"Not that I don't love you for it all," she would say, "but there's really nothing to fear."

On the day when he sat in the parlor with Dr. Nathaniel Bedford, however, listening to the subdued cries and moans from the bedroom above, he was wild with it.

"I've got to go up there, Doctor!"

"No, no. That's no place for you. Prudence is as good as any midwife, and I'll go up again presently."

"But how long is this . . . this likely to go on?"

"Can't tell with the first one. Could be till tomorrow morning."

"My God! She couldn't stand that!"

"Oh, yes. Women do. Don't ask me how, but they get through it. Most of them."

O'Hara pounced. "What do you mean, *most of them?*"

"Well now, be reasonable. Considering the number of babies born there's not too much goes wrong. But of course once in a while . . ."

O'Hara leaped to his feet. "I'm going up," he said. "I certainly had a part in the beginning of this and I'm going to stand by her now at the end of it."

"Tut! Tut!" the doctor said. "Sit down and behave yourself. *I* know husbands. You're likely thinking now there'll never be another if it's like this, but when the baby's safe here you'll forget all about that and have your wife pregnant again in two or three months. *I* know. I've seen it happen too often."

O'Hara gave him one terrible look and made for the stairs while the doctor muttered, "Most cantankerous young man I ever ran into."

Prudence, on her way down, tried to fend him off.

"No, Mr. O'Hara. That ain't any place for you up there. The doctor's the only man . . ."

He pushed her aside none too gently and took the steps two at a time. At the bedroom door he paused a second to quiet the beating of his heart, before he went in. Mary lay, already white and spent, her face dripping with the sweat of her travail in the unseasonably warm May afternoon. As she saw O'Hara she reached her arms with a pitiful cry.

"Oh James, you've come to me! Prudence said it wasn't seemly . . ."

"Seemly or not, darling, I'm here and I'll not leave you for a minute until this is all over."

"I can bear it better when I have you. Will it be . . . much . . . longer?"

"No," O'Hara lied stoutly. "Of course not. Oh my dear Delight, hold on to me if it helps. Can you smell the locusts?" For the fragrance was sweet upon the air.

"No," she whispered weakly.

The anguished hours went on through the evening, through the night, until before the dawn Dr. Bedford's face was as grave as O'Hara's own. Then at daybreak with a last expulsive agony while Mary's arms held tightly around her husband's neck and his own supported her, the baby was born and a new cry was heard upon the earth.

"It's a boy," the doctor announced, now with calm assurance. "A fine boy. Here you are, Prudence, clean him up and then they can have a look at him."

Mary lay unheeding, her eyes closed, small shuddering breaths coming from her. "Will she be all right?" O'Hara asked anxiously without glancing toward his son.

"Yes, yes," Dr. Bedford smiled at him. "Let her rest a while. When she sees her baby she'll perk up fast enough. What about you? You'd better get yourself a good slug of whiskey. You look as though you'd had the labor pains yourself."

When the new parents finally looked together upon the small creature born to them, O'Hara gave the name. Before this Mary had evaded any selection. "Let's wait," she always insisted. Now O'Hara spoke it plainly. "I would like to call him William Carson if you are agreed."

"Oh, Father will be so pleased! But would you not like to have a *James,* after you?"

"Perhaps," he said smiling, "in due time." Then as though Dr. Bedford were listening, *"in due time,"* he repeated with emphasis.

It was that fall that they had their first overnight guest. The second smaller room upstairs had been nicely fitted out, for the store was prospering as O'Hara's friends had predicted, and Mary's fine taste made good use of the money available.

In addition to the newly furnished bed-chamber another piece of fine living now graced their home: this was the Irish table which had come over sea and mountains in time for their first wedding anniversary. O'Hara was tremendously moved at sight of it, and Mary was thrilled beyond measure. She even knelt to caress the shamrock feet.

"There's such an elegance about it," she kept saying, "and such a difference from anything I've ever seen. I'm so *proud* of this, James!"

One afternoon when O'Hara was working in the store with McGrady a man walked in. It was John Wilkins from Carlisle. O'Hara wrung his hand for they met as old friends.

"What a surprise!" he said. "What brings you here?"

The other man looked grim.

"Glad to see you again, O'Hara, but I'm a bit discouraged. I decided a while back to move to Pittsburgh. More opportunity here, I heard, so I came ahead to spy out the land as it were before I brought my family. From what I've seen so far I think I'll stay in Carlisle."

O'Hara laughed. "Don't be hasty. I suppose you've noticed the dirt."

"*Noticed* it!" Wilkins exclaimed. "There's a hog in every mud puddle. There's a poor seedy look about the whole place. Plenty of taverns I can see with drunken Indians rolling out the doors and not the sight of a *church*. Is there one?"

"Not yet," O'Hara admitted, "but we . . ."

"What makes you think this town will ever be anything more than it is now?"

O'Hara drew him outside and pointed to the confluence of the two great rivers at the Point.

"That!" he said.

"Oh, you mean the location here?"

"I do. I doubt if there's a better one in the country outside of the eastern harbors. And look over there." He pointed across the muddy Monongahela to the hill which rose mountain high just beyond it. "That hill is full of coal. And some day . . ." His keen eyes narrowed as if he already saw into the future. "Some day I hope to get into manufacturing and if I do I'll use *coal*. I hope I'll be the first man to do it, but," he added laughing, "you can bet I won't be the last!"

"Well," Wilkins conceded slowly, "there may be something to what you say but I'm still quite disappointed in the town."

"Come home with me to dinner and we can talk it all over. I want you to meet my wife."

"Agnes Denny says she's a beauty."

"She's that and more. Have you engaged a tavern room yet?"

"No. I inquired for you and came right here."

"Good. We've got a guest room. I want to hear all about

Carlisle so we'll make a night of it. Come back to the store now and I'll send a message to my wife to put an extra potato in the pot."

He dispatched two notes, as a matter of fact, with McGrady, the second being to Hugh Brackenridge.

Hugh: Come to dinner and help convince John Wilkins of Carlisle that Pittsburgh is more than a pigsty. Bring all your eloquence and *wear your best breeks*. J. O'H.

When O'Hara and his guest reached the house in the King's Orchard the latter's eyes opened wide. They became still wider as dinner was served in the parlor at the Irish table with Mary in a tight bodiced rose dress, O'Hara in a fresh vest and Brackenridge in *knee breeches!* The conversation was lively from the start. A skimming of national politics first; the necessity for a strong central government with a President. Jefferson? Hamilton? Franklin perhaps? General Washington topped them all, they agreed. Hugh and Wilkins discussed pro and con the beginnings of a *party* to be made up of those who championed a Constitution. Alexander Hamilton and John Adams were at the head of it and if it finally got organized the members were to be known as *Federalists*.

"I'll join up with that," O'Hara said quickly. "I'm for a Constitution as fast as we can get one. Something's got to hold us together now or we'll fall to pieces. In spite of the *peace*," he punned.

There was, indeed, between more serious topics a great deal of witty chaffing from Brackenridge and O'Hara and the recounting of jokes, the one from Wilkins, though, being pronounced the best of the evening.

"You remember, Mrs. O'Hara, when your husband went

back east a year ago to do some buying for his store?"

"I surely do," Mary answered. "It was the first time we had been separated since our wedding."

"Well, he stopped over night in Carlisle and a few of his old friends — Eb Denny, Dicky Butler and I — went to the tavern after dinner to visit with him. There were several strangers stopping there, officers, who joined the group. One of them, a right handsome young blade, spoke up and said to your husband, 'Captain, you talk of Philadelphia. Did you ever happen to meet pretty Polly Carson when you were there?' Of course Eb and Dicky and I were biting our pipe stems, waiting for the fun. 'Oh,' says your husband, 'you haven't heard that she married last spring?' 'The devil she did,' said this fellow. 'Who married her?' 'Why,' said O'Hara here, cool as you please, 'Parson Brown, I believe, of the Locust Street Presbyterian Church.' 'Come, come,' says the fellow, 'you know I don't mean that. Whom did she marry?' 'Well, if you must know, sir,' says your husband, 'she married *me!*' "

After the laughter Mary looked across the table.

"You never told me that story, Mr. O'Hara."

His eyes twinkled. "I guess I was afraid the man was one of your old beaux!"

"And there were plenty of them, I'll warrant, eh Mistress?" Wilkins said with admiration.

"Perhaps," Mary answered demurely, "but there was only one that ever mattered."

Hugh slapped the table. "By my faith, prettily spoken, that! For the thousandth time I congratulate my friend here."

With this, Mary rose, on pretext of attending to her baby, and left the gentlemen to their port. When they were settled finally in the easy chairs, O'Hara gave Hugh a side glance and he began at once to speak of Pittsburgh and his own ambitions for it.

"Of course we do need a *church!*" he said.

Wilkins was at once interested.

"Now, that's the thing I missed as I first looked around. You think there is the possibility of one?"

"Definitely," said O'Hara. "A group of us have been planning already. One of our most prominent families here are the Nevilles, but they're Episcopalians. However most of the others are Scotch-Irish and if you scratch their skins you know you'll find Presbyterians."

"The Penns reserved lots for the various congregations," Hugh put in, "and ours has a fine big tree on it which I picture standing by the side of the front door of the church. If you come to reside here, you would be of enormous help I know in promoting a building."

"It would certainly be a project of the greatest interest to me," Wilkins said slowly.

"Good!" said Hugh. "We'll count on you," as though Wilkins' coming was now assured. "But I have two other irons on the fire," he went on. "I want this town to have a *newspaper* and an *Academy!* I think I've got a Philadelphia printer lined up already, but he can't come out for another year. Then we'll have to have an editor . . ."

"Mr. Brackenridge, may I ask what your business is?"

"I'm a lawyer, sir."

"You mean you have enough work to keep you busy here?"

"Pretty much. And I'm not the only one either. You see, Mr. Wilkins, the *law* whether broken or kept is an integral part of the life of every civilized community. And, I might add, the degree of civilization in any place depends upon the quality of the citizens and not," here he grinned at the older man, "upon the number of hogs running loose."

"You've hit me fair!" Wilkins said. "I judged hastily. But you'll admit the general outlook here leaves much to be desired. But go on, Mr. Brackenridge. You speak of an *Academy?*"

"Oh, that's the thing nearest to my heart. *Liberty and Learning!* That's my motto. You know the only type of school we have at the present? A Mrs. Pride opened classes for girls, spreading the word that she would teach needlework, and *Reading, English and Knitting* if required! There's education for you. Well, I've got a beginning made for an Academy though it may be several years before we can incorporate. I've got some trustees promised and we have our fingers on two lots between Second and Third streets, off Smithfield. It will be small at the start, but so was Princeton. Who knows but my little Academy may turn into a University one day, too! That's what I like about being a part of a young, growing town. The possibilities of the future are unlimited."

The port was excellent. The men mellowed. As the hours passed Pittsburgh grew, industry developed, learning flourished, elegant brick houses took the place of ramshackle log cabins, great vessels left the docks to sail around the world . . . the picture grew more vividly real as midnight turned into morning. When at last Hugh got up to go Wilkins had reached a decision. He would find a place to live and bring on his family. O'Hara handed him his candle and wished him good night.

"I'll walk Hugh to the end of the lane to be sure he doesn't get lost in the city we've just built," he said, grinning.

When they were out in the crisp autumn air under the

apple trees he went on, "We've got ourselves a fine new citizen tonight. Thanks for your part in it."

"I've had too much port," Hugh said irritably. "My head is fuzzy and my legs aren't steady. For the love of heaven, you'd think my Scotch blood would take care of me better than this."

"You should have mixed it with a little Irish," O'Hara rejoined, grabbing his arm.

"What I want is a *wife*," Hugh burst out suddenly to O'Hara's surprise.

"Best wish in the world. Anyone in mind?"

"Yes, but it's hopeless."

"Don't ever say hopeless to me in matters of love," O'Hara said. "Do you want to talk about it?"

"Yes. Maybe it's the port, but anyway I'll tell you. A few weeks ago a farmer from out here, fifteen or twenty miles back, came to see me about a boundary dispute with his neighbor. Well, I rode out one day to look over the land, and — the man had a daughter."

"Some men do," O'Hara murmured.

"Now the Lord never cut me out for a celibate. I've proved that in plenty of predicaments but I tell you, O'Hara, I never felt about any girl as I feel about that one. Just looking at her, mind you, I knew I wanted her for my wife. She's the opposite of Mary, dark instead of fair, but as pretty in her own way I think, and with such a spirit in her eyes! I think she felt something too, for if my blood was hot so were her cheeks. But . . . I'm trying to be sensible."

"*Sensible!*" O'Hara fairly shouted it. "When was a man in love ever sensible? What's wrong with you? Go after her and never stop till you get her!"

"It wouldn't work, O'Hara. She's completely unlettered. She can read and that's about it. All she knows is to milk a cow. And I've got ambitions. I'm going into politics. I want a nice home eventually and a wife who can preside at my table and speak the King's English. Put yourself in my place. You can see then that I must forget her. And yet . . . as we stood in her father's pasture looking at each other, something struck fire between us. So, you have my story."

The young men had stopped on the edge of the Orchard and stood now in silence. The little town itself was still except for the mournful tinkle of a cowbell occasionally from the field beside Suke's Run. At last O'Hara spoke.

"If I were you, Hugh, I would go back to see this girl. Often. Make sure that you love each other. If you do I'd marry her and then send her back to Philadelphia to a good school for a year."

"What an utterly mad idea," Hugh groaned angrily.

"No, it isn't. She has looks you say and a spirit that would indicate intelligence. Able to pick things up quickly. She probably has common sense and good womanly qualities. What she lacks is the outward polish. In the right kind of school she'd get this in a year. *You* know. Manners, speech, some social graces, with a little literature and such thrown in! Mary would know the right place. Well, if I had this problem that's the way I'd handle it."

"Do you suppose a girl would agree to such a plan?"

O'Hara chuckled. "You're not unattractive Hugh, my lad. Marry her first and show her what love can be like. I think probably then she would do anything to please you."

"Well," Hugh said after a pause, "you're either a damn fool or a genius, O'Hara. On second thought I believe you might be the latter. In any case I'll go home now and sleep on it."

"Can you make it back alone?"

"Oh, sure. The night air has cleared my head. If it hadn't, your suggestion would have knocked me stone sober. Thanks for everything. Good night."

The guest room, which Mary had so charmingly furnished, continued to be occupied with such frequency that the tavern keepers twitted O'Hara about stealing their custom. It was all in good sport, however, for it was generally conceded that elite strangers should be directed to O'Hara's store from whence they would eventually be taken to the house in The King's Orchard. This, not only for the greater comfort of the guests, but for the greater glory of Pittsburgh.

One stranger scared Mary out of her wits at first. Upon answering a knock at the kitchen door she saw a large man with a face so swarthy it was almost black, accoutered with four belts around him, two brace of pistols, a sword, a rifle over his shoulder, a pouch and a huge tobacco pipe! He introduced himself as General Peter Muhlenberg whom O'Hara had sent on to the house since he himself was detained at the store.

But the odd looking man proved most entertaining. He was on his way to the Falls of the Ohio to locate lands in Virginia for the officers and soldiers of the Virginia line in Continental service. His interest in the Indians was deep-seated for his grandfather was Conrad Weiser who had held conferences with the red men forty years before! There was, naturally, much to discuss between him and O'Hara.

So the picturesque transients came and went, contributing as O'Hara and Mary agreed, a richness to their living and a new meaning to the hospitality for which they were growing famous.

One afternoon O'Hara came home to find Elliott sitting on the back stoop whittling a small horse. He glanced up and gave a characteristic greeting.

"Started this damn thing on too small a piece of wood. Not going to have a tail for the beast."

"Elliott!" O'Hara exclaimed. "Man, I'm glad to see you! Where have you been all this time? When did you get in? Are you going to stay a while?"

"Hear you've got a store."

"Yes. It's not bad either and business is growing. Want a job?" He laughed as he said this, but Elliott was serious.

"My gammy leg's been kickin' up lately. I'm afraid I'll have to give up tradin'. But behind a counter now I might look right smart. You know I'm a devil with the ladies."

O'Hara sat down and threw an arm round his shoulder.

"You're always heaven-sent, Elliott. How do you know to turn up just when I need you?"

Elliott didn't answer this. Instead he looked up and smiled. "I've met the Missus an' I must say you've done yourself proud, O'Hara."

They ate in the kitchen and then settled comfortably afterwards around the fire, the men with their pipes, Mary with her knitting listening avidly to their stories, especially the ones of their first trip to Pittsburgh. Of those details she couldn't hear enough: the death of the moose, the shooting of the bear *and the panther* which still in rug form lay beside her bed. She let her knitting fall idle as O'Hara told of their night in the pioneer cabin where he had described the Bingham ball.

"I suppose," she remarked with a twinkle, "you didn't tell *everything*."

"Oh, I omitted a few details," he said, and even as they

looked at each other Elliott did not seem to be shut out, as he joined in the laughter too, guessing the reason.

A closeness fell upon the three. When the fire grew low it was Elliott who got up casually and put a new log on, as though after long wanderings he had come home.

"Ever run into Guyasuta since I saw you?" O'Hara asked.

"Yep. Once. He mentioned you, by the way. Said he'd like to see you again but didn't know whether he would be welcome."

"You heard about Hannastown?"

"Yes. I don't know how the old buck got into that but do you know what he's got in his craw now?"

"No more depredations, I hope," O'Hara said sharply.

"No, no. I think he's mebbe quietened down a little. He told me he's decided to settle over here across the Allegheny and spend the rest of his days there. I don't know how the town will take to that."

"Not very kindly, I imagine. Is he coming soon?"

"Not for a couple years, he said. Ever seen him, Mrs. O'Hara?"

"No. I've just heard of him many times. What's he like?"

As the two descriptions continued they were decidedly at variance.

"A crafty lookin' customer," from Elliott.

"A really noble face!" from O'Hara.

"Just plain Injun if you ask me."

"I think he's rather handsome! Oh, I guess you'd better wait till you see him, Mary," O'Hara added, laughing. "Then you can make up your own mind."

With the perceptiveness that constantly surprised and delighted her husband Mary sensed the bond between the two men, and when Elliott rose to go back to Semple's she held out her hand.

"I want you to know, Mr. Elliott, that you will always be welcome in our home."

He looked down at her, his keen eyes softening.

"Those are nice words, ma'am, for a lonely man to hear. I thank you."

The next morning he was at the store when O'Hara got there. By noon it seemed as though he had been there from the start. He ambled around, learning the stock, making suggestions, greeting customers in his easy fashion. In between busy moments he and O'Hara talked of Indian affairs which were in a bad way. In spite of the fact that peace was concluded and a treaty signed, the British still held fortified posts in the north and west, and the officers stationed there were evidently encouraging the Indians to stop the American advance if they could, for the attacks kept growing in number and ferocity all the time.

"Even here it's been too close for comfort," O'Hara said. "The settlers around have been having trouble, and a month ago a band of the Senecas, we think, tried to shoot up the Fort! There aren't many men on duty there now but they managed to scare the Injuns off."

"What do you think it's going to be? More treaties an' speeches or an all out war?"

"Both would be my guess. I hear some Commissioners have been appointed to go out and talk things over. But the trouble is, Elliott, there's too much right on each side to make the one or the other give way. Here are the Americans, veterans of the Continental Army, paid off in western lands instead of cash. They're going to go out there and claim them. And they should. The West has to be settled. On the other hand there are the Indians pushed out of what they naturally feel are *their* lands. Never sure the promises made to them will be kept. They've been fooled too often. A bad business all around."

"And you think it'll be a big fight at the end?"

"I don't see how things will ever be quiet without."

"What if the Injuns win?"

"They can't in the long run but it'll be bloody bad in between. I got word General Josiah Harmar is going to come out with some troops to safeguard the Commissioners and then stay to take command of the federal forces north of the Ohio. Elliott?"

"What?"

"I'm more glad than I can tell you that you're here. If I should have to be away you could run the store and keep a watch over Mary. I still think it's a miracle that you always appear at the right time. Is it because you keep track of what I'm up to?"

"What makes you think you'll have to be away?" Elliott parried.

"Oh," O'Hara grinned, "my prophetic Irish soul, and a few hints in letters from back east. I may get mixed up with this thing. Well, anyway, it won't be for a while, I imagine."

But the call came sooner than he expected in the shape of a message from General Knox of the War Department, requesting that O'Hara become contractor for furnishing provisions to Harmar's western army as well as providing things "necessary for the table and support of the Commissioners" during their negotiations with the Indians.

He read the letter to Mary who looked back at him with astonishment and alarm.

"What would this mean, James?"

"Well," he said slowly, "it would mean the hardest appointment I've ever had so far. To provision an army in the wilderness is a tremendous undertaking. To collect the supplies will be difficult enough but the transportation problems will be the worst. I wonder," he added consideringly, "if it can partly be done by boat."

"Will you be among the Indians?"

"Oh, yes, of course. Somewhat. The idea of having the Commissioners go out is to talk with them and try to make treaties, and I'll be with these men sometimes at least. I know the dialects."

"Will there be danger?" she pursued.

He smiled at her tenderly. "Dear Delight, there is always a certain amount of danger in the wilderness. I suppose," he said, his visional eyes looking off beyond her, "that even when the country is built up with towns and cities there will still be dangers. Not rattlesnakes nor Indians but others. Why, darling, you laughed at me for thinking there might be danger for you in childbirth. Well there will only be about the same degree for me in this project."

Mary had been sewing quilt patches together. She laid her work on the kitchen table and walked over to the fire, and stood, looking into it.

"It is settled then?" she said, without turning. "You have no choice in the matter?"

"I'm afraid not. After all, I've been an officer in the army. This order comes from the War Department. I couldn't respect myself much if I refused it."

He went over to her and took her in his arms. "Is it all right? I will have to be away of course but not for too long at a time. By the very nature of the work I'll have to come back to Pittsburgh often for supplies. So, you see, it won't be too bad."

Mary met his eyes.

"You *want* to do this, James, don't you?"

He hesitated. "I needn't tell you that I don't want to be separated from you even for a little. But as to the work, I would like to try it. It's a tremendous thing they've asked of me. It's a challenge sure enough and I like the feel of that. Then — not to blow my own horn — it *is* a pretty big compliment. It implies the government liked my work before. Yes, I want to do it if it's possible."

"And besides you are bored with the store."

He looked down at her in amazement. "How did you ever guess that?"

"I know you pretty well by now, Mr. O'Hara," she smiled.

"You're uncanny. Yes, I'm bored with the store even though it's doing well. Now, Elliott can look after it with McGrady's help and make himself a living and we'll still get some income from it. But about this contractor business, I'll naturally be honest, scrupulously honest, but I'm sure I'll still make money at it! Will it really be all right with you if I go ahead?"

She stood as she had done years ago in the library back home, twisting a button of his waistcoat.

"I told you once I'd be willing to travel to the world's end with you," she said. "Now I guess my part as a wife is to be content at home while you do the traveling. That's harder but I'll try."

Events from then on moved so swiftly that even O'Hara with his predilection for speed was staggered. His own letter of acceptance was followed by others from the War Department, one from Robert Morris in Philadelphia relating to his salary and one from General Harmar.

But most thrilling of all was information about the Commissioners themselves who under the protection of the troops would arrive in Pittsburgh in a month's time, before going on to their conferences at the western forts. For he learned then that among these men were Dicky Butler and *George Rogers Clark!* It was incredible, O'Hara told Mary jubilantly, that he was going to see Clark again and oh, certainly have him in their home. But in this new world it was the unbelievable which always happened! Clark did not write. He wouldn't. But Dicky Butler whom O'Hara admired deeply said in his letter that he and Arthur Lee, another of the Commissioners, had written to Robert Morris, the Secretary of Finance, to be sure there would be no slip-up, asking that "the articles which we have noted as necessary should be purchased by Mr. O'Hara, *in whom we can confide.*"

Mary read this aloud over and over and while her husband told her she was unduly proud it was evident that his own heart was warmed by the praise.

The work was heavy. In addition to the order for army provisions the state, wishing to convince the natives that she could furnish the best assortment of goods for them, demanded that O'Hara procure a goodly supply of suitable articles for the Indians. So once more he was combing the other local stores and sending back to Philadelphia for brooches, arm bands, knives, bridles, ribbons and finger rings. He added coats, blankets and ruffled shirts from his own stock. All of these he packed, marked, numbered and placed in the back of his store until the arrival of the Commissioners.

When they came with their guarding troops, General Harmar elected to camp on the level ground on the other side of the Allegheny, and O'Hara ferried across at once to see them. His meeting with Clark was almost violent in its mutual delight. They gripped hands, they slapped each other on the back, they laughed uproariously in sheer pleasure.

"Dad Drabit!" Clark kept saying with his red hair rampant, "if I ain't glad to see you, you old son of a gun! And when we're not up to our chins in water, either!"

O'Hara and Mary had carefully planned the entertainment they wished to give. It would be impossible to have *all* the Commissioners to dinner, so it was decided to invite Clark, Dicky Butler and Harmar for the meal itself at which Mary would be present. Then she would retire as she had done before and the guests from the town, General John Neville, Major Isaac Craig, Devereux Smith, John Wilkins and of course Hugh Brackenridge, would be asked to come in for port and an evening's talk.

"We can't have the wives," Mary said as they discussed it. "In the first place we haven't enough chairs and in the second place you men will be freer to visit without us. While you are away I'll entertain the women. I'll have teas and maybe a nice quilting party for them. So that will even it up."

"You're right, as usual," O'Hara agreed and proceeded at once with his invitations which were promptly accepted.

On the night itself Mary bloomed as she always did under excitement, the parlor was fresh from its extra dusting and polish and the Irish table bore with grace her finest china and silver. The dinner guests were all impressed, but Clark was ebullient. He was all over the house. He must see everything. Then he would come back to gaze at Mary.

"You've a fine place here and no mistake. And you've got a good man too. I've seen him in some tight fixes and he stood up mighty well. Whether he deserves anything as nice as *you,* Ma'am, I wouldn't know. Dad Drabit," he added turning to wink at O'Hara, "you'd better behave yourself pretty good the rest of your life or I'll come back and knock the gizzard out of you."

Dinner was gay with many reminiscences of the war, some of which made O'Hara look a bit anxiously at his wife. But Mary took them all in good part and laughed with the rest. The one which amused them all the most was Clark's description of the night the Governor of Kaskaskia and his wife had wakened to find four men surrounding their bed.

"And of course we all looked like the devil," he said. "Dirty and ragged and beards an inch long. All of us over six feet and Simon Kenton and me with red hair sticking out all over to make us seem wilder. But you didn't look too smart yourself, O'Hara, as I recall."

When the laughter died down, he went on. "But the thing I never got over was how Madame Rocheblave foxed us. We took him right into custody but we left her by herself to get dressed and all. Felt that was only polite. And Dad Drabit, if she didn't steal all the British papers and we never did find them! Well, it taught me one thing. It don't always pay to be a gentleman."

When Mary rose at last to leave them the men bowed as low over her hand as though they were in a Philadelphia drawing room. Then there were knocks both at the parlor and the kitchen doors and the guests from the town arrived. When General Harmar talked to O'Hara a few days later he spoke with amazement and pleasure of that evening.

"I had no idea," he said, "of the quality of your leading citizens here! The East couldn't produce any better. I think this town is going to grow, Captain."

The first conference was to be held at Cuyahoga on the bank

of Lake Erie in November and O'Hara had finally decided that
since the waterways did not quite connect he would have to
transport everything by pack horses and go across the country
with the troops. He was working each day from dawn till dark,
coming in at night exhausted, for a late supper during which
Mary entertained him with little William's latest accomplish-
ments, the town news or letters from the east. Agnes Denny
wrote that Eb was definitely coming to Pittsburgh that fall; her
father said that Philadelphia was moving now in its old groove,
business fairly good, society very gay, politics on the rampage
with him and most of his friends in favor of getting the Federalist party under way and a Constitution drawn up. Here in
Pittsburgh the biggest excitement in Mary's eyes was that Hugh
Brackenridge was actually *going to see a girl!* Out in the country!

One night when O'Hara came in late Mary was nowhere to
be seen. Prudence merely said that Mrs. O'Hara was tired and
had gone on up. He swallowed his food quickly and a bit anxiously, and hurried after, glad to be settled early for the night.
When he entered their room Mary was sitting white faced and
fully dressed on the edge of the bed.

"Darling, are you sick?"

He went over to kiss her but she pushed him gently away.
"No, I'm not sick," she said. "It's just that I would prefer tonight to be alone."

"Alone? You mean you don't want me to . . . to sleep
here?"

"If you please."

"But why? Mary, what is it? You're not . . . not . . ."

"No," she said. "I am not. And I'm not sick. It is just that I
would like to be by myself."

He stood staring at her, incredulous. Then as she gave no sign he turned, got his night things from the closet and moved toward the door. Here, he looked back.

"But darling, *what have I done? Tell me!*"

It was an anguished cry but it did not move her. She sat still as stone, and after a moment of waiting he went out. He lay down in the guest room, stricken, going over and over in his mind all he could remember of the past few days. They had been as far as he could recall, perfectly normal except for his longer hours and greater weariness at night. But Mary had seemed so understanding, and so really interested in all his efforts to get the flour, biscuit, candles, and the rest. She had even given him good advice on several occasions. More and more he was finding that she had business acumen, strange in a woman. She was her father's own daughter. But most mystifying of all was that their breakfast together on that very morning, while hurried, had been a happy one. They had laughed together over Elliott's remarks on the finger bowls of which there were now, according to Mary's original prediction, only a few left. Elliott after a hasty explanation from O'Hara did some experimenting on his own but was discouraged.

"Course I'd never have any call to use one," he said, "but I couldn't get one of my big paws all in it, anyway. I guess they're just for the ladies."

Mary was still chuckling over this as he had said goodbye. He had been gone all day down the river at a gristmill to get more flour, so had not seen her until just now. Something must have happened during those intervening hours, but what, what could it have been, so grievous that she would not tell him? That she would *shut him out* with this devastating coldness.

But another thought finally pierced him. Could her present

attitude represent the accumulation of hidden loneliness, fears, and even resentment at his leaving her? If this were true it would be the most serious of all reasons to combat. For how could he assuage these feelings without giving up the work he was now committed to do?

When he finally fell asleep from sheer exhaustion it was with a last thought that on the morrow everything would surely come right. There was always healing in the daylight.

But it was not so in Mary's case. She remained pale, stony, distant. To all his frantic questionings, to all his attempts at caresses, she withdrew into an impregnable silence.

At the end of the fifth day he could stand it no longer. He drew her, half resisting, into the parlor and shut the door. She sank down on the sofa and he stood before her.

"Mary," he said, "when we were married one of the vows you took was that you would obey me. As a gentleman I would never dream even of referring to that except in some extreme emergency. I feel it is that now. We can't go on this way. You will be sick and I will be ruined for I cannot, I will not leave you until this is cleared up between us. I ask you now to tell me exactly what is lying on your heart. *What happened?*"

She shook her head but his voice was stern.

"I expect you to answer."

She looked down at her hands as she kept threading them together.

"It was the day you were away down the river," she began slowly. "You know the new little Bake and Sweet Shop where the saddlery used to be?"

"Of course."

"The stoop is at the side instead of in front of the door. I went in to get some seedcakes as a little treat for your supper . . ." She swallowed with difficulty. "And as I was coming out I heard women's voices on the stoop. They couldn't see me and I couldn't see them. But I heard them."

"Yes?"

"I stopped right in the doorway when I heard one of them say, 'Poor little Mrs. O'Hara!' "

"What?"

"The woman said she'd never want a daughter of hers to marry a man who had been an Indian trader. She said . . . she said they all had a wife somewhere in the wilderness and even when . . . when they were really married to a white woman they would find a way to get back sometimes to . . . to the Indian. And the other one said . . ."

"Go on!" His voice was choked.

"She said, 'Look at O'Hara. He's going back amongst them now with these Commissioners and you can see he's happy as a king over it. You'd think he'd be satisfied with what he's got,' and the other one said, 'They're never satisfied.' And then I . . . I ran through the store and out the back door. The man ran after me for I dropped the seedcakes but I never stopped till I got home. And that is . . . what happened." The tears were running down her cheeks.

It was O'Hara's face now that was white; it was livid with anger. The torrent of his words poured from him. Mary had never heard him swear before. She heard him now. When he finally checked himself he raised her to her feet.

"Look at me!" he said. "Look into my eyes."

She raised her own brimming ones to his.

"Mary, since the time I kissed you in Mrs. Bingham's Greenery until our wedding night I never," he paused as though searching for the right words to use before her, "I was never with a woman. I will not insult us both by giving my oath on that. I think you will accept my word," he added bitterly.

A great light flooded her face. "James!" she cried, reaching her hands to him. "Oh, James!"

But he moved back, his own countenance unchanged.

"To think that you could believe this loose, evil gossip *about me!* To question my life in this regard before we were married would be bad enough. But for you to think that I would now leave you, my wife, to go to the arms of *any* woman, let alone a savage, this has cut me to the very quick."

"But the women sounded so sure! And I don't know about . . . about men." Her voice was piteous.

"I'm not *men*," O'Hara said, still with bitterness, "I'm your husband and you should never have doubted me."

He turned on his heel, went out of the parlor, shutting the door with finality behind him, and went up again to the guest room. This that he had just learned was worse than anything he could possibly have imagined! He felt wounded beyond healing. His pride in his own integrity had been destroyed, and his resentment was devastating. How could Mary, in the face of his utter devotion, have been affected by the accusation in the first place? But even though she was troubled by it, how could she have *believed* it to the extent of refusing even to give him a chance to speak in his own defense, until she was forced to do so? It seemed to him in his anger that all his love up to this point had been unavailing. He lay, drowned in a black misery.

Just beyond the King's Orchard as the night advanced, he could hear the rolling waters of the Allegheny for a high wind had risen. Then in an hour's time the rain came, beating against the many-layered paper window panes. He listened to the threat of the storm upon them and muttered, for a moment forgetting the grief of his spirit, "Some day I'm going to make glass!" And even as he voiced his resolution it brought to him the poignant thought of all Mary had given up in leaving her old life in Philadelphia for the one in Pittsburgh. She had brought her grace and beauty to the rough, sprawling, unkempt pioneer village and borne its limitations without complaint. Even with the joy of her child and the small diversions possible, he knew she had times of discouragement and loneliness for the friendships and surroundings to which she had been accustomed. He knew this because occasionally his cheek, moving against her pillow as he roused from his initial sleep, had found it wet as it had been on their first night here. But always in the morning her smile had once again made bright the place of their habitation. Oh, he had taken her cheerful acceptance of this life too much for granted!

But something else smote him sharply now, something he had refused to admit before because of his own hurt pride. He had cursed the women who had brought this unspeakable distress upon him and Mary; he had branded their words as loose and evil gossip, but he knew as he forced himself to honesty that beneath their exaggerations there was a strong element of general truth. Mary did not "know men" as she had said piteously, but he did, and he knew fur traders. He remembered, too, the night a certain Chief had offered him his daughter in marriage, and that the girl was beautiful enough to quicken a man's desire. And he knew something else which he had never told Mary and never would. Elliott, in spite of all his words against the natives, had an Indian wife! If he stayed on in Pittsburgh there would be times when upon one pretext or another he would ride off into the wilderness and be swallowed up there for days or weeks . . .

Was it perhaps the existence of such burning facts as these below the women's speech that, unconsciously sensed, must have overwhelmed Mary's normal repudiation and seared her tender heart?

Suddenly he leaped to his feet and hurried to the door. Even as he opened it, above the wind and the rain, he heard the sound of sobbing. And there in the hallway was Mary, coming to him.

"James," she cried brokenly, "I can't *live* if you're angry with me!"

He picked her up, enfolding her small, shivering body in his arms. He carried her to their own bed and there beside her, cradled her against his heart while their tears mingled and the words, *Forgive! Forgive!* from each of them, were smothered by their kisses.

They had never been closer than on that night.

It was the beginning of the following week that the trip to Cuyahoga was begun. In the early morning the troops, the Commissioners on horseback and O'Hara with his pack train set out. He and Mary had said their last goodbyes, but as she stood at the top of the kitchen steps watching him out of sight down the lane, he turned suddenly and came hurrying back until he stood below her, looking up into her face. All the tenderness, all the passion of their love had come flooding back, stronger than ever during the intervening days and nights, but his eyes now, at his departure, were still anxious. She kissed him very gently on the forehead, the eyelids, the lips as if in blessing.

"I'm glad it all happened," she said softly in final reassurance. "Before, perhaps I wondered a little without realizing it. But now I *know*. I will always know. Hurry along now," she added with a brave little laugh. "The sooner you go, the sooner you'll come back to me!"

CHAPTER TEN

I T W A S early evening of a hot July day the following summer
when O'Hara rode out of the forest and into Pittsburgh on
his fourth trip home. In spite of his eagerness to get to Mary
he reined Pitt in for a minute at the edge of the Orchard and
surveyed the town. There was a noticeable change, a pleasant
one. John Wilkins, he knew, had been the chief instigator of it
with Neville and Craig to back him up. Some of the usual
roving hogs were now apparently in pens; the roads had been
worked upon and presented a somewhat smoother, if dusty
appearance; front yards for the most part were fairly neat and in
many cases planted with flowers from the precious little seed
packets brought over the mountains; and several log cabins had
been whitewashed like his own! Behind it all rose Grant's Hill,
always greenly pleasant, where the townspeople strolled of a
Sunday.

"Well, well," O'Hara said to himself, "we're getting on a
little and no mistake!"

He rode quickly down the lane, flung the reins over Pitt's
head, and ran up the steps. The horse had long ago learned to
stand, waiting his master's pleasure. Prudence appeared from
the stairway and greeted him calmly.

"Oh, you're back, I see, sir. Well, the child has just gone off to sleep and the mistress is dining with Mr. and Mrs. Wilkins. I believe Mr. Brackenridge is there too. Have you supped yourself, sir?"

"Not a bite. Anything you happen to have will taste fine. I'll do some work at my desk until Mrs. O'Hara returns."

He went up stairs first to look at his boy, who stirred only slightly under his father's kiss, then came down and settled himself with his papers at his newest acquisition, a tall secretary which had been made in Pittsburgh. While he chafed under the delay in seeing Mary he would be glad to have a little start on his accounting which was always intricate and time consuming. Except for the one big disaster last December he knew that his work had been praiseworthy, and in certain respects almost incredible, so his record-keeping, while laborious, brought satisfaction too. But the remembrance of that one ghastly incident, error, accident, whatever it might be called, was still galling him.

It had happened on the way to Fort McIntosh where the second parley with the Indians was to take place. This post was situated where the Beaver River joins the Ohio and since there was of course continuous waterway from Pittsburgh to that point he had secured a large flatboat and loaded it heavily, but he felt safely, with the needed supplies. The weather had been sunny and only moderately sharp the first of the month but when they were well on their way they ran into bitter, freezing, deadly cold. The vessel was driven aground on a fish dam by the ice, with its broadside battered in. There was no way of getting it off with the weight it bore, two of the crew were already dangerously frostbitten, and there was no hope of relief; so he had done the only thing possible. He had ordered thrown overboard twelve thousand-weight of flour, five hundred-weight of bread and biscuit, the rum, the soap, the candles and the rest! As the valuable stores, secured by him with unceasing labor and awaited with need by the troops and Commissioners, dropped into the icy river O'Hara's own heart had sunk with them. This was his first real failure and it was a desperately serious one.

It had been morning before the men were able to float the boat off the dam and get her battered remains to shore. Eb Denny, who had been sent out to join the Commissioners at Fort McIntosh, was with him, and seeing O'Hara's black mood had tried to comfort him.

"It was an accident, man. I can testify to that."

"They will say I should have started earlier."

"Well, why didn't you?"

"I was trying to get more flour. It's a hard job, Eb."

And there had been criticism. Plenty of it. Especially from Arthur Lee, one of the Commissioners. O'Hara had gritted his teeth and said nothing after stating the facts themselves. But he had made himself very clear to General Harmar. He pulled now from a secret drawer before him a paper which he reread for his comfort each time he got back home. It was a copy of the statements between himself and the General. His own concluded:

> As these losses of provision may probably be considered under the fifth article of my contract with the Secretary in the War Office, and you being acquainted with the circumstances, I shall esteem it a particular favor if you will please to furnish me with the necessary certificate thereof.

The General's reply had been prompt to the effect that—

> the above statement of facts relative to the loss of the contractor's boat and cargo is just and true agreeable to the best information that can be obtained.

So, the War Office had accepted it, absolved him and the whole thing was pretty well forgotten now by everybody but himself. To him, in spite of Mary's wise comforting, it remained a scar in his memory. Well, he thought, I've been pretty lucky. I guess when a man gets to feeling too sure of himself the devil gets in a crack at him.

It was nine o'clock before he heard voices in the lane. He had eaten his supper, chatted a moment with McGrady — who always reported in the evening and now had taken Pitt to his usual stall in Semple's stable — and had covered several long sheets with his neat, careful writing and figures. He leaped to his feet now and went to the door where he could see John Wilkins and his wife with Hugh and Mary approaching the house. When he stepped out and down the steps to meet them Mary rushed toward him with a cry of joy and there was general exclaiming and welcome.

"Come in! Come in!" O'Hara said hospitably, even as he hoped they would refuse.

The Wilkinses did decline, but Hugh, when the others had made their farewells, entered the kitchen eagerly.

"Go ahead! Kiss her!" he said, applying himself to the fire. "Don't mind me. As a matter of fact . . ."

"Oh James," Mary said as she finally released herself, "we have such news for you! Tell him, Hugh."

Hugh turned then, grinning from ear to ear.

"I'm about to become 'Benedick, the married man!'" he said.

After the medley of excited questions and answers they all sat down while Hugh told his story.

"Her name is Maria Wolf and you know the first of it, O'Hara, for it was your advice that brought it all about. I've been going to see her regularly, and a few weeks ago she promised to marry me and also to go to Philadelphia to school. In fact she agreed so quickly to that that my feelings were hurt at first. Then I found it was because she wants so much to be . . . be . . ."

"Worthy of you?" O'Hara prompted.

"Well, that sounds pretty bumptious but she does want to fit in with whatever kind of life we may have. You know I'm running for the Legislature and I've a pretty good idea I'm going to be elected. If I am I'll be in the East too, and I can see her betimes."

"Who's going to marry you?" O'Hara said.

"You might well ask! Parsons are as scarce here as hen's teeth. But I've got on the trail of a young theolog from Princeton who's roaming around. He's got some idea of converting the Indians. You know, all that kind of business. So, next Tuesday he's going to tie the knot. Just her father and mother there. Meanwhile, blessings on your wife here!" He paused to look fondly at Mary as she took up the tale.

"Prudence and I have been cleaning Hugh's cabin and fixing it up a bit. Oh, it's such fun! And on their wedding night, James, I thought we'd give them a supper. Just us. To invite more people might . . ."

"Yes, that would embarrass her," Hugh said. "She's not really shy but you must remember she's had no advantages. She's a fine girl, though!" Then he added, ruefully, "But guess what she's afraid she's going to miss? *A cow!* My God, I want to be good to her but I won't have a cow in my back yard. I hate the dirty beasts. I had enough of them when I was a boy. Try to convince her, Mary, that I'm much better than a bovine, won't you?"

There was great laughter and hand-shaking and good wishes

as Hugh said good night. Almost immediately, however, he stuck his head again in at the door.

"This will prove I'm in love all right, O'Hara! What do you suppose I forgot to tell you? After working on the thing for nearly three years, too. Listen to this!" He emphasized each word with a pointed forefinger. "On the twenty-ninth of this month of July, 1786, there will be published the first issue of *The Pittsburgh Gazette!* Put that in your pipe and smoke it."

Oh, the bliss of union after absence! Warm heart against warm heart! Peace, even though transient, instead of the love-laden fears born of danger or loneliness! And the unburdening of all the mind had stored against the meeting. There was, indeed, more than usual this time to talk about. Mary had much news from the east, the biggest being that her sister, Elizabeth, had a little son, Christian Carson Febiger!

"So the *Carson* name is getting its just due!" O'Hara observed.

Then there had been letters from old friends, one from Mary Vining which was very sad. She said she and Anthony Wayne had tiny snatches of happiness like spots of blue in a storm-swept sky but that after these brief meetings they felt worse than before. Her heart ached more for Anthony even than for herself, but what could she do? she had asked pitifully.

"What *can* she do, James?"

O'Hara was pacing the parlor floor as he listened. "Nothing!" he said emphatically. "Nothing! Wayne as a man and a gentleman has made the decision himself as he ought to do. She must abide by it."

"She says his hair has gone almost white. It will make him very handsome."

"I'm afraid he's paid a bitter price for his looks, then. Well, any more news of the social set?"

"Several girls have heard from Peggy Arnold in London. She has a second baby. But the General is terribly unhappy and quite bitter. He expected to be an important man there, and Peggy writes that nobody pays any attention to him."

"I could have told him that! The British respect an honest enemy but they'll have no truck with a traitor. Well, let's get back to Pittsburgh and pleasanter topics. Now, about Hugh's wedding. Did I understand you to say you were having them to supper on their wedding night?"

"Why, I thought so," Mary said innocently, "wouldn't you like that?"

"It isn't what *I* would like but I think they'd rather be by themselves that evening."

A flash of understanding recollection spread over Mary's face with a blush. "Oh, James," she said, "how stupid of me! I should have thought of that."

He smiled mischievously down at her. "Yes, I certainly think you should!"

"Prudence was talking to me the other day," Mary went on with a small giggle. "She says when a man *makes* too much over his wife it's likely to spoil her."

"Fancy that!"

"And that she knew a man once who was always hugging and kissing his wife like . . . well she said she would mention no names."

"Very discreet of her."

"And that this woman got so spoiled and above herself she ran off with another man!"

"Well, well," O'Hara said, kissing her soundly, "I must really be more careful. And by the way, if Prudence opens up the subject again, tell her to mind her own business. Politely, but make the meaning clear. Get your hat now, dear, and we'll go out and have a look at the town."

They stopped at Hugh's cabin and O'Hara was amazed at the transformation. It was now *clean* with a couple of braided rugs on the floor; the books, English, French, Latin, Greek, set neatly on new shelves; a dresser along the wall back of the table; and two rockers and a settle beside the fireplace.

"I got the extra furniture cheap from a man who's moving on west to the Ohio country. What do you think of it?"

"It looks like a real home, Hugh," O'Hara said.

Mary had a few more touches to put upon the bedroom so the two men stood outside looking over the town and commenting on the changes a year had brought. A new growth had come upon it, a new era, indeed. The days of Indian trade which had supported it from its first cabins had almost passed. While there would, of course, still be some traffic in furs the chief business now was selling goods to passing travelers. For the movement westward was gaining momentum every month and Pittsburgh lay directly on the route to the farther lands. It was the last place where the immigrants could purchase supplies before they "jumped off," as it were, into the unknown wilderness.

"You'll hardly believe how many stores have sprung up," Hugh was saying, "even in the last few months. Nineteen we have now, by actual count! Two bakeries, a ropewalk, a gold and silversmith, — though how he's going to make a living I wouldn't know. And of course the printshop. I want you to see that and meet my men. It's just back here at Ferry and Water. Can you come now?"

"Let's make it afternoon, shall we? I really ought to see Elliott first. Can you keep a secret, Hugh?"

"I've been known to."

"Well, I've got an idea. It may be years before I can carry it out, but when I can get shed of this contracting business I want to get into manufacturing. Some day *I'm going to make glass!*"

"Glass?" Hugh said. "Did I hear you right?"

"You did. I'm sick unto death of oiled paper window panes, and what's more to the point with me, so is Mary. They're a continual annoyance to her. I don't know how long it will be before I get to this but I plan about it every night out in the wilderness before I go to sleep. I'm going to buy up some land soon over here at the foot of Coal Hill. Good place, I figure."

"Well," said Hugh, "if you're set on it, I guess it's as good as done but may the devil admire me if it isn't the craziest scheme I've ever heard. Why the secrecy?"

O'Hara grinned. "I don't want any other man to get the idea first."

Hugh roared. "On that I think you're pretty safe. No other fool big enough, I'd say."

Mary came out and went on to do some shopping; O'Hara made his way to his own store and since there were no customers at the moment he and Elliott settled for a chat.

"How's business?" O'Hara asked.

"It's damned good. More strangers goin' through here now than you'd believe. We're makin' money."

"Well, that's the object. Do you think we could put prices up a bit?"

"I was just goin' to suggest that. You can check over things while you're here. How long are you stayin'?"

"Three weeks or more. I never know how long it will take to raise the supplies."

"Run any more boats aground?"

O'Hara gave him a sharp look and then laughed. "You're the only man I'd take that question from. It's still a sore spot. No, I've been pretty lucky these last months. I've been able to get cattle out there, one way or another, and that seems to impress the Commissioners. I needn't tell you it's a tough job though. It takes all the ingenuity I've got."

"How's the Injun business goin'?"

O'Hara shook his head. "I don't think it's going at all. And the worst of it is that it may be years before the Commissioners realize it. We've all gone from post to post while they've made treaty after treaty . . ."

"I can see it," said Elliott. "The Injuns all sittin' around in their best beads an' feathers an' noddin' an' takin' their presents an' goin' off, an' God only knows what's in their skulls."

"Right. Elliott, do you know about Gnadenhutten?"

"Yep. I know all about it."

"Why didn't you ever tell me?"

"We was both down in the south when it happened. By the time I got the story we was separated. It's all past anyway."

"I want to hear it. It's one of the pieces of this whole ghastly picture. Go ahead. I want to know."

"Well, to put it in a nutshell things had been pretty bad for the settlers round north an' a little west of here. Plenty killed. One man's wife an' children all taken; so after that, they got about eighty men together an' set out for Gnadenhutten on the Muskingum, where the Moravians lived. *They'd* all got converted somehow an' they was peaceful but the settlers found out that the warriors that did the depredatin' had their winter quarters in this village. To clinch it, when they got there, one of the men in the party who'd lost his wife found her clothes in one of their houses. They were pretty bloody. Well, I guess I know what *you'd* have done under them circumstances."

"I guess you do," O'Hara gritted.

"Well, they done it, all right. Killed every man, woman an' child of them. A fella that was along told me about it. Said he got pretty sick before they was through for them Moravians was prayin' to Jesus Christ while they died."

There was silence for a minute, then Elliott went on. "I spose you heard about the next raid out to Sandusky. Colonel Crawford's?"

"I heard what happened to him."

"I guess everybody has. An' while the Injuns were killin' him by slow torture Simon Girty was sittin' on a log watchin' it. Crawford kept beggin', 'Shoot me, Girty, for God's sake, shoot me!' An' this fella that got away said Girty just laughed an' said, 'Sorry, Colonel, I haven't got a gun.' An' I'll tell you what was back of *that!*"

"What?"

"Why some good while ago, Girty took an' awful shine to one of Crawford's daughters. He went to the house one night full of business an' Crawford showed him the door, pretty definite. There was enough Injun in Girty to make him want revenge. He had to wait a while but he got it, all right. Well, there are a few more pieces for you. If you can fit them together, you're a better man than I am."

"I think I'll go take a walk," O'Hara said, getting up. "Has everything been quiet round here? Indians, I mean?"

"Why, pretty much. Course we get some bad stories from the settlers as they come in, but here in town we've had no call to take our guns off the hooks."

"I worry about being away. Would you be willing to sleep in the house?"

"Sure. Only not in that fancy guest room. I can be mighty comfortable on the kitchen floor. I don't look for no trouble here at all, but if ever there was any, well as to your wife — my life for hers any time."

He held out his hand in a rare gesture and O'Hara grasped it, then stepped out into the sun, his eyes misty.

The wedding day was fine, bright and midsummer mellow. Mary had been busy since they had seen Hugh ride away, dressed in his best. At her suggestion their wedding gift was a pretty set of dishes from the store which she now arranged to their best advantage on the dresser. From her linens she made up the bridal bed, set on the mantel a pair of candlesticks from her own wedding gifts, and surveyed it all with satisfaction.

"From what Hugh told me confidentially," she said to O'Hara as he stopped for her, "this may seem almost elegant to Maria compared to her parents' cabin."

"Could be. It looks cozy enough. I hope the marriage goes well, for in a way I feel responsible."

The supper next evening for the newlyweds presented a problem. Should she, Mary asked her husband, array the table with her best Philadelphia silver and crystal which Hugh had often seen, or with her plainer settings in order not to overcome the bride by luxury unknown to her? They both decided that for Hugh's sake they should use the best they had to do honor to the occasion. So when the guests finally appeared *at the parlor door* (after being out of sight all day) they found a gleaming table awaiting them. Hugh's swift glance toward it justified the earlier decision.

Maria was in the main a pleasant surprise. She was prettier than either O'Hara or Mary had expected and on her the usual

frontier linen dress and folded white neckerchief were becoming. Her dark eyes sparkled, she laughed easily and there was
about her a certain alertness which bespoke an active mind.
But her few remarks showed frequent lapses of English, her
hands were rough and reddened by farm work and her movements had an uneasy awkwardness as though she was, quite
naturally, embarrassed at meeting her husband's fine friends.

Dinner conversation was fairly easy with Mary keeping up a
cheerful line of small talk and O'Hara and Hugh filling in with
light comments as they could. The state of the refurbished
cabin was discussed at length with Maria expressing her pleasure in it. But when they all sat down for the evening a heavy
quiet fell. Mary with a side glance at her husband conveyed
the fact that she had done all she could by way of verbal exchange; Hugh, the eloquent, the ever talkative, now sat in a
sort of bemused and wordless surprise, with constant possessive
glances toward Maria, while she in her turn was smilingly and
continuously silent.

O'Hara cleared his throat and clutched at an inspiration.

"I've just thought of something," he said. "This would be a
perfect time to present a problem I've been considering. Here
is a lawyer and here are two intelligent ladies to voice their
opinions. How about it?"

"Go ahead. Shoot!" said Brackenridge.

"It was Eb Denny who raised the question in my mind. You
met him, Hugh, when he was going through here?"

"Yes. Fine chap."

"Mary liked him too. He is now with the Commissioners.
Does your wife know of their work, and mine?" O'Hara asked.

"Oh yes. I've told her all about it," Hugh said.

"Well, here are the facts. There was to be a parley at Fort

Finney on the Miami River. Captain Beatty, the paymaster, got sick on the way down so he turned the money over to me and went back. I always have with me everywhere a big line of articles for the Indians in case they are needed, so I picked out all the things I thought would interest the troops and after I had paid the men I spread out my wares in front of them. They bought everything I had! So, as Eb Denny pointed out, half in a joke, I brought back with me about the same amount of money I took out. Now, was there anything wrong in that? What do you say, Hugh?"

Brackenridge laughed and slapped his thigh.

"You're a good one, O'Hara. That was the neatest trick of the year. But," he went on seriously, "you were entirely within your legal rights. You didn't even urge them to buy, did you?"

"Heavens, no! They were all bored to death and they fell on the articles like children."

"Your prices were reasonable?"

"They were, indeed."

"Well, I give you a clean bill on that. You were just confoundedly clever to think of it. What do you say, Mary?"

"As long as the men were satisfied. . . ."

"Oh, I give you my word they were! And now, Mrs. Brackenridge, what are your sentiments?"

Maria looked embarrassed, glanced toward her husband and shook her head.

"Oh, come," said O'Hara, "I would like to hear from you. Pro or con. Please!"

"Go ahead, Maria," Hugh said, "speak up!"

"Were the troops mostly married men?" she asked hesitantly.

"I imagine so."

"With families?"

"Very likely," O'Hara said, a faint color rising in his cheeks.

"Their pay I s'pose usually went to their wives. It's awful hard, like, for a woman with her man away. An' her with little childer mebbe. So I thought . . ." She gave a frightened glance toward Hugh. "I just thought mebbe you shouldn't ought to have tempted the men to spend their money."

There was a second of hushed silence during which Hugh turned scarlet. But O'Hara went across suddenly to Maria and held out his hand.

"Thank you," he said, "for saying honestly what you thought. And I wouldn't be surprised if you came nearer the truth than the rest of us."

They all, except Maria, put forth a sudden effort at conversation on other subjects then, Hugh apparently feeling more responsible than before to carry his end of it. So he spoke now of the coming newspaper and the two young easterners, John Scull and Joseph Hall, whom he had persuaded to come from Philadelphia to Pittsburgh for this adventure.

"Hall isn't a very rugged man. I hope our winter here won't be too hard on him. Scull is tough as a nut. He'll carry the biggest load. Everybody is excited about the paper, but whether they'll pay their subscriptions remains to be seen. Well, it's a start anyway, like our church foundation. You've seen that, O'Hara?"

"Yes, John Wilkins and I inspected it yesterday. He's going to work on the building himself. I wish I were here more to help. I'm glad it's going to be a sizable structure. Even if it's only a log one with a good oak floor and walnut pews it will have some dignity. And I'm going to hold out for a good strong ceiling if I pay for it myself."

"I'm so glad they left the big oak tree at the front," Mary

said. "I can picture people coming out of church in the summer and standing under it to discuss the sermon and . . . and everything."

"Chiefly the *everything*, I imagine," Hugh said, smiling, "but I stipulated that the tree should stand. Well, Maria, I think we must be leaving after a very delightful evening."

There were hearty good wishes and congratulations and Mary impulsively kissed the bride who whispered, "I'm glad you're going to be nigh-hand me. You can tell me things."

When the new couple were lost to sight in the summer darkness O'Hara turned to his wife.

"Well, what do you think of her?"

"I like her," Mary said slowly. "After a year in Philadelphia she'll be a very charming person. And I think she can stand up to Hugh if she needs to."

O'Hara laughed. "So you feel my friend might be a bit dictatorial?"

"Perhaps, but she'll manage him. The one thing I *didn't* like about her was her criticism of you."

O'Hara sobered instantly. "Well, frankly I didn't either but she may have been right. I didn't tell quite all the story. I had liquor to sell too. The General gave the troops permission to buy it and toleration to get drunk if it didn't interfere with their duty. Lord, how they responded! For three days there wasn't a sober man in the garrison. But there again I was within my legal rights. The General himself gave me permission to sell and at first I was pleased over the whole transaction."

He stopped and then said with a wry smile, "Until Eb Denny said, 'Well, O'Hara, between the wet and the dry you're going to take back as much as you brought.' And that was true, except for the Officers' pay. It's hard for me to resist a chance to make money, if it's honest, and I made a good deal on this. But after Eb's speech I had a twinge of conscience, and Maria added to it."

They put out the downstairs candles and went up to their room. Once there O'Hara said, "Dear Delight, it's so illogical of me. I want *you* to criticize me when you feel you should, only . . ."

"Only you would rather I didn't?" she smiled.

"I'm afraid that's the amount of it. Let's just say I'll try not to give you cause."

On the eve of the 29th, a group of men gathered in the print-shop at Ferry and Water streets with a bowl of negus as a treat on the table. There was of course Brackenridge himself, O'Hara, John Ormsby, Isaac Craig, Presley Neville, Devereux Smith, and John Wilkins, together with the two young printers, Scull and Hall. It was by way of being a send-off for the first issue of *The Pittsburgh Gazette*. Hugh did most of the talking.

"We want your support for this project and we hope you'll discuss it with all your friends. We intend to give you each a sample copy tonight so you can peruse it before you sleep." He pointed to the bench behind him where, neatly stacked lay the first papers, four pages each, ten by sixteen inches in size, printed with care on the hand press the young editors had brought over the mountains.

"Each week we'll try to have some foreign news. Who of us wouldn't give half a guinea to know what is going on at Smyrna and Amsterdam or how many armies are on foot in Europe? Then closer home in our own state," he went on, "heretofore we haven't known much about what our representatives were doing. Like boys creeping into a haystack we could see only their heels while their heads were hid away amongst the cabals of Philadelphia. Well, we hope to remedy that, and tonight we invite you to give us suggestions for general subjects to be included. For most of our subscribers, as you know, have no reading matter except the Bible and an almanac and we trust the *Gazette* will be an educational influence in their lives."

The negus went down in the bowl as the men voiced their opinions. There should be articles on religion, politics, agriculture, essays in praise of this or dispraise of that . . .

"And don't forget," O'Hara said, "to sprinkle a few witty anecdotes through the pages to brighten them up."

The men all laughed for O'Hara's own lambent wit was more or less proverbial.

At the end of the evening there was one glass left for each man. Hugh raised his. "To the success of *The Pittsburgh Gazette!*" he said. And the men drank the toast with heartiness.

Until O'Hara left again with his supplies, his days were full from dawn till dark. But as he worked his mind was busy also on his own affairs. He wanted to buy up more lots. He pointed out to Mary one evening the sketch he had made of the Woods plan.

"Here at the Fort is the apex, you see. Now, the only place the town can expand due to the rivers is at the back here on the legs of the triangle, as it were. So I'm going to buy up land at both sides in order not to lose out, no matter which direction the march of progress takes." He laughed as he said it.

"You're so clever, James."

"There's another thing. I wanted our first house to be here in The King's Orchard. A log one was all I could afford at the time but in a few years I can build you a bigger one."

"But I love this one."

"I know, but you'll love another one still more. There's no question in my mind but that the best residential section is going to be along Water Street. You know where Major Kilpatrick's house is now?"

"Yes. It's a nice one."

"Well, I hope to build one next to his, finer yet. The best for you, Mary."

She considered. "That would be along the Monongahela and I like the Allegheny so much better."

"So do I, really. But the view from the place I've picked out is worth the change in rivers. You see, darling, we will want a bigger house one day."

"You guessed, then?" she said, surprised.

"Guessed what?" he asked quickly.

"I've been afraid of upsetting you but I think there is a chance for little *James* by another spring."

He stared at her in dismay.

"Don't look that way," she said. "Aren't you pleased?"

"The question is whether *you* are."

"But of course I am. I'm happy about it. I want a big family."

"Women are brave," he said under his breath.

"Don't worry. All my friends here tell me the second is much easier than the first. And I lived through that."

"But to be away from you so much just now! Oh, that will be distressing."

"Well," Mary rejoined, "it distresses me, too. But I'll tell you something, Mr. O'Hara, if it doesn't make you vain."

He leaned over and laid his cheek against her hair.

"I'd rather be married to you, even if you're away most of

the time, than to any other man who was always with me."

They walked slowly along Water Street the next Sunday, past Major Kilpatrick's fine house.

"There," O'Hara said, "you see these lots just next to his? They're the ones I have my eye on. If you like the location I'll take an option on them at once. Look at the view!"

It was a nearer and more magnificent vista of the marriage of the rivers than they had from the Orchard and while the Monongahela did not have the clear swiftness of the Allegheny nor the bordering locust trees, it too was a great rolling stream and edged by spreading sycamores.

"It's a beautiful spot!" Mary said.

O'Hara made an expansive gesture. "No more logs! A big frame structure is what I have in mind, with a stable and carriage house too. After all I've begun to make money and I expect to make a great deal more before I'm through. And," he added quickly, "in the doing of it I hope to serve my country and help my city grow. I'm really not as selfish as I sound."

As they walked back home Mary spoke seriously. "James," she said, "I wish you would take me into your confidence about your business affairs."

He looked at her in amazement. "Why, darling, it never occurred to me you would want to be bothered with such things."

"But I would," she said. "And it wouldn't be a bother. I might even be able to help you in some small ways. I'm not a merchant's daughter for nothing and I'm really rather good at accounts."

"I know that. I've seen your housekeeping ones. Tonight, if you like, we'll sit down together and go over all my . . . my *assets*," he said, laughing.

At bedtime when they had finished, O'Hara looked up at her in mock gravity.

"It's not fair," he said. "It's definitely not fair."

"What isn't?" she asked in alarm.

"For any young woman to be as beautiful as you and still have a business head on her!"

The next morning early O'Hara went to see Dr. Bedford whose generous house stood along the Monongahela where Water Street ended in country. He had to wait a few minutes in the small office and while he paced the floor he stopped now and then to read again one of the framed diplomas on the wall as though to give him courage.

London, April 3rd, 1770

These are to certify that Mr. Nathaniel Bedford
hath diligently attended our Lectures on the
Theory & Practice of Midwifery and on the
diseases of Women and Children.

WM. MOORE   THOS. DEBMAN*

When the doctor came in he was brisk, cheerful and discerning as usual.

"Well, you've done pretty well with your timing. Better than I expected."

"You know why I'm here?" O'Hara asked in surprise.

"My dear young man, it's written all over your wife as plain as a pikestaff. We doctors can read the signs. Now, what's bothering you at the moment?"

"It's my having to be away so much during these coming months," he burst out. "I'll have to go on with my contracting . . ."

---

* This diploma hangs now in Carnegie Library's Pennsylvania room in Pittsburgh.

"I should hope so. A man has to do his work and a woman has to bear the children. The Lord ordained it that way from the beginning. I don't quite see how you could further the matter now if you were at home. May be as well if you're away, as a matter of fact."

O'Hara removed some bills from his pocket and quietly slid them across the desk.

"I know a woman doesn't see the doctor until her . . . her time has come but in this case I wondered if you would be willing to stop in once in a while and check . . . just be sure everything is all right?"

Dr. Bedford as quietly slid the bills back toward O'Hara.

"Why, I'll do that, Captain. Always a pleasure to talk to your wife. I wonder if you know what a spot of brightness she makes in this town. Mrs. Bedford was at her quilting and what a party that was apparently! Just the *elite* there, of course. But your wife makes everybody welcome, high and low. I know, for I hear about it from some of these poor bedraggled critters when I go round amongst them. Do you know what they do when they get to the end of their rope? Well, they go to your kitchen, Captain, and your wife gives them tea and talks to them and cheers them up and by the time they get home they think they've been to Philadelphia and back."

Dr. Bedford held out his hand.

"Glad to keep an eye on Mistress O'Hara. Maybe she'll give *me* a dish of tea betimes. So get along with your business. It's pretty important."

As O'Hara made his way from one gristmill to another along the rivers he had an idea one day. If he owned a gristmill himself and made his own flour he would have one steady source he could count upon. He could sell his output to the government at the same price other mills charged *and,* here he smiled to himself, make a good deal of money doing it! He studied each mill at which he stopped and finally decided upon the largest of these about three miles down the Ohio. It was in good condition but the owner was not young and at that moment looked hot and weary. Would he be interested, O'Hara asked him, in selling the mill at a good price if he were kept on at a salary to run it?

"And with another man perhaps to help you," O'Hara added. "This is a pretty big job, and I think we could make it still bigger."

The miller stared at his questioner in amazement, then slowly, each feeling his way, the bargaining began. John West, the owner, showed O'Hara around the property, pointing out the great wheel, the smaller cogs, the solid granite foundation.

"My father built this mill," he said, "and I've kept it in good order. I dress my own mill stones," he added proudly, "but I'm getting along and no son to come after me!"

In the end O'Hara had the mill, or would have when he brought his first payment, and West was hard put to it to conceal his satisfaction. He would get an assistant and then would have to turn no grain away.

"No, no," O'Hara said, "never do that! I want the output of flour doubled if you can. We've got a market for it."

Within a few days of his leaving O'Hara had a strong feeling of accomplishment. Once again a great flatboat was loaded with supplies but at this season the waters would be safe. On his own account he not only owned a gristmill but he had bought ten lots on the legs of the triangle and had an option on the two on Water Street. Greatest food of all to his ambition was the purchase of a parcel of land at the foot of Coal Hill across the Monongahela. *There,* he thought to himself, *as soon*

as ever I can get to it I'll start Pittsburgh's first real manufac-
turing. I'll make my glass if it breaks me!

He woke very early the second day before he was to set off.
He raised himself on one elbow and looked his fill at Mary's
sleeping beauty as the first light came hesitantly through the
oiled paper panes. Prudence was not yet stirring he knew, and
yet his trained ear caught small sounds at the kitchen door. He
threw his clothes on quickly and went down. It was Elliott.

"Get your gun, O'Hara. There's trouble an' I think we've
got to go," he said in a low voice.

"What is it?"

"It's Porter. You know the fellah we got the pill for? He's
over at Semple's an' he's as near crazy as he can get. His boy's
took an' his wife . . ."

Elliott made a swift gesture across the top of his head. "He
wants us to go back an' help him."

"What can we do now? The Injuns will be gone far enough
by this time."

Elliott swallowed. "He wants us to bury his wife for one
thing. He says he can't, an' his brother's laid up sick again."

"I'll be with you in a minute."

O'Hara went up to the bedroom and leaned over Mary.

"I have to leave early, darling. I'll be home as soon as I can.
You go back to sleep."

He went down, took his rifle from its hooks and joined Elliott.

"Semple's up. He says he'll give us a bite of breakfast before
we start."

The men did not speak again until they reached the tavern.
Here they found Porter shaking as if from palsy and Semple
trying to force whiskey into him.

"Drink up, man! It'll settle you. You can't go on like this!"

O'Hara took the glass and spoke to the white-faced man before him.

"Porter, we're going back with you to do what we can. Try to pull yourself together." He held the glass close while he grasped one of Porter's hands in his own. "Drink it," he said, and then added to Semple, "Something hot if we can have it."

"We can't wait," Porter broke in. "They may come back and take her."

"No," Elliott said, "I can promise you, they won't do that. We'll get on our way soon but we'll all need something in our bellies first."

During the meal, when even Semple was speechless, the silence was broken only once.

"She didn't want to come out here," Porter said quaveringly. "She only done it to please me because I was so set on it. She never wanted to come." And it was O'Hara's face then that turned white.

The three men rode through the dawn, tense and watchful, O'Hara beside Porter, Elliott behind. Little by little the distracted man told his story. It had happened the afternoon before while he had been in one of his cleared fields a little distance from the cabin. He had heard screams and come running. His wife lay dead, scalped, at the back doorstep; the boy was gone. At first he had been so sick he could do nothing even with the little children's terrified crying behind him. When he was able to stand up he had called and called for the boy until he realized that the Indians must have captivated him. Then he had taken the younger ones over to his brother's and returned to sit by his wife's body until he had determined to come for help. Even now, as he finished, a hard retching shook him.

"What can I do now, Mr. O'Hara?" he asked when he could speak. "I'd take the little 'uns an' go back to Philadelphy to-morrow, but how can I leave my boy with the savages?"

"Don't think of this at the moment, Porter. We'll talk it all over later. Just keep a sharp eye out now to your right and ahead of us. We may be in plenty of danger ourselves."

But they reached the cabin in safety. Even before he had seen the ghastly work of the marauders at the back, O'Hara felt a sharp pang as he looked at the small home before him: the rude logs, felled and put together by a man's bare hands; the little clearing, wrested from the wild, with its precious crop; the signs of all the hardship of daily struggle against the threat and encroachment of the forest. Why? *Why* did men leave safety and comfort and cross the mountains for this? But even as he asked himself the question, his own heart answered it.

Elliott got off his horse and came close to O'Hara. "I've seen this before but you haven't. It ain't pretty. Keep your teeth tight shut and look away as much as you can."

They tied the horses and followed Porter around to the back step. There at the sight of what lay before them O'Hara turned quickly, a terrible nausea overwhelming him. With a tremendous effort of will he mastered it, gritted his teeth and fastened his gaze on the lower part of the woman's body. Elliott was taking charge.

"Have you got a clean sheet, Porter, or a blanket or anything?"

Porter brought a sheet, his hands shaking as he held it out. "She'd just ironed yesterday."

"You go off to the clearing now an' work as hard as you can. We'll do what has to be done, an' then we'll call you."

They found a shovel and another digging tool in the small shed, and when they had selected a spot on the opposite side from the clearing, Elliott and O'Hara began their work. They dug the grave deep and when it was done they wrapped the woman's body in the sheet and lowered it as gently as they could into its resting place. O'Hara was thinking of her face, a lovely face indeed, as he had last seen it, raised in a white agony of supplication. Elliott was evidently remembering the same.

"She prayed hard enough to save him," he said. "But I guess there wasn't anyone round to pray for her when she needed it."

"There's got to be a prayer here today," O'Hara said. "There's *got* to be."

"Well, you'll have to make it, then. It ain't in my line an' you can't expect Porter to do it."

They filled the grave, making its surface flat with the forest floor, and then deftly with their hands scattering over it bits of dried leaves and withered acorns, moss and twigs that made the summer carpet. At the head of it they stuck a living branch. Except for that it was indistinguishable.

"I'll go an' fetch Porter now an' you can be thinkin' up something to say."

O'Hara's mind was distraught. To utter any words of his own before Porter and Elliott would be to him intolerable. And try as he would he could remember no other except the Lord's Prayer and he knew his control would not hold out for the length of that. Just as the others returned the last words of the burial service came suddenly to him.

The three men stood in silence beside the leafy bough. Porter drew a long shuddering breath and then straightened as though the outward sign of the inevitability of earth as the mother of all had in a measure steadied him. And then O'Hara spoke.

"May she rest in peace, and may light perpetual shine upon her soul."

They sat for a little while inside the cabin, needing the rest and the corn pone Porter offered them.

"It's the boy we've got to think of now," he said. "What can we do about my son?" The words were anguished.

"How old is he?" Elliott asked.

"Just bare eight."

Elliott looked off through the door.

"Tell you what we'll do. You've had about all you can take for one day. You get along over to your brother's an' stay there while O'Hara, here, and me hunts round in the woods to see if we can pick up a trail or anything."

They saw Porter, pathetically submissive, ride away, his face still stony white but his hands able to grasp the reins. When he was gone Elliott voiced his opinion.

"If that's all the age the boy is I'd say he's gone with his mother by this time."

"You mean they haven't captivated him?"

"Doubt it. If he was older they'd take him all the way. But a little chap like this would likely cry an' if he couldn't keep up with them they'd knock him on the head an' go on. Leastwise that's the way they mostly do. If we go out through the forest, with any luck we'll find him."

"Ride or walk?"

"Have to ride. I'm afraid to leave the horses here. You see there may still be some of the devils lurkin' round. I don't just relish this job. If I was sure the little chap was safe dead . . ."

"What do you mean?"

"We wouldn't need to bother then. But they could have hit him an' . . . O'Hara, why don't you stay here an' behave yourself an' let me see what I can find. I've got nothing to lose, live or die, an' you've got a damned lot."

"You mean the child might be lying out there, still alive?"

"Well, there's a chance of it."

"Come on then. We've no time to waste."

They bestrode their horses and set off into the forest warily, every moment on their guard, watching for the faintest sign which might indicate which way the Indians had passed. They turned in this direction and that, their eyes sharp, their ears quickened. But there was only the strange pulsing sound which is not sound, the silence of the wilderness.

It was two hours later when Elliott got off his horse and peered at the ground. What he saw was only a folded leaf and a broken twig. He held up his hand and O'Hara joined him. Their long training gave them discernment as they walked slowly along, leading the horses. Other subtle signs appeared. They felt sure they were on the trail. And then, suddenly they found what they were seeking. The child's body lay to the side of their path, his small tear-stained face showing white against the forest floor. But the blow had been strong enough. There was no life in him.

It was O'Hara who carried him back in front of him on Pitt. It was his eyes that were wet as once again he and Elliott did their unspeakably hard task. When at last all was finished the two men rode over to the cabin of Porter's brother without speaking until they drew up at the door.

"You're better with words than me, O'Hara," Elliott said. "I guess you'll have to tell him."

But the telling was not as hard as they feared. Porter met them, his face distorted with anguish.

"You didn't find him?"

"Yes, Mr. Porter, we found him. We brought him back and did . . . what must needs be done. It was a blow that killed him apparently. I'm sure he knew nothing afterwards."

"He wasn't . . . not like her?"

"No."

Porter moved back and sank into a chair beside the table. "I guess I'm thankful it was that. If they'd taken him I'd never have slept thinkin' of him so little among the savages, mebbe abused, an' him lost an' homesick for his mother. Now, he's with her an' he's safe. I'll stand it some way."

He dropped his head upon his arms, his shoulders shaking, but no sound coming from him.

The family was stricken quiet but the woman set hot mush before Elliott and O'Hara, which they were glad to eat. Before they left Porter stood up to bid them goodbye.

"I can't even thank you for what you done today. I might ha' gone clear crazy if I'd had it to do myself. An' I've never paid you your pound yet," he added to O'Hara.

"Just forget it. I don't need it. What will you do now?"

"I'll take the little 'uns an' go back where I come from. I've a sister there will look after them. I'll mebbe wait till I can sell the cabin." His voice broke on the words.

"Oh, he'll sell it all right," his brother spoke from the bed. "They keep comin' out here all the time. God knows why. Many's the time I've wished . . . Course if I didn't get these doncy spells every once in a while we'd get on pretty good, unless . . . unless . . ." His eyes rested on his brother and the words trailed off.

It was sunset now as the two men rode back along the river. They took the hours in silence as the darkness overcame them. It was when they entered the town that O'Hara reined Pitt while the words burst from him.

"Elliott, I can't do it! Not after all I've seen today. I won't go off and leave my wife and child in danger. I'll break my contract with the government. Someone else can supply the troops. I tell you *I won't go!*"

There were only two lights visible in the little town. One was at the tavern, the other in a cabin where one could guess Dr. Bedford was ushering in a new life.

"Well now," Elliott drawled at last, "might be worth while to think this over a little. First place I can tell you this. I know the Injuns about as well as any man does an' I can promise you they won't come into the town here. Not now."

"What about Hannastown?" O'Hara asked sharply.

"All right. What about it? It wasn't a town like Pittsburgh is. The men there worked out in their fields. The day it was burnt every last son of a gun of them was out helpin' Mike Huffnagle take in his harvest. Now here there's business to keep the men in the town every day. The Injuns know that. Another thing . . ." He paused.

"Such as what?"

"Well, it's kinda hard to put. You an' me both believe these parleys an' treaties ain't goin' to solve the whole problem. But while they're goin' on they certain sure keep a good few Injuns round these parts out of mischief. A good many lives may get saved by them in the meanwhile. Do you get what I mean? An' you're a pretty big part of this treaty business. Well, go home an' think it over. An' don't forget I'm sleepin' in the kitchen every night you're away. If you go," he added.

O'Hara made no reply for a long minute, then he said, "You're a good man, Elliott."

"Same to you," Elliott answered and turned toward the tavern.

O'Hara dismounted quickly and handed him the rein. "Take my horse along, will you? I'll walk home."

The house was dark and silent when he reached it. He went into the kitchen, lighted a candle and then stood by the fireplace leaning his head against the mantel. He was shaken as he had never been before in his life. The ghastly experiences of the day had stripped him of his normal strength. He felt too weak, too distraught to make a decision and yet it had to be made. Remade, rather, for his mind had been fully settled as he rode the miles between the cabin and the town. Yet he knew Elliott spoke the truth in so far as any man could apprehend it. He knew too, that his work was important and realized without vanity that no other man would be able to do it as well. General Harmar and the Commissioners had often told him this. The hard discipline of fact and of duty bore down steadily, irresistibly upon him as the minutes passed. He would have to go.

But even as he knew it he saw again the body of Porter's wife as it lay on the doorstep. Would he ever be able to forget that sight? He heard again Porter's words which had pierced his own heart: *She never wanted to come. She only did it because of me!*

"Oh God! Oh God! *Oh God!*" he cried aloud, and it was a prayer of supplication.

At last he blew out the candle, went softly upstairs and undressed in the dark. With his first movements near her Mary woke.

"James, are you back at last? I tried to wait up for you but I got so sleepy. Was it a hard day for you?"

He didn't reply at once and she asked him again.

"Was it a hard day, darling?"

"A little," he said, as he drew her close.

CHAPTER ELEVEN

M ARY and her women advisers had been right. Little James entered this world with a minimum of trouble for his mother. O'Hara had planned his trips with care so that he would be home for the event and was now happy, proud and relieved.

"And I can go on and have my *six?*" Mary asked him roguishly.

He laughed. "I'm not Providence."

"You come close to it. I only hope," she added, glancing at the cradle, "that the times will grow settled and that there will be peace for our children to grow up in. How are things going now? Please tell me the truth. You always evade my questions."

"It's largely because I don't know how to answer. Most of the tribes come to meet with the Commissioners and there are speeches from our men and speeches from the chiefs, White-Eyes, Captain Pipe and so on. No sign yet of Guyasuta, by the way. Then the Indians take their presents and go off. The Shawnees are the ones we're most anxious to pin down to a treaty but they keep hanging back. General Harmar, I may say, is considerably discouraged. But, we'll see. Don't worry your little head about it all."

"How can I help it, when you're in the thick of it? I'd like to know more details about your work too. I thought you were taking me on as a partner in your affairs."

He bent over and kissed her. "I am," he said, "but in another line."

When they finished laughing Mary persisted in her questioning. "Can't you be specific about what you do? You come back here, are away most of the days and then leave, and that's all I know."

"Well, let's see. Maybe this would seem more concrete to you. As of the present the daily ration for each soldier is eighteen ounces of bread or flour. If I run short of that I use a quart of rice or a pound and a half of Indian meal. Then each man gets a pound and a quarter of fresh beef a day or a pound of salted beef or three quarters of a pound of salted pork. When fresh meat is issued we have to provide salt to keep it and that means two quarts for every hundred rations. Soap is at the rate of four pounds per hundred rations and candles a pound and a half. So that's the way it is. I have to know how much is needed for each post for say, three months in advance, and provide it."

Mary's eyes were wide. "Somehow this makes me realize more than ever before what an enormous job it is and how wonderful you are, darling."

"I like business," he smiled. "If I didn't have to be away from home so much I'd really be enjoying all this. It's a challenge and no mistake. The easiest thing to provide is the liquor. When the officer orders it the men get half a gill of rum or whiskey. That and the flour I can get around here, locally. The candles and soap come mostly from New York. The meat is the hardest. I intend while I'm back here this time to ride down into Kentucky and see if I can buy a herd of cattle.

I can pick up some men there I know to take them out. I'd like to get them to Detroit and fatten them there. Of course there is always the problem, too, of pack horses for the wilderness and boats for the rivers depending upon where we're heading. I should have told you that for every ration I receive one cent. As my contract says, 'for full compensation for the trouble and expense in issuing the same.' And it counts up, darling! I'm making money! Well, enough for now of my business. Let's look at my namesake."

More even than a year ago O'Hara was conscious of the changes in Pittsburgh itself and drank in the signs of growth and new activity. Flatboats and keelboats were more numerous along the wharf, new taverns and stores had sprung up it seemed on every corner, and on the cultural side, the Presbyterian congregation was now incorporated by legislative act, and the log building completed with the Reverend Samuel Parr installed as the first pastor. More extraordinary still perhaps was the incorporation of the *Pittsburgh Academy* with a fine list of trustees, a tract of five thousand acres in the wilderness and the block of lots bounded by Smithfield Street, Cherry Alley and Second and Third Avenues. Hugh Brackenridge was full of this latter triumph when he brought Maria over one afternoon to call upon the new baby and its parents.

Although Mary had prepared him somewhat O'Hara was still startled at the change in Maria. She wore a modish dress, was now free from embarrassment and self-consciousness, and made few slips in her English. Her bright eyes attested to the eager mind which had made her improvement possible. *So!* O'Hara thought to himself, *my suggestion was a good one.*

Hugh, as usual, was full of talk and filled in the news O'Hara had not heard.

"Yes, we've really made the first start for the Academy. In

another year or two we'll get some sort of building ready and a principal and then we'll open."

"How was the Legislature, Hugh?"

"Oh, so-so. I enjoyed it and I suppose I'll always be in and out of politics. I'm changing my views though. At first I was a Federalist through and through. I wanted a strong central government like Alexander Hamilton, but I'm getting interested in this new Democratic-Republican party that Thomas Jefferson is starting. Well, at any rate the Constitution has been adopted. That's the biggest piece of news."

"Ah," said O'Hara. "That's wonderful. Now if we can elect a President . . ."

"Are you for Washington?"

"I certainly am. Who else could be thought of?"

"Well, I've heard John Adams spoken of here and there."

"Capable man but nothing to Washington."

"Of course after those dozen champagne glasses he gave you for a wedding present you'd have to stand by the General!" Hugh laughed. "Come on. Let's leave the girls to gossip while we look over the town."

Once outside the Orchard O'Hara turned toward the Point. The noble old Fort was falling steadily into disrepair. Its Bastions were breached, its turrets toppling.

"Well, its glory has departed, sure enough," Hugh said meditatively, "and it can never be rebuilt. What the town needs now is a smaller fort near the center which can really be manned in an emergency."

O'Hara looked at the great fortress with narrowed eyes. "Good bricks there. I think when the teardown really comes I'll buy them."

"I wouldn't doubt it," said Hugh. "What for?"

"This town could stand a nice neat row of brick houses. Give it tone. Yes, I think I'll see to that."

"Anything else on your mind at present?" Hugh's voice was ironical but O'Hara didn't seem to notice.

"Yes," he said. "I'm going to try to get a sawmill started while I'm here. With all the increased building — boats and houses too — the place can stand another one. Then, later on when I can manage it, I think I may build a brewery! Down here on the Point wherever I can get the land. After all, drinkables are a big product around these parts, and the one most easily marketed east or south. Wouldn't you say so?"

"I'd say something more. There's a greater amount of drunkenness round here than the east would ever dream of. But O'Hara, there's a little cloud gathering. No bigger than a man's hand yet, but by crickey some day it's going to make trouble."

"What's that?"

"Taxes," he said. "We're a new country and we're in debt. Back east they're sniffing round every corner to see how money can be raised. I've heard more than one man say, 'What about all this whiskey coming in from the Back Country? How about an excise on that?' Well, it won't come for a few years, maybe, but some day, we'll be in for it."

"But the farmers can't send their wheat and rye back east as *grain!* The only way they can market it is after they distill it!"

"I know. I'm only telling you what's in the wind. Come on, and I'll show you what *Marie* has done to his new tavern this summer. And I'll buy you a glass of whiskey, speaking of the stuff."

They moved slowly through the town, O'Hara stopping

often to greet those he passed: old Major Kilpatrick, still jaunty
at ninety with his knee breeches and cocked hat; Dennis Lochy,
the blind ballad singer who improvised a few lines for his benefit.

> *"In songs and rhymes I'll sing the praise*
> *Of Captain O'Hara all my days."*

O'Hara dropped some coins in his hat as Brackenridge muttered, "Well, I've heard him do better."

"Probably with a better subject," O'Hara grinned, and then
he raised his hand in quick salute as General John Neville's
commanding figure emerged from a store. It was a friendly
meeting as far as O'Hara was concerned. He summed up the
Indian situation in answer to the General's questions and heard
his plans for an Episcopal church next to the Presbyterian.
Hugh, meanwhile, maintained an aloof silence. When they
passed on O'Hara said, "What have you got the wind up about
Neville for?"

"I don't like him. He's too much the aristocrat for my stomach. Then he's got such a damned clique around him. There's
his son, Colonel Presley, his brother-in-law Abraham Kirkpatrick, his son-in-law Major Isaac Craig, and his lawyer John
Woods, my biggest rival, by the way. If they saw old Neville
caught here *in flagrante delicto* they'd all swear he was back
east at the time!"

"Come, come, Hugh! That's a nasty comparison for a man
like the General!"

"All right. I'll withdraw it. But I will say they all make up a
pretty strong little cabal if anyone had to buck them, politi-
cally. Well, here we are at Marie's. What do you think of
it?"

O'Hara exclaimed with pleasure. He had seen the new tavern itself before but not the gravel walks with their bordering shrubs and early flowers. John Marie, with his French blood, had both business and esthetic sense, and here at the foot of Grant's Hill, which was the only *pleasance* the town could claim, he had built a spot of beauty. While the men were finishing their drinks O'Hara voiced his praise of Maria. He had hesitated before for fear it might reflect upon his first impression of her, but Hugh had evidently been waiting for his reaction.

"You notice a change in her then?" he said eagerly.

"I do. You have a very charming wife, Hugh. I congratulate you."

"And I thank you again, my friend, for your advice."

All the way back to the house Hugh extolled Maria's qualities. She was proving to be a great reader and he was helping her to continue her studies now under him as teacher. He was boyishly exuberant.

"What do men *do* who have stupid wives?"

"I really wouldn't know," O'Hara said, laughing. "Of course I fancy there are a few stupid husbands in the world too."

"*Touché,* old chap. Well, let's just say we're among the blessed."

Maria was ready to leave when they got back to the house and O'Hara stood at the kitchen step watching them down the lane, satisfaction upon his face. All at once Hugh turned.

"Mind your P's and Q's, O'Hara."

"What's that? What are you talking about?"

Hugh hurried back. "There! I'm glad I was the first to introduce you to the new catchword. Did you notice that board on the wall behind the bar at Marie's? Well, all the taverns have them now. When a man is drinking hard all evening and treating too, the tavern keeper writes his name on the board and puts *P* for pint and *Q* for quart after it and then checks how many of each he orders. When the number gets up he calls the man to the bar for a reckoning. So someone lately started the expression and it's spread like wildfire. No one ever says *Watch out!* or *Be careful,* now. They say 'Mind your P's and Q's.' Pretty good, eh?"

"Excellent," O'Hara said. "I'll take that one back to the troops!"

The gristmill was flourishing. The output had indeed doubled and O'Hara had engaged another man in the hope of increasing it still more. For his own flour he charged the government exactly what he had to pay to other mills, and made a handsome profit doing it. The idea of a sawmill had been in his mind for some time. Now on this trip home he decided to put it into action. One of the many boat builders was an Irishman, Dennis O'Keefe, and on this afternoon when Hugh and Maria had left, O'Hara made his way toward the wharf. Dennis was a brawny man but, as O'Hara had sized him up before, he had brains as well and he *knew wood.* The plan proposed was simply this: if O'Hara put up all the capital would Dennis see to the building and operating of a sawmill? The Irishman stood for a moment as though stupefied, then he drew his hand across his brow.

"*Would* I?" he said. "It's the opportunity of me dreams an' me never expectin' it. I know how to go about it, Captain. I've been round sawmills off an' on all me life. I pledge you'll never be regrettin' this. When do we start?"

"At once," said O'Hara firmly. "I own a couple of lots down here. We'll take a look at them now, and then I'll order whatever machinery you'll need." His eyes roved over the forest clad hills beyond. "At least there is no shortage of raw timber."

That night Mary was able to be downstairs and she and her husband sat together in the parlor while once again he went over with her his assets, explaining just what money was with Robert Morris in the Philadelphia Bank, and how much he was leaving in one of the secret drawers of the desk for all her needs and any sudden demand of his own.

"I'm almost getting to be a banker, myself," he said. "General Harmar has asked me to keep some of his funds. They are in the other secret drawer, in an envelope bearing his name. You see, I do consider you my partner in everything, in spite of my little joke."

He told her then of the plan for the sawmill. "My idea is to develop a number of industries here. First of all, naturally, I want to make money. But along with that I want to stimulate business production. I want to make Pittsburgh grow and before I'm done I want to make some of those smug easterners take notice of the possibilities out here. I've got a far-reaching plan . . ."

There was a soft sound, less than a knocking, at the back door. O'Hara went quickly through the kitchen. On the back stoop in the darkness he could discern an Indian! For one quick moment a chill struck his heart; then he recognized the man before him. It was Guyasuta! With a cry of welcome he drew him into the kitchen, grasping the Chief's arms with his own.

"Where have you come from?" he asked, falling easily into the Seneca dialect.

Guyasuta looked at him impassively.

"You are glad to see me? Even remembering . . . Hannastown?"

O'Hara paused as he studied the strong figure before him. The face, while beginning to show signs of age, had the same nobility he remembered.

"Yes," he said slowly. "While I may be very sad at some of your actions, I am still your friend."

The Indian nodded. "And you are my son. I stay away because I fear you would not receive me. Now my heavy heart is light."

"Sit down," O'Hara said eagerly. "You must meet my wife. You must break bread with me at my own table. Oh, Mary?"

She came a little hesitantly but with a smile which her husband knew to be a brave one. He introduced the two and Guyasuta studied her without speaking for some moments. At last he turned to O'Hara and said in his own tongue, "She is beautiful as a young willow in spring beside the water courses!"

"I'm afraid she's a little tired now for we have a new baby. Why don't you go on up now, Mary, and I'll set some supper out for Guyasuta."

As she nodded assent O'Hara lifted her in his arms and carried her up the stairs. When he returned the old Indian wore a puzzled expression.

"How many days has your new child?"

"Eighteen."

Guyasuta shook his head. "When Indian baby has *two* days mother is chopping wood and waiting on husband. I have now two wives. Old squaw takes care of me by day. Food and clothes. Young squaw for nights. Indian ways are wise. Huh?"

O'Hara kept a sober face. "White men's customs are a little different. Now for some food."

He took down a flitch hanging beside the fireplace, cut generous slices for the long handled skillet, brewed a pot of tea, and set out cornbread and butter from the cupboard. He could see the Indian's nostrils dilate at the good smell of the frying meat. When all was on the table Guyasuta fell upon the viands ravenously while O'Hara made a pretense of eating with him. When it was finished they both lighted their pipes.

"I am very glad to talk with you," O'Hara said in English. "I suppose you know what is going on in the west."

"A little," the Indian said, as O'Hara restrained a smile. He knew the system of communication among the red men was well-nigh perfect.

"We are honestly trying to make peace with your people. We are spending much, much money, much hard work to get treaties signed by all the tribes. Will you tell me what you think the result will be?"

Guyasuta smoked on as if he had not heard. At last he spoke.

"When white man first come he had *one fire*. Now he has *thirteen*. When he first come he say he want only as much land as a buffalo hide could cover. Now . . ." he gestured widely with his pipe. "Moons will rise and set and year will follow year and still he will take our land, and never keep a promise. What good is a treaty? Your men might as well come back home."

"There is only one other way."

Guyasuta slowly nodded his head.

"Your people then will fight?"

"We will do what we must."

"How will the *Six Nations* go?"

"As against the white man we all go together."

And then there was silence as the smoke slowly filled the kitchen.

When a heavy hour had passed in which O'Hara had felt

there was nothing for him to say, Guyasuta again removed his pipe. He leaned over the table and touched O'Hara's arm.

"I have no son of the flesh. *You* are my son of the spirit. I come tonight to ask a favor. The lands beyond the Allegheny were once my hunting ground. I want to end my days there near to you and be buried there, by your hand. Will you promise me? You, I trust."

O'Hara looked startled but he slowly rose — as did the Indian — and held out his hand. Guyasuta looked at it for a moment and then grasped it.

"I promise on my honor to see to your burial as you request, if I live longer than you. And if in your old age you need care you will have it in my own home."

The Indian looked steadily into O'Hara's eyes, drew a deep breath, pressed the hand he held again and started to the door. Then he turned and with a faint relaxing of countenance pointed upstairs.

"Young love — best love," he said, and went out.

The next morning O'Hara told Mary all about the visit, including the details of the two wives. She pretended great alarm.

"I do hope as years go on his influence over you in that line won't be too great!"

O'Hara smiled. "I rather think I can stand up under it. But I did make a promise to him I probably shouldn't have without consulting you. He wants me to bury him across the Allegheny when the time comes, and I added that if in his old age he needed care I would give it to him in our house."

"Mercy!" Mary ejaculated. "I can't fancy having an Injun at my fireplace!"

"Don't worry. He'll probably be hale and hearty till he's a hundred. For some reason I have a great fondness for the old fellow. And he calls me his *spiritual son*. It touches me, rather. I hope you understand, dear."

"Of course. And I don't wonder he loves you. Oh, I wish to-day we wouldn't have any callers. Just us. You'll so soon be going again, won't you?"

"To Kentucky, yes. But I'll be back here after that. I'm with you, though, in hoping no callers come."

But they did. At least two. The first was a thin, unshaven man with worn clothes and his feet sticking out of his shoes, who remained on the stoop as O'Hara went out to talk to him.

"Captain," he began, swallowing hard in his embarrassment, "I'd think shame to come here like a beggar if I wasn't in awful need. I was a keelboater but I took lung fever an' it nigh did for me. Then the Missus has a new baby an' Doctor Bedford says we all ought to have a . . . a . . . bit more to eat an' it was him said to come to you an' tell you just how it is. Course he's helped us by not chargin' us an' a lot like us, but . . ."

"You did right to come," O'Hara said quickly. "You know my own store?"

"Yes, sir."

"I'll give you a paper for Mr. Elliott there and he'll give you groceries. Wait a minute."

When he came back he had some money besides the paper and Prudence was already putting bread and butter in a basket and ladling out soup from the big pot over the fire into a kettle.

"There!" O'Hara said as the man took his various gifts. "Carry this carefully. It will give you all a little food before you go to the store. And let me know if you get in a pinch again. Could you work now at something easier than keelboat-ing?"

"I ain't too strong yet but I could do something. Captain, I need to work . . ."

"Well, when you go to the store tell Mr. Elliott I said to give you some little jobs, and we'll see what happens."

The man's eyes were wet with weak tears. "I can't thank you, Captain . . ."

O'Hara waved him off. "No need. We all have to help each other. Good luck and let me know how you get on."

When he told Mary about it she confessed she had often been tempted to give money aid to some of the women who seemed in hard plight, but had not been sure how he would feel about it. She did often press food upon them.

"In most cases probably food is best but if you ever find there is real need, feel free to give money too. You remember," O'Hara smiled, "the night we sat under the locust trees and agreed upon the motto for our home?"

"How could I forget? *Where friend and stranger, rich and poor, will be welcome,*" she repeated, musingly.

"I believe I said 'the decent stranger uninterrogated,' " he amended, "and we've certainly stuck to it. I wonder how many travelers we've entertained over the years? And we've had plenty of elegant guests, too, like Colonel John May of Boston a few months ago."

"He told me he would write in his Journal that he had had an elegant dinner at Captain O'Hara's home!"

"I believe I'm more proud of our reputation for hospitality than of all my land holdings. And they're pretty considerable at the moment. But it's you, darling, who make it possible and I love you for it."

The other caller was a surprise and a pleasure. He came in early evening to the parlor door, his uniform neatly brushed, his hair freshly powdered, and the gray eyes in his slender handsome face sparkling. It was Ebenezar Denny.

O'Hara sprang to meet him. "*Eb!* How on earth did you get here? Come in! Come in, man!"

Eb greeted Mary with smiling courtesy, settled himself comfortably in one of the wing chairs and looked content with life.

"What's up? Why are you back?" O'Hara kept asking.

"Give me time," Denny said, "and I'll tell you all my news. I'm here because I foxed the General into giving me a little furlough. Good man, General Harmar. If I ever have a son the General will have a namesake! Of course I have a message or two for the powers that be, back in Philadelphia. That's excuse enough on the surface, but what I really wanted was to get a few days in Carlisle."

"To see your mother, I take it?" O'Hara asked wickedly.

"Naturally," Eb answered. "To see her . . . and others."

"All right, we'll let it go at that. We'll give you our big news now and then I want to hear what's been happening at the Post. Could I bring the baby down, Mary, and show him off?"

"Oh, bachelors aren't interested in babies, dear!"

"Egad, they'd better be or the race might become extinct. Can I bring him? I'll be careful."

So little James was brought down, sleeping, by his father, examined shyly by Eb, pronounced remarkable in every respect, and conveyed, still sleeping, back to his cradle above.

"And now," O'Hara said urgently, "what's been going on? I can't wait longer to hear."

"Well," Eb began, "we've had the devil of a time — excuse me, Mistress O'Hara — with the Shawnees these last weeks. First of all they announced that a big delegation would come to the Council House to treat. It would be quite a thing, you

know, the first real overture we've had from them, so the officers got together and decided we'd receive them royally. That
we'd cook and serve them food, ourselves!"

"Oh, *no!*" O'Hara ejaculated.

"Well, you'd have known better but you weren't there."

"Wasn't *Clark* there?"

"No, he'd gone down the river. So, we went ahead and after
the gun salute we brought out the food. You should have
heard them hoot! 'The old women!' they said. 'The old
women dressed up as soldiers!' "

"That's the way it is with them," O'Hara put in. "Only the
old women do the cooking."

"Well, we found it out all right to our sorrow. They listened
to Harmar, made a speech or two themselves, and then went
off as sassy as you please."

"I'll wager they did!"

"Clark got back a few days later and just after that in
marched the Shawnees again. Some of them recognized him
and their countenances changed a little but their chief walked
up to the table bold as brass and laid a wampum belt on it,
mixed white *and black*. Peace and war, you know. Clark was
standing there with a sort of cane he had cut from a thorn tree.
Know what he did? He took his stick and skited the wampum
belt off the table on to the ground and set his foot on it!"

O'Hara threw back his head and roared with laughter. "And
his red hair bristled?"

"I swear it stood on end. Well, the damned — excuse me,
Mistress O'Hara — Injuns left with their tails down and in a
few days they came back and signed a treaty!"

Mary gave an exclamation of joy. "Oh, now the trouble's all
over, isn't it? There won't be any real war?"

Eb started to speak but O'Hara quickly forestalled him. "That's what we'll hope for, certainly, isn't it, Eb?" Then he looked at his watch. "Dr. Bedford sets the rules here just now and we have to keep hours. Shall I take you up now, Mary? Then Eb and I can mull things over and have something to 'wet our thrapples' as Semple says, and even use a cuss word now and then if our feelings for the red brethren get the best of us. All right, dear?"

"You must take my love to your mother," Mary turned back to say to Denny. "I write her about all my problems as she told me to." She gave a little laugh. "She's advised me already how to make a mustard plaster and when to start a child on the Shorter Catechism and how to test pound cake by breaking a piece against your ear to see if it sings! You'll be sure to give her my message?"

"I won't forget. I know she likes to hear from you and I might add she was born to give advice. You should see what she writes *me!*"

When the men were alone with their whiskey noggins they settled to serious discussion of the Indian affairs.

"I didn't say it in front of your wife but a few days after the treaty those sons of bitches fell on a little settlement just down the river and wiped it out. So, there we are again. Harmar's got his craw full and he'd like to get out of the whole thing if he decently could. But of course he'll stick till something's decided."

"'If it were done when 'tis done,/Then 'twere well it were done quickly,'" O'Hara quoted, musingly.

"How's that?"

"Oh, if we could be sure that a big battle would finish it all up, then we ought to get at it right away. It's this year after year prolonging, waiting, dillydallying, that frets me. I had a call from Guyasuta last night!" he added.

"No! What's *he* up to?"

"Oh, nothing particular that I know of. But he says we might as well bring our men back as far as treaties are concerned. He says the tribes will all join with the Six Nations in a war, and he evidently thinks it's inevitable."

"You know what Harmar told me out there? Congress is about to appoint General St. Clair as governor of the Western Territory!"

"No!"

"You don't care for the General?"

"Oh, he's a fine man I'm sure personally but I don't have much faith in his ability in Indian affairs. Eb, there's just one man who in my opinion could go out there and clear the whole mess up. Mad Anthony Wayne! You know his watchwords? *Silence, surprise and cold steel.* That's just what would do the trick. Congress may come to him finally but in the meanwhile they're just dumb enough to waste a lot of money and good men!" He sighed. "Oh well, if we will have a democracy we've got to put up with the frailty of our lawmakers."

"Better than a bad king at that, isn't it?"

"Oh, absolutely! I'm just restive at the moment. Selfishly so. I'd like to have the Indian business ended so I could get on with my own affairs. You know, Eb, when the old Fort comes down there's going to be a chance to get some fine building material. Want to go in with me on that?"

"I'd like it fine. As soon as I'm free of a uniform I want to settle here and get into business and . . . and get married."

"Ah," said O'Hara, "how is little Nancy Wilkins of Carlisle?"

"As sweet as ever but young, too young yet."

"Well," O'Hara laughed, "that's a fault she'll get over. Take heart, Eb. I had to wait till Mary grew up. Now about this building idea of mine . . ."

They talked on till morning and in their plans a row of brick houses rose to replace log ones. "When the time comes, O'Hara, I'll be glad to be your partner in this. The idea 'likes me well,' as the saying goes. Now, I've got to get back to the tavern for I start on tomorrow."

"As to sayings, here's a new one started round here." And he told him about the *P's and Q's.* "Take that one back east with the compliments of the Back Country," he said as they chuckled together.

Day by day O'Hara had been negotiating as usual for the needed supplies; he had also taken up his option on the lots on Water Street for more and more he dreamed of a great spreading house there one day, in keeping with his growing family and his own ambitions. He often looked at the coat of arms which hung on the parlor wall. It signified his descent from the Barons of Tyrawley, the O'Hara ancestors of County Mayo, Ireland. The rampant lion looked back at him, he fancied, a little reproachfully. *You deserve better than logs behind you,* he would think, *and one day you'll have a place worthy of you, old fellow.*

The last night before he left for Kentucky to purchase cattle he and Mary for once had no interruptions. She lay curled up on the sofa and O'Hara sat in a wing chair beside her with the candle stand close.

"I've been so busy I haven't read the papers for two weeks," he said, leafing through them. "I wonder how Scull is getting on with his news. Hugh says the subscriptions are going well but people forget to pay for them."

"Read to me," Mary said. "I'd love that."

"All right. I'll just pick the lighter items for you. Oh, here's my own little advertisement:

> Just received at the store of subscriber a complete cargo of West India goods, groceries and dry goods.
>
> JAMES O'HARA

"Simple and to the point," he commented. "But listen to this one:

> Just received from Philadelphia to be sold by Wilson and Wallace at their store in Water Street, will dispose at reasonable terms for flour, beef, cattle, butter or cash: Coffee mills, Testaments, Bibles, groceries, axes, sadlery, dishes, hats, sickles, Tea kettles, ribbons, wash basins, muffin plates, wagoner's tools and many articles too tedious to mention.

"Well," O'Hara said, "that ought to pretty well cover it. Here's an item about *Ginseng:*

> A quantity of good Ginseng wanted by the subscriber for which a generous price will be allowed in merchandise.

"What is Ginseng?" Mary interrupted.

"Oh, it's primarily an American root, I guess, and there's a big trade going on in it round here. It's supposed to cure all manner of ills. And," he added, with a sly side glance toward her, "it's reputed to increase a man's sexual powers. I wondered whether I should get some."

"*James!*" Mary said with a shocked giggle, "you are really dreadful!"

"Just thought I'd inquire," he said imperturbably. Then he cried out, "Why here's something I sent in myself months ago!"

"I didn't know you'd written anything!"

"Well, I didn't really. I got this out of an old London paper and thought Scull might use it, as an *Anecdote.* I'm strong for those. Listen. I think this is amusing.

Doctor Sheridan, the celebrated friend of Swift, always had his pupils to prayers in his school. One morning in the middle of prayers one boy saw a rat descending the bell-rope, and laughed aloud. When pointed out Doctor Sheridan was so angry he called him up and had his posteriors bared for the rod, when the witty schoolmaster told him if he could think of anything tolerable to say on the occasion he would forgive him. The trembling culprit addressed his master with the following beautiful distich:

> *"There was a rat for want of stairs*
> *Came down a rope to go to prayers."*

Sheridan instantly dropped the rod and instead of a whipping gave him half a crown."

"Oh, that's wonderful!" Mary laughed. "Mark that and I'll look it over when I want to be entertained. But do go on reading."

"Now let's see:

The famous horse DOVE will cover, this season at . . .

Um . . . um . . . um."

"What was that?"

"Nothing. Just stable talk. No interest to us. But here's something! The first Pittsburgh Almanac is soon to come out, and ah, here's a poem! By Brackenridge, I'll wager. It's called *Poetic Blossoms by a Western Swain addressed to his Mistress,* no less.

> *Ye powers divine assist in softest lays*
> *My first attempt to sing my Anna's praise.*

(He couldn't very well say Maria!)

Sublime the theme, sublime ideas rise
Depict the radiance of her charming eyes;
Charmed by those eyes, in unison conspire
All Ovid's softness and all Pindar's fire.

"That's Hugh all right. No one else knows Pindar and Ovid. There's an article on Advice to Young Men, and one on Drunkenness. I don't think we need to read either of those. I see there's a Negro wench offered for sale! I'm against slavery. You know what Hugh said one day? He said there were men around here who wouldn't for a good cow shave their beards on Sunday and yet would keep slaves and sometimes abuse them. Well, enough reading for one time, dear?"

"Perhaps, but I enjoyed it. Talk to me, now. Something I can think of when you are away."

O'Hara sat watching her. She had not yet regained her color but the paleness enhanced rather than detracted from her delicate beauty. At last he spoke.

"Hugh's verse is very nice but it's not real poetry. It doesn't go to the heart. But I know one that does. Should I repeat it for you?"

"Oh, *do,* James. That would pleasure me greatly."

"One Christmas afternoon I was sitting in Semple's Tavern at sunset thinking of you, and an old song my mother used to sing came to my mind. I always liked it so much as a boy that the words have never left me. This is it:

Have you seen but a white lily grow
Before rude hands had touched it?
Have you marked but the fall of the snow,
Before the earth hath smutched it?
Have you felt the wool of beaver
Or Swan's down ever?

Or have smelt of the bud of the brier,
Or the nard in the fire?
Or have tasted the bag of the bee?
O so white, O so soft, O so sweet,
So sweet, so sweet is she!"

There were happy tears on her cheeks when he finished and his own were misted in tenderness.

The passage of some years could be described as the "slow and steady march of time." During other periods the months in their succession seem as swiftly moving as though driven by the very spheres, because of important events crowding upon each other. The latter was the way O'Hara felt about the years which followed that quiet night with Mary in the King's Orchard.

Through bitter weather in late January of 1789 he rode once again along the Forbes Road, this time on a horse other than Pitt who was now old. O'Hara was headed for Reading with a new and peculiar glow in his heart, for he had been selected as one of the Pennsylvania electors, who would vote for the first President of the United States! His own interests had of late years been so entirely wrapped up in business, that this honor, which might be termed political, had come to him as a surprise and an enormous pleasure. He had often wakened in the night, thinking of it. More than all his service in the War, this appointment made him an *American* through and through. He gloated upon this fact as he rode along, even as he saddened at thought of his native Ireland. For one item in the *Gazette* headed *Irish Affairs*, which he had lately scanned but had refrained from mentioning to Mary, was that by Royal Proclamation any soldier who persisted in tacking on the barracks the sign *No King and Liberty* would receive 500 lashes! And a note below had struck him even more forcibly. It was to the effect that any foreigner detected in having the book entitled *The Rights of Man* by Thomas Paine, should be indicted as a felon.

"Poor Ireland," O'Hara muttered as he rode along. "I'm glad I'm out of it! I'm glad I'm in a free country."

The Pennsylvania delegation with General Hand as chairman voted unanimously for General George Washington at their February 4th meeting, and O'Hara finally returned home with satisfaction and fourteen pounds, five shillings pay for his trip! But the experience had wakened a new idea within him. This great game of politics was a challenge too, and he liked any sort. He decided to run that year for Representative in the Assembly!

It was desperately hard to fit his campaigning in with his regular work as contractor for the Western army, but he applied all his great energies to the task. Mary encouraged him, for she was thrilled over the possibility of a year in the east; but Hugh Brackenridge was openly pessimistic.

"You haven't a chance, O'Hara, if you remain a Federalist. I tell you the Democratic-Republican party is the popular one. If you had changed . . ."

"I would no more change my politics than I would change my wife," O'Hara said shortly.

"All right. Have it your own way but you'll lose as sure as shootin'."

And he did. It was a bitter pill to swallow for he was accustomed to bending events to his will, but as it happened he had plenty of other matters just then on his mind. It was clear now apparently even to Congress, that the Indian troubles could not be solved by treaties; and General Harmar was ordered to make an expedition of war against the Maumees, the renegade Indians who were then infesting the frontiers. A thousand militia were ordered from Kentucky and five hundred troops from the Pennsylvania back counties.

And O'Hara, along with the other provisions, loaded two hundred and twelve horses with flour!

The Indians won; the losses were sickening; General Harmar resigned, and a new expedition was ordered under General St. Clair. Harmar on his way back stopped in Pittsburgh and he and O'Hara talked it all over.

"St. Clair's gathered up five thousand men, but what an army! Most of them are collected from the streets and the city prisons and hurried out to the west with no more knowledge of Indian fighting than rabbits. And his officers are as ignorant, except for Dicky Butler who has no confidence in St. Clair. My expedition was disastrous enough, but I predict St. Clair's will be a slaughter."

"There is just one man . . ."

"I know. I've recommended him to Congress."

"So have I."

Harmar's prediction was all too true. When the news of the next great defeat reached Pittsburgh, the town shivered with fear. The situation was now desperate. Running like a chant of death through the streets was the nasal voice of the blind rhymester, Dennis Lochy:

> *Come gentlemen, gentlemen all,*
> *Ginral Sincleer will remem . . ber . . ed be,*
> *For he lost thirteen hundred men all,*
> *In the Western Tari . . to . . ree!*

A few days later O'Hara helped draft an appeal to the President and was one of those who signed it:

In consequence of the late intelligence of the fate of the campaign to the Westward, the inhabitants of the town of Pittsburgh have convened and appointed us a committee to address your Excellency. The late disaster of the army must greatly affect the safety of this place. There is no doubt that the enemy will now come forward with more spirit and in greater numbers, for success will give confidence and secure allies.

We seriously apprehend that the Six Nations, heretofore wavering, will now avow themselves. Be that as it may the Indians at present hostile are well acquainted with the defenseless situation of this town. At present we have neither garrison, arms nor ammunition to defend the place. If the enemy should be disposed they would find it easy to destroy us. The safety of this place being an object of the greatest consequence not only to the neighboring country but to the United States as it is the point of communication to the Westward it must be of the greatest consequence to preserve it.

The reply was speedy. General Knox of the War Department wrote Major Isaac Craig to procure materials for a picketed fort to be built in such part of Pittsburgh as would best cover the town and any stores kept there. And with this order old Fort Pitt died forever and the new Fort La Fayette was born.

O'Hara spoke again to Elliott. "Why don't you eat at the house too, when I'm away? I'll tell Mary and Prudence you're tired of tavern fare. How about it? I'd feel safer."

"Couldn't refuse good vittles."

"You know Guyasuta?"

"Sure. I know the old goat."

"He's my friend. If he should ever turn up at night, watch out. He'll be on a peaceful errand."

"If you say so."

"I do. But if any hostile Indians should ever come near . . . for God's sake, Elliott, aim straight."

"Well now," he drawled, "it ain't hardly necessary to tell me how to use a rifle. I've a general idea which end the shootin' comes out of. But I'll take care of things. I still think the Injuns will study a while before they come into the town here but the new fort's a help. It's goin' up fast, I tell you."

"How's the new man working out at the store?"

"Why, damned good. Takes to it like a duck to water. Oh, we'll get along fine here. But what do you think's goin' to happen now in the west? Something's got to be busted up, huh?"

"And pretty soon," O'Hara said grimly.

As a matter of fact several things happened in quick succession in that April of 1792. First, a quiet letter but one filled with potential significance came to Mary. There was a Post Office now in Pittsburgh and the inhabitants listened on certain days for the blast of the post rider's tin horn which announced the arrival of the mail. So on this day Mary, upon hearing it, had sauntered up to where the letters were dispensed and returned with her own which was from one of the Chew sisters in Philadelphia. She read its news eagerly as she walked along, and then at one sentence stopped in her tracks.

Mrs. Wayne, Anthony's wife, died last week at their home in Paoli, after a long illness. It is said he cared for her most faithfully. Only now of course we wonder . . .

Mary could hardly wait for O'Hara to get home that evening. She told him at once.

"Oh, James, it would seem so wicked to rejoice and yet how can we help it a little? Will you write him? Should I write Mary Vining?"

"I would say no to both," he replied thoughtfully. "It's a delicate situation. I think we should wait until we hear the facts from one of them. Of course if what I hope for comes true, we may see Anthony here before long."

The two appointments came close together: Major General Anthony Wayne was chosen at long last to snatch victory from the Indian tribes of the West; and James O'Hara was appointed by the President with the advice of the Senate to be Quartermaster-General in the Army of the United States!

When the dignified certificate was received O'Hara and Mary pored over it that evening with pride on both their faces.

"This is the biggest thing that has come to me yet. I can't help feeling elated that His Excellency has such trust in me. You see this means that I'll be responsible not only for provisioning all Wayne's troops but for every post we have, even up into New York." O'Hara drew a long breath. "It will be a tremendous job, but somehow I think I can do it!"

"Of course you can," Mary agreed. "You can do anything! But I suppose this will mean you will be away from home more than ever?"

He looked steadily into her eyes. "I'm afraid that will be true, dear."

She managed a smile. "I'll try to do my part too," she said.

Although as beautiful as ever, Mary had changed in the last five years. Two more babies had come to her, very close together. One, little Butler, named for General Dicky whom O'Hara greatly admired, lay sleeping safely now, upstairs; the other, alas, lay in a tiny grave behind the Presbyterian church. "There are so many *little* graves," Mary had whispered piteously to her husband on that tragic day.

O'Hara had known a sharp grief at the time, but the rush of work and the lively children still in the house had dulled it. But he knew Mary's heart still mourned. It showed in the

white silences that occasionally fell upon her and in the weeping that sometimes overtook her in the night when she clung
to him. But, perceptive as he always was toward her, he realized that the sorrow had deepened her nature. She was no
longer merely the lighthearted girl; she was a woman, and now
essentially his helpmeet. She had learned more details of his
government work and his private business. She studied carefully the information he gave her, and was ready with practical
advice now and then which, to his surprise, he found himself
taking seriously. Of course due to O'Hara's native wit there
was between them the same constant flow of laughter and small
jokes; but each was finding new depths in the other as the
years passed.

At once, as was his habit, O'Hara began to plan for his new
duties. There must be, he realized, the erection of magazines
and granaries for the storage of dry forage at various points;
he would need to hire blacksmiths, wheelwrights and carpenters, and, perhaps most important of all, secure a deputy quartermaster for each large post. He began this latter selection by
talking with Major Isaac Craig. The news of his own appointment had soon swept Pittsburgh and O'Hara found the daily
greetings of his neighbors tinged with new respect.

"You'll come out of this a *General*," Hugh predicted as he
congratulated his friend.

"Just so *I come out of it*," O'Hara said, "I'll be willing to
forego the title."

"Um," Hugh was meditative. "You do get yourself into the
damnedest jobs. This new one will be plenty dangerous one
way and another, I suppose."

"Plenty," said O'Hara, "but I'm like Oliver Goldsmith, 'I
have a knack at *hoping*.' Well, just don't give Mary the other

idea, nor Maria either, for that matter," he added. "Women do talk together, you know."

His conversation with Major Craig was highly satisfactory.

"Isaac, will you Q.M. for me in Pittsburgh? I'll need a good deputy here. It will be a case of receiving and distributing the public stores as they come in. It's all going to be big business, Isaac."

"Well, I'm glad I don't have the whole responsibility. But I'll take over for you here, gladly."

They paid their respects to the old fort as they walked toward it, and discussed the new one. It would be the center now for the supplies. O'Hara's eyes were fixed across the Monongahela.

"I'm going to tell you something, Isaac, which I've told only to Brackenridge and, of course, my wife. When General Wayne finishes the Indian business I want to get into manufacturing."

The Major laughed. "You'll need something of course to occupy you. All you have now is a store, a gristmill, a sawmill, a tannery and plans, I hear, for a brewery here at the Point."

O'Hara made a deprecative gesture. "Oh, I like to keep Pittsburgh busy. But this other is my special dream. I own land over below Coal Hill. I want to put up a plant there one day to *make glass.*"

"I'll be damned!"

"Is that so strange?"

"No. The surprising thing is I've thought of it myself."

O'Hara reached for the other's hand and gripped it. *"Good man!"* he exclaimed. "When we're ready to start, will you be my partner?"

The Major looked rather dazed. "You're a hard one to refuse, O'Hara. I guess I may as well agree to this too."

So, the bargain was sealed.

A few evenings later there was a knock at the parlor door after supper, and there stood Major-General Wayne. *Mad Anthony!* Handsomer by far than either O'Hara or Mary remembered, with ruddy cheeks, chestnut brows and golden brown eyes below the white hair. A great warmth of friendship enfolded them, with the pulsing under current of the future's beckoning joys always present but never quite breaking through. There was all the general Philadelphia news to discuss though one name was not spoken. Then when all the light gossip was over Mary rose and extended her hand prettily.

"It's delightful to see you again, General. Of course we met on my wedding day but I was so excited then . . ."

"Of course you were. I've always heard that love is a great beautifier, and you, who needed least to prove it, have done so!"

"Oh, what a gallant speech! I thank you, General, and we'll expect you tomorrow night to dinner. Now I'll leave you both to discuss the big matters."

They were indeed big and the two men settled to them with stern faces. The troops would be arriving soon, and the westward march would begin. Wayne's questions came, sharp, intelligent, determined, and O'Hara answered them from his wider experience with the Indians and the wilderness. When the General rose to go at last a slight grimace of pain crossed his face.

"Do you remember that damn fool sentry that shot me the night we were going to La Fayette's camp?" he asked.

"I do, indeed. Do you mean you still have trouble from it?"

"I do, a little. The doctors have probed around as if they were digging potatoes but they can't find the bullet. Still in the fleshy part of the upper leg, I guess. Oh, well, as long as it behaves itself there I'm all right."

He stood a moment as though uncertain how to proceed, then he said slowly, "Have you heard anything recently about my . . . family?"

"We have," O'Hara answered. "Mary had a letter from a friend in Philadelphia. I . . ."

Wayne raised his hand. "I do not wish to speak of that. It has its own sadness. But since you know my story I will tell you that when a sufficient time has elapsed Miss Vining's parents will announce our engagement and then . . ." All at once his golden brown eyes fairly blazed with light. "As soon as I'm finished with this campaign, we will be married!"

O'Hara wrung his hand, still forebearing comment for fear of choosing the wrong words, but he did say quickly, "Come, I'll walk along the lane with you. The apple trees are almost in blossom and there's a moon."

They went slowly and in silence through the faintly perfumed air with the pale light glancing upon the new, young leaves. O'Hara wondered if Wayne was thinking as he was of that other spring night at York when they had sat together and spoken of the soldiers sentenced to die the next day. He shook off the memory. At the end of the lane he said, "Anthony, this night is too beautiful to think of Indians! Let's just concentrate on whatever brings joy to our hearts, shall we?"

"Even so!" the General answered, smiling. "Even so."

They parted then, both strong, virile men in their early prime, tested in many fires and not found wanting. And both in love.

CHAPTER TWELVE

IF GENERAL WAYNE'S mission was a desperately difficult
one: to win complete victory from the Indians who now
were more than ever confident because of their successes over
Harmar and St. Clair; throw the west open for civilization; and
indirectly compel the British to yield the posts they still held
on the American side of the Great Lakes; O'Hara's problems
loomed at first all but insurmountable. He knew moments when
the weight of his vast responsibility seemed crushing. But his
years of experience in this particular field along with his natural
determination and confidence bore him up. So he wrote firmly
to Secretary of War Knox:

"I can now take the liberty of assuring you that no motive
nor consideration can possibly interfere with the duties of my
station, which I feel myself most religiously bound to execute
agreeable to your instructions and my own judgment."

Thus, he dedicated himself to the task.

One of his first problems was that arrangements had to be
made now for handling large sums of money. One early con-
signment of cavalry horses alone cost $25,000. O'Hara decided
that not more than $10,000 should be sent to him at one time.
Then he talked the matter over with Mary.

"These packets will come to *you*. You will open them,'

count the money, make a record of it and then turn it over to
Major Craig. If I am out at a post at the time and need it there,
he will forward it to me."

Mary was aghast. "*I* am to receive this money?"

"You are. I trust a great many people. Most of them in fact.
But there is only one person in whom I have perfect and absolute confidence. Give you one guess," he added with his usual
warm smile. "This way we will always have a double check.
Now, can you ever say again you are not my partner?"

There was one personal matter to consider now when they
were together. O'Hara was eager to have the big house on
Water Street built as soon as possible.

"We're cramped here," he said. "Look at our family already, and I can't trust you not to add to it!"

"I hope to," she said demurely.

"So," he went on, "since you and I have already agreed upon
the plans, I'll try to get the workmen started at once. I'll look
things over from time to time when I'm back and it will give
you something interesting to do, to supervise while I'm away.
You're happy about it, aren't you?"

"Yes," she said slowly, "though I will always like the King's
Orchard better than Water Street."

"Ah, but I have a surprise for you! How would you like it if
we should keep this house? I'll use it for my office and we can
come over to it whenever we wish. When the apple trees are in
bloom, for instance."

She threw her arms around his neck. "Oh, James, you always read my heart."

Once more O'Hara rode through the trackless forests where
danger always lurked, for he considered it his duty to visit all
the posts at least once a year as he transacted his enormous
business. There were the ever pressing and vexing problems

of supplies and transportation, but even more wearing was the keeping of accounts for the War Department. In a leather package fastened to his saddle there were the long sheets upon which by candlelight in all sorts of strange places he wrote in his precise hand the endless records of money received and expenditures listed.

Wayne at this time was comfortably camped at a place he had named *Legionville* from the "Legion" he had organized. Word had come back to O'Hara that the General had inaugurated the strictest discipline with the troops. Two soldiers had been shot for sleeping at their posts (hard necessity, he would say again); whiskey was forbidden in the camp; cleanliness and regularity of diet was insisted upon; there was drilling every day including the use of bayonet and sword; Wayne dined with his officers, carefully explaining to them all the details of the expedition; and most remarkable perhaps of all, he had secured the services of some friendly Choctaws and was using them to sow dissension among their hostile brethren.

These facts all helped to answer a question often put to O'Hara. Why did Congress not appoint George Rogers Clark to lead this expedition? Who knew the Indians better than he? O'Hara in answering tried to be fair to both his friends. Clark was the most fearless, the most ingenious of leaders when his troops consisted of a band of frontiersmen who could endure incredible hardships and "shoot a squirrel through the left eye." But this battle that was slowly but inevitably building up was one which would demand a seasoned general of trained troops. The Indians now in their warfare had come a long way from the time of Braddock, when they shot arrows from behind trees! They had learned much of the art of war and now, supplied by the British, had guns and bullets.

While O'Hara working with his various deputies was supplying all posts, his greatest concern of course was for Wayne's encampment, as his neat records showed.

19404 lbs. flour	$1940.40
18750 lbs. fresh beef	468.75
9500 lbs. salted beef	1045.00
30 head beef cattle	440.00
1 yoke oxen	66.00
1 Brown steer	235.00
1 Kentucky boat 30 ft. long	41.80

And notations. *Furnish 270,000 daily rations in advance on December 1st. Purchase 1400 more horses and equipment . . .*

O'Hara often thought with a wry smile as he scanned his accounts that mere figures could not list the miles he had traveled; the deals he had effected; the contracts made, broken and restored; the difficulties with recalcitrant wagoners and boatmen; the ingenuity (he admitted it!) by which he achieved the well-nigh impossible. And with it all, while he tried to keep the thought underneath, he realized he was making a great deal of money.

Upon one subject Wayne had twitted him playfully. O'Hara's love of horses was ingrained. When he wrote the General anxiously about the care of certain invalid dragoon horses Wayne had replied that he believed O'Hara was more interested in *equus* than in *homo.*

But their letters were as a rule serious in nature and couched in conventional language. They were both angry and frustrated when Congress decided even now to attempt another parley and sent Commissioners to Fort Erie to sue for peace! The result was that the Indians gained the time they wanted, then refused to treat at all, and the burden fell upon Wayne to see that the Commissioners reached their homes with their scalps on their heads, for which they formally gave him thanks.

In the fall of 1793 a new anxiety fell upon Pittsburgh and especially upon O'Hara. A contagious fever had broken out in Philadelphia. Most of the clothing for the army came from there and an order from the War Department was received at once by Major Craig to open, air and repack all the bundles! The Pittsburghers were frightened. O'Hara came back when the news reached him, his heart torn within him. He felt he must help Craig but in doing so he forfeited the opportunity to go home. He spoke to Mary from outside their door, slept in the fort and prayed as he had not often done. The reports from Philadelphia grew worse and then there were none at all. Secretary of War Knox had fled with his family to Boston, Major Stagg, also of the department, had gone to New York, so there were no communications from the War offices. There was nothing to do but work, wait and hope.

O'Hara's great solace during these weeks was the sight of the new house on Water Street. "There must be *stabling,* too," he had once said to Mary. "That's what it's always called in the old country. For I intend to have a nice place for Pitt to end his days in and also room for two carriage horses."

"Are we to have a carriage then?" Mary had asked in pleased surprise.

"Indeed we are. I fancy seeing my wife ride out on a summer day, holding a little parasol over her head. A coachman on the box, of course."

"Won't you be along?"

"On Sundays. Then we can pretend we're driving once more to the Garden of Delight! You had a pink dress on that day."

"I'll get another."

The house and stables were now finished, ready for the last painting and the planting of the grounds. The place had a spacious dignity even O'Hara had not expected and he thrilled with the pride of it. Inside beyond the wide reception hall there was a great drawing room, a dining room of generous dimensions and a library, with kitchen and pantries behind. Prudence had some misgivings about cooking on a *stove* but her devotion was such that she was ready to try anything. Besides there would be, of course, another servant. Over the stables were adequate quarters for McGrady who, while his indenture period was long since up, was a fixture in the family and a possible coachman.

" 'It likes me well,' as Eb Denny would say," O'Hara murmured as he went over his property.

New furniture had already been ordered, with the dining-room pieces a surprise for Mary. These, O'Hara had written his father-in-law, were to be the handsomest that money could buy and he and Mary's sister Elizabeth were to select them. He mentioned in his letter that their house in the King's Orchard, while modest, had already become famed for its hospitality; so it was his desire that the new dining room should be meet to receive even the most distinguished guests.

By the end of November the epidemic had subsided as suddenly as it had come; the exiles returned to Philadelphia; mail began to come through bringing a letter to Mary from her father that all was well with the family; Pittsburghers relaxed as there was now no further danger of contagion from the army clothes; and O'Hara, scrubbed and brushed at the fort, went to spend his last nights with Mary.

As he rode off again he was thinking seriously of his conversations with Brackenridge which had taken place here and there on street corners. Hugh was violently worked up over the proposed excise tax on whiskey and its possible results.

"I tell you, O'Hara, these farmers around here are oiling their rifles. They mean business. They're going to fight this like hell. They've got David Bradford, a young Washington County lawyer, for their leader and when the time comes they'll stop at nothing, even to *invading Pittsburgh*."

"Oh come, Hugh," O'Hara had said. "Aren't you pulling the long bow?"

"I am *not*," he replied shortly. "I've studied this thing and the root of the trouble is far deeper than a mere quarrel over the excise. As these people see it, it's a stand by the Democratic, poverty-ridden West against the encroachments of the aristocratic Money Bags of the East."

"And may I ask where you stand on this?"

"Well, I'll answer indirectly and please keep it to yourself. General Neville is backing up the excise tax for all he's worth, and I was born to be an enemy of the General's!"

"Well, mind your P's and Q's, Hugh," O'Hara said with a grin.

"Mind your own. Oh, good luck, old man. I know you have enough on your mind just now without my bothering you with this. What a lot of problems there are in the world!"

There were plenty for O'Hara during that winter, and few visits home. By April he had to go to Philadelphia to await the passage of the Appropriation Bill in order to get more money and the chance to buy there in the city much that he needed for the West. It was good to see Mary's family again and exchange all their news. Christian Febiger, Elizabeth's husband and his own erstwhile groomsman, was going to ride back with him, on his way to the Legion. He was a soldier, eager to serve in this new crisis and most of all to be once again under General Wayne. Ever since Stony Point his admiration for Mad Anthony had mounted to near worship.

The bill passed, the Secretaries of War and Treasuries were not only helpful but loud in their praises of O'Hara's work; and to his great relief he was able to secure certain supplies he needed for the western country right there and order them forwarded as quickly as possible without further intervention from him.

The ride back to Pittsburgh was one of the most beautiful O'Hara could remember. A soft blush was creeping up the stalks of the sumac and sassafras, the small green leaves were unfolding on all the trees, the tiny wood folk scampered about, and the fresh scent of new growth rising from the forest floor was all around them. It was a comfortable trip too, compared with those he made constantly to the various posts, for now the Forbes Road was well traveled and inns had sprung up along its route. A contrast indeed to the one upon which Elliott had taken him on his first journey west! Between stops, however, there were still long hours of forest solitude. One day O'Hara broke the silence.

"I've got a new bee in my bonnet, Febiger."

"I wouldn't doubt it from the news I get about you. What's this one?"

"Salt," said O'Hara laconically.

"*Salt?* What are you talking about?"

"Well, it's like this. Salt has always been most devilish expensive in our parts. It all has to be brought over the mountains either from Baltimore or Philadelphia with a very high freight rate. *We've* always been able to afford it ourselves, but there are plenty of settlers around and people in Pittsburgh too, who can't. I tell you there's still many a sprinkling of wood ashes used to take its place."

"Good Lord! I never heard of such a thing!"

"You never lived on the frontier," O'Hara returned grimly. "Now I've found out on my trips around the posts that there is a big saltworks at Salina, New York, not far from Niagara. The Onondaga works, it's called. If I could manage to get salt shipped from there I'm sure it would eventually be cheaper than from Baltimore."

"How would transportation be?"

O'Hara laughed. "Now you've asked the *real* question. All I would need to do, as I see it, would be to buy a good many wagons and teams, build a couple of vessels at the Lakes, improve a few roads and portages . . ."

"I think you'd better forget it!" Febiger said, highly amused.

But O'Hara knew that the idea once having entered his mind would never leave it. He added only one more comment now. "If I can ever bring this about it would benefit not only Pittsburgh but all of Western Pennsylvania."

By June a letter came from Wayne which was both amusing and pathetic. He said that the war had now assumed so serious a complexion that O'Hara should be with the Legion. That at the moment they had no deputy at Greenville, their present encampment, "except the most trifling thing, whose utmost stretch of abilities will not reach across the counter." O'Hara and Mary laughed over this together. But in a few days a more urgent message came. Wayne wrote that he considered O'Hara's presence there "indispensably necessary."

So there was another goodbye, this time fraught on O'Hara's part with the knowledge that the great battle, after the long skirmishes, preparations and delays, was at last about to be waged. And he would be there. The new house stood ready but the occupancy must wait perhaps until fall.

"Couldn't you take over a few linens and little things?" O'Hara asked. "I fancy Maria would like to help and it would give you pleasure to begin your moving in small ways. It will all have to be done sometime, you know."

"I think I would like that. Oh James, don't you suppose it would be proper now to tell Anthony that I've heard from Mary Vining and that I send him my warm congratulations!"

"I'm sure it would. I'll have a good deal to tell him myself." For the word in various letters from Philadelphia was that the social set was completely agog over the news of the engagement and coming marriage. All reports said Mary Vining had never been so beautiful, never so radiant, never, of course, so happy. She shone like a star in every group. Even the thought of an imminent battle did not seem to frighten her, the dangers of war being apparently less absolute to her than those of the unending bonds of honor had been. "My Anthony is invincible!" she had said once proudly.

As O'Hara held Mary for the last time before he left he wondered with pain in his heart if farewells would ever cease, if perils would ever end, for he knew, unlike Mary Vining, that no man was invincible.

When he finally reached the camp at Greenville on the Miami River he received a touchingly warm welcome from Wayne who looked tired and careworn but brightened immeasurably as he received Mary's message and heard O'Hara's further reports.

"I can hardly believe it!" he said with a sudden boyish smile. "And thank heaven we're coming toward a climax here at last, by the reports my spies bring in. You see we can't have a real battle until the Indians actually line up against us. So it's been skirmish after skirmish with nothing conclusive. My word, I'm glad you've come, O'Hara! This fellow here doesn't know a flapjack from the sole of his shoe." He laughed. "As a matter of fact I can't tell the difference either, as things are."

"I'm sorry about him. He was well recommended. Have you fared pretty well up to this?"

"Excellently. I think you've saved the army! I know what a job it must have been. One of those impossible things that somehow gets done anyway."

"I'll get to work at the Commissary at once."

"Oh no. Wait till morning. Come into my tent and let's talk. We both deserve that much respite."

So they talked again chiefly of happy matters: the wedding and where it would be; O'Hara's new house; details of dress for a military bridegroom; the charms of their respective Marys upon which each could expatiate with full sympathy from the other. As the hour grew late Wayne filled their noggins again with whiskey. "Not good for the troops," he said with a twinkle, "but excellent for the General."

"As a matter of fact, O'Hara," he went on, "I don't see why we shouldn't admire ourselves a little! We damned well deserve it. I'm pretty proud of this last record. I've marched nearly four hundred miles through the country of the most watchful and most vindictive enemy! I've cut a road through the woods the entire way, a lot longer and more remote and more dangerous, too, than Braddock's ever was. We've built three forts and now at last we've got to a position where the issue is really going to be joined!"

O'Hara raised his cup.

"And *you!*" Wayne went on. "Look what you've done, man! You've supplied this army all the way, through practically insuperable difficulties. Without you the whole thing couldn't have happened!"

He raised his own cup. "Here's to us! As the Scotch say, *'Who's like us!'* "

O'Hara set to work at once the next day and with something of Wayne's own disciplinary powers, reorganized the Commissary department. There was food enough there if it was properly sorted and prepared. The staff soon learned they were now working under a master who meant business and improved accordingly. The meals at once grew better and Wayne spoke his satisfaction.

"Nothing puts spirit in an army quicker than decent food. I was growing desperate before, for in these next weeks I want to hold the men up to fighting pitch."

"More supplies ought to arrive any day now. I started them out weeks ago," O'Hara said. "One thing I want to ask. When the final engagement comes, be sure to put me in it. I can shoot as well as most."

"No," Wayne answered. "We'll need to eat after the battle, whenever it comes. You stick to your own job and the rest of us will attend to the shootin'."

"I feel rather a coward, staying in the rear."

"*You!*" Wayne laughed. "You're the last man I'd ever accuse of that. Besides, if it's any comfort to you, there won't be much safety anywhere at that time. And you can keep your rifle loaded."

O'Hara was amazed at the encampment itself, the neatness, the order! There were close to three thousand soldiers here but their movements were a pattern of disciplined training. He watched the bayonet drills with interest. *This* weapon was the one thing, he knew, against which Indians would not fight. Good old Anthony! He knew his job.

As the weeks wore on more supplies arrived and there was through the camp the murmur of full-bellied satisfaction. In addition, the reports from the spies indicated that the Indians were collecting in earnest some miles away along the Miami.

"We'll move up, now," Wayne told O'Hara, "and build another fort. The men can knock one up in a hurry. I think we'll name it *Fort Defiance*."

"You'll wait to build a fort?" O'Hara asked in surprise.

"It won't take long and it will be a good thing to have. I don't expect to *fall back* to it, but we might need it for the wounded."

The order to break camp and march was given early in August. O'Hara's work was in a way the heaviest of all, for the removal of Commissary and supplies was always a difficult one. He talked the night before with Febiger.

"If either of us should stub a toe in this business it might be wise to leave a few last words . . ." They took it lightly but certain messages from each were carefully written down.

"I'm sorry Eb Denny is missing all this. He was sent up to Fort Erie with a contingent some time ago. He'd like to be with Wayne, I know that."

"We all like to be with Wayne," Febiger replied.

The march was through the very heart of the Indian country but there were no incidents, further proof that the enemy was concentrating farther on. When the stop finally came, the fort, as Wayne had predicted, was quickly built: a rude log structure but capable of protection and defense. A thrill like that of a tingling nerve was now sensible amongst the men. In the officers' mess there was rejoicing. After their long, intolerable waiting there was to be decisive action at last. For the report of the scouts was that the Indians, probably about two thousand of them, were now lining up about five miles distant in regular battle array.

"Good!" Wayne gloated. "Couldn't be better!"

The order to march again was given early the next morning and the five miles were covered speedily with the army moving in its fighting positions, the Miami River to the right of them until they came upon a spot where a tornado had evidently swept through the forest, leaving twisted trunks and uprooted trees in enough profusion to impede the cavalry. Wayne, as always in the van, led the way around the fallen timbers, and when the army was all at last on level ground, formed his forces in two lines with cavalry leading the first. Suddenly the Indians opened fire upon the mounted men in front, so concerted and murderous as to drive them back to the main army. There was a rain of bullets from the Legion, only to be answered steadily by the Indians. O'Hara in the rear where he had been ordered to stay felt sheer terror grip him. "This is worse than York-town!" he kept muttering. "Much worse."

The Indians, though in more or less conventional formation, still practiced their ancient art of deploying behind trees. The battle grew more and more merciless as the hours passed. Life or death, that struggle, with the Indians fighting at their last stand for their lands and their homes; and the Legion of the United States fighting for a country that would stretch from the mountains to the western sea.

At last O'Hara from his vantage saw what Wayne was about to do. He was sending one force to turn the right of the enemy, and another at the same time along the river to turn their left. And in the center, there was advancing a heavy brigade with *bayonets fixed,* to press by direct charge, the enemy from their coverts.

The Indians could not withstand this mode of attack. They broke in utter confusion and were driven two miles in the course of an hour with, as O'Hara heard afterwards, dead bodies and British muskets scattered in all directions. Before the sun set their villages and cornfields were burned for miles around. The forty-year struggle with the red men was ended.

O'Hara had no time to talk as he supervised the hot supper the soldiers sorely needed. Meanwhile the wounded were taken back to Fort Defiance where General Hand, with the army now not as a military man but in his own profession as a doctor, ministered to them. Wayne and the other officers were seeing to the burial of the dead.

The last smoldering embers were dying out in the sky when O'Hara went into Wayne's tent at his request to join him at supper. The General looked white and exhausted but with a spark of triumph in his eyes.

"Well, it's over, thank God," he began.

"And what a victory!"

"Yes, I guess we'll call it the Battle of Fallen Timbers when we send in a report. Good a name as any. What a place that was! I'll tell you something, O'Hara. I've fought my last battle. I think I've done my duty for my country. What I want now is to go home and get married and make love and lead the life of a country gentleman the rest of my days. I don't ever want to hear the word *war* again."

"I don't wonder. After today I certainly don't myself. But now you can leave soon for the East, can't you?"

Wayne stared at him. "Let's eat first and wet our whistles well, and then I'll tell you how the immediate future looks to me." As he moved an expression of pain escaped him.

"General, you're not wounded!"

"No, no. I don't know how I always escape. Mary says I'm 'invincible.' No, it's that damned old bullet that gives me a twinge sometimes. I'm fit as a fiddle, really. Just tired. Dog tired."

When they had eaten and drunk well, Wayne leaned back and began to speak, slowly.

"You remember after Yorktown, O'Hara? Well, I'm afraid we're caught in the same way, now. The big battle is over, true, and I'm sure the Indians will never take concerted action again, but there are still a lot of them around. If we pulled out our troops completely now it would be unwise. I want to see a *real* treaty signed this time. One that will stick, and this time it may take a while. Then of course there is the matter of the judicious and orderly dispersion of several thousand troops. Poor devils! They all want to get home as much as we do. I don't let myself think how much longer I may have to stay. You'll get back sooner of course, but I will need you for several months more at least. How about it?"

O'Hara smiled. "I think I can still take orders, *mon général.*"

"Do you remember after Yorktown when we had to accept delay I spoke one note of comfort?" Wayne asked.

"I'm afraid I don't. I guess my mind at the time was not too receptive to comfort."

"Well, I said that at least from then on letters would get through. And it's the same here, only better. It's amazing what work the messengers have done. So, let's count on that. One pleasant fact to me is, I'm still *alive.*"

O'Hara sobered as he looked into Wayne's eyes.

"After what I saw you doing today I can't account for it, but I give hearty thanks."

So the weeks went on. As the General had said, letters came with surprising regularity. A brief one from Brackenridge gave O'Hara the keenest anxiety. The "Whiskey Rebellion," as it was now being called, had reached a point of near violence. Commissioners appointed by President Washington were in Pittsburgh, including Brackenridge himself, William Bradford, the attorney general of the United States, Thomas McKean, chief justice of the state supreme court, and Congressman William Irvine, once commander of Fort Pitt. On the other side were David Bradford and his fire-eating followers of Washington County, including the stiffest of those resisting the tax on their own distilled whiskey. Brackenridge wrote:

> I trust you to keep this under your hat, O'Hara, but for the moment I'm running with the hare and the hounds both. My sympathies are with the western farmers, but I feel I can do more for them by appearing to side with the law until things get quieter. If the foxy Nevilles find me out, I'm as good as done for. The girls don't seem to realize the seriousness of the situation yet and I don't enlighten them. Mary, of course, is completely out of it since you are, yourself. Better stay there a while longer.

As a matter of fact Mary's letters were very cheerful. She and Maria were having the greatest pleasure in the leisurely move to the new house. It was becoming more and more like home to her and she really had to curb her feeling of *pride* in it. The house in the King's Orchard *did* look small now. And wasn't this strange when it had seemed ample before? She would never cease to love it because it had been their first home and was so relieved they were to keep it. She had started the older little boys on the New England Primer and had found them to be *so* bright. Little Butler had been left with a cough after the measles but Dr. Bedford said it often happened. She read his letters over and over and slept with the latest one under her pillow, and just exactly where *was* he now?

One night he sat at a camp table and wrote her in detail.*

Headquarters
Miami Villages
Oct. 3rd, 1794

MY DEAR WIFE

I had the pleasure of writing you last from Cincinnati, on the 19th. Ultimo. On the 20th. I left Fort Washington and on the 30th. arrived at this place with my convoy in perfect order and very acceptable. This march was by no means disagreeable.

The Army arrived here from Fort Defiance on the 17th. of September, and the Legion is now employed in erecting a Fort which will be strong and regular. A Garrison of three Hundred and fifty will be left, and about the 15th. the remainder of the Army will return to Greenville, and the business of my department being completed in the Quarter for six months, I shall then proceed to Fort Washington. This will probably be about the first of Nov. I shall in the meantime embrace every opportunity of writing you.

The intentions of the Indians yet remain a mystery, their long and total silence in respect to us is considered as very extraordinary. I am however convinced that they are awaiting the result of more refined and corrupt councils than their own, which may terminate in the confusion and disgrace of the Incendiaries concerned.

I am greatly concerned for the Doctor's state of health, and have some apprehension for Febiger, who would also be an irreparable loss to the whole connection, *hope for the best.*

I see your curiosity to know how far we are from any place.

I inform you that Recovery is one Hundred miles from Fort Washington, the General Course with 16 Degrees West, that here the Army faced to the Right and marched to Grand

* The original of this letter is in possession of Mrs. H. E. H. Brereton, the great-granddaughter of James O'Hara.

Glaize where Fort Defiance now stands, seventy four Miles and and a half, General Course North, 10 Degrees East, and from that point the Army marched on the 13th. Ultimo, ascending the Miami river forty eight Miles and a half, General Course, South, 69 Degrees West, and with the last Escourt I kept the old Course by Fort Recovery to this place which I reckon fifty four Miles from Recovery, then 24 Miles to Greenville, then 76 to Fort Washington, and about 500 to *home.*

It gives me a great deal of pleasure to hear that my dear little boys are such clever fellows and learn so well. I am in hopes my Butler will grow bold and strong with the change of the Season.

God bless you and them,
and preserve you, the
delight of your most
tender

JAMES O'HARA

He got home in late November earlier than he had expected, on an Indian summer afternoon. He rode quickly through the town and dismounted, his heart beating fast, at his own door. Here Prudence met him.

"Oh, you're home, sir," she said with her usual calmness. "Well the Mistress is over at the Big Place!"

He thanked her and hurried to Water Street. Before him stood the house of his dreams, painted white now, making it look even larger than it was, with the new grass still green upon the lawn and the young trees at the sides and back showing sturdy growth. He stood for a minute looking at the noble view of the rivers, then with his heart high, he bounded up the steps and opened the front door. There was no sound within.

"Mary!" he called. "Mary!"

There was a cry then and the sound of running feet and she threw herself into his arms, but not with the usual joyful welcome. She was crying as he held her, sobbing even.

"Oh darling, my Delight, what is it? Tell me!" His voice was terrified.

"It's your being away so long. I can't stand it. I've tried to be brave and do my part but it's been too hard, with all this Whiskey War going on. James, they almost burned down this house!"

"*What?*" he cried.

"It's true. It was only Hugh that saved it. You know Major Kirkpatrick right next us here has been working with General Neville for the government and the Whiskey people hate him and they came one night, a crowd of them, to set fire to his house. And of course that would have taken this one. And Hugh came and talked to them. He said you were away, serving your country and they mustn't do this harm to you. And finally they went away. But they did burn the Kirkpatrick farm build-ings up on Coal Hill. We could see the glare all over town. Oh, I've been so *frightened!*"

There were a few chairs already there and he drew her to one and held her on his knee, smoothing her hair as he tried to com-fort her, making strong resolutions within himself.

"Darling, listen. You've been so brave, so uncomplaining these past years. But now my plans are going to be different. I will not leave you this time until all this *Whiskey* trouble is over. And even after that I promise you my trips will be shorter. The big battle is won now and I can delegate more of the business to others. Would you care to hear a little piece of news?"

She raised her head and he wiped the tears away.

"I've been made *General* O'Hara. Do you like the sound of that?"

She kissed him for answer, her face suddenly all alight. "I never was so proud! How long have you known it?"

"Not long. I got word before I left the Post. As a matter of fact I feel a bit 'lifted' myself as they say in the old country. Well now, dear little *Mrs. General O'Hara,* would you join me in a tour of the house?"

So the tears and their own dark days of separation were once more forgotten, but Mary had a quick question.

"What about General Wayne? When will Anthony get home?"

O'Hara's face sobered. "I don't know," he said. "You see he's just done a tremendous thing. He's made a complete conquest of the Indians for the first time in forty years. Now he naturally wants to oversee the Peace Treaty. He practically has to, and the Indians are delaying. We think they're waiting to see what the British will do about the forts they still hold. What do you hear of Mary Vining?"

"Oh, she's *so* happy, everyone writes me. So relieved he got through the battle safely. She pretended she wasn't worried but of course she was, terribly. Now she says when their happiness is so assured she can wait as long as she has to. The girls say she's doing the most exquisite needle work for her bridal chest. Well, I hope it won't be too long. Come now, and see the dining-room rug. Father sent it addressed to me, so I had it laid. And the furniture is all here in crates at the back of the store! Of course it was all sent to you, but since the rug is mine . . ."

"But dear Delight, everything I have is yours!"

"Oh yes, but I wanted us to be together when the furniture was set in. Can we have it done soon?"

"As soon as tomorrow we'll begin."

When they had made their tour and stood in front of the house ready to start back to the Orchard, Mary said slowly, "When this is all furnished as we plan I believe it's going to be even more beautiful than my old home in Philadelphia!"

O'Hara tucked her hand under his arm and gave it a little squeeze. "You musn't hate me for it, but that's been my ambition all along."

The next day before he began upon the furniture O'Hara felt he must learn for himself just how serious the "Whiskey War" had been or indeed might still be. He could see the presence of strange troops in town and they filled him with consternation. He went first to talk with Samuel Semple, always a repository of information and common sense. He went into a couple of other taverns, where he asked a few questions but listened more, then he talked with Elliott. From it all he pieced together these facts. Alexander Hamilton, author and head of the Federalists, had apparently seen in the uprising of the Democratic western farmers, who resented paying a tax on the whiskey they were selling, a fine chance to dramatize his own party with its emphasis on the control of the central government. So he had urged the raising of troops, marched them over the rough Alleghenies and fanned them out over Pittsburgh and the surrounding Monongahela country with the idea of ferreting out all traitors, Hugh Brackenridge suddenly becoming the chief! For the Nevilles had consciously or unconsciously misrepresented his behavior in every way possible and were ready to see him arrested for treason.

When O'Hara stopped at the Brackenridge house Hugh met him with a very lopsided smile.

"Well, well, O'Hara! Glad to see you but you'd better not come in. I've been poison round here."

"I guess I'll risk it," O'Hara said, stepping over the threshold. "What the devil's been going on, Hugh?"

"Plenty. How much do you know already?"

"The background, but I want details. Go ahead, man. Out West I had no idea how serious it all was, for you especially."

"Maria's out doing errands so sit down and I'll let you have it. I wrote you my sympathies were with the farmers but I certainly stand for law and order. The Nevilles, though, twisted everything I did. I went out to Mingo Creek once to try to calm down a violent group there. And once when they came up here to shoot up the town I bought three barrels of whiskey *out of my own pocket* to quiet them. But to the Nevilles I was 'consorting with the insurgents.'"

"I can hardly believe this!"

"True, just the same. You know General Neville was one of the tax collectors and the farmers hate his hide. They came up one night to demand his papers. Of course he didn't give them and there was a little shooting. One good man, McFarlane, one of the farmers, was killed in the fracas. So things got worse."

Hugh's face was thin, O'Hara saw now, with dark circles under his eyes.

"You know Hamilton, don't you?" he went on.

"Slightly."

"Well, he came with the troops and had a little band of judicial inquisitors. General Henry Lee was at the head of the army, and damned if they didn't quarter him *on me!*"

"In this house?"

"Exactly. I guess they thought if he was here I wouldn't run away. Like young David Bradford did. I knew Lee years ago. I tutored him at Princeton, but I don't like him. Well, we did our best by him. I was pleasant as a basket of chips and Maria nearly killed herself cooking for him and waiting on him. And what do you suppose happened? Two weeks ago he told us that 'for the sake of retirement' he was moving to a less central part of town, and *left!* You can see what that made us look like. Maria was heartbroken after all her work and thinking she was helping me! I'd like to kick that fellow across the Alleghenies, even if I broke both legs doing it!" His voice was bitter.

"Well, what now?" O'Hara persisted. "Have things quieted?"

"They had to. What could the farmers do against all those soldiers? But there's plenty of rancor still. They arrested sixteen men a few weeks ago at night. Didn't even let them get dressed entirely. Marched them out into the country, kept them in a pen out there for days till they nearly died of exposure and then found out that most of them had been falsely accused! How they missed me in that group I'll never know. Oh, there's been dirty work done. But as to me, want to hear the climax?"

"I needn't tell you I do."

"Just a week ago Hamilton summoned me for an interview. He's a reasonable man. We talked it all out and he ended by giving me a clean bill!"

"Thank God!"

"And they tell me old Neville nearly exploded when he heard of it. He talked about it everywhere and a man told me he said 'Brackenridge is the most artful fellow that ever was on God Almighty's earth! He's deceived everyone and now he's even put his finger in Hamilton's eye.' Not a bad epitaph, eh?" Hugh laughed.

O'Hara was sober. "This is all so much worse than I ever imagined. You've been through bad times, Hugh. I'm glad it's over for you, and that you're cleared. Mary told me how you saved our house. How can I ever thank you enough? You must have pretty well taken your life in your hand to do it."

"It was a tough crowd but they really listened when I expounded on you. If you'd heard me you'd have been convinced you're quite a fellah. They were dead set to fire something that night so they went up on the hill and burnt Kirkpatrick's farm buildings and a pretty blaze they made! Of course you know he's worked hand in glove with Neville."

"How is Maria now after all the anxiety?"

Hugh's face lit up. "She's feeling pretty happy that I've been cleared especially since now we'll be eligible for the ball. Has Mary told you about that?"

"Oh, yes. I heard the news last night."

"Well, if anyone deserves an invitation to this affair in honor of Lee, she does. There have been a good many social events the last couple of months but of course we've been out of them. And your Mary didn't seem to have much heart for going, with you away. Now we can go together and show off our pretty wives. They're planning their dresses already, I think."

O'Hara got up to go. "We're putting the new furniture over on Water Street today, so I've got to leave. I'm still stunned by all you've told me."

Hugh lowered his voice though no one was near. "There's one thing I didn't mention. It still haunts me. Just after the troops came when feelings ran pretty high, I looked out of the bedroom window one night and saw some dragoons advancing on my house here *with a rope*."

"You can't mean that!"

"I do. But I'll say this for the Nevilles. They headed them off. I guess even they decided they'd stop one short of hanging me! But it's not a pleasant memory. Oh, O'Hara, I'm ashamed never to have mentioned your big victory! What must you think of me?"

"I'll tell you all about that later. Just now I wanted to hear exactly what you've told me. My news will keep."

"When are they going to make you a General?" Hugh asked with a chuckle.

O'Hara colored. "Well, as a matter of fact they've already done so."

"Ho! Ho! So, that's the reason you weren't afraid to come into my house. As a *General* you can . . ."

O'Hara's gray eyes shot sparks. "Take that back, Hugh!"

"My God, the man's touchy!"

"On some points, yes. Things like honor or friendship . . . Take that back!"

Hugh grasped his arms. "Why you damned fool!" he said affectionately. "Surely you knew I was joking. But O'Hara, I'm glad you flared up like that. I'm good and glad. It comforts my heart after all I've been through. I've got one true friend in Pittsburgh, at least."

The moving to the Big Place, as Prudence called it, was accomplished in a week's time with McGrady and Elliott helping while Lewis, the erstwhile keelboater, kept the store. Other men in need of work were pressed into service so that a steady stream of loaded wagons traversed the short distance between the King's Orchard and Water Street, while from the store the heavy crates were transferred to the grounds at the back of the new house and opened there. O'Hara planned that the last things set in place would be the dining-room pieces, so that room was left empty for the time being.

It was Mary's decision to leave enough furniture in their old home so that it would not look *forlorn,* as she put it. The big secretary of course remained in the parlor and O'Hara had a larger and plainer desk set in to give more working space. The large wing chairs, now showing signs of wear, remained, with a couple of candlestands. But the beautiful table* from Ireland with its shamrock feet was the first thing to be removed to the

---

* This table is now in the home of James O'Hara Denny, of Pittsburgh.

new drawing room, and above it O'Hara hung the Tyrawley coat of arms with a feeling of satisfaction.

"I think the old lion will feel more content here," he said to Mary.

The guest room in the old house was to remain intact. "We might have an overflow of visitors some time, or a stranger might need a bed," Mary said.

"Or," said O'Hara with great seriousness, "I might be working late in my office and decide it was too much trouble to go home and I'd just sleep there."

Mary looked up startled and then seeing the twinkle in his eyes, laughed. "Oh you!" she said. "What a tease you are!"

When it was time to say the last goodbye to the log house Mary's eyes were full of tears. "One reason I insisted upon keeping a bedroom here was that some time when the apple blossoms are out, or the locusts, perhaps we might come over ourselves for old sake's sake and stay the night," she said.

"We might," O'Hara said tenderly. "We might do just that." And then they kissed, as they closed the kitchen door for the last time and left the King's Orchard.

But in the great new house there was no chance for tears or regrets as its welcoming beauty surrounded them. For their first night there O'Hara had ordered fires in every room and plenty of candles lighted; so in the late afternoon he and Mary walked through their new domain in a gentle glow. The drawing room had long yellow satin sofas which picked up the color in the wallpaper that Mary had selected from samples sent from Philadelphia. The chairs were striped blue and gold and the candlestands and side tables were polished cherry wood. At the end of the room near the library stood a small spinet.

Mary paused to finger the puckered blue silk pockets at each end.

"This is the best place for it, I think. For if we should ever have a soiree the violinsts could stand here at either side and be out of the way."

When he felt the time was ripe O'Hara led her to the dining room where for a moment she was speechless. It *was* unbelievably handsome! The long table with its eighteen chairs, the massive sideboard, and the serving table, all in richly carved mahogany. Prudence had to call them three times for supper before they could cease admiring; then they sat down at last with the children, in the big comfortable kitchen. Prudence was cooking over the open fire but promised to try the new-fangled stove soon.

"After all, a good, sound kitchen is the heart of the home," O'Hara said, looking about him, relaxed and content.

That night before she slept, Mary said, "Do you know, James, what I believe I like best in the whole house?"

"Me?" he suggested.

She moved her head on his arm with a little laugh. "Well, of course, *you,* but I mean the house itself. I think I'm most thrilled over the real glass window panes!"

"And the devil's own time I had getting them," he answered. "About half the first shipment broke coming over the mountains and when it was finally all here I found it had cost about as much as the furniture! But some day . . ."

"What do you mean, *some day?*"

"Oh, some day I hope everyone in Pittsburgh will have glass window panes."

Through the coming days O'Hara discovered that a delicious under-current of excitement was running through the conversation of the women who belonged to the town's elite. The main subject at tea or at casual meetings in stores or street corners was apparently the coming ball in honor of General Lee. Since no private house was adequate it was to be held in the new fort and James Brison, prothonotary of Allegheny County, was the manager and would issue the invitations. Maria and Mary discussed their dresses and tried them on for masculine approval, before hanging them up, ready for the great night. The two couples were to go together and Maria's cheeks always flushed red with anticipation as they spoke of it, for the ball would be in the nature of a triumph and public vindication for Hugh.

Meanwhile O'Hara had gone to see Major Craig. They discussed in detail the great victory in the west and exulted over their own success with the supply lines, then O'Hara turned grave.

"There's something I have to say to you, Isaac."

"All right. Say on."

"I'm a Federalist, as you and your immediate connections are, and I'm your friend and theirs. But I am also a friend of Hugh Brackenridge. He's been through a pretty little hell over this *Whiskey Rebellion,* and I don't think all of you can take much satisfaction in what you've done to him. For myself, I don't like it."

"Well, well," the Major said, somewhat embarrassed, "you were away and couldn't know all the facts. But shall we just say it's past now, Brackenridge has been cleared by Alexander Hamilton, so let's get on to our own business."

"I had to make myself clear, Isaac."

"You have," he smiled grimly. "You usually do."

So, this being understood they fell to planning the future.

"I doubt if we can really get started on our *glass* for another year or so," O'Hara said, "but at least we can be thinking about it. I heard that a glassworks near Philadelphia has a fine man as manager and I've made some inquiries. He's a Peter Eichbaum, a German. Family, glass cutters for generations. Now, why can't we at least keep a finger on him until we're ready? You write him, and ask his advice as to how to go about building a glassworks. That will flatter him and he'll remember our names. Sign mine with yours, will you, Isaac?"

"Easy enough. Good idea."

"As for me I've got something else I have to start on at once."

"What now?"

"I'm going to ship salt from the Onondaga works up at Salina, New York, down to Pittsburgh."

"That's impossible!"

"I know it. That's one reason why the thing attracts me," he grinned. "We've got to find a cheaper way than getting it across the mountains and I think this will be it. Don't look so shocked. After what we've done these last two years in Quartermastering I should say it's reasonable to tackle anything, wouldn't you?"

"That depends very much upon who tackles it," said the Major.

A few days later the invitation to the ball arrived for *General and Mrs. James O'Hara.* They were both proud of the wording and happy over the prospect itself. "I'll have to check over my own wardrobe," he said, "and stop in at the wigmakers. My old one looks as though the rats might have been in it. Oh, from the way this reads we're invited to the dinner too! That *is* an honor."

"Then we can't go with Maria and Hugh, can we, for they won't likely be at the dinner. But we can meet them before the dancing starts. It's a wonder Maria hasn't been over. I'll run in tomorrow and we'll make final plans."

But before she had a chance to go, Hugh came there. His face was set.

"The invitations are all out," he said, "and the Brackenridges did not receive one."

"Oh, Hugh!" Mary cried in distress.

"It was James Brison! He had it in his own hands. And I'll tell you something. I'm not through with politics yet by a long shot, and if it's the last thing I do in this world I'll get even with him for this!" And he turned and walked out.

"This is cruel!" O'Hara said. "It's not just the disappointment of missing a ball, though to Maria that will be great enough. But it's another blow to Hugh personally. I'm very sorry about this."

"Couldn't you do something, James? Couldn't you speak to Mr. Brison or General Lee or . . . or even to Mr. Hamilton?"

He shook his head. "I don't think so," he said. "It's not too good an idea to use your own spoon to stir another man's broth."

"This is going to take the pleasure out of it for us, too," she said mournfully.

And to a considerable extent it did, though the affair was the most socially ambitious in the town's history. O'Hara listened to many comments from the easterners to the effect that they had not expected such entertainment in the Back Country! He was glad to renew acquaintance with Hamilton and meet the other officers but his special gratification was in seeing Mary holding her own little court, as beautiful, he felt, as on the night of Anne Bingham's ball in Philadelphia. As the silks and laces and powdered wigs began to move to the strains of a minuet, however, O'Hara was thinking of the deerskin breeches and linsey-woolsey dresses he had seen rollicking in the square dance at the old Fort on his first Christmas Eve here, over twenty years ago. *Pittsburgh has really grown up,* he smiled to himself.

They left early. "When your heart is a little heavy, your feet seem a bit heavy too, don't you think, James?" Mary said on their way back. And as they passed the dark and silent Brackenridge house, he agreed with her. Once at home they went directly to their room where O'Hara lighted the fire and drew the small sofa of many memories close. There as they discussed the evening the thing took place which often happens between married people in love: they thought of the same thing at the same time! It was that *they* would give a party at which Hugh and Maria would be honored guests!

"It won't be the same as being at the ball tonight but it will be something to salve their wound," O'Hara said.

"And we *should* give a housewarming in any case. Just for our particular friends, don't you think?"

"The crème de la crème!" he smiled.

"And just before Christmas we can have the house trimmed with pines. Oh, it will be beautiful. Let's plan!"

The fire had to be remade three times before they finally went to bed. But because of all their decisions Mary wrote the invitations one day in her delicate hand: *General and Mrs. James O'Hara will receive . . .*

And receive they did one evening the week before Christmas in the wide center hall carpeted with roses and with the curving stairs behind them twined with greens. Movement and laughter and admiring voices filled the rooms as the logs in the fireplace crackled and flamed and the candlelight shone soft and golden from every mantelpiece and table.

There had been one anxiety in connection with the party. This was that the Neville "cabal," as Hugh called it, had to be invited. Not only, as O'Hara had pointed out to Mary, were they perhaps the town's first family, they were also his friends and Major Craig, the General's son-in-law, was his close business associate. Whether bringing the erstwhile enemies together in the confines of four walls would be disastrous or not, had remained to be seen. But as it turned out there was no open indication of feud. O'Hara did some clever manipulating as a host and the principals themselves kept out of each other's way. With it all, Hugh and Maria had reason for pride in their position that night, for it was patent to all that they were valued friends in the house. So the music from the violins and spinet flowed on in the drawing room, the elegant buffet and hot spiced rum punch was dispensed in the dining room, and the general gaiety continued without a break.

When Mary and O'Hara had bade the last guest goodnight, he put his arms about her. "Well, it was delightful, dear, wasn't it?"

She looked into his eyes. "You've given me *so much*, James!"

"Not a fraction of what you've given me! That is beyond price. But at least you're in your proper setting at last."

They moved slowly through the rooms, putting out the candles, placing the shields before the fires and recounting all the evening's successes.

"I'm sure we brought happiness to two of our friends with the party. If we could only know that Mary Vining and Anthony Wayne were together now how wonderful that would be! I was thinking of them as I dressed tonight. Surely he will be through in the west before too long, won't he?"

"I have no idea. One thing I do know. The General will always do out the duty."

"But the waste of it, when they could be married now after all the long delay. The terrible waste of time!"

"There's one thing you can always count on about *time.*"

"What is that?"

"It passes."

And it passed swiftly for O'Hara during the months that made up the following year! Ever since the idea of transporting salt from New York State to Pittsburgh had entered his head, he could not rest until he had put it into execution. The situation was simply this. Money, as always, was scarce with most people and salt — that infinitely precious commodity, the preserver, the essence of all flavor, the very life of taste and appetite, lending zest to the palate and savor to all living — was brought now from the east or from Baltimore over the mountains by laden pack horses for *eight dollars a bushel!* O'Hara was convinced that he could bring it from the Onondaga works to sell at half that price and make a good profit. But the difficulties in the way were stupendous. A whole transportation route would have to be built. Could it be done?

He went up to Salina right after the New Year and with his shrewd eyes narrowed and his contractor's invaluable experience to give him assurance, he began his negotiations. First for the salt itself and then, practically, for the barrels. He would reserve some in his contracts but he ordered others from a cooperage to his exact specifications: "good pork barrels, with not less than twelve hoops on a barrel and not to be nailed with less than ten nails and to be delivered to Oswego in good order." Then, the route! Roads and portages would have to be improved and wagons bought; and there would *have* to be two small vessels built, one for Lake Ontario and one for Lake Erie!

He did not quail. The very magnitude of the task exhilarated him. He examined all the terrain; he drew precise plans; then he proceeded as he had done with all his other smaller undertakings. The idea and the entire capital were his own; but after that came the selection of capable men to take charge at each step of the way, with himself checking and overseeing both on the ground when he could, and from a distance when he could not. Relentlessly he pressed his plan; steadily the idea took palpable form; apparent impossibilities smoothed out; delays and discouragements were overcome, as the year grew older and at last, old.

By December O'Hara, back in Pittsburgh, stood at the wharf one bright, cold day to receive his first shipment of two hundred and fifty barrels of salt which had come safely by keelboat from French Creek down the Allegheny on the last stage of its long journey. It would sell at the rate of *four dollars a bushel!*

A crowd gathered as the keelboats were unloaded. Men and women with pans and pails waited jubilantly to buy the precious grains when the first barrel was opened. They shook hands with O'Hara and tried to express their thanks.

"This is a great day for us, General!"

"You're the only man could have done it!"

"No more wood ashes now!" one shabby woman said happily.

When the salt was finally removed to O'Hara's own store, he went back home to exult with Mary over his achievement. He had kept his promise this year to come back oftener, though the times with her had of necessity been short, except for one visit in the fall when a new baby had come to the big house on Water Street, this time a little girl. O'Hara had not known how greatly he desired a girl-child but now his whole strong being seemed to melt at the touch of the small rosebud creature. She had been named *Elizabeth* for Mary's sister and would soon be three months old. There was a newcomer also in the Brackenridge home, a boy! So, he was thinking as he walked briskly along, compared to the other events of the year the shipping of the salt could be reckoned as less important. But he would not belittle it. It had been a great and successful undertaking, a benefit to his town and to himself.

There was another reason still why this coming holiday season would bring joy to him and Mary. Vicarious but very real. Anthony Wayne had at long last been released from western service and would be back in Philadelphia by Christmas!

When O'Hara reached the house, pausing first as always to gloat over the handsome structure and the view upon which it faced, he poured out to Mary all the details of the scene at the wharf, and then with pencil and paper showed her just how much he himself would be making on the venture.

"Couldn't you bring the salt price down still further then?" she asked.

"Ah, my little conscience!" he said, laughing. "Later on when I've recouped the money I've had to lay out, I *will* bring down the price. But even now, don't forget I've halved it from what it used to be. Letters from the east today?"

Mary's face was aglow as she laid two before him. "They are both filled with news of Mary Vining. She's going to give a big dinner in honor of Anthony's return and they'll be married at the New Year! She is almost beside herself with joy, they say, and no wonder!"

"And imagine Anthony! I can picture what *he's* feeling."

They discussed their own holiday plans and decided to have a large afternoon reception just before Christmas instead of a soiree such as they had had last year. But, as Mary said, no matter what' they did this would be an unusually happy time for many reasons.

It was two days before the party, merrymaking was in the air and the house was hung again with greens when O'Hara came in suddenly, his face white. He found Mary in the library and pressed her gently into a chair.

"Sit down, my dear," he said. "I've just had dreadful news. *Ghastly* news!"

She looked up at him, terrified. "What?" she breathed.

"Anthony Wayne died on the fifteenth out at Erie. On his way back!"

CHAPTER THIRTEEN

Pittsburgh was indeed growing up. True, there were still a few cows pasturing comfortably at the foot of Grant's Hill and an occasional hog running wild, but for the most part an almost urban decorum had replaced the raw frontier atmosphere of earlier days. Most of the log cabins were gone now with the frame and brick structures taking their place. When the old Fort was demolished O'Hara and Ebenezar Denny had used the bricks according to their plan, and with the neat row of dwellings they put up the number of houses rose to over eight hundred! At the same time O'Hara had bought the small "Block House," built by Colonel Bouquet, in order than it might be a permanent landmark in the town. While the newer buildings were devoid of any architectural beauty and even lacked the picturesqueness of the old, their miscellaneous outlines were all softened by the profusion of locusts, sycamores, Lombardy poplars and weeping willows which had spring up in the wake of the primeval forest.

Certain attributes of the Pittsburghers themselves were discernible to strangers who came there. These qualities may have derived from the prevalence of Scotch-Irish blood which, as always, had a large percentage of *iron* in it; or perhaps they were the result of the former bitter struggles with nature, the elements and the Indians, but there remained a core of strength, of determination and also of self-esteem quite removed from egotism, in these men who were founding a city.

The *Academy* was at last a flourishing concern and there were also several schools for younger children. A small courthouse had been built, and two more churches established, the Episcopal and the Methodist. The ironic comment by a traveller that in Pittsburgh "taverns were more plentiful than churches and whiskey purer and stronger than the faith" could at this point be more successfully challenged. The King's Gardens were now largely covered with houses instead of vegetables and flowers as of old, but the *Orchard,* while somewhat smaller, remained. The keelboats still poled up and down the waters, with Mike Fink, after his congenial practice with Wayne's Indian fighters, continuing his supreme sway among the boaters. It was a colorful day when he visited his native Pittsburgh, making his rollicking rounds of the taverns, fighting any man willing to fight with him and some who weren't, testing their courage by first shooting tin cups off their heads and subsiding by night into hidden but quite as turbulent orgies!

There was another colorful spectacle, however, of a peaceful nature. Little by little the roads over the mountains had been improved and now even more anticipated in the town than the Post rider's horn was the sound of the bells which heralded the approach of a Conestoga wagon! It *was* a beautifully impressive sight, for the wagon boxes were painted blue with the running gears red; above, flared the great white covering canvas. Six powerful coal black "Conestoga" horses, of a special breed, pulled the wagon and each was provided with hame bells so that the loud, ringing music of their chime became synonymous with safe arrival. It was not long before another catch phrase sprang into common use. "I'll be there *with bells*," one townsman would say to another.

Within the big house on Water Street the changes had been happy ones. There was to keep Elizabeth company a second little girl now, at O'Hara's insistence, *Mary*, and the boys were growing tall and strong. There was also a chambermaid and another kitchen helper for Prudence. In the stabling there were housed, besides the aged Pitt, a young riding horse and a spanking team of bays which drew the only carriage in the town! Mary prayed earnestly to herself as she rode out in it that she might be delivered from vanity and pride!

Their hearts still ached over the tragedy of Anthony Wayne's death, due, as they had learned later, to a flare-up of his old wound; and even more continuously for Mary Vining who, as the letters from the East told, had never left her home since the news came. She had been writing the invitations for the dinner of welcome when the word had been brought to her and she, too, had seemed to die then, though still in life.

Both O'Hara and Mary missed the Brackenridges who were living in Carlisle to be nearer the center, for Hugh also had a title now. During the last big gubernatorial campaign he had worked zealously for Thomas McKean, who was elected. His reward was his appointment as justice of the state supreme court! It was a signal honor and the very position for which Hugh was eminently fitted. His fame had spread also because of the publication of the first two volumes of his work, *Modern Chivalry*, upon which he had been concentrating for years; so O'Hara felt sure that the old hurts in his heart were now pretty well healed. One evidence, however, that he still remembered them was that upon his appointment he had at once prevailed upon the governor to dismiss James Brison as Prothonotary and replace him with one of Hugh's own relatives! So was the revenge complete.

While they missed Hugh and Maria, they now had the Dennys, who in a large measure took their place. Ebenezar had at last married his little flower-like Nancy Wilkins back in Carlisle, and had come with her to make their home in Pittsburgh. So O'Hara had a congenial friend and onetime comrade-in-arms with whom to smoke his pipe and exchange reminiscences, and Mary had another young bride to take under her wing. When they supped with the O'Haras it was often by common consent in the big home-like kitchen where Agnes Denny's pewter plate still graced the mantel.

But though O'Hara seemed the same to the casual eye as he walked the streets receiving respectful greetings from his townsmen and exchanging witty sallies with a favored few, and while he checked with satisfaction upon his various industries, which now included *The Point Brewery,* he was, within himself, a seething mass of anxieties and nerves. For the first time in his life he could not sleep and woke up in the mornings tense and unrefreshed. The trouble was that he was now launched upon the greatest of all his undertakings, the fulfillment of his most cherished dream: the manufacture of glass. And the difficulties involved were more intricate, more overwhelming because of their unfamiliarity than any he had heretofore encountered.

He often thought of the night the idea had first come to him with force. It was as he lay in the guest room of the Orchard house, heartbroken and estranged from Mary, listening to the beat of the rain upon the oiled paper panes. He knew then that he must one day make glass for her, for Pittsburgh, and of course for himself. And now he was in the midst of it and for the first time in his life he had doubts of his own power to succeed.

They had begun, he and Isaac Craig as they had planned, by enlisting the interest of William Eichbaum, a Westphalian glass cutter considered the best in this country. His first demand while still in Philadelphia had been for samples of clay from the countryside around Pittsburgh to see if any was suitable for the making of *pots*. This took time. Finally Eichbaum admitted that one sample "was not amiss" and ordered the digging and ripening of twenty-five tons!

"Why doesn't the man come on out and oversee everything himself as we want him to do?" O'Hara had fretted. "I'll pay him! What's the matter with him, anyhow?"

But Eichbaum was canny. Until the O'Hara glassworks were really started he would remain where he was. The next problem had been the location of coal. O'Hara had been determined from the first that this was to be the fuel instead of wood, but it took much time and labor to find a vein of sufficient depth.

"We'll be the first in the country to do this," he kept telling Craig, "so don't let's give up on it."

At last the proper depth was found and the factory itself built, at the foot of Coal Hill below Jones Ferry on the Monongahela almost opposite the point where the two rivers met. Then, at last, Eichbaum came on. O'Hara invited him to stay at their home until he became somewhat settled before bringing on his family, and had quite looked forward to the visit, but they had found him a difficult guest. He was a Continental gentleman of great refinement and regarded Pittsburgh with a patronizing eye. He had left Germany for France in pursuit of his trade or *profession* as he termed it and had been most successful there, even to supplying some of the glass for the Palace of Versailles under Louis XVI! After the fall of the Bastille he had come to the United States but he still managed somehow to affect the air of the court. This all infuriated O'Hara who bore his own honors lightly and spoke to all, high and low, with the same easy friendliness. So annoyed was he that he would not speak French with Eichbaum though the latter kept urging it.

"Oh," O'Hara would say innocently, "my French is rather rusty. And besides, my wife does not speak it." He could see Mary turning her back on these occasions to hide her amusement. But the more he saw of Eichbaum the more convinced he was that the man knew his business. "And that's the only thing that matters," he told Craig.

O'Hara was still involved with government business though he was trying hard to be released from it; so the Major had to be the acting manager of the glassworks. When the building itself was finished O'Hara stayed on in Pittsburgh until the furnace was built. This contained eight pots for window glass which, they hoped, would turn out three boxes to a blowing, each box containing one hundred square feet. Two pots of the furnace were to be used for the making of *bottles*. At this point O'Hara's spirits soared. He had engaged workmen, a few experienced ones from Philadelphia; he and Craig had learned much of the process themselves from Eichbaum, who seemed to be growing more and more interested; the coal was dug and waiting with a crew to keep it in supply; everything now, in fact, was ready for the great experiment. And O'Hara had to leave!

"This is one of the hardest things I've ever done!" he told Mary the night before he set out. "But I can't in all honor delay here any longer. Until I'm free from my contracting I can't take a chance on letting a post get low in supplies. I've got to inspect them. I think I'll be gone only a few weeks, and we'll celebrate when I get back! This is going to be a big thing, darling."

He had explained to her in detail the business arrangements, and as before, left in her charge the money to be paid out. As he rode off that next morning he watched the building beyond the river upon which the great hope was set. In a few days now smoke would be pouring from those chimneys!

But when he returned one late autumn day, his eager eyes saw the factory just as he had left it, the chimneys empty! He rode quickly to his own home, found Mary out but assured himself from Prudence that all was well there, then hurried to the Ferry and on to the factory which stood now, cold, empty and silent. He found Craig and Eichbaum in the small lean-to office and burst in upon them almost with violence. "What happened? What went wrong?"

Craig shook hands and set a chair. "Now calm yourself, O'Hara. We're all disappointed, I can tell you. Explain it, Eichbaum."

"It was the clay," Eichbaum said. "I chose the best of the samples you sent me and I was sure it would do. It was not right. When we first fired the melting pots, they broke. New Jersey is the only place where I am *certain* the clay is right. It would have to be shipped in barrels over the mountains if you decide . . ."

"I have a feeling, O'Hara, that we should give up the whole thing. You know better than anybody else what that expense would be," Craig said.

O'Hara looked back at them in white astonishment and anger.

"Give it up? What do you mean? I'll never give it up. We

started out here to make glass and we're going to make it! Let's get the order in for the clay at once. Come on over to my office where we have better writing materials. We can send the letter by tomorrow's post."

"Have you any idea," Eichbaum said slowly, "of the amount of money you'll have to spend on this?"

"I don't care how much I have to spend. I guess I'm able for it. The only thing I'm interested in is getting on with it. Let's go."

Over in the house in the King's Orchard Eichbaum dictated the letter. In it the matter of haste was emphasized though at the best they all knew it would be four or five weeks before the clay arrived. When they had finished their consultations and Eichbaum had received permission to go back to his family during the interim, O'Hara detained him after Craig had left. He had a question which had risen in his mind on one of his solitary rides, along with a great resolution.

"Could you tell me," he asked now, "which glass manufacturing house in all Europe you consider the best?"

Eichbaum told him. "You're not thinking of *importing* glass if we fail here?" he asked.

"We're not going to fail. But thank you very much. Just curiosity," he added.

When he was alone O'Hara wrote a second letter, this one to the Westphalian Glassworks. In it he stated he was interested in purchasing the largest and finest crystal chandelier the house could make, with description and price to be sent him as soon as possible. For this was the idea that had come to him in the forest. He was now President of the Board of Trustees in the Presbyterian Congregation of which he and Mary were members. He was also the wealthiest man in the town. It would be fitting then for him to give a gift to the church, and what more suitable, more to his liking, than one of *glass*, glass in its most delicate and resplendent form. Practical, too, for the flickering light from the poor side sconces and the one candlestick on the pulpit left the room now in a semidarkness at any evening meeting. He sat picturing with pleasure the glorious change his gift would make, and then added a postscript to his letter. asking for a sketch along with the estimate and the approximate date at which the chandelier, if ordered, could be shipped.

As he left the King's Orchard for Water Street his heart, because of his new plan, was eased a little from his first bitter disappointment over the cold chimneys of the factory; besides, he would soon see Mary!

She was waiting for him in the library, eager as always, quick to comfort him for the momentary failure of his hopes, but full apparently of excitement.

"What is it?" he asked when he released her from his arms, "what's the big news?"

"How you do *know* me, James!"

"I should hope so, by this time. What's happened?"

"It's really quite extraordinary! Sit down and I'll tell you all about it. General Neville was over and he says that Prince Louis Philippe, Duke of Orleans, I think he called him, and his two brothers from France are touring the United States! They've been visiting in Philadelphia and are going down to New Orleans and will come by way of Pittsburgh!"

"Good heavens!"

"The letter came from General Washington addressed to either you or General Neville — of course he knows how much of the time you are away — asking if between you, you would entertain the princes. The Nevilles would like to accommodate them at night but the General wondered if you — we — would have them for the dinners, probably two, and make quite a ceremony of them. I think," she added, "that he is impressed by our dining room."

"Indeed, he'd better be," O'Hara grinned. "Well, this *is* news with a vengeance. We've already had some pretty distinguished guests but these will top them all. When are they likely to arrive?"

"That's a difficulty. We can't be certain but General Neville says he thinks they may be on their way now and he will check on every wagon that comes in. So we'd better start on our arrangements right away. I do think it's thrilling, don't you?"

"Very much so! Now let's see whom we should have as the other guests with them. For the first dinner the Nevilles of course, and the Craigs, and perhaps the Devereux Smiths. He has French blood in him. Oh, I wish Brackenridge could be here! He's always such a dinner table asset. Mr. Arthur of the Academy I would like, for he's versed in history and literature and a good conversationalist. And the Dennys certainly. Then we can have a second group for the next night. Well, you go ahead, dear, and plan your part of it. Needless to say we'll spare no expense. I'll invite the guests conditionally when we decide on them but I've an idea none of them will mind holding their time open!"

He paused considering. "Do you realize the Duke of Orleans is heir to the throne? I wonder why they are here. My guess would be that with all that's going on now in France they may feel it is wise to be as far away as possible for a time. The Duke's father was among those executed a few years back."

"Oh how dreadful," Mary said. Then she added, "I suppose you will deign to speak French *with the Duke*."

"I may, if I remember any," he chuckled. "And who's the tease now?"

"I'm so glad I've just gotten new gowns from Philadelphia! If we have several dinners I can wear a different one each night."

The arrangements went forward apace. The house shone, for McGrady had been impressed to polish the brasses and the silver. There were still chrysanthemums in the garden and Mary decided upon a large bouquet on the Irish table and an epergne for the dining room as soon as the date was fixed. Already on the buffet the decanters were filled with the best Monongahela rye and the finest Philadelphia sherry, Madeira and port. The food was planned, with O'Hara insisting upon something distinctively American. So, since the season was fall they settled on the main viands as roast turkey with baked apples stuffed with fresh sausage, Prudence's superlative cornbread and pumpkin pie for dessert.

"That will be practically an all-American menu for them, and they'd better like it!" O'Hara said. "Only I wish to heaven they'd soon get here. My lips are getting stiff on my smile of welcome!"

"And I'm so nervous I could jump out of my skin!" Mary said.

He was instantly all solicitude. "You mustn't be worried about the dinners. No Prince is worth that. If you just smile at them they won't know what they're eating. Now do relax. I can't have you worn out over this."

But after another week the news came. General Neville sent over a note to the effect that the guests had arrived that afternoon and as they were very weary from the trip Mrs. Neville would serve a light supper and allow them to retire early. But on the next evening if convenient they would be pleased to dine with General and Mrs. O'Hara, and also on the one following.

The activity on Water Street began at once. The turkeys were secured, plucked and dressed for the oven. The pumpkins were cooked ready for the morrow's pies. The flowers were cut and put in water and Mary went about trying to make the already perfect house more perfect. O'Hara meanwhile informed his guests both for the first night and the second, and then on his return managed to get Mary to bed at a reasonable hour. They both woke early in the morning, however, with a strong inner excitement.

"It's almost treasonous for us to make so much over the fact that we're about to entertain royalty," O'Hara said dryly. "After all we live in a democracy where all men are born 'free and equal.' "

Mary's reply was not relative to any political philosophy. "I do hope you'll like the dress I'm wearing tonight. You haven't seen it yet for I've been keeping it as a surprise. It's cut in the very latest fashion."

"What color?"

"Red. Red satin."

"Whew! That ought to raise the temperatures of our guests!" He laughed, easily.

Through the day the big kitchen was filled with delectable odors as Prudence and her younger helpers went about their preparations. McGrady had been well trained in waiting on table and Joseph, the coachman, was equipped to double as butler whenever occasion demanded. So the service was assured. Mary arranged the flowers and set the great table with O'Hara near, assisting when he could. The doilies of Madeira lace, the tall silver candelabra, and the crystal glasses and epergne added elegance to elegance.

"You were so right to order eighteen chairs," Mary said. "I would never even have thought beyond a dozen."

"What made you choose red?" he asked suddenly.

"For my dress? Oh, I don't know. It's a nice warm fall and winter color and I've never had a red one before."

Mr. Cox, who taught a singing school two nights a week in the courthouse, had been engaged to play the spinet, bringing with him two violinists.

"Be sure to tell them this is not a musicale," Mary had reminded O'Hara. "We only want a soft background for the conversation, as the evening advances."

"I think," said O'Hara now, as he arranged the General Washington champagne glasses with some of their own on a silver tray, "that I'll tell them to start playing when these are passed. They can wait in the library until then. Did I tell you I'm serving cider? The princes will be used, of course, to champagne and this will be different. I don't recall ever tasting cider in France."

At last everything was in readiness and it was close to the time when the guests would arrive. O'Hara was dressed in his best: a blue rounded dress coat, a rose velvet vest, and white satin breeches, fastened with his ancestral knee buckles. He paced the hall floor nervously now, calling up to Mary who had been delayed because of a ripped flounce in her lace petticoat. It was the very moment of the hour when she finally came down the stairs. As O'Hara looked up at her his heart jumped. The lustrous red satin basque, dropping off the shoulders and cut to a very low point in the front, seemed molded to her form. Her cheeks from the excitement were as scarlet as her gown, while the rest of her skin was as purely white as winter snow. The whole effect was ravishing.

She had just taken her place beside him when the great knocker sounded and Joseph opened the door to admit the Nevilles and the honor guests, three young and distinguished looking men, the Duke of Orleans by far the handsomest. O'Hara greeted them warmly and saw them bow with a sort of startled admiration before Mary as they kissed her hand. The others came soon after and there was general talk in the drawing room as the rye and sherry were passed and repassed. When Joseph announced dinner Mary led the way to the dining room on the arm of Prince Louis Philippe with his next younger brother following with the daughter of Devereux Smith and the youngest with Nancy Denny, O'Hara himself taking in Mrs. Neville. There were subdued exclamations of pleasure as the great table with its glittering appointments came into view; the food, as course followed course, was beyond praise and the conversation throughout was bright and entertaining. Opposite him O'Hara could see Mary at the far end of the table, glowing and seductively beautiful in her red dress, smiling up at the princes on either side of her while they apparently could not for long turn their eyes away.

When the ladies retired to the drawing room at last and the gentlemen were left to their port O'Hara moved to be nearer the princes and with an apology to the others began speaking to them in French. They thanked him for the courtesy and began eagerly to respond. He found, however, that they did not wish to dwell upon France and the tragic years that lay behind. After touching lightly upon Napoleon and the Egyptian campaign in answer to a remark of his, they came swiftly to a discussion of their visit in the United States. They had been agreeably entertained in New York but had felt most at home in Philadelphia. They had been to Mount Vernon and greatly admired General Washington. They had seen Niagara Falls, what a marvel! but most of all they wanted to ask questions about the new country here: its government, its political parties, the *Indians,* and finally about their proposed trip down the Ohio to New Orleans. O'Hara had long been a master of self-control so he chatted now with ease and charm.

When they rejoined the ladies the royal guests gallantly made a point of conversing with those whom they had not been near before: they professed themselves enjoyably regaled by the *cider* and found the soft music most pleasing, as it was. All in all as the evening ended there was writ large not only upon their faces but upon those of the other guests, that it had been an enormous success.

"I will find it difficult to wait for tomorrow night, Madame," the Duke said as he bowed over Mary's hand.

When the great door closed for the last time Mary turned, radiantly, to her husband. "It was perfect, wasn't it?"

"I think it went off well enough," he answered.

She looked at him anxiously. "You're tired, James. You've looked worn out ever since you started this glass business. I'll go now and thank the people in the kitchen and then we can go right up. Joseph and McGrady will see to the lights and fires."

He followed her slowly up the stairs, still in silence. Even in their own room when Mary dropped down on the little sofa he did not come to join her as was his wont but seemed to be busying himself at his highboy.

"What is the matter, James? Did anything go wrong? Please tell me."

He turned, his face flushed and stern.

"Yes, I'll tell you what was wrong. It was the way those men looked at you! I don't care if they are royalty. They're

Frenchmen first of all. I could read every thought in their eyes and I could have killed them for it! And you, smiling up at them!"

"Smiling at them!" Mary echoed. "Why you *told* me to smile at them. You said if I did they wouldn't know what they were eating!" Then she added slowly, in astonishment, "Why, James O'Hara, I do believe you are jealous!"

"Jealous!" he flared. "Of course I'm jealous. Every man is if he's in love. And that Louis Philippe is so damned attractive!" Suddenly a delicious sound filled the room. It was Mary's laughter. She leaned her head against the back of the sofa and gave way to it utterly while O'Hara stared at her.

"You find that so amusing?" he asked.

"Of course I do! And *so* nice! So wonderful!"

"I don't understand you," he said, amazed.

"Oh, any *woman* would understand. To think that I, past forty, with five children and my first gray hair pulled out today, should have a jealous husband! Don't you see it makes me feel so young and so . . . so *desirable!*"

His face softened as he came over and sat down beside her. "Have I ever given you any reason to doubt the latter?" he said, with his old smile breaking through.

"Mercy! I should say not! But you know any woman likes admiration any time. We're just made that way. You do forgive me for laughing at you?"

"As a matter of fact, I'm glad you did," he said slowly. "If you had argued or reasoned or explained I might still have had a little hurt in my heart. But when you laughed you drove it all away. I'm sorry I spoke sharply. It's just because I love you so terribly. Always have. Always will. But there's something I have to ask you, darling."

"What is it?"

"I don't want you to wear that dress again."

"This *dress!* But it's so beautiful! I was sure you would like it. Why don't you?"

"It's cut too low. It's too revealing."

"But that's the very latest fashion. I've had pictures from a Philadelphia magazine. All the women are wearing them this way!"

"Not you," he said. He bent swiftly and pressed his lips to the curving white flesh. "This beauty is for me, alone. I won't have it even suggested to other men's eyes!"

She looked at him in wonder. "I never thought of anything like that. But I could . . . put . . . a . . . little . . . lace in the dress I plan to wear tomorrow. If you insist."

"I'm afraid I do, and thank you."

It was a good while before they settled themselves for slumber that night. O'Hara spoke once again.

"A man is a jealous beast," he said.

"And a woman is a vain thing," she replied.

Then they both laughed, kissed again and went to sleep.

There was a second newspaper in Pittsburgh now, this one, also of Hugh Brackenridge's sponsoring, called *The Tree of Liberty.* Scull, still editor of *The Gazette,* had according to Hugh become so partial to the Federalists that he did not give fair space to the political propaganda of the Democratic-Republicans. Hence, the new sheet, edited by young John Israel from Washington. Hugh's interest in fanning the life flame of the new journal was so great that he made fairly frequent trips back from Carlisle to see how all was going and to contribute in person his own vitriolic articles. O'Hara, knowing this, had haunted the office for the past two weeks hoping to hear that Hugh either had arrived or was expected. On this, the day of the second dinner for the visiting princes, he made one last call at the office and was hailed by young Israel at the doorway.

"He's here," he said, pointing to the back room.

O'Hara gave a shout and fell upon Brackenridge as he sat writing at a desk there. "I've had some great coincidences in the course of my life, but this is one of the best. How are you? How's everything? Can you come to dinner tonight with French royalty?"

They talked fast, catching up on all their news. Maria and the boy were well. They were all enjoying Carlisle. As to tonight's dinner, Hugh's eyes sparkled, until he thought of clothes.

"I've nothing to wear but what's on my back!"

"I can fit you out. We dine at eight, so get around to the house about seven. This is to be a smaller group so the talk can be general. My word, Hugh, I'm glad you got here. Working this afternoon?"

Hugh nodded. "Why?"

"Oh, it's the opening of the county fair and Neville and I thought the princes might like to see it, and go to the races. Couldn't you join us?"

"Too much to do here, I'm afraid. But I'll turn up at your house by seven. What about your *glass*, O'Hara?"

"No go, for the moment but I'm not giving up. I'll be through with my contracting in another month and then I'll devote my whole attention to it. See you then at seven!"

If possible the second dinner surpassed the first. The smaller number both in the drawing room and at table would have made conversation more easy and intimate in any case but with

Hugh present it became scintillating. There was plenty of laughter as the afternoon at the fair was discussed.

"And the *racing!*" the Duke exclaimed. "It was excellent. I was surprised that you have a Jockey Club here!"

"It's been in existence for several years," O'Hara replied. "We're just as eager to lose our money on the horses as they are in larger places. Makes us feel very cosmopolitan, you know."

Even as philosophy and politics were touched upon, the lighter note was preserved until at last Hugh began to dilate upon his idol, Thomas Jefferson, and then his eloquence captured them all.

When the last goodbyes were said Mary in yellow brocade with a little white cascade of lace upon her bosom looked up at her husband mischievously.

"Will you not say this time that everything was perfect?"

"Absolutely."

"And you're not jealous tonight?"

He shook his head. "Only proud. Proud as Lucifer."

O'Hara's position as Quartermaster of the United States had been ended some time before, and now at last and upon his request, his work as contractor for the armies was finished also. It gave him a strange feeling. The long, exacting burdensome weight of responsibility with its dangers and problems was now removed. He was, he kept telling himself with relief, a free man. Free to pursue his own interests and to live without interruption in his own family. But the custom of years could not be shaken off in a moment. Instinctively he found himself often considering transportation, or waking up at night in a sweat of fear because he must have forgotten to order *flour!*

So he had upon him still the stamp of old anxieties in addition to the new ones pertaining to his great dream.

The precious clay from New Jersey was long in coming. Delay after delay was questioned, partially accounted for and then added to by another. Craig, Eichbaum, who was now back, and O'Hara stormed or swore according to their various natures — and waited. Meanwhile the workmen had to be paid to retain them.

One day O'Hara received a letter from the Westphalian Glassworks, containing a sketch of a chandelier. It hung from a circle with a double row of candles, below which were pictured a myriad of crystals. O'Hara studied it for a long time during which some of the new lines in his face seemed to smooth out. This was what he had in mind, and the price did not deter him. This would be his gift. He wrote the order, and then sat on in his office imagining the effect of the chandelier in the plain log church. It would transform it even in the daytime. But at night, lighted . . . He began, with a smile, to write out possible presentation lines, and finally after many tries came up with a sentence that pleased him because he found a faint humor beneath the words: *In token of a glowing desire to promote the lustre of this enlightened society.*

He chuckled over this and laid it in the drawer. He had decided to tell no one of the gift, not even Mary. He wanted particularly to surprise her at the last. He went out now taking quick look-ins at the tannery, the brewery, the sawmill, the gristmill and last of all the store. Elliott, a little more lame but blandly casual as usual, sat down for a chat.

"Well, how does it feel to be out of the woods permanent?"

"Pretty good. Only I'm still contracting in my sleep. The

best part of the thing is that I won't have to be leaving my family now."

"Nice lot of children you got there, General."

"I'm pretty fond of them."

"Wonder to me is they've growed up so well with you away so much."

"They have a good mother."

"They have that. But them boys. They told me when you went off you left them *in charge*."

"I did. Every time."

"Well by gum, they seemed to take it serious. That Butler. You know he's goin' to be the most like you."

"Think so?"

"He's got your wit. Ever hear about the day he whistled in school?"

"No, I don't believe I did."

"It was while I was stayin' at the house. They told me Butler whistled right in the middle of class. The teacher pounced on him an' asked him why he done it. An' he says as cool as you please, 'I was just whistlin' down my sums.' "

They laughed together and then Elliott went on. "An' them little girls of yours . . . well if they wanted my *skin* they could have it. They sort of make up to me for some things I've missed. By the way," he added as though there was a logical sequence, "your friend Guyasuta was round."

"Where?"

"Oh, he was down by the ferry the other day. He'll probably be to see you. I wouldn't know what's in his craw. He don't look too good to me."

"Sick, you mean?"

"Well, when an Injun's not up to snuff he gets the funniest

damned color. I've seen it often and Guyasuta's got it now."

"If you see him again tell him to come to me at once, will you? I wonder why he hasn't done so before. Could he be frightened out by the new house, do you suppose? Well, I must be moving along now." The man he had once helped came toward him as he got up. "Oh, how are you, Lewis?"

"I'm doin' real well, General, but there's something I'd like to tell you."

"Go ahead."

"I know you've helped a lot of people besides me but there's a family livin' near me now that's in awful bad straits. He's been sick an' she's just had another baby. Seems as if there's always a new baby."

O'Hara smiled. "Pittsburgh has to grow," he said.

"I know but it's hard when there ain't enough to eat."

"All right. Now let's get to work on this. Elliott, get out your biggest basket and fill it up with groceries and Lewis, you take it now and one like it every day to this family till the man's working again. And here," he added, feeling in his pocket, "take a little money to them. Make them feel safer."

He waved away the thanks and started out, but looked back from the door. "And Lewis," he said, "when you hear of anyone else in real trouble, let me know."

He was concerned at the news of Guyasuta, especially since it reminded him of a decision made and temporarily forgotten to buy some land across the Allegheny. There, he had solemnly promised to bury the old Indian, and he must not be laid in alien soil. Besides the idea had occurred to O'Hara that they should have a summer home. A dank heat rose from the Monongahela during July and August; but up on the low bluff above the Allegheny there would be cooler days and evening breezes. He made his way now to the office of Devereux Smith.

When the two men late that afternoon crossed the ferry and rode their horses over the land beyond the river, O'Hara cried out in surprise.

"To think that I've lived all these years across from this spot and never actually seen it. This would be an ideal location for a house!"

"What! Another one?"

"A summer home," O'Hara explained. "Look at that orchard! Some long-ago hands planted that. Mary and I are rather sentimental about orchards, so this would delight her, I know. This tract could all become valuable farm land, Smith. I'm going to buy it. Will you arrange the sale?"

"How much would you want?"

O'Hara scanned the land around with a careful eye. The virgin forest had been cleared but there were good trees here and there in addition to the orchard. The ground was level and he knew what richness lay in the soil. In one way and another it would be a good investment.

"I would want some real acreage," he said. "About three hundred, I should think."

Smith whistled, and then they talked terms of sale. "I'll have to check on just who the proprietors of all this are at the moment. Some of it still belongs to the Penns, I think, but I haven't much doubt that it can be bought. You'll soon own this whole end of the state, O'Hara."

"I'll stop a pinch short of that, I guess," he laughed.

As they rode back to the ferry O'Hara reined his horse before a magnificent spreading oak tree, the finest he had ever seen.

"Not thinking of cutting that up for your sawmill, are you?" Smith asked.

O'Hara shook his head. He had decided that this spot should be Guyasuta's grave when the time came.

When he told Mary that night of the idea for a summer house she was at first amazed and then gradually enthusiastic.

"It would be nice to have a real farm with plenty of out-door space for the children. You say there's an *orchard?*"

"Quite a sizable one. If we get this place I'd like to give it a name as they do with homes in the old country. My word, it ought to be a lovely spot in the spring!"

Mary considered. "Why not *Springfield* then," she suggested.

"I like that!" he said decidedly. "I like that very much. Let's stick to it."

So to their amusement and satisfaction the O'Hara country estate had a name before it was even bought!

On a gray November day the first barrels of clay arrived. At once the factory became active. The workmen were rounded up; Eichbaum began his careful supervision of the making of the new pots; and Craig and O'Hara watched and lent a hand everywhere they could. O'Hara felt a vast elation. Now, all would surely go well. The excitement seemed to have spread even to the workmen, for they proceeded with unusual zeal. Too much, as was later proved.

It was not until late December that the pots were all completed. Now again the great furnace was put in blast and the result awaited tensely. O'Hara lay awake nights and felt his hopes unaccountably drowned in new fears. And his dark intuition proved correct. One after another the pots were lost, sometimes at the first melting. Eichbaum was strangely humble.

"The trouble must have been in the drying," he said. "The men were over eager. They didn't give the pots time enough. Perhaps I was too eager myself. I am sorry, gentlemen. I'm afraid this is a serious loss. What shall we do now?"

"We'll go ahead. We'll try again. What did you think?" O'Hara exclaimed. "Have you any new suggestions?"

"Yes. I would like another man who really knows the business to be secured to help me. I cannot oversee all the workmen myself, as I should. I've heard of a man back east, named Wentz. If we could get him as an operating foreman . . ."

"Do you know where to reach him?"

"I have his address."

"Then send for him at once. I'll write him also. Can you start things up here again until he comes?"

"I'd rather wait," Eichbaum said.

O'Hara drew a heavy breath. "So be it. We'll have to let the furnace go out again then, and lay the men off."

"You can still withdraw from the whole venture if you wish," Eichbaum suggested, looking at the others.

"We'll go ahead," they both said at once.

"Glad you're sticking with me, Isaac," O'Hara said as they left that night.

So another long wait began.

Christmas passed with outward merriment but, as far as O'Hara himself was concerned, inner frustration and Mary worried over him even as she tried to comfort him. On New Year's evening a low knock was heard at the back door which O'Hara opened himself. On the steps stood an Indian wrapped in a blanket. It was Guyasuta! O'Hara drew him quickly in out of the cold, seeing upon the ravaged once handsome face the peculiar pallor that was not pallor of which Elliott had spoken. He seated the old man by the fire and began to chafe the thin hands.

"I have come," Guyasuta said weakly, "as you told me to do."

"You are sick!"

The old man nodded. "I will not trouble you long."

Mary had come out and the Indian looked at her doubtfully. "You will not be angry?"

"Oh, you are welcome, Guyasuta," she said warmly. "And you must have food, now."

"Have you any corn-meal mush left, Prudence?" O'Hara asked. "Thin a little down to a gruel and put some sugar in it."

Then he and Mary conferred as to where they would put their guest. "He won't be comfortable in a fancy bedroom," O'Hara said with concern.

"How about my little sewing room? It warms quickly and we could put the cot Butler used to sleep on, in it."

"That would be best. I'll go up with you . . ."

"No, you stay with him. The boys will help me. We won't be long."

So O'Hara waited until the older boys came down and then amongst them they half carried the Indian up to the room Mary had prepared. She had just now brought in one of her husband's own warm bed gowns. O'Hara signaled the others to leave, then removed the old man's blanket and started to take off his deerskin clothes. But Guyasuta shook his head, and lay down on the bed as he was, with a small grunt of relief at its comfort. O'Hara put more wood on the fire, drew the fresh blankets over him and saw that already he was asleep.

During the night each time O'Hara woke, which was often, he went in to make up the fire and check on the sick man's condition. He still lay motionless upon his back, eyes closed but whether in sleep now or not, was not plain. In the morning he seemed weaker and reverted entirely to his own tongue.

"Would you like some of your people to come here to see you?" O'Hara asked anxiously. "Perhaps your wife . . . wives," he amended hastily. "Elliott knows where they live. He would go and fetch them."

The Indian shook his head. "All my long years I live with my own people. Now, I die with you."

He looked off across the room. "You have never harmed an Indian. You have been to all a friend. To me you have been as my son. From that first night when our eyes met. We have seen each other seldom but always I carry you in my heart. You feel this also?"

"I feel it also," O'Hara repeated.

"Then I am at peace."

When O'Hara went to the store that afternoon leaving Mary to watch the sickroom for an hour, he ran into General Neville.

"Well, so I hear you have Guyasuta with you!"

"Yes, I have."

"Do you not know that he was a prime leader at the awful siege of Fort Pitt in '63?"

"I do."

"And the chief leader at the burning of Hannastown?"

"I know that."

"And yet you dare harbor the old bastard in your own house?" His voice had risen in anger.

"And since it happens to *be* my own house, General, have you any objection?" O'Hara's eyes were cold.

Neville sputtered a bit. "Now, now, no real offense meant. But I certainly can't understand this situation."

"As a matter of fact, I can't myself. What I do know is that this man is my friend and I have an obligation to him which I intend to fulfill. Good day, General."

By another evening Guyasuta was very weak indeed. He had refused O'Hara's suggestion of Dr. Bedford with a determination that could not be questioned, so the hours passed and his pulse grew fainter. Elliott had been in and spoken in easy Seneca which the Indian had answered. Since he knew the time was near O'Hara told him gently of the land beyond the Allegheny, now his own, and the great tree there. From beneath it could be seen the meeting of the rivers. It would be a noble resting place.

"It is well," Guyasuta whispered, and by morning he was dead. The strange, tender, continuing bond between the Indian and the white man was now severed.

O'Hara's heart was heavy as he made the few necessary arrangements. The man who always dug the graves in the churchyard went out with him to be shown the spot under the oak tree. In the afternoon Guyasuta's body, wrapped in his own blanket and in another fresh one upon which Mary insisted, was placed in the undertaker's spring wagon; O'Hara with Mary and the boys, who had been deeply affected by all that had passed, rode in their own carriage while Elliott followed on horseback. This completed the small cortege.

When the grave was filled they all stood for a moment looking across at the icy rivers, as the wind moved among the bare branches overhead.

"I wish it could have been spring for him," Mary said softly.

"Perhaps it is," O'Hara answered. "That is what we do not know."

With the coming of Wentz, affairs at the glasshouse became both better and worse. To O'Hara and Craig he seemed a reasonable, capable man, with whom it was easy to get along, but for some reason not apparent on the surface he and Eichbaum took an immediate dislike to each other. They covered it, but the other men knew it was there, and felt the situation would not make for steady progress. However, Eichbaum needed Wentz; Wentz needed the job; so an armed truce prevailed.

The next great experiment of melting also failed, and Wentz was certain the trouble now was in the kind of *sand* being used. Eichbaum reluctantly agreed. It was decided then to secure samples from all the sand pits around, and let the furnace go out while the outcome of it all hung once again in the balance. The delay drove O'Hara into an inward frenzy. In all his tremendous undertakings heretofore, there had been along with the difficulties and discouragements a constant, steady movement of overcoming. Now, these blocking standstills to him were well-nigh unbearable. Mary watched him with keen anxiety for there was white at his temples now and the first lines in his face were growing deeper. One day she spoke seriously to him.

"James," she said, "have you thought that perhaps you may never have success with the glass?"

"I won't tolerate that thought! I will never give up on this. Why do you ask that? Don't you have faith in me?"

"Yes, I really believe that you will achieve what you've set out to do. But I also believe . . ." She stopped as though embarrassed.

"Go on," he said, looking intently at her.

"It's hard for me to put my feeling into words, but I think any man worthy of success should also be able to bear defeat. If it should come," she added.

He did not speak and she went on. "If you accept this possibility you can still try just as hard as ever to . . . to make the glass but maybe you wouldn't then be so tense, so . . . sort of bitter over the setbacks . . ."

He watched her for a moment and then still without answering turned as though to leave the house. She ran after him.

"James! I haven't offended you, have I?"

He smiled at her. "You couldn't offend me," he said. "I just want to get out by myself and think over what you've told me."

He walked along the river, keeping his eyes away from the factory. He knew himself to be a strong man, both of purpose and execution. He had had up till now what was perhaps phenomenal success. The idea of failure was foreign both to his nature and to his experience, and perhaps because of this he had grown to consider himself infallible and ready to war with any circumstances that threatened to prove him otherwise. This, he slowly realized, was less than good. This attitude, which had in it something at least of stubborn pride, was not one he would admire in another man. He thought again of Mary's words. If he now without bitterness could accept the *possibility* of failure in this his most cherished dream, perhaps the tension would indeed go out of him and he would once again be able to sleep at night as he used to do, and rise in the morning strong and willing to meet whatever the day brought. But more importantly, he might be a better and a humbler man.

He walked for an hour pondering this until he began to feel some of the strain leaving him. How wise Mary was! All through the years she had not only given him the joy of her love and her tender womanliness, but had supported him many times by the soundness of her judgment. She often made him think of his own mother who had seemed outwardly all feminine beauty, but who had an inner strength that he knew his father had respected and depended upon. He decided now to do his best to follow Mary's suggestion to which he had with difficulty reached agreement in his own mind. "But," he muttered to himself, "I'll still never give up while there is a shred of hope!"

He took a short cut through to the store, for a chat with Elliott always relaxed him. He found that gentleman swearing steadily as he wrestled with three large boxes which he said had just come in on the last horse train of freight.

"They're addressed to the store here so McGrady brought them over but what in hell's in them, O'Hara?"

O'Hara's heart leaped as he read the lettering on the boxes. They had come from the Westphalian Glassworks in Germany!

"If anyone asks you that, Elliott, just tell them you don't know," he said, laughing.

"Well, that'll be no damned lie. But I can't help wonderin' what you've been up to now. Ain't we goin' to open them, then?"

"Not yet. But don't worry. Next after Mary, I'll tell you what's in them."

When he got home he didn't refer to their recent conversation, instead he poured out his great secret and had the satisfaction of seeing Mary's delight in the idea. One thing he still withheld. This was his plan, conceived from the beginning, of making the gift synonymous with the first success in the glass manufacture. To this he would still hold, as long as he could.

The last slow, disheartening winter months passed. New sand was substituted for the old but *still* there were failures. O'Hara brought Wentz to his office one day to talk it all over with him in private.

"What is *wrong?*" he asked peremptorily. "I want the truth."

"Well, a good many things. We haven't got the best workmen you know. Some from round here are just new to the trade. The last few failures have been because somebody bungled, but they're all learning."

"Should we try to get more workers from Philadelphia?" O'Hara asked.

Wentz shook his head. "Good glass men are hard to come by. We'd have to break new ones in and even then we wouldn't be sure. Better stick to what we have."

"You think you've got the right sand at last?"

"I think so. We've had trouble with the coal, as you know. I'm convinced it *is* the best fuel but neither Eichbaum nor I have used it before and we have to learn how to adjust the heat. We had two failures because the pots got too hot."

O'Hara leaned forward. "Tell me, Wentz, honestly, whether you think I'll like it or not, do you believe we have a chance of ultimate success?"

"I do, if your money holds out."

O'Hara smiled. "That's my responsibility. What about yours?"

"It's a tricky business, General, but I don't see why we can't win out with it *sometime.*"

"Eichbaum seems pessimistic."

"Oh, that's his nature. Don't pay any attention to him. What I've got him to agree to now is to forget the window glass for the present and just keep the two melting pots for the bottles fired. If we can finally produce *one perfect glass bottle,* we've got it! We can go on from there and do anything we want."

O'Hara rose and shook his hand. "You've cheered me up, Wentz. Go ahead as hard as you can."

"I only hope we don't break you up doing it, General."

"I'll manage," O'Hara said, smiling again.

On a late afternoon in April some sober Pittsburgh residents were astonished to see their first citizen now in his early fifties tearing hatless up from the ferry at a speed his own sons might have envied! James O'Hara did not slacken his pace along Water Street nor at his own front steps which he took two at a time. If the puzzled eyes of the neighbors could have followed him indoors they would have seen him rushing through the front hall.

"Mary! Mary! Mary!" he shouted.

She came in fright from the back of the house to see her husband throwing his arms wildly in the air and executing the steps of what she learned later was an Irish jig.

"We've done it!" he yelled. "We've done it! We've *won!* Today we've made a perfect green glass bottle!"

Suddenly he sank down in one of the hall chairs with an expression, half wickedly gleeful and half ashamed.

"At a cost," he added, "as I reckon it, *of thirty thousand dollars!*"

The news swept the town and there were many callers at the house on Water Street that evening offering congratulations.

"Well, we hear you've done it again for Pittsburgh, General!"

"The first glasshouse west of the Alleghenies, we can say now!"

"We knew success would finally come, with you at the head of it!"

"And Major Craig says window glass will be made before too long."

For Craig came in for felicitations too, though all the town knew that it was O'Hara's foresight, capital and determination which had made the achievement possible. For the first time, that night, O'Hara spoke to Mary about her advice to him.

"I honestly tried to hold in my mind an acceptance of whatever might come, but the odd thing was that as soon as I'd done that I was surer than ever that we'd succeed! Odd, wasn't it?"

"Maybe that's the way it happens," Mary said, "and I'm so happy for you."

"Now, I'll get to work at once on the plans for the chandelier," he said jubilantly. "I was just waiting . . ."

"I surmised that."

"So? Who is it knows whom now?" he teased.

He confided the secret of the boxes to Elliott the next day and also to his associates at the glassworks for he wanted Eichbaum's help in assembling the piece. He sent notes by McGrady calling a meeting of the Trustees at his office for the following week. By that time he expected to know how long it would take to have the chandelier ready for hanging. Eichbaum came over to the store that afternoon after work, filled with curiosity and a marked irritation that he had not been told before this. But when the space there was cleared and blankets spread to receive the delicate contents he began to unpack the boxes with a skilled and sensitive hand, his enthusiasm rising above his former annoyance.

"So this was what you wanted the address for," he said.

"Yes," O'Hara answered, "but I planned to keep the matter secret for a while. Do you like what you see, so far?"

"Beautiful! Exquisite!" he exclaimed, gently unwrapping one prism. "But we must work here only when we have good daylight. Better to do only a little each afternoon than to rush it."

"How will you get it to the church? Will you assemble it all here and then take it over?"

Eichbaum shook his head. "The main part we'll put together here, but all the crystals I will want to hang in the church itself when the framework is already up. We can carry them over wrapped carefully in baskets, then if we three could work together, I'll attach them if you men hand them up to me. You won't want the public to see this for the first time until it's lighted, will you, General?"

"That's my idea. Could we have it all ready by the week after next?"

"I'm sure of it. You'll have to keep people out of this part of the store, though."

"I sorta think I can see to that," Elliott drawled.

"Shoot a few if need be," O'Hara suggested cheerfully. "I hope none of the pieces have been broken in the shipping."

"I don't think so. Not from the Westphalian works. This must have cost you a pretty penny, General."

"Well, well, if you give a gift, give a good one. And this, I hope, will last for a while."

O'Hara's spirits soared as the next days passed. Wentz had been right. After the first perfect glass bottle, the difficulties that had nagged and blocked them disappeared. The clay, the sand, the temperature had all now been finally proven correct. The blowing had always been the least uncertain part, for Eichbaum and Wentz (who now seemed almost congenial in their new success) were both experts as well as two young Philadelphia workers; so the bottles were steadily turned out as the chimneys smoked, the furnace glowed, and an air of assured activity filled the glasshouse.

At the meeting of the Trustees O'Hara told of his proposed gift and the men were loud in their expressions of surprise and pleasure. They listened respectfully to his plan. The chandelier would be hung early the following week. Could there, following this, be an evening meeting at which time he would present it formally to the congregation who would then see it for the first time, lighted? His idea would be to have the meeting something less than purely religious under the circumstances, with a *talk* or *address* by someone, rather than a sermon. What were their views on this?

There was then animated discussion which O'Hara directed skillfully.

"Would you not have Reverend Barr take charge then?"

"By all means. He would preside, announce a hymn maybe to start with, offer prayer, and introduce all the speakers. That should give him enough to do."

After more discussion this was conceded. "But who would you get to give the address?" one man asked.

O'Hara brought forth an idea as though it had just occurred to him.

"Well now, let's see. What would you think of Reverend Arthur? He's President of the Academy and a born intellectual. He has a very easy, pleasant manner of speaking and I think he might give us an interesting talk. How does that strike you?"

After more discussion everything was settled exactly as O'Hara had previously decided it in his own mind.

"And now, gentlemen," he said, "I'm going to depend upon you to inform Reverend Barr upon the matter and allow him to set the evening. Any one will suit me. And also will you speak to Mr. Arthur about his part? I'm sure among you, you can arrange this all tactfully. I wish the church was big enough to invite the other congregations but I fear that would be impractical."

"Never fear," one man said. "When the news spreads we'll have a crowd, that's sure. Well, some can stand if they can't all get seats."

"Funny thing!" one of the Trustees remarked as the men were leaving, "for you to be giving this glass chandelier to the church at the very time your own works start going in earnest!"

"Yes," O'Hara agreed innocently. "Odd coincidence, isn't it?"

The work of assembly went on steadily in the back room of the store each afternoon. Eichbaum was in his element. His fingers seemed more and more to have the artist's touch as he handled the delicate crystals.

"Two rows of tapers!" he exclaimed one day as he lifted out the framework.

"Yes, it's going to make quite a light, I hope," O'Hara answered.

By Monday of the following week they were ready to begin work at the church. The meeting had been set for Thursday night at eight, so there would be no need of haste. Eichbaum had been relieved of all duties at the factory until the chandelier was completely hung and had now developed a possessive feeling toward it which was both amusing and touching.

"Would you rather have two of the men from the glasshouse over to help you hang the crystals?" O'Hara asked, as they left the store one day.

But Eichbaum shook his head.

"We've worked together with the unpacking, the three of us, and I'd rather go on that way. I want you there in any case, and this Elliott person has a surprisingly sure and gentle touch for an . . . an *uncultivated* man," he said.

O'Hara tried to hide a grin as he agreed.

The following day he met Mr. Arthur who was on his way

to Water Street. "Come on back to the house, then," O'Hara urged.

"Let's walk as we talk," the older man answered. "It's a beautiful day. The apple trees are in bloom in the King's Orchard. Did you notice that?"

"Oh yes, I never miss them."

"Lovely fragrance. Essence of spring. Well, General, I hear we are to have a wonderful surprise next week."

"I hope it will be . . . pleasing."

"And I also hear that I, alas, am slated to make a speech. I feel honored to be a part of the happy occasion but I don't know what to say. That was why I was on my way to see you. I wondered if you could suggest a selection from the Bible perhaps that I could use as a starting point? Oh, I know I'm not to preach a sermon, but I will have to have a *topic*. Do you have a favorite verse, for instance, General?"

O'Hara shook his head. "I'm not an Elder, Mr. Arthur. My work is on the financial side so I'm hardly prepared to give any spiritual suggestion."

"No verse you can think of?" he persisted. "This meeting is built around you, and you are the one who should suggest the theme."

O'Hara did not reply at once, then he asked, "Do you know Bunyan, Mr. Arthur?"

"Ah yes, very well. Don't tell me *you* do?"

"I had to read *Pilgrim's Progress* when I was a boy and more than that, I had to commit two of the short poems. The two best ones, I think."

"Yes, yes. *He that is down need fear no fall*, for instance?"

"That one and the other which I liked better. *Who would true valour see . . .*"

"And a fine one that is for any boy to learn. I must have my

Academy students memorize that. So you still remember it?"

"Yes. Many and many a time as I rode alone through the wilderness I recited it to myself. You see I had a feeling that there was a strong similarity between a *pilgrim* and a *pioneer*. But," he shrugged, "I doubt if this would have any bearing upon your problem."

"As a matter of fact," Mr. Arthur said slowly, "I think it might have an extraordinary one. You've given me an idea, General. Thank you!" And he turned abruptly and walked away.

Before he reached the church O'Hara was stopped again. This time a shabby man touched his hat and began to speak at once.

"I've been wantin' to run into you, General. Everybody's talkin' about the glass these days but I'm still thinkin' more about the *salt*. That's meant an awful lot to us. You know when you can get a good hunk of beef, a quarter mebbe, in the winter, it has to be salted to keep it, an' the brine has to be strong enough to *float an egg*. Did you know that, General?"

"I don't believe I did," he admitted.

"Well, that's the truth. An' before, we never could afford enough salt to do it an' so our meat never kept right. Now we're goin' to have good eatin' right along. I just wanted to thank you, General."

O'Hara reached his hand. "I'm glad you told me. I appreciate this."

As he went on he smiled to himself picturing the egg floating in a tub of brine. But that would be the rule and the recipe, he had no doubt, born of long pioneer experimentation. He must remember to tell that to Mary. But as he sat that night with her in the library, there was something more important of which he wished to speak.

"When we moved here," he began, "you said you wanted to go back sometimes and sleep in the old house just for old sake's sake. Do you remember?"

"Of course. And I would still like to. I wonder why we've never done it?"

"I thought perhaps this Thursday night might be a nice time after the meeting. It will be, I think, rather a memorable occasion, it's not long after our wedding anniversary . . ."

"And the apple trees are in blossom now. Did you notice?"

"Yes," he said, for the second time that day. "I never miss that. Then there's still another reason I would like to do it now. And that's because there is a definite connection between the guest room there which we would use, and my manufacture of glass."

"There *is?* What?"

"I'll tell you that night!"

"Oh, James," she said earnestly, "I'm *so* glad you are sentimental. I don't think many men are, do you?"

"It's me Irish blood, darling," he said with a twinkle.

By Wednesday noon the work at the church was completed. From a central circle hung the immense glass chandelier with its double row of sperm candles. From their holders depended a myriad of crystals which gleamed even in the daylight. There had been less trouble than O'Hara had feared with curious onlookers during these last days. He had passed the word around that by Thursday night *and not until then* all would be welcome. So the wholesome respect in which he was held coupled with the human pleasure in anticipation of an ultimate surprise kept people away. General Neville wandered in once; Isaac Craig and Wentz came over and Tuesday afternoon John Scull, editor of the *Gazette*, entered the church, looked at the chandelier from all sides and left, saying nothing. O'Hara was slightly nettled by his silence but soon forgot it in the general excitement.

Thursday evening was one of May's finest, with a delicately fragrant warmth abroad and a lighthearted western breeze blowing. Eichbaum had promised to see to the lighting of the candles himself so the O'Hara carriage with all its family occupants rolled up to the stake-an'-rider fence enclosing the churchyard at exactly a quarter to eight, with the arrangement that the children would return home in it when the meeting was over. Even now the congregation was pouring in and at the door itself people were standing, waiting for a chance to enter. O'Hara glanced back to be sure the children were all close behind them and then as soon as was possible went inside with Mary on his arm. Once there they all stopped short. O'Hara, himself, had not seen his gift lighted until this moment, and his heart seemed to turn over in his breast. He could feel Mary's hand trembling as she looked first at the chandelier and then at him, for the sight was dazzling, unbelievable. Every tiny facet of the crystals caught and reflected the light of the hundred candles burning above them!

They all walked slowly up the aisle to their pew in the block of six to the left of the pulpit and from there could watch the congregation as they kept coming in. Some were awe struck, speechless, at the blaze of beauty before them; others kept exclaiming softly as though they could not stop. The church was soon full and still the people came. They stood in the side aisles and in the back, and when there was no more room they stood on the outer steps peering over each other's shoulders and changing position so that all had a chance to see the glory inside.

At last Mr. Barr and Mr. Arthur ascended the pulpit together and the meeting began, as indeed, most services did, with the singing of the Twenty-third psalm. For this there was no need of printed page nor precentor. Everyone had known the words from childhood. So now, strong and full the volume of voices rose:

> *The Lord's my shepherd, I'll not want;*
> *He makes me down to lie*
> *In pastures green, he leadeth me*
> *The quiet waters by.*

When the singing was over, the Reverend Mr. Barr offered a prayer, a very lengthy one. During it at times O'Hara's lips twitched, for, as was his wont, the pastor gave detailed information to the Almighty which it was reasonable to assume He might already know. The little girls, sitting on either side of their father, grew restive and he put an arm around each to steady them. But at last the prayer was ended and Mr. Barr called upon General James O'Hara to make the presentation speech.

O'Hara moved out to the front of the pulpit, faced his townsmen and told briefly of his pleasure in conferring the gift, ending with the sentence he had thought of and written down months ago. "I give this," he concluded, "in token of a *glowing* desire to promote the *lustre* of this *enlightened* society."

There were some smiles. It was to be expected that the General's wit would in some small measure break through. Then John Wilkins, representing the Elders, accepted the gift in behalf of the congregation, reading from a resolution of thanks already prepared, which he then handed to O'Hara. It was now time for the address of the evening.

Mr. Arthur came slowly forward, leaned upon the big pulpit

Bible, waited for silence, and then began very simply to tell a story. It was about a pilgrim who had set out on a hazardous journey to reach a Celestial city. He pictured vividly the dangers and tribulations with which the pilgrim had been beset: how he had been attacked by the dragon, Apollyon, been plunged into the Slough of Despond, overcome lions, fought with Giant Despair, languished in Doubting Castle.

"Oh," Mr. Arthur said, "according to the author of this story, *'the way was very wearisome.'* But what I want to emphasize now is that the pilgrim never once gave up until he had reached the end of his journey. Listen! Listen to the words which gave him courage!

> *Who would true valour see,*
> *Let him come hither;*
> *One here will constant be,*
> *Come wind, come weather;*
> *There's no discouragement*
> *Shall make him once relent*
> *His first avowed intent*
> *To be a pilgrim.*

"This that I've been telling you," the speaker went on, "was a fanciful tale written by John Bunyan over a hundred years ago. Now I wish to speak of the true story of another type of pilgrims."

He told then of how these, the pioneers, had crossed the mountains, a feat of incredible courage in itself; of the graves large and small which marked that terrible path over the Alleghenies; of the bitter privations and hardships in the little log cabins of the settlers; of the dangers from wild beasts; and at last he spoke of the deadly struggles with the Indians. As the word fell from his lips a quick breath, like a sigh, stirred the audience.

"But," Mr. Arthur continued, "you, too, and your fathers and mothers before you, never gave up even though 'the way was very wearisome.' You never went back. You pursued your avowed intent. And now here is our town, no more afraid of the destruction by night nor the arrow that flieth by day. All around is peace and growth and prosperity. And here tonight before us is this glorious, dazzling gift of beauty which we can accept as a symbol of the fact that those hardest times are past, and as an earnest of what Pittsburgh may one day become."

And then he closed with prayer. A very brief and quiet one but it seemed as though the congregation hushed its heart to listen.

He prayed that they might all remember that they were still pilgrims journeying to another, a heavenly city in which there would be no need of a candle, neither the sun to lighten it, for the Lord God was the light thereof.

For a long minute there was no sound, and then slowly the movements began and the voices, until all restraint was lifted and there was everywhere laughter and loud acclaim. O'Hara and Mary stood at the front and shook hands with the steady stream of men and women who came to express their thanks and admiration. Those who had had to remain outside during the service now came in and looked their fill. Everywhere there was manifest that exhilaration which comes from pure pleasure and satisfaction.

At last the church was emptied of all but a few. Eichbaum put out the candles, even as he had lighted them. Goodnights were said and then O'Hara and Mary, arm in arm, walked slowly through the spring darkness. When they reached The King's Orchard she spoke suddenly.

"Oh, James, I have a lovely surprise for you!"

"You have? What is it?"

"The *Gazette* came today and I saw an editorial in it about your gift so I slipped it over here to the office when I came to arrange the bedroom. I thought it would make such a nice climax for the evening."

"An *editorial* about it?" he said. "Why Scull came in the other day and looked it all over and never said a word!"

"Maybe he was just saving up for this. Oh, you'll like it!"

They sauntered along the lane between the blossoming trees. His arm was around her now as they neared the kitchen door. They went on through to the office where he made a light.

"Here it is!" Mary exclaimed, picking up a paper from the desk. "I have it folded at the place. Read it aloud, James. I can't wait."

He took the paper eyeing it with surprise. "An editorial, eh? *Splendid Present!* Well! Well!"

"Read on. It gets better the farther you go."

"A chandelier of elegant workmanship has been presented to the First Presbyterian Church of this place, by Gen. James O'Hara. This beautiful ornament, which was imported at great expense and trouble, reflects as much credit on the taste as on the magnificence of the generous donor, and adds one more instance to the long list of liberal acts, performed during a most useful life by this worthy citizen."

"There!" Mary began. "Isn't that . . ." But she stopped short, seeing something she had never seen before. There were tears rolling down her husband's cheeks.

"This . . . this," he stammered, "touches me. To think of Scull's writing this way about . . . about *me!*"

Mary spoke quickly. "I feel it's beautiful, too, but it's not half of what you deserve. It would take a whole paper to tell of all your kindnesses, and the amazing work you have done, James. All the incredible things you, alone, have accomplished! I . . ."

"No," he said vehemently. "No!"

She looked at him, startled, as he crossed to where she was standing. Then with infinite tenderness he cupped her face between his hands, and gazed into her eyes.

"Not alone," he said. "Oh, my dear Delight, not *alone!*"

EPILOGUE

THE FOLLOWING WORDS are cut upon a flat stone which covers a grave on a gentle hillside in the old Allegheny Cemetery of Pittsburgh, Pennsylvania:

> Here lies the body of James O'Hara who departed this life Dec. 16, 1819 in the 67th year of his age. Born in Ireland in 1752, came to America in 1772. Served in the War of the Revolution, was commissioned Quarter Master General of the Army of the U.S. in 1792. As a pioneer he did much to develop the vast resources of this country And was highly esteemed by his contemporaries for his sagacity, intelligence and wit.

These lines are culled from *American Families of Historic Lineage*, The Americana Society, New York:

> General O'Hara died in the sixty seventh year of his age, on Dec. 16, 1819, at his home on Water Street, Pittsburgh, and the entire town mourned. It is said that the tears of the rich and the poor were commingled, for he had been the firm friend of both, treating all with justice.